Jesus Triumphant

Chronicles of the Nephilim
Book Eight

By Brian Godawa

JESUS TRIUMPHANT
1st Edition

Embedded Pictures Publishing
Los Angeles, CA
310.948.0224
brian@embeddedpictures.com
www.embeddedpictures.com

ISBN: 978-1-942858-02-7 (paperback)
ISBN: 978-1-942858-03-4 (ebook)

Scripture quotations taken from *The Holy Bible: English Standard Version.* Wheaton: Standard Bible Society, 2001.

Other books by the Author

Hollywood Worldviews: Watching Films with Wisdom and Discernment (Intervarsity Press)

Word Pictures: Knowing God Through Story and Imagination (Intervarsity Press)

Myth Became Fact: Storytelling, Imagination & Apologetics in the Bible

Chronicles of the Nephilim

Noah Primeval
Enoch Primordial
Gilgamesh Immortal
Abraham Allegiant
Joshua Valiant
Caleb Vigilant
David Ascendant
Jesus Triumphant
Jerusalem Judgment

Chronicles of the Nephilim For Young Adults

Enoch Primordial: Young Adult Edition
Noah Primeval: Young Adult Edition
Gilgamesh Immortal: Young Adult Edition
Abraham Allegiant: Young Adult Edition
Joshua Valiant: Young Adult Edition
Caleb Vigilant: Young Adult Edition
David Ascendant: Young Adult Edition
Jesus Triumphant: Young Adult Edition
Jerusalem Judgment: Young Adult Edition

When Giants Were Upon the Earth: The Watchers, Nephilim, & the Biblical Cosmic War of the Seed

For more information and products by the author:
www.godawa.com
www.ChroniclesOfTheNephilim.com

Dedicated to the apostates
Of the Jesus Seminar, and the Jesus Project,
and to
True believers whose imagination
is in need of resurrection.

This is spiritual war.

ACKNOWLEDGMENTS

Special thanks to my wife, Kimberly, always; to Doug Van Dorn for his giant encouragement and theological input, including material on the satan; to Michael Gavlak for his valuable input; to Sarah Beach for her editing.

NOTE TO THE READER

Jesus Triumphant is the eighth in the series of novels, *Chronicles of the Nephilim* about the Biblical Cosmic War of the Seed. Though it can be read as a standalone novel, there are characters, motifs, storyline histories and themes that have been carried over from previous novels in the series. Therefore, the true depth and riches of the story can be best appreciated and understood in that context.

And in the days of those kings the God of heaven will set up a kingdom that shall never be destroyed, nor shall the kingdom be left to another people. It shall break in pieces all these kingdoms and bring them to an end, and it shall stand forever, just as you saw that a stone was cut from a mountain by no human hand, and that it broke in pieces the iron, the bronze, the clay, the silver, and the gold. But the stone that struck the image became a great mountain and filled the whole earth.

Daniel 2:44-45, 35

For Christ also suffered once for sins, the righteous for the unrighteous, that he might bring us to God, being put to death in the flesh but made alive in the spirit, in which he went and proclaimed to the spirits in prison, because they formerly did not obey, when God's patience waited in the days of Noah, while the ark was being prepared, in which a few, that is, eight persons, were brought safely through water. Baptism, which corresponds to this, now saves you, not as a removal of dirt from the body but as an appeal to God for a good conscience, through the resurrection of Jesus Christ, who has gone into heaven and is at the right hand of God, with angels, authorities, and powers having been subjected to him.

1 Peter 3:18–22

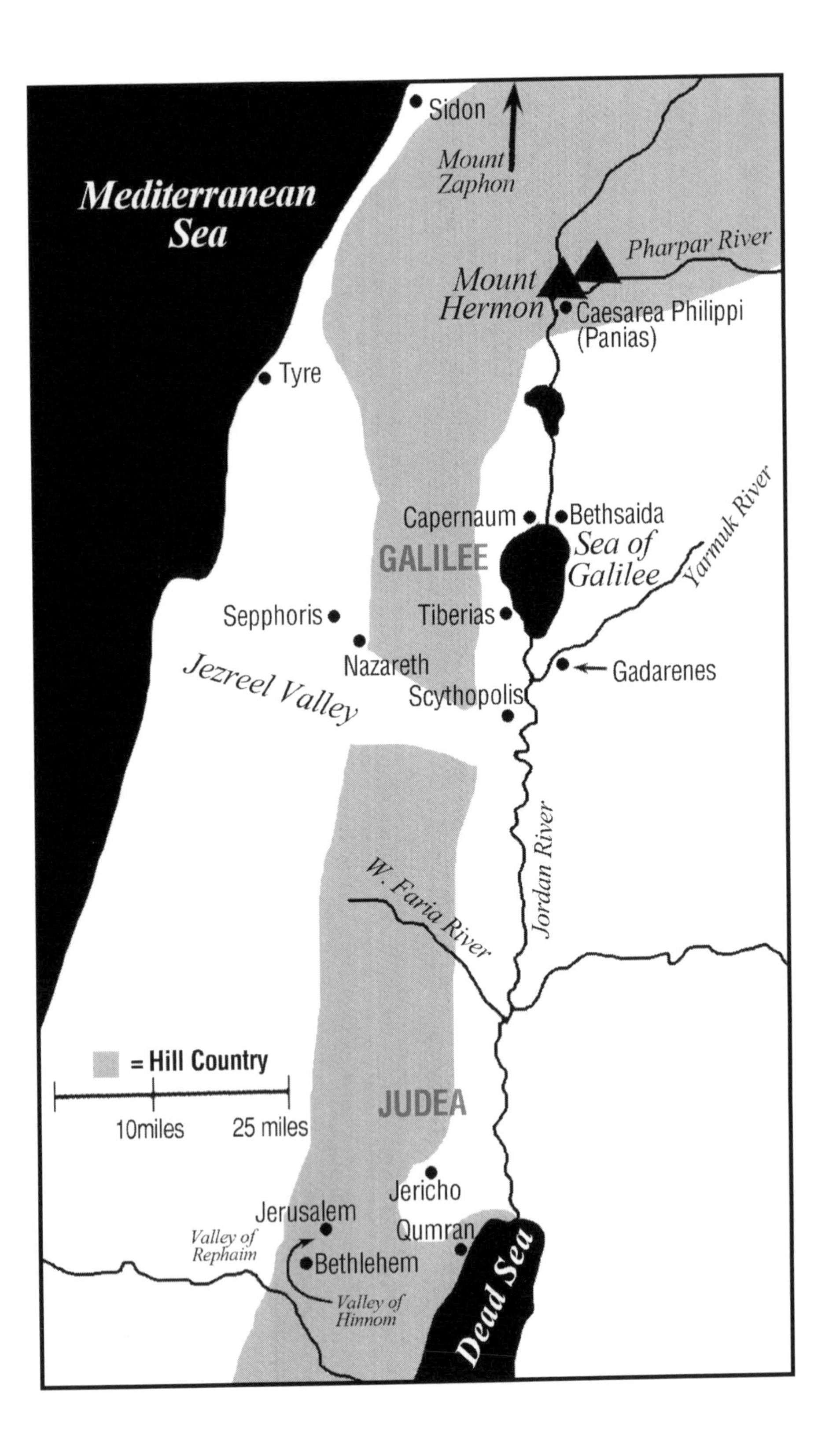

Sidon
Mount Zaphon
Mediterranean Sea
Pharpar River
Mount Hermon
Caesarea Philippi (Panias)
Tyre
Capernaum
Bethsaida
Yarmuk River
GALILEE
Sea of Galilee
Sepphoris
Tiberias
Nazareth
Gadarenes
Jezreel Valley
Scythopolis
Jordan River
W. Faria River
= Hill Country
JUDEA
10miles
25 miles
Jericho
Jerusalem
Qumran
Valley of Rephaim
Bethlehem
Valley of Hinnom
Dead Sea

PROLOGUE

Tohu wabohu. Formless and void. The desert of Azazel was the haunt of jackals, the habitation of *siyyim* and *iyyim* demons, Lilith the night hag and her serpent Ningishzida. Here the night creatures howled, the centaurs dwelt, and the satyr goat demons danced upon the ruins of desolation. Chaos and disorder.

But it was not night, it was day. The demons seemed held at bay, their whisperings carried only by the winds.

Jesus bar Joseph stumbled on the rocky wasteland. His staff kept him shakily on his feet as he leaned on it for support. His hood barely shielded him from the scorching bright sun high above. The howling winds felt like waves of heat from a blacksmith's furnace. His sandaled feet pained at each step with sunburnt exposure. His lips were parched, cracked and bleeding.

Water. He craved water. He had a headache, a backache, his entire body ached. He had been fasting for over thirty days now, he couldn't remember exactly how many. He had lost track. Dizziness finally brought him to the ground, his knees stinging on the gravelly desert floor.

"Had enough?" The whisper penetrated him with a sweet malice.

He ingested dust from a gust of wind and coughed. It stuck in his dry throat and he suffered a coughing fit that made the burning even worse.

When he had finally calmed down, his blurred and watery eyes looked up at the being before him: At almost six feet tall, cloaked in a desert robe that could not hide the gaunt figure beneath. Deliberately androgynous with long flowing hair. A disturbed blending of male and female characteristics. Make-up accented serpentine eyes that melded beauty and malevolence. This being was confusion and chaos incarnate. It stared down at him with cool contempt.

"Nachash," croaked Jesus. It was the name of that ancient tempter in the Garden, the first of many names through the ages; Accuser, Mastema, Sammael, Diablos, Helel ben Shachar, the Serpent.

"I am going by Belial these days. It has a nice ring to it." *Belial* meant the personification of wickedness, treachery and rebellion.

Jesus' throat hurt to speak. "I see you are disguising yourself in more humble appearance these days. Afraid of something?"

"The jester from Galilee. I am impressed you can maintain your wits after so many days in my little home away from home." Belial spread his hands out, gesturing to the dry deadly expanse around them. "I will admit that the advance of civilization has made it somewhat disadvantageous for the Watchers to reveal our true nature or presence. Yes, we are working more behind the veil than we did in primeval days. On the other hand, the way things are going, I can foresee an age when humanity has turned religion into pretty fictions, and blinded themselves to our reality. Imagine the influence we will then have on ignorant fools who no longer believe in us."

In the days of Jared, before Noah, two hundred Sons of God had rebelled against the Creator, Yahweh Elohim. They left their habitation of a multitude of heavenly host that surrounded the throne of Yahweh. They came to earth at the cosmic mountain called Hermon in the northern reaches of Canaan. They were the Watchers who masqueraded openly as the gods of the earth. At eight feet tall with serpentine skin of beryl and bronze that would shine with emotion, they earned the additional name of Shining Ones.

But as the primeval past faded into memory, mankind's knowledge expanded and its hubris grew with the promise of the Serpent that humans would become as gods. The Watchers became less obvious with passing time, as they sought to work more behind the veil of the supernatural world. As divine beings, Watchers could exert hypnotic effect on humans to see them in any appearance they desired. Thus, the eight-foot tall shining Belial made himself appear to be a mere five-foot ten being, both male and female, neither male nor female, a dissolution of gender, an abomination in the Law of God. But to Belial, such intolerant condemnation would not stop him from looking good. Unlike the ordinary, quite uncomely human before him, Belial still wanted to stand out from the crowd. He reveled in abomination.

Belial said, "Let us stop wasting time, Nazarene. I know who you are. I saw the entire circus show in the desert. The dreadfully smelly and theatrical Baptizer, the Holy Spirit descending like a vulture, Yahweh blathering from heaven, blah, blah, blah."

Jesus drifted off in his memory to a mere month ago, where he had been baptized in the Jordan River not too far from this hellish wasteland. John the Baptizer had left the communal sect of Qumran by the Dead Sea to become a lone voice crying in the wilderness to prepare the way for Messiah's advent. He was baptizing people in preparation for that arrival. But when he saw Jesus, he protested that he was not worthy to tie the thong of Jesus's sandal, and that it should be Jesus who baptized John instead.

Jesus could remember the precious look on John's face. A mixture of revelation and confusion, like he doubted what he had been proclaiming might actually be coming true. Jesus had chuckled and thought of dunking John in the water as a playful prank, but thought better of it because of the seriousness of the moment.

Baptism was a serious sacrament indeed. It was a symbolic ritual that recapitulated the cleansing waters of the Great Deluge. In the days of Noah, the fallen Sons of God had not merely come to earth to draw worship away from Yahweh. They also sought to corrupt humanity by violating the holy separation between heaven and earth. They mated with human women who gave birth to unholy hybrids of human and angel. These offspring were giants called Nephilim, and they were mighty warriors of old. The angelic/human crossbreeding had a second purpose: to corrupt the bloodline of the Messiah that was promised through the fully human bloodline of Eve. In the curse on the Serpent of the Garden, Yahweh had said, "I will put war between you and the woman, and between your seed and her seed; he shall crush your head, and you shall strike his heel." The violent sins of men and angels brought the judgment of Yahweh to cleanse the earth from abomination. But it was only the beginning of a war that would not cease until the promised Messiah came to crush the Serpent's head.

Baptism was recruitment into that supernatural holy war that reiterated the waters of the Flood cleansing unholiness and evil from the individual's life, in preparation for a new messianic world. But in the case of Jesus, it was much more. When Jesus was baptized, the Holy Spirit had come upon him, which was foretold by Isaiah the prophet, "Behold my Servant, whom I uphold, my Chosen One, in whom my soul delights; I have put my Spirit upon him; he will bring forth justice to the nations."

Yahweh the Father then spoke the words from heaven, "This is my beloved Son, with whom I am well pleased."

Those words were an allusion to a well-known messianic psalm of David where Yahweh spoke to the coming King.

> *"You are my Son; today I have begotten you.*
> *Ask of me, and I will make the nations your inheritance,*
> *and the ends of the earth your possession."*

But justice and inheritance were not merely a passive receiving of land rights. It was a hostile takeover from inhabitants that would not give up without a fight. The second part of that prophecy did not bode well for the powers of the earth.

> *You shall break them with a rod of iron*
> *and dash them in pieces like a potter's vessel."*
> *Now therefore, O kings, be wise;*
> *be warned, O rulers of the earth.*
> *Serve Yahweh with fear,*
> *and rejoice with trembling.*
> *Kiss the Son,*
> *lest he be angry, and you perish in the way,*
> *for his wrath is quickly kindled.*

But that was not the only Scripture of such ominous foreboding.

And the faithful were not the only ones privy to the prophecy. Even from the earliest of ages, the heavenly principalities and powers used the Seed of the Serpent to hunt down the Chosen Ones in each generation to try to kill them. Enoch, Noah, Abraham and others were protected by Yahweh from this murderous plan. The oracles of the pagan diviner Balaam and others foretold a divine star coming from the line of Jacob, a kingly scepter from Israel, a lion from Judah who would crush the skulls of the enemy and dispossess his inheritance.

Snapping fingers and a voice brought the delirious Jesus back to the moment. "Jesus. Hello, Jesus. Stay focused now. Look at me."

Jesus looked at the creature. He wanted to gag as much from the ugliness of evil as from his spasming shrunken stomach.

Belial sniffed long and deep and said, "Just smell that. It's heavenly."

Jesus's senses came alive with the sweet warm smell of freshly baked bread. His stomach cried out ferociously.

Belial's words were sing song seductive. "Well, look what we have here. I believe it is exactly the stone ground wheat bread your own mother, that blessed Virgin, used to bake for you."

Jesus was still on his knees. He looked over to see a loaf of steaming hot bread, fresh from the oven, sitting on a group of rocks not three feet from him. It had been pulled apart ready to eat. He could see the flakey crust, some of it floating away in the damnable breeze. Steam rose from the soft light brown interior. It took everything in Jesus's soul to keep from reaching out and stuffing his mouth with the tempting sustenance of life.

But it was not real. Belial was not a creator, he was a mimic and a master of illusion. He could manipulate the senses to create just about any hallucination with which humans could deceive themselves by.

"If you are the Son of the God, command these stones to become loaves of bread. I want a worthy adversary, not a sickly weakling."

Jesus had the power to do so. He had after all provided manna for the children of Israel. That was true heavenly bread, the food of angels. And he had provided water out of a rock to satisfy the thirst of thousands of Israelites as they wandered in the wilderness. He could taste that sweet cool refreshing water right now in his memory. He had gone so very long in his fast already. Perhaps it was time to feed himself and get to work with his plan.

No. He had to finish what he started here. He replied to Belial, "It is written, 'Man shall not live by bread alone, but by every word that comes from the mouth of God.'"

The mirage of bread faded away.

"Oh, aren't you a holy self-righteous Torah-thumping zealot. You think you are the only one who knows the Scriptures by heart?" Belial spit out in Jesus's native Hebrew, "'The earth was without form and void, and darkness was over the face of the deep.'" He paused venomously. "I know what you are doing. It's all so pathetically typological. And over the heads of common Israelites I might add." Typology was Yahweh's technique of repeating spiritual truth through repeating patterns in the Scriptural story he was unfolding in history.

"Yahweh is obsessed with his Exodus as if it is the only miracle ever accomplished in history. Now, you are setting yourself up as a new Moses to deliver the Israelites out of my worldwide empire of Rome."

Belial was evil, but he was not stupid. Jesus sat up on the ground to listen. He pulled his hood down and placed his staff at his feet.

Belial continued, "Yahweh has sought to hide his plan from me since the beginning of creation. But then, like an idiot, he writes his little hints all over his Scriptures, that he leaves out in the open for any angel or *elohim* to read—and he thinks I am too ignorant to figure out the narrative."

Jesus listened expectantly. He was patient, even with such condescending bluster.

"When Yahweh created the heavens and earth, the land was a desert of chaos, *tohu wabohu*, formless and void. Just like Moses was in the desert wilderness with Israel, and you are in the wilderness of Azazel right now. And all that desert chaos is what Yahweh seeks to push back to create his covenant order. Am I right so far?"

Jesus gave a slight nod of approval. Not bad. But there was so much more to it than that. Moses had wandered forty years in the desert for Yahweh to prepare him for the exodus, Israel wandered forty years in the desert before she could enter her Promised Land of the covenant. And now Jesus had fasted for forty days in the desert in symbolic unity of preparation for his entry as king of the new exodus of Yahweh's people out of their latest slavery under the new Egypt.

Belial continued his rant, "Yahweh pushed back the sea and crushed the heads of Leviathan in order to establish his covenant with Moses and Israel, which was the creation of order out of chaos. Then he pushed back the waters of the Jordan for Joshua's armies to cross and slay the Anakim giants of Canaan. It's that mythical thing of gods conquering the sea and river to establish their new world order, or should I say tyranny? So I gather you have yet to conquer your body of water. What will it be, drink up the Dead Sea? That will leave you thirstier than when you started, you know. With all that salt leftover from Yahweh's childish temper tantrum over Sodom and Gomorrah."

Jesus managed a slight smile at Belial's accusations. There was always a certain silliness to the self-righteous blame-shifting of evil. But his lips cracked open with pain, reminding Jesus of his purpose here. Belial could see it and was delighted with the slightest of suffering in his nemesis.

He continued, "Oh, and let us not forget the whole Son of David motif. That one is a real hoot. And I quote, 'I will raise up your seed after you, and I will establish his kingdom. He shall build a house for my name, and I will establish the throne of his kingdom forever. I will be to him a father, and he shall be to me a son. My steadfast love will not depart from him. And your house and your kingdom shall be made sure forever before me. Your throne shall be established forever.'" He had quoted it with exaggeration to make it sound ridiculous. He concluded. "Can it *be* any more obvious?"

Jesus shrugged. Maybe, maybe not.

"No, wait, yes it can. I do believe it can. How about this one,

Yahweh says to Adonai, my Lord:
"Sit at my right hand,
until I make your enemies your footstool."
Yahweh sends forth from Zion
your mighty scepter.
Rule in the midst of your enemies!
Yahweh has sworn
and will not change his mind,

"You are a priest forever
after the order of Melchizedek."

Jesus finally spoke up. "You had better be careful, Accuser, quoting so much Scripture may have a deleterious effect on your accusations."

"Well, well, 'the Messiah' has a second wind. Nice to see you listening, starved attention though it may be. May I complete the narrative?"

Jesus gestured with his hand to continue.

"So, King David, that vanquisher of giants, and Seed of the Serpent, takes down the Philistine champion Goliath. He enters Jerusalem in a triumphal procession with the head of his giant foe, and proceeds to wipe out the last of the Rephaim giants in the land. Now, I wonder what city the 'Son of David' is going to enter in triumph to claim his universal kingship? Why, Jerusalem of course, where he will claim the holy temple and demand eternal priesthood according to the order of Melchizedek. And there you have it. The Messiah as prophet, priest and king. But why wait? Let us go there right now."

The wind whipped up around Jesus. Sand got in his eyes. He closed them tight and stood up from the ground. When he opened his eyes, he found himself standing at the pinnacle of the holy temple in Jerusalem with Belial beside him smiling. Beneath this roof, the holy of holies resided, where the cherubim images guarded the ark of the covenant, the very royal throne and footstool of Yahweh Elohim on earth. And that throne room was a shadow, a mirror of reality of Yahweh's true throne room in the heavens above the waters. Thus, the saying, "On earth as it is in heaven."

It was a hundred and fifty foot drop to the bottom of this temple. He could see the priests going about their daily sacrifices in the court below. Beyond, in the women's courtyard and in the outer court of the Gentiles, Jews were milling about engaging in temple duties, completely unaware of these two observers peering down from the golden trimmed roof.

Belial's previous sarcasm turned smooth and testy. "Prove now you are worthy of your Scriptural claims. If you are the Son of God, throw yourself down, for it is written, 'He will command his angels concerning you,' and 'On their hands they will bear you up, lest you strike your foot against a stone.' Or are you not God's new Melchizedek?"

His sarcasm carried particular venom when he mocked Jesus's phrase, "it is written."

Jesus swallowed and replied, "On the other hand, it is also written, 'You shall not put Yahweh your god to the test.'"

Belial scoffed, "Oh, how petty."

Another gust of wind blew from below. Jesus's cloak flew up and obscured his vision. When it came down, he saw he was on the precipice of a deep ridge back in the desert. Had he ever left?

The gust of desert wind suddenly went still. Jesus found it difficult to breathe in the stifling deadness of the heat. Was he dizzy from the height or from his malnutrition? Now, he heard whispering voices of malignant evil all around him. The cacophony was enough to make a human go insane. But Jesus was no mere human.

Belial said, "My children. My minions. No, the Nephilim are not gone from the land. They are still here. And they will rise up."

The unholy Nephilim had been purged from the land, first by the Flood, and finally through the holy wars of Canaan by Joshua ben Nun and King David. There was only one thing Belial could mean by their return.

Belial changed the subject. "Yahweh has protected his chosen seedline of Messiah through all the ages. I must say however, that I am not impressed with his choice of a final vessel. You have neither the constitution nor the military skills of your namesake, Joshua." Joshua was Hebrew for Jesus. "Now there was a ballsy warrior. I hated that godlicker and his tail-wagging dog, Caleb.

"But you, you are but a simple carpenter. Pshaw! I fail to see how you will fulfill his conquest. The only thing you have going for you is the Covering. Apparently, the heavenly principalities and powers cannot touch you." Belial paused. The bodiless demonic horde faded back into the howling desert rocks. A subtle smirk grew on Belial's lips. "But the earthly humans over which we rule *can*."

He let that one linger with a sense of foreboding. Belial was good at delivery. He was after all the Accuser in the very courtroom of Yahweh's divine council. He challenged the Laws of Torah and prosecuted heavenly lawsuits against Yahweh's people.

"I almost had you in the hands of Herod when you were born. How you escaped Herod's slaughter of the innocents at Bethlehem, now that I must congratulate Yahweh on. The whole flight to Egypt and all. And there you have it, that exodus connection again. Just like Moses escaping the slaughter of Hebrew infants by Pharaoh. Nice touch. If it had not been for those Babylonian Magi literally coming and pointing out the star prophecy to Herod, that rock head would never have figured anything out."

The star prophecy that Belial alluded to had a long history of importance. When Yahweh had originally created the heavens and earth, he placed the constellations of stars and planets in the sky not merely for seasons but for signs to mankind. And the most imaginative sign was the story of redemption that he embedded within the very structure of the twelve constellations that revolved around the earth. The narrative was of a virgin (Virgo) who would bear the promised seed and pay the price of justice (Libra) to overcome the "wounder of the heel" (Scorpio). This promised one would be a conqueror (Sagittarius the archer), who would be the scapegoat of atonement (Capricorn), and bring living waters for his people (Aquarius the water-bearer). Those people would be blessed though bound (Pisces the fish). Their blessings would be consummated through a ram of sacrifice (Aries) who would become a ruling leader (Taurus the bull), a king with two natures (Gemini the twins). He would hold his people fast in his grip (Cancer the crab), and would ultimately reign as king over the earth (Leo the lion).

Yahweh's enemies eventually subverted the original intent of the constellations and twisted the entire system into a form of idolatry that worshipped the stars instead of Yahweh as the determiner of destinies.

The Babylonian Magi, whose tradition was influenced by the teachings of the exilic prophet Daniel, had followed the final sign in the heavens that pointed to the birth of Messiah. It was written that when the constellation Virgo was on the horizon, clothed with the sun and the moon under her feet, with twelve stars above her head, she would give birth to a divine king. This was because the king planet Jupiter aligned in conjunction with the king star Regulus over her head creating a bright star. The Magi observed that sign in the year 750 AUC, seven hundred and fifty years from the founding of the city of Rome. The star Regulus is in the constellation of Leo the Lion.

The Magi were taught by their Hebrew prophet that this King of the Jews would be called the Lion of the tribe of Judah. And they were taught he would come from the small town of Bethlehem in Judea. Unfortunately, the second part of the sign was the constellation of Hydra, the red dragon, whose tail was just under Virgo's feet and entailed a third of the horizon line called the elliptic. This prefigured the Serpent and his fallen ones seeking to devour the Messiah at birth.

Warned by Gabriel, the Magi never returned to Herod and Jesus's parents escaped to Egypt until after Herod died. By the time Herod, that son of a serpent, murdered all the young male children of Bethlehem, Jesus was already gone.

Jesus knew that Herodian mass murder was a mere portent of the battle he had in his future. And this monster before him was the heavenly architect of his earthly opposition. Jesus swayed in his stance. He reached down and with a grunt picked up his staff to hold himself up.

But when he arose, he now found himself on the peak of a mountain range, the tallest in the region. It was cold and snowy. The wind, no longer hot, but bitterly cold, rushed into his folds and chilled him to the bone. He pulled his cloak tighter and raised his hood.

Belial stepped up beside him. "It is so much colder without food in your belly. Here, let me help you." He took off his cloak and draped it around Jesus. "There, there. Are you warmer?"

Jesus said nothing. But he did not refuse the cloak. He shivered and felt his toes already going numb. Belial stood unfazed by the freezing winds despite his bare skeletal chest.

"Do you know where you are?" asked Belial.

"Mount Hermon," said Jesus.

"Very good," he condescended. "Believe it or not, I did not bring you here to freeze your little toesies. But rather to share my change of heart from my mount on high."

Mount Hermon was the original cosmic mountain of the gods. The original location of the Watchers' descent. At the Flood, most of the two hundred rebel gods had been bound into the earth and imprisoned in Tartarus by the archangels to await the Judgment. Seventy of them and their minions escaped the catastrophe and used this original site of their falling to earth as their sacred headquarters of rebellion against Yahweh. They even organized themselves into a pagan imitation of Yahweh's own divine council of heavenly host, several of them vying for chief position as the most high.

Deep within the bowels of Hermon was a cavernous hall of assembly where the seventy met in counsel to deliberate their plans and administer their own twisted form of justice upon the earth. A lake of pitch black infernal waters in the cavern led to the Abyss that connected to the mouth of Sheol, or Abode of the Dead, called *Hades* in Greek. Thus Hermon was a holy mountain that connected the three tiers of the cosmos: the heavens, the earth and the underworld.

Jesus was standing on the high place of the stronghold of supernatural evil next to the Prince of the Power of the Air.

Belial swiped his hand and the clouds appeared to part, enabling Jesus the ability to see all the known world below and their cities of men. Belial's contempt melted into a seductive whisper in Jesus's ear. "Do you see all these kingdoms and their glory? They have been delivered to me, and I give them to whom I will."

Though he was the Father of Lies, in this, he told the truth. After the Flood, the Great Nimrod of Babel had unified all the world under his sovereign authority. He built a ziggurat tower, a sacred cosmic mountain to the heavens where humanity sought divinity in their godless unity to storm heaven. But Yahweh divided their tongues and spread them upon the earth as seventy nations. Because of the incorrigible evil of men's idolatry, Yahweh allotted each of the nations and their territories under the authority of the seventy Sons of God, as their inheritance. They would worship the rebellious heavenly host.

But Yahweh saved the sons of Israel for himself, through Abraham, Isaac, and Jacob, and claimed the land of Canaan for their inheritance. The only problem was that Canaan was already under the dominion of Ba'al, Asherah and other gods. And Canaan was the land of giants, the Seed of the Serpent. Joshua ben Nun and David ben Jesse had cleansed the land of its unclean inhabitants with the Wars of Yahweh. But Israel's constant adultery with the gods of Canaan lost them their inheritance, and over the years, they were chastised by one nation after another. Assyria, Babylonia, Media-Persia, Greece, and now Rome.

Over a millennia, Belial had built up the small Latin republic in the west that ultimately became an empire. As the heavenly Prince of Rome, Belial's ownership eventually dominated the entire world as Rome conquered all under her power. Since earthly powers and heavenly powers were linked in their spiritual reality, Belial was the chief archon, the god of this world. He parceled out land and power to the other gods out of his own bounty and rule.

Belial whispered, "All of this power and glory is mine. All of it. Caesar is my puppet, his governors are my whores, and his undefeated military machine is my right arm of power. You stand no chance against me, Messiah."

Jesus shivered with more than cold. This serpent had become monstrous in his power and no less insidious in his intentions since the Garden. He had been preparing for the ultimate War of the Seed for millennia, and he was ready for a fight.

But then Belial changed his tone. "And yet, I have an offer of shalom between us." Shalom was the Hebrew word for peace, a peace that was not mere cessation of hostilities, but was true enduring wholeness and unity. Jesus looked up into his eyes.

"All of this, all the kingdoms of the earth and their authority, I will give to you as a peace offering. Is that not what Yahweh has promised you?"

It was Yahweh's promise that the Messiah Seed of Abraham would bless all the nations and inherit the earth. But this is precisely why Belial's offer was completely out of character. Why would he conquer nations and fight for eons of time to gain control of the whole world, only to hand it over to his arch nemesis? There had to be fine print in this covenant offer.

Belial continued with the sincerity of a politician. "You will have your earthly inheritance without all the death and destruction and bloodshed of the Day of the Lord." And then he spilled the barley. "All I ask is one teeny tiny thing in return. All you have to do is fall down and worship me."

Jesus looked Belial in his eyes, deep dark pools of malevolence. He whispered back, "Be gone, Accuser. For it is written, 'You shall worship the Lord your God and him only shall you serve.'"

Belial sighed and said, "Fine, have it your way. But just let it be written, I gave you the chance to avoid Armageddon and you blew it." He grabbed his cloak off of Jesus and swung it around in an arc, creating a whirlwind of snow that blinded Jesus for a moment in its swirling white coldness.

Jesus found himself in the desert again. But now he was alone. Belial was gone. But his haunting words of warning lingered longer than the cold in his extremities as the desert heat overtook him again. "Armageddon" was a word that meant a climactic battle for the "mount of assembly," the very seat of divine power in the heavens. Hermon was the mount of assembly for the gods of the earth. Zion was the mount of assembly for Yahweh in Jerusalem. Belial had used the term to express the clash of kingdoms that was coming between the kingdom of heaven and the kingdoms of earth. A clash of cosmic mountains. The prophet Ezekiel called it the Battle of Gog and Magog.

Jesus knew that right now, Belial was most likely already informing his divine council in Hermon of their exchange. The gods were already preparing for war. Belial's words echoed in his memory: "The heavenly principalities and powers cannot touch you. But the earthly humans over which we rule *can*." Though they had no authority to touch Yahweh's anointed, they might do so through their human vessels.

Jesus trembled with the weight of responsibility that now overwhelmed him. But the pain was lessened when he heard the familiar sound of his favorite angel echo in his mind.

Jesus, be strong and courageous.

"Jesus, be strong and courageous." It wasn't in his mind, it was being spoken to him from behind.

"Sound familiar?"

Jesus turned. He looked up into the smiling face of Uriel the smallest of three angels now standing before him.

Uriel finished his thought, "The words you spoke to Joshua at the threshold of the Promised Land. Funny how it all comes full circle."

Gabriel, the second angel, and Uriel's constant bickering companion, responded, "Uriel, I think your humor is once again in incredibly poor taste considering his suffering. Where is your compassion?"

"Nonsense," said Uriel. "Jesus has done it. Victory is a cause for celebration, not sadness. He made it forty days without food, which is more than I can say for you, chubby." Uriel patted Gabriel's stomach. Gabriel moved away annoyed at the jab. Sure, he was heavier than the lightweight Uriel, but he certainly didn't see himself as "chubby."

Mikael, the largest and best groomed of the three, was the guardian prince of Israel, and tended to be protective of his ward. He offered a wineskin to Jesus, who took it and gulped with gratitude.

After a moment of silence, Jesus wiped his beard of the wine and said, "You need a better sense of humor, Gabriel."

Gabriel pouted with frustration at being ganged up on. Uriel, his perpetual nemesis was one thing. But being teased by the Master was quite another.

Jesus said, "And Uriel, you had better deliver on that bread you promised."

Uriel smiled again and held out a loaf of Mary's best bread. "Baked two hours ago by your mother." Jesus grabbed it.

Mikael said, "Remember, do not eat too quickly. It is bad for your digestion after fasting."

"Thank you for your ministering spirits," said Jesus, and took a big hungry bite out of the loaf.

Uriel muttered, "Your mother should open a bakery. Can I have a bite?"

Mikael was not so lighthearted. He knew that the challenge had been declared. The road to war had begun.

CHAPTER 1

Demas stepped out into the arena. The iron barred gate clanged shut behind him. He looked up at the spectators encircling him in their amphitheater seats. The sound of their cheers shaking the stadium did nothing for him. He cared nothing for them or for their pathetic empty lives driven by bloodlust to the circus.

He was a bestiarius and he had a job to do.

At twenty six years of age, he had nothing to live for—or die for. A Hellenized Jewish citizen of Scythopolis in southern Galilee, he was a man between worlds who used both but believed in neither. Hellenism was the term for the Greco-Roman cultural influence on other nations throughout the world, something the Jews were normally hostile toward. He both detested the imperial oppression of his adopted Roman occupiers and despised the belligerent intolerance of his Jewish kinsmen. To satisfy his frustrated anger, he filled his time with what he did well: killing beasts. It kept his mind busy and his body strong. And it paid well.

While many gladiators were criminals and other enslaved fighters, bestiarii were voluntary hunters for spectacle. A good bestiarius could draw ten denarii per hunt, as much as an elite scribe might make in a week. Demas made fifteen. He was the best in the Decapolis, the ten Greek cities surrounding the Roman precinct of Galilee. But he refused to join the bestiarii guild of animal baiters, so he was shunned as an outcast.

He didn't care about those greedy thugs either. He only cared about killing. In killing beasts, he could take out his aggression and feel alive facing his own death every time he entered the ring. His opponents were exotic predators brought in from near and distant lands: lions, bears, tigers, leopards, panthers, rhinoceroses, even hippos.

Demas was the best at what he did because he knew animals better than anyone. After his parents had died, he and his brother had been adopted by a Hellenistic couple in Scythopolis. Demas took up animal tending and eventually became a trapper. When his life bottomed out years back, his fateful anguish drove him to become a bestiarius even as he maintained his animal tending duties for the spectacles. He got to understand the animals as he took care of them and prepared them for the ring.

Animal hunts, called *venationes*, were more popular than gladiator fights. They had begun in the early days of the republic as peaceful parades of exotic animals discovered by Roman expansion. As the republic turned into an empire, the Caesars turned the parades into hunts. Victory over the exotic animals became a symbol of the emperor's power over the newly conquered territories from which the animals came. The spectacles would vary. Sometimes it would be animal against animal, sometimes animal against hunter. Sometimes it would be multiple animals and multiple hunters or single hunters against single animals. Sometimes the animals would be used as means of executing criminals or captives tied unarmed to stakes or sewn into the skins of dead animals. The predators were starved before events to increase their aggressiveness and ensure maximum entertainment for the masses.

Today would be a fateful day in Demas's life. He tried to forget about what he had to do later by taking on a more difficult venatio. He secretly hoped he would fail and die in the contest, which would make this a symbolic day for him indeed. But if he triumphed, at least he would make twice his normal wage. But then again, what difference did that make? He didn't care about the money either.

He only cared about the Thessalian black bull that bore down upon him from the center of the ring.

He gripped his whip handle tightly and gathered the ten foot long thong in preparation. At the end of the thong was the cracker or popper, within which he had embedded several pieces of sharp iron for ripping flesh. He was a master with the whip. He could rip out an eyeball from a victim with precision or yank a limb out from under his prey with ease.

A charging Thessalian bull was a different matter.

He crouched in preparation as the bull was almost upon him. Its head lowered, its thick long horns pointed in his direction to gore him.

Just before contact, Demas ducked and rolled out of the way of his attacker. It took moments before the animal realized what had happened and turned for another attack. This time, it would not be fooled.

Demas got back up to face the monster. He did not wear a helmet or other traditional gladiator garb so that he could move more quickly against his animal adversaries. Dexterity was as important as weapons skill. He wore only a leather tunic with belted leather over his abdomen, a key attack area for most animals. His only armor was a segmented metal shoulder and arm guard for his left arm. In his sheath he carried the common Roman gladius straight sword, about three feet in length. He picked up a javelin at his feet and ran to the edge of the stadium.

The sound of the crowd told him the bull was chasing him and about to ram him.

He felt the hard skull make contact with his buttocks. He launched into the air and flew a good ten feet. He released the spear before he hit the dirt so he would not break it.

The crowd went wild. He did after all have to put on a good show.

But it was not without calculation. The bull's hit had thrown him to within eight feet of the edge of the arena, where he had wanted to be.

He peered at the bull that had already turned and prepared to run him down again. It snorted and kicked the dirt with its front hoof.

As Demas stared down his adversary, he thought of the god Ba'al, so ubiquitous throughout the land of Israel. Ba'al was often symbolized by a bull. Demas hated Ba'al. He despised the gods. Killing this bull would do more for him than mere physical victory.

The bull charged again. The crowd cheered.

As it closed the gap, Demas didn't move. He just stood still.

He started to move backwards at a slow pace calculated to match his predetermined point of impact.

The bull did not have a highly attuned depth perception. As it sprinted down upon Demas, it zeroed in on its visual target. It lost its background awareness.

It could not calculate the slow move that its quarry was engaging in.

By the time it hit its target, Demas had backed up to the wall. The two long horns were much longer than the thickness of a human body. They plunged deep into the painted wooden wall of the arena on each side of Demas. The force sent a shockwave through the body of the beast and a loud crunching snap rang through the amphitheater.

The crowd went wild again. This was good circus.

Demas didn't even have to use his sword. The nasty brutish black monster had broken its neck and fallen dead. But Demas would have plenty of opportunity to use that blade in mere moments. This venatio was a mere warm-up, an appetizer to the full course meal of flesh and blood, tooth and sword that was about to be served up for the hungry audience.

Demas despised the masses. He saw them as a mob, carried away by their own bloodlust, and just as easily manipulated by their rulers as their entertainers. A crowd of otherwise intelligent or moderate individuals, could become a hive of unthinking insects, hornets incited by a wave of the hand or the proclamation of a meaningless slogan.

These masses were a peculiar crowd. The citizens of Scythopolis, as in much of the region of Galilee, were a mixture of Greek and Jewish heritage. This created a unique set of problems because the Greco-Roman worldview was polytheist and imperialist, while the Jewish religion was monotheist and theocratic. Jewish laws stressed the rule of God and separation from Gentiles or non-Jews. Many of them were driven by contempt for their Roman occupiers. But many of them had also been deeply compromised by the powerful influence of their captive culture of Hellenism, an assimilation of the Greco-Roman worldview.

Herod the Great, the first Jewish client king under Augustus Caesar, had been a conniving sell-out to Rome. Because of his Idumean or Edomite ancestry, he claimed Abrahamic heritage. But in truth, the Edomites were sons of Esau who were prophesied to be in perpetual hostility with the sons of Jacob, or Israel. Herod's contempt toward the seed of Abraham was evident in his absorption of pagan Hellenistic culture. He had poured millions of shekels into Greco-Roman building projects all around Judea and Galilee. He had even put a Roman theater and Hippodrome for chariot racing and games into the holy city of Jerusalem. Though he was loathed by many Jews for his Roman sympathies, he established a Hellenist influence within the land of Israel that would no doubt last for generations. The rabbis condemned the games and circuses, but many common Jews still attended them, just as many commoners still worshipped Asherah and Ba'al, despite the pleas of their prophets and priests. Mobs were not easily swayed from their depraved appetites by the elite.

Demas picked up his spear and whip to face his next adversary—or more accurately, *adversaries*. An iron gate lifted and two huge black wolves padded their way toward him. They spotted their human prey and immediately froze low to the ground, preparing to strike.

Behind Demas, the rusty sounds of another iron gate cranking open drew his surprise. A gigantic monster lumbered out. A nine foot tall, twelve hundred pound brown bear. A very hungry bear, who now spotted its meal.

Demas panicked. He was supposed to hunt these animals one after another in sequence, not all at once. Someone must have betrayed him. Maybe one of the other jealous bestiarii. Or maybe someone who just wanted a darker thrill at seeing the animal baiting champion be taken down in a fury of fang and claw. None of that mattered now. Now, he had to think. He had to strategize.

His planning was pierced through with the sound of yet another iron gate lifting. A fourth predator? He wouldn't stand a chance. He glanced over his left shoulder to get a glimpse of the new enemy. An African lion. The king of the arena. What was worse, he recognized the huge seven-foot-long feline from his animal keeping. He had nicknamed him Crueldis. The giant lion had killed so many bestiarii he had become a legend. Demas had gotten familiar with the creature while caring for it. He fed it and nursed its wounds from previous hunts. But now, that big pet cat was going to eat him for dinner.

Oh well, he was ready to die anyway. The crowd was already in a frenzy. The only thing that would stop this approaching violence was Demas' death. He decided to make this the most glorious death in the arena for decades to come. He would give the mob their entertainment.

He would go down fighting.

He held his spear in his left hand and unfurled his whip to face the wolves. The bear would watch and take its time, the lion might even be next. Take out the smallest foes first.

But "small" did not capture the essence of these ferocious wolves. They were orchestrated and vicious. And they were ravenously hungry.

The thinner one snarled in front of Demas as the other one circled to his rear.

He thrust his spear out, the skinny one backed up.

He twirled his whip overhead and snapped it behind him without even looking. It was one of the tricks he had developed over the years.

The crack of the whip drew a howl and a large piece of bloody flesh from the wolf. The ragged iron cracker tips did their job.

Uh oh. The bear approached cautiously from the left.

The lion circled the battle, looking for a way in. He circled closer and closer. This would not go well.

The thinner wolf advanced to draw Demas' attention, at the same moment that the wounded rear one launched onto his back.

Demas felt fangs dig into his whip arm shoulder. He yelped in pain and went down to the ground. He could hear his attackers' angry growling at his ear.

The thin one attacked.

But Demas saw it and raised his spear as the thin one was upon him. It did not veer in time and the spear plunged into its chest, piercing its heart. It yelped and fell to the ground, drawing the spear out of Demas' hand.

Demas rolled in order to pin the other animal beneath him.

But he was shocked to see the twelve-hundred pound muscle-bound bear lunging at him with its huge jaws wide open. The guttural growl echoed through the stadium and the crowd went hushed with shock at their hero's sure demise.

Demas only had a second to respond. He did so defensively. He raised his left armored arm and the bear's teeth bit down onto steel. If his arm had not been so protected, the creature would surely have crushed the bone, ripped through flesh, and tore his arm off. But the steel had just enough guard to stop it for the moment.

The wolf kicked its way out from under Demas. Demas knew he was himself mere moments from death.

In that moment the lion attacked from Demas' right.

But he didn't attack Demas. He jumped onto the back of the bear and held on with his huge claws as the bear reared back in shock and defense.

Demas could not believe his luck. The lion must have had some kind of memory, some kind of connection to the human who had fed him and cared for him in its captivity. It was rescuing him instead of attacking him.

Demas rolled to his feet, his left arm numb from the bear bite, his right shoulder stinging and bleeding from the wolf. He picked up his whip and snapped it at his growling nemesis.

Behind him, the lion had sunk its teeth into the back of the neck of the bear as the ursine beast continued to twirl around in a confused circle trying to shake the big cat off its back.

Demas spared no second. He aimed for the left eye of the wolf and ripped it out of his enemy with a well-placed snap.

The crowd rose to its feet with wonder and applause.

But the beast would not stop. It turned to look at Demas with its good eye.

Demas snapped again and shredded half of its right front leg. Another aim and hard yank, and the back of its skull was popped open, exposing the brain. The animal stumbled toward Demas and fell dead at his feet.

A deafening cheer roused his hopes.

He turned to see the bear reach up with one of its paws and drag the lion off its back onto the ground. They tumbled in the dust with voracious claws and fangs.

But it was not an equal match. The bear was much bigger and heavy.

It reared back with a roar before stomping on the feline.

A leather lash wrapped around the bear's neck from behind and iron bits dug into its flesh. This kind of move would not choke the bear, and it could not even do a bit of harm to it. It would only allow Demas the ability to hold on tight and ride its back.

The bear pulled away from the wounded lion and tried to free itself from the flea that now rode it like a bucking bronco.

Demas held on with his weakened left arm and pulled out his gladius with his aching right arm. He aimed to plunge it into the brain of the behemoth.

But his grip loosened. The sword flew from his hands. He lost his hold and followed the sword with a big thud into the dirt. The landing knocked his breath out of him. His ribs were bruised.

He looked up to see the bear standing over him on its hind legs to its full nine-foot-plus height. This thing could defeat a Nephilim. It roared. Demas could see blood and saliva splashing from its flapping jowls. He expected it to crush him any moment.

From out of nowhere, the lion leapt. It grabbed the unsuspecting bear right in the throat and pulled it to the ground.

Demas rolled out of the way as the crowd erupted in applause.

He looked around desperately for his sword. He spotted it and limped over to it.

The bear was on top of the lion. But the bear was still.

The lion struggled to pull itself out from under the dead monster that had crushed it with its weight. The lion's jaws were dripping with the blood of the bear's esophagus ripped from its throat.

But it could not get out.

Demas approached the lion.

The crowd gave a standing ovation. This was true entertainment worth the price of admission.

He walked up to his fighting partner with heartfelt sadness. He said to it, "Thank you, old friend," and plunged the sword into its heart. The lion opened its mouth in a silent roar and died.

The crowd fell silent. Their cheering stopped almost instantly at Demas' surprise finale. They could not believe it. Booing peppered the crowd. It was anticlimactic. It was animal cruelty to the very creature that had saved him from the claws of the bear.

Demas looked around him at the mob. He didn't trust their passions. They were fools carried along by their lust for blood and circuses. Of course he had to kill the beast. No amount of partnership against a common enemy could change the fact that this beast was still ultimately an enemy. It would turn on Demas, kill him and eat him after it had killed the bigger enemy. No temporary friendship would change its inbred natural instincts. The masses were idiots to project a relationship between man and beast. In the long run, a lion is a lion and a human is its enemy.

Damn the mob to Gehenna. He limped out of the arena to his iron gate.

When he arrived inside the gathering area for fighters beneath the stadium, he was accosted by the sight of two bestiarii hanging dead by their necks from the rafters. They were beaten bloody. One of them had his tongue hanging from his mouth in a hideous contortion. A gladiator in iron armor stopped on his way out to the arena. “Those are the two culprits who released the animals upon you.”

Demas stared with amusement at the hanging corpses. The gladiators had discovered the betrayal and reinforced their code of honor. Maybe this gang of guilded thugs was not so bad after all.

CHAPTER 2

Demas made his way through the graveyard of tombs just outside Scythopolis. His wounds had been dressed. His shoulder ached with the pain of vicious animal punctures. His ribs and left arm were bruised from the bear brawl, but he was whole. He was not too sure he was glad to be alive though.

He found a tomb marked with his adopted family name, "Samaras."

He paused, unsure if he could follow through with this. It would have been so much easier had he just been mauled to death in the arena. Then it would be his brother here, bringing Demas' body, or what remained of it, to lay in the crypt. Demas would no longer have the dark shadow over him that followed him everywhere he went.

He had to do this. He used a large wooden post as a wedge to move a circular stone that covered the grave opening.

He bent down and entered the four foot high entrance.

Tombs were the luxury of the upper classes in society. The average poor man was buried in a shallow grave with nothing but a mere stone with markings to indicate who it was who awaited their resurrection from this spot. The rich were able to afford crypts where entire families would be able to "go to sleep with their fathers," as the saying went. Sleep was the common metaphor used to express their hope that one day Yahweh would return and resurrect the dead for judgment. There was a debate within the Pharisee and Sadducee circles about resurrection. The Pharisees believed it, but the Sadducees did not. Demas was inclined to agree with the latter, more liberal group. But in the end, such petty debates over dogma didn't really matter to him anyway. He would never get his beloved back.

The burial chamber was just tall enough for him to stand with a slight stoop, and wide enough to contain several "beds" carved out from the walls to lay corpses upon. Enough sunlight leaked in through the entrance to light the interior with few shadows.

He walked up to a carved out shelf at the back where several ossuaries rested. They were small stone boxes, about three feet long and two feet wide, marked with prayers that housed the bones of his deceased parents. These were his adopted parents who lost their lives in a plague years back.

This world was cold and brutal, like the edge of a gladius. Not many lived into their thirties or forties with all the sicknesses, thuggery, war and revolution under Roman oppression. Demas and his brother Gestas had survived too much in this life, and that was one of the reasons why Demas had given up. Their birth parents had been lower class Jewish citizens of Sepphoris, not too far from Nazareth in the west. Their father had been a stone mason who helped build some of the Herodian structures that he and his brother had ended up performing within later in life.

In the thirty-third year of the reign of Augustus Caesar, a Jewish rebel named Judas the Galilean rose up and led a revolt against Rome. The Roman governor had ordered a census of Judea in order to increase their taxes. Judas and a fellow Pharisee, Zadok, were driven by a holy zeal for the Law of God and used as their model of inspiration the Maccabean revolt of a hundred and seventy years earlier.

Jews had a particular animosity toward censuses because they felt it was an encroachment upon Yahweh's right to number his people and upon his ownership of the land. Judas considered armed rebellion the only option for faithful Jews and even started a slogan, "No king but God." "Caesar" was Latin for emperor or universal king. Such slogans were therefore a denial of the emperor's universal rule. And for Romans, such insurrection would not be tolerated.

Judas gained two thousand followers, but was ultimately defeated in Sepphoris when the Romans sacked the city. They crucified all the rebels on poles along the thoroughfares of Galilee as a warning sign for the disobedient. The Imperial legions were not known for respecting innocent civilians and killed too many of them as collateral damage in their frenzied retribution. Demas's parents were among the victims of this barbarous atrocity. He and his brother were but two and one-years old respectively. They were then adopted by their Hellenistic Jewish parents in Scythopolis, which remained their home to this day.

But this evil of Rome was only the half of his grief.

In response to this provocation from Judas, Caesar placed Judea under direct provincial administration from Rome. The Herodian rulership over the Jews was restricted to Galilee, but the Roman army made its presence felt with quartered troops all over the territory. They delivered harsh punishments for every minor offense. The people lived in abject fear for their lives with the grip of Imperial Rome around their throats. It was within this disarray that Demas had grown up.

His face grew flush with hatred of these vile memories as he picked up an empty ossuary box. He breathed a sigh and turned to face the body that lay on the other side of the crypt.

He could not hold it back any longer. Tears flooded his eyes as he looked upon the bones of his beloved wife, Natasa. She had been dead over a year. The flesh and blood had decayed from her bones, leaving an intact skeletal form in quiet rest on its burial chamber bed. It was now time to take her bones and place them in the ossuary as was the custom.

He knelt before her and set the box next to him. As he looked upon the remains, he thought what a tragic pity it was for this to be the end of all men. Everything that made her unique, her beauty, her loving and kind personality, her creativity and talent, had all melted away, leaving the same bones that every other worthless and cruel criminal had. In the end we are all the same—dead bones.

He now really hoped the Pharisees were right and that there would be a resurrection. His beloved Natasa deserved it. Demas would, no doubt, burn in the fires of Gehenna, but at least she would have a reprise of existence.

He gently lifted her forearm bones to place them in the ossuary. Touching the bones of his beloved triggered memories of that fateful day. He broke down in a trembling howl.

They had been married but a few short years when Roman legions quartered in his city's homes again. One of the soldiers had seen Natasa's beauty and had come back one night to take her. When Demas was out of the home, the soldier broke his way in and tried to rape her. But in her defiant struggle, he accidentally broke her neck and killed her.

By the time Demas had tracked down who it was, and what company he belonged to, he was too late. The soldier had been killed in a battle with wilderness brigands.

Not only was she taken away from him, and made to suffer horrific terror, but Demas was denied the ability to exact revenge on her behalf or to receive even a shekel of satisfaction. From that moment on, he lived a life of eternal emptiness and despair.

That was why Demas no longer retained a belief in a just god. Yahweh was not just. He allowed terrible suffering to the good and innocent, while rendering satisfaction to the guilty and evil. No, Yahweh was not just. He was a cruel jokester of death and suffering in whom Demas could no longer maintain faith.

Will these bones live? If he could only find the bones of her killer, he could at least grind them to dust and cast them into the flames of Gehenna, so that he could insure the evil would not resurrect along with the good and somehow find forgiveness. That would be the worst mockery of all.

He placed the forearm and humerus into the box.

He stared at the skull. Her precious skull. He lifted it gently, as if it were a glass object of inestimable value. He looked into the sockets, trying to imagine the face that once filled his life with grace, beauty, and love.

"Demas." The voice came from the grave entrance.

It was Gestas, his brother. A year younger, and a more passionate soul than Demas. He was more handsome as well.

"I knew you would be here."

Demas placed the skull softly into the box.

Gestas said, "Here, let me help you, brother." Gestas stepped in and took a place next to Demas to help him respectfully place the bones in an orderly pile in the box.

Gestas felt terrible for his brother. He knew how deeply he had loved. In fact, he envied Demas. As an actor in the theater, Gestas had become quite well known and allowed to frequent the elite circles of Herodian power. He developed a reputation for being a philandering cocksman, seducing the women of wealth. But he saw that his immoral frivolity resulted in an aching emptiness of soul. He didn't believe in love. He only saw it from a distance in his brother.

Until he fell for an Herodian princess. A brunette beauty unlike any he had ever encountered. She was a rare and honest soul in a pit of immoral snakes, as he considered these treacherous Herodians. He wanted her purity to save him. When Gestas sought to marry her, he came to realize the delusion he had been living. He was suddenly cut off from the inner circle, disinvited from the palaces and parties. He, a lowly actor, no matter how famous he became for his talent in the theater, was still a lowly craftsman. He had never been and would never be nobility. They had been using him as much for their pleasure as he had been using them for his ambition. But in the end, it could never be. He could never transcend his social class. He had believed the masquerade he had been playing, and it had blindsided him.

His one chance at being known and loved by a woman had been dashed forever on the rocks of the Herodian ruling class. These were the traitors that fornicated with Rome and exploited the Jewish poor. These were the wealthy who bought and paid for the priesthood of Israel, turning the holy into an abomination. These were the bastards who were responsible for his brother's loss.

They finished placing the last of the bones in the ossuary.

Demas placed it on the stone bed and fit the top onto it.

"She was a good woman," said Gestas. "I still do not understand why she chose you and not me."

Demas forced a smile. There had been no competition. He was only trying to cheer him up.

"I could not make it to the venatio," Gestas interjected. "I had preparation for the play tonight. Did you slay the audience?"

"You could say that," muttered Demas.

Then Gestas spoke what he came there for. "Come to the play tonight, Demas. I want to take you somewhere afterward."

"Where?"

"Just trust me, brother." Gestas looked at the ossuary before him and pressed his palm against the engraved prayers and images along the exterior. "Opportunities for justice and retribution have a way of presenting themselves when you least expect it, when all other avenues have been exhausted."

Demas looked askance at Gestas. "What do you mean, 'retribution'?"

Gestas got up and stopped at the grave entrance. "Just come tonight. You will not regret it." And he left him.

CHAPTER 3

Fifty miles north of Scythopolis, the city of Caesarea Philippi was a hive of buzzing merchant and religious activity. Herod the Great was the first provincial ruler to embrace the cult of the emperor instituted during the reign of Augustus. He poured hundreds of talents of gold into rebuilding the city, still called Panias at that time, in Greco-Roman fashion to honor Augustus Caesar. A brilliant white palace he called the Augusteum sat above the city on a raised platform dedicated as a temple of Rome. The city's location was just twenty-five miles north of the Sea of Galilee, placed at the crossroads of east-west traffic between Damascus and the port city of Tyre, and north-south traffic between Syria and Galilee. This prime real estate made it a nexus of economic and cultural interchange.

When Herod split his Jewish kingdom into tetrarchies before he died, he gave Galilee to his son Antipas, Samaria and Judea to Archelaus, and the northern regions, which included the old city Panias, to Philip. Philip renamed Panias after himself as Caesarea Philippi.

Its population was a hybrid mixture of Greek, Roman and Semitic residents. Its religion, a fusion of Greco-Roman polytheism. But its real power lay just outside the city, up the hill, a brief walk away to a sacred grotto, the cave sanctuary of Pan. When Philip had renamed the city, the local priesthood retained the title Panias for their holy site. Its location in the foothills of the cosmic mountain Hermon, in the ancient land of Bashan, made it a spiritual nexus. Bashan meant, "place of the serpent," a heritage that went back to Og of Bashan, the last of the Rephaim giants that Joshua defeated. Bashan became the inheritance of the Jewish tribe of Dan, and the location for Dan's idol worship of the golden calf of Ba'al. This area would forever be the bane of Israel, as prophesied by their forefather Jacob, "Dan shall be a serpent in the way, a viper by the path, that bites the horse's heels."

It was to this sacred grotto that the two large eight-foot-tall beings walked as they passed the outskirts of Caesarea Philippi.

One was an overly built muscular male carrying a mace and wearing a conical cap of Canaanite deity. The other was a mature battle-maiden with buxom breasts and blood-stained battle skirt.

They walked along the river banks, up to its origin in a cave opening below a three hundred foot tall rock face. All along the face of the cliff, Greek-looking architectural frontispieces appeared carved out of the rock, creating a small necropolis of stone. What lived inside those elevated entrances was not readily apparent.

The beings came to the mouth of the grotto, where a large pool formed outside the cave as the headwaters of the Jordan River, a reflection of Eden's own cosmic mountain and rivers of living waters. Lush bushes and trees all around hid a thousand eyes that watched the beings approach the cave's entrance.

A small group of six nymphs met them to escort them inside. The nymphs wore transparent gowns and exotic jewelry. Nymphs were the seductive sexual courtiers of Pan, the god of passions and nature. The High Priestess, dressed in an exotic silken robe, embroidered with gems, had been expecting them.

"Welcome to our sacred space," she said, "I am the Ob of Panias."

She continued with a deep bow, reiterated by the others with her. "The sacred order of Pan welcomes, with humble submission, the most high god, Ba'al and his escort, the mother of the gods, Asherah."

The gods were not so formally inclined. They had a job to do, and no time to delay. "Ob, we need your skills with necromancy," said Ba'al. "The time is come to call up the hordes of the dead."

They entered the large cave opening and followed the river back into the dark recesses. It had been so many ages since their primordial fall from heaven, that Ba'al and Asherah had forgotten their original names as Sons of God. Their gender was male, but some of them, like Asherah, were masquerading as goddesses, so they played the part to the full by modifying their bodies to appear female.

Ba'al had come so far in his quest for power. He began as an upstart deity before the Flood, when Anu and Inanna ruled the pantheon in Mesopotamia. When the Flood ravaged the earth and most of the gods were bound in Tartarus, Ba'al began to build his skills and strength until he became the most formidable of divinities, calling himself Ninurta, and then Marduk. It was not until he arrived in Canaan that he was able to ascend above the stars of heaven and become Elyon Ba'al, the Most High.

During the time of Israel's forefather, Abraham, the archangels invaded his palace on Mount Sapan in the far reaches of the north and cast him into the molten magma that flowed beneath the earth. But he came back with a vengeance when he was vomited out of the great volcanic island of Thera during the time of King David, their anointed one.

Ba'al had been nursed back to health by Asherah on the shores of Tyre, and she conspired with him to betray Dagon, chief god of the Philistines, in order to renew Ba'al's place as head of the pantheon. Over the generations of Israel's growth in her Promised Land of inheritance, Ba'al and Asherah had managed to worm their way into the hearts of Israelites like a couple of parasites. Though Jews were expressly forbidden by Yahweh from worshiping other gods or making images of them, the populace nevertheless became infatuated with them and whored after the Canaanite deities. The extent to which Jews gave them obeisance is the extent to which the gods had freedom and power to occupy the land and keep it from being inherited by Yahweh's people.

Ba'al was called by other names in various locations. He went by Ba'alzebul in the Philistine coastal cities, which meant, "Ba'al the Prince." He had various Israelite locations named after him such as Ba'al-Berith, Ba'al-Gad, Ba'al-Peor, and others. When his palace on Sapan was destroyed by the angels, he decided not to rebuild it and took as his own the holy cosmic mountain where the gods assembled, and in whose foothills lay this very Cave of Pan. Mount Hermon was now called Ba'al-Hermon.

Asherah, on the other hand, had been a great support to Ba'al. She did not seek to usurp his authority and became his ally in the pantheon. She worked patiently through subterfuge and cunning intrigue. In the days of the Israelite monarchy, she had managed to infiltrate Israel with her cult prostitutes and Asherim poles placed right beside the Yahwist altars of sacrifice on the high places.

She and Ba'al had both cursed the day that the pious prig King Josiah of Israel uncovered long lost scrolls of the Law of God they had neglected in their backslidden ways. He reformed the culture, cleansed the holy temple, and purged Israel of her high places and cult objects of idolatry. The gods' previous control diminished. Asherah and Ba'al wanted to ring Josiah's neck for the inestimable damage he had done to their stronghold of dominion.

Belial then pushed Assyria to decimate the ten northern tribes of Israel and guided Babylon to exile Judah for seventy years. With the Greek Hellenizing effect of Alexander the Great and then Rome's hegemony of worldwide control, Belial got his talons on Israel in a way Ba'al and Asherah were never able to. They were still delegated authority within the region, but as god of the world, Belial was the chief prince whom they supported.

Belial liked to rub it in their noses with the chores and responsibilities he gave them. Thus the current task at hand.

They arrived at a towering twenty foot tall golden statue in the center of the cave. The six nymphs held their torches high in adoration of the being: a satyr god with horns on his head, the torso of a man, and the hairy legs and hooves of a goat.

The Ob bowed before the graven image of Azazel, the ancient one. God of the desert wastelands and lord of satyrs. Jews called satyrs goat demons, but that was far too harsh and judgmental. The satyrs were almost all gone now, as a result of the Jewish desacralization of nature. Yahweh's creation narrative was different from all the others in that it had divested the world around them of gods and spirits. It spoke of a natural world tamed in the hands of the Creator. Rather than revere the elemental spirits and see themselves as slaves of Mother Earth, the earth was instead seen as a wilderness of chaos that was to be harnessed and domesticated by man. Yahweh had the gall to command mankind to take dominion over the earth and subdue it by pushing back the chaos and bringing order through agricultural, economic and energy technology. Yahweh had depersonalized nature, which lessened the captivity of man to the gods of nature.

Pan was a god of nature, the last of the satyrs. He now stood before the group of nymphs and their visiting divinities. He had stepped out from a crevice in the rocks to meet with them, the sound of his hooves clacking softly on the rocky floor.

"Welcome to my lair, Most High Ba'alzebul, and Lady Asherah of the Sea." Pan's eyes moved greedily over Asherah's voluptuous body. *What I wouldn't give to ravage this bitch*, he thought. She was a goddess of sexual vigor and fertility, and he was a god of passion and sexuality. He would give her an experience of ecstasy she would never forget, with some bruises and marks to remember him by.

There was something about this satyr's hairy primal nature that appealed to Asherah. She could smell his musty odor, and reveled in his lustful observation of her every move.

But she was here for an important job to do. If the goat touched her, she would crush his skull with Ba'al's mace.

"Let us get to the Abyss," she said with cold resistance.

Pan lifted his eyebrow, impressed with her bravado. He thought, *Such feistiness could prove more deeply satisfying with the conquering. I wonder if Ba'al would be up for a gang rape?*

"This way," said Pan. He turned and led them deeper into the cave's darkness. The torches were not all that necessary for the gods, since their eyes could see as well in darkness as in bright sunlight.

They came upon a large dark pit that cut deep into the earth. The nymphs circled the edge and used their torches to light incense censers before securing the torches in stands. The incense drifted hazily around the cavern and made the nymphs light-headed. The gods stood back and watched as the six nymphs poured chalices of honey, milk, and wine into the dark pit as a libation to the gods. They never heard the liquids hit the surface below because it was too long a drop.

What they could not see in the pitch black darkness at the bottom of that cliff were the primordial waters of the Abyss. These waters were both below the earth and above the firmament of the heavens where the throne of Yahweh rested on the waters. Leviathan, the seven-headed sea dragon, swam in this domain that gave it access to the many lakes, seas and rivers of the earth. Leviathan was the force of chaos that Yahweh had tamed for his purposes. He had emptied the sea monster's jaws at the War of Gods and Men before the Great Flood. He crushed the heads of Leviathan at the Red Sea in order to establish his covenant with Israel, a covenant that was understood as a creation of the heavens and earth. Subjugation of the dragon and the waters was the mark of sovereign authority and the power to create order out of *tohu wabohu*, the formless void.

The gods were not here for Leviathan this evening. They were at Panias for another purpose. The waters of the Abyss also operated as a passageway that linked the earth above with the underworld below. Panias had a nickname throughout the land. It was called the Gates of Hades.

The Ob entered a trance-like state and swayed like a serpent amidst the floating clouds of incense. Her pupils expanded to fill her eyes. No whites were left, only black pools of darkness. Obs were necromancers who called up the dead. The Ob and her nymphs were opening the Gates of Hades.

The gods went to the ledge and cast a piece of silver into the pit as a payment for their request. Then, one after the other, they used a sacrificial dagger to cut their palms and squeeze their blood into the pit.

Next came the sacrifice. Usually, a black pig or other special animal was slaughtered and laid at the edge for its blood to mix with that of the supplicant, to aid in calling up the spirits. But there was none. The nymphs were confused. They were normally given the dead pig to lay at the edge. But there was no pig to offer.

The Ob twitched and spasmed and spoke in foreign languages in a voice not her own. It was the language of Babel.

The three gods approached the nymphs like feline predators, their eyes fixed, their steps smooth and ready to spring. Then the nymphs realized why there was no animal to sacrifice. *They* were to be the sacrifice.

Each god grabbed two nymphs, one in each hand, and broke their necks. One of them got out a scream before being stifled by death.

Pan was disappointed. That poor slave was his favorite. He would never be able to embrace her sexually again. He considered doing so with her dead body as a last goodbye, but thought better of it when the howling sounds ascended from the pit deep below. They had to complete the ritual.

They cut the throats of the nymphs and placed them at the edge of the cliff. Their blood dripped down the ledge from their limp, broken forms.

The howling increased.

The Ob fell to the floor in a fit of seizure. She called out in her magnified croaking voice, "NEPHILIM, ARISE! COME FORTH FROM THE DARK EARTH TO FULFILL YOUR DESTINY!"

The ground around the precipice rumbled and all went quiet. Deathly quiet. The air had been sucked out of the cave and down into the pit, and all sound with it.

They waited in the vacuum of silence.

The Nephilim were the Fallen Ones, the Seed of the Serpent, and because they were heavenly hybrids, when they were killed in the Flood and thereafter, their spirits became disembodied demons. Now they were being called up *en masse* to finish the war they had started in primeval days, but this time as unclean spirits who inhabited the land and the people.

Demons could only possess those who invited them in. But unfortunately for Israel, many Jews violated the first commandment of Yahweh's Ten Words from Sinai, and worshipped the Canaanite gods. This failure gave the spiritual forces of this present darkness a grip of influence over Israel. She was infested with demons.

Another rumble, followed by the reverse of the sucking wind, and a gust of unimaginable force blew out of the pit, like a huge corpse reviving with breath. The gods fell to the ground before the whirlwind. It was like opening a crypt that sucked the surrounding air and began to breathe.

And then, it all stopped dead.

A new rush of sound took its place. A myriad of thousands of whisperings came out of the deep recess like water overflowing a cup. They washed over the Ob and the gods like angry waters. The ears of the summoners were pierced with the painful cries of violent Nephilim spirits suppressed for millennia, now freed to roam the earth.

The gods stood. Asherah belted out, “Come forth, my children! Fill the land with your presence!”

Ba’al added, “Inhabit its people and every dark corner! Messiah has come to claim the land and crush the head of the Serpent. But you must take hold and fight back! You must strike his heel!”

The whirlwind of voices kept coming like a flood, passing over them on their way out to the land. A deluge of demons in search of bodies to inhabit.

CHAPTER 4

Demas felt uncomfortable being a member of an audience. He was used to being the sole entertainer in the ring with thousands cheering him on. Other than the pain of battle wounds, his heroic animal baiting seemed to be the only other thing that made him feel alive in his dark reality.

Now, sitting in the theater of Scythopolis, amidst seven thousand cheering idiots, he felt the meaningless despair of being but one of a myriad of passive onlookers, manipulated and carried away by the pathos playing out on the stage before them.

The Greeks and Romans loved their entertainment. They spent so much time in the theater, the amphitheater, and the hippodrome, amusing themselves with sport and entertainment. Amusement was the way to avoid thinking about the sword of Damocles that hung over them all, waiting to drop at any moment and take their lives. The fools.

The theater was the largest in the Decapolis. It was built semicircular with stone seating that rose high above the stage on the hillside upon which it was built. Down below, between the audience and the stage, an orchestra played the music that stirred the pathos of the soul, while the chorus sang the logos of narration that captured the mind. The proscenium stage was three hundred feet wide with a massive "scene" backdrop behind it, constructed as the façade of a building. Various painted backdrops were hung to provide change of story location.

The audience seats were organized and separated by social rank, the plebeians naturally finding their place toward the rear. Since Demas was related to the lead actor on the stage, he found himself in the enviable location just behind the senators, equestrians and knights of the few front seats.

He didn't care for the theater, and he rarely attended, but tonight, his brother had requested it. Thank heavens pantomime had become more popular than the boring philosophical pontificating of the Stoic plays. Seneca was the worst. They amounted to little or no action with characters standing around giving speeches. Demas knew that the fine art of rhetoric could twist words to justify any immoral behavior known to man, from the anarchy of lawless barbarians to the tyranny of empire. But if they were going to do so, at least provide some kind of interesting visual and dramatic entertainment along with it.

Pantomime on the other hand, was wildly popular with the masses as its actors performed silent drama and dance to the accompaniment of narrating chorus and musical instruments. The audience wanted spectacle. If they wanted a sermon, they could go to synagogue. This evening's program was fortunately interesting to Demas: The Labors of Hercules. The story went that Hercules was required to serve penance for murdering his family, by engaging in twelve epic labors in service to King Eurystheus. Each episode was an astonishing feat such as slaying the huge Nemean lion or the many-headed Hydra, capturing a monstrous boar, or the Cretan Bull among others.

Demas related to the god-man hybrid protagonist Hercules. He too felt hated by the gods and cursed with the labors of his life. Every victory over monsters in the arena made Demas feel as if he was one step closer to that ever elusive sense of purpose. But he never arrived.

There was an inexorable struggle between fate and human will in the Stoic tragedies that Demas also understood deeply. They enacted stories of enduring heroes with upright spirits achieving victory over internal and external evil. Thus the solution to the universal dilemma of evil could be found not in the gods above to save humanity, but in man freeing himself from the ignorance of passionate excess and emotion. Demas' Jewish heritage however filled him with an opposing emotional passion, gusto for life, and righteous anger for justice. He felt as if two spirits fought within him for dominance, and these plays triggered that gladiatorial combat.

On stage, Gestas performed as Hercules achieving his twelfth and last labor, capturing alive the three-headed demon dog, Cerberus, the guardian of the Gates of Hades. Demas watched his brother wield his sword dramatically against various Shades of the dead in the fiery darkness. He observed with a critical eye because he had taught Gestas how to fight so that his acting would carry authenticity as well as prepare him for the dangers of real life. Six men operated the large monster suit of the hound of hell that frightened the female observers in the audience. As musicians played and narrators sang, Hercules captured the monster and dragged him out of the underworld offstage.

Demas wondered what the world of the dead was really like. All nations and peoples had their myths and stories of just what the "Land of No Return" held out for the destinies of men. Ancient Sumeria and Egypt told stories of gods who died and returned from the dead as mythical representations of the cycle of nature. Many other narratives of heroes like the Babylonian Tammuz or the Greek Odysseus, told tales of those who descended into the underworld in order to free a loved one from death. They all tended to portray a gloomy dark world where the unrighteous dead suffered in one form or another. The righteous dead, however were taken away to garden paradises, or "Isles of the Blessed."

Demas preferred the contrary voice of the Stoics. Although they were terrible entertainers with their plays, they were nevertheless more insightful with their rational philosophy. Hellenistic thinkers like Zeno and Seneca considered such myths of descent to be mere imagination, attempts to placate fears and speculate about what no one could possibly know. No one had in fact ever come back from the dead to reveal what happened to the soul upon its escape from its prison house of the body. Aeschylus the Greek Stoic playwright wrote, "Once a man dies and the earth drinks up his blood, there is no resurrection."

Demas decided he would not stay to watch the mimes. They would mock the Jews in their audience by parodying their religious observances. He got out of his seat during intermission to wait for his brother back stage.

"What did you think?" Gestas asked Demas, as he disrobed from his costume backstage.

"I think you need work on your swordplay," said Demas.

Gestas shook his head with a smile. "Come with me, and you'll get your wish. But we have to hurry. We are already late."

"Where are we going?" said Demas.

"To the scribal collegium," said Gestas.

The collegium was not the gym where they could practice sparring, but the school where scribes practiced and teachers educated students.

Demas continued confused, "What do scribes have to do with fighting?"

"More than you realize," said Gestas.

The sun was already setting when they arrived at the collegium in the upper class district of the city. They snuck in the back way so as to avoid being noticed. They slipped past large Corinthian columns into the atrium in the center of the school. No torches were lit. It was a secret meeting. Fifty Jewish citizens from all kinds of social classes and backgrounds filled the benches where students usually sat. Blacksmiths, carpenters, an equestrian and even a politician listened with rapt attention to the charismatic speaker before them.

Demas and Gestas stayed back in the shadows of the pillars. They watched the orator, a clean-shaven young man in his late twenties, with a handsome square jaw, long wavy black hair, and intense eyes. He was clothed in ruffian garments and armed with sword and dagger. A distinctive scar crossed his left cheek from his ear down to his chin, an obvious battle wound. But he spoke with eloquence and education, which was strange for a brigand and rabble rouser. He gave a rousing exposition intended to inflame his audience's passions. An immediate concern for Demas.

"The nation of Israel has been the slave of Gentile pagan forces for far too long. The Assyrians, the Babylonians, the Greeks, the Medes and the Persians, and now the Romans. My brothers, do you not remember Phinehas the priest during the time of the Exodus? The people of Israel were committing idolatry and playing the harlot with Ba'al at Peor. They were whoring with the daughters of Midian. And one man dared to bring a Midianite woman into the holy congregation. Yahweh's anger burned against Israel until Phinehas went and thrust through the man and his woman with a spear. This holy action of zeal atoned for the sin of the people. Yahweh withdrew his anger and made covenant with Phinehas to be a perpetual priesthood. Phinehas is our example of the zealots we must all become."

Demas and Gestas were familiar with the Torah story of Phinehas. They had heard it in synagogue while growing up. Demas leaned in and whispered to his brother, "Who is this man?"

"Shh," hushed Gestas. "Just listen."

The speaker continued. "Zeal for Yahweh. That is what I speak to you about tonight. We must all be zealots for Israel's holiness. For the prophecies have all pointed toward Messiah coming to free us from the yoke of the Kittim." Kittim was a derogatory reference that Essenes used of their Roman oppressors.

"The prophet Daniel spoke of this day. He said that there would be seventy weeks of seventy years from the decree of Cyrus to rebuild Jerusalem until the time of Messiah the prince. Seventy times seven years decreed to finish the transgression, to put an end to sin, and to atone for iniquity, to bring in everlasting righteousness, to seal both vision and prophet, and to anoint a most holy place. My brothers, that prophecy was four hundred and ninety years ago. Seventy weeks of seventy years."

A rumbling went through the audience of men, indicating agreement. Demas however was not so agreeable. This man sounded a little crazy. And dangerous to have such control over his sheep-like hearers.

"My brothers, do you not remember the Maccabees? When that despicable king, Antiochus Epiphanes, dared make our traditions illegal and tried to force our people to eat swine and violate our Sabbath. And worst of all, he set up his image in the holy temple, an abomination of desolation. But Mattathias Maccabeus refused to bow the knee and killed his own countryman who would worship false gods. His son, Judas the Hammer led a revolt that destroyed the pagan temples, and reinforced the Jewish covenantal sign of circumcision. He entered Jerusalem in triumph and cleansed the temple of the abomination of desolation, returning authority to Yahweh. The Maccabees pushed back their Greek oppressors like Leviathan the sea dragon, and Yahweh's inheritance was returned."

Demas knew that story well. It was the origin of their festival of Hanukkah. But now he saw the agenda. He shook his head and muttered, "Interesting. Will he mention the more recent uprisings of Judah ben Hezekiah and Judas the Galilean?"

Gestas gave him a sour look. But Demas would not back down. "Those revolts ended in thousands of Jews crucified." Such failures were not so inspiring to cite, but they happened, and more recently than the Maccabees.

The speaker continued. "My brothers, everything that the Maccabean revolt gained for us, the purity, the holiness, the zeal, was lost when the Herods took over the priesthood. The Herodians are the betrayers of our countrymen. They are not even true Jews. They are Edomites, sons of Esau. Pretenders and betrayers. They rob the common Jew and control the majority of the wealth of Israel. They conspire with Rome to keep us enslaved while they sit in their extravagant palaces drinking wine and eating pig. I ask you, do such rulers deserve their riches? Do they deserve to live when so many of us die?"

Demas knew Gestas had special hatred for the Herodians. That, no doubt, was what drew him to this eloquent desperado. They were the ruling class of Judea and Galilee. From Herod the Great to his sons who currently reigned as client kings of Caesar, the Herodians masqueraded as Jews, but were Romans in their loyalty. When Gestas was spurned for his attempt to marry into that aristocracy, he had gained a bitterness that plagued him and now blinded him to the maniacal dangers of this charismatic outlaw with a silver tongue and bloody hands. Demas became agitated. The speaker kept saying "my brothers, my brothers." But when such a man incited violence against their own kinsmen who would not join their cause, that man was dangerous indeed.

The speaker concluded. "I was a scribe. An Essene. I have spent my whole life studying the Scriptures and the holy texts, my brothers. I am telling you, the War of the Sons of Light against the Sons of Darkness has arrived. Are you ready? Will you be a zealot with me or will you stay chained in your slavery to Rome? Will you join the fight against our Herodian traitors or will you be cowards? I already have hundreds of followers hiding out in the wilderness. Join our band of Zealots and share our holy calling, "No king but God."

Ah, there is the reference to Judas the Galilean, thought Demas. Stripped of all reference to his failure, but promoting the slogan Judas became known for. No king but God. It was a call to revolt and return to their Mosaic theocracy, the rule of God. Caesar had pretended tolerance in allowing subjugated peoples to worship their own gods, just so long as they also worshipped Caesar as their ultimate King of kings and Lord of lords. This cunning brigand was trying to revive a movement begun by Judas and he had even given it a name: Zealots.

The speech was over and the men milled about. Gestas grabbed Demas. "Come with me. I want to introduce you."

Demas reluctantly followed his brother up to the charismatic speaker.

They were the first to approach him. Others seemed intimidated by the man's presence.

Not Demas.

"Gestas," said the speaker with a delighted look, "I see you have brought your famous brother."

Demas cringed. A master of flattery as well.

Gestas said, "Demas, I want you to meet Jesus, the leader of the Zealots."

"Call me Barabbas."

Demas gritted his teeth with distrust. *Bar Abbas* meant *Son of the Father*. Was this religious fanatic one of the delusional messiah pretenders?

Barabbas said, "We could use a good fighter like you for the cause."

Demas replied, "I am afraid I do not share your enthusiasm for lost causes."

"Lost?" said Barabbas. "On the contrary. Messiah is the only winning cause there is."

"Excuse me," interrupted Gestas. "I will leave you two to argue. I have to speak with Jacob and Demetrius." Gestas left them.

Demas said to Barabbas, "You are one of many brigand leaders and their messianic claims to such zealous devotion."

"Indeed," said Barabbas. "There is more than one shepherd who is sounding the alarm. But eventually, we will all unite in purpose."

"I am not so sure you would find me an obedient sheep," said Demas with a smile. He saw Barabbas as the same kind of controlling tyrant as all the others.

Barabbas smiled back. "An independent spirit. I like that. But do you really believe you belong to no community, obedient to no one but yourself?"

Demas felt like a man without a country, caught between two worlds, both of which he did not feel fully a part of.

"I distrust lawlessness as much as tyranny."

Barabbas continued, "In this very city, they hung the decapitated corpse of Israel's first king, Saul, on the walls of a temple to Ashtoreth." Demas knew his history. Scythopolis had been Beth-Shan in those days. Barabbas was using the word "Ashtoreth" as an insult that combined the goddess' name Asherah with the Hebrew word for shame, *bosheth.* His zeal filled every word he used.

Demas said, "Why did you leave your community at Qumran?"

Barabbas felt the sting of the challenge, but rose to it. "I got tired of a bunch of whining talkers who sat around attacking everything with their words but doing nothing with their actions. Nothing. They think Yahweh will come and save them, so they neglect their god-given duty to participate in real change. We Jews are a contentious lot. Essenes, Pharisees, Sadducees, Herodians. We spend more time fighting amongst ourselves as to who is the true people of God, while the godless take away our liberty to *be* the people of God."

Maybe this arrogant upstart wasn't all bad.

Barabbas challenged Demas, "Do you consider yourself a part of the people of God?"

"What do you consider the mark of membership?" said Demas.

"Circumcision and Sabbath to begin with."

Demas grabbed his outer garment and began to pull it up. "Do you require verification to listen to your sermons?"

Barabbas smiled. "No. But then there is the first commandment from Sinai. 'No king but God.' Do you agree?"

Before Demas could formulate his dodge for that one, they were interrupted by a man screaming. "Run! Roman Vigiles!" Vigiles were the watchmen of the city, established by Augustus to keep the order and police urban crimes.

Demas and Barabbas were by a pillared exit. They looked into the atrium and saw a cohort of Roman soldiers burst in from all around them. They were surrounded by twenty or more. The Jews scattered.

A Centurion called out, "You are under arrest for sedition!"

They knew the punishment for sedition: crucifixion. They had to get out of there.

Some men had drawn their weapons to protect themselves. But Demas could not see Gestas.

Suddenly, two Roman soldiers were upon them. Demas drew his sword and without hesitation cut them both down in swift, easy moves.

He looked over at an impressed Barabbas, who whispered. "Follow me. I know a way out."

"But my brother."

"He will be fine. He knows the rendezvous."

Barabbas slipped through the shadows into a passageway. Demas hesitated. But he could not see Gestas anywhere. He must have already left. Demas followed Barabbas into the darkness.

They made their way through corridors, avoiding a few Roman soldiers rushing about. Then they were out in the moonlight of the city.

Barabbas took him down dark alleyways to where some horses were tied up. They leapt upon them and raced out of the city to the desert hills.

Barabbas and Demas galloped their horses into the highlands of Samaria a couple miles outside the valley and the city. As they approached a rocky pass, Barabbas stopped and held Demas back. He made a whistle call, and Demas heard a response.

He looked above them and saw a dozen brigands, with arrows pointed at them, relax their aim to allow them through.

They approached a group of small, hidden caves with a hundred men milling about. Many of them recognized their leader and came to hear his report. Demas got cautious looks from most of them until Barabbas said, "He saved my life. He is with us."

He is with us. Demas didn't protest, but it angered him that this smooth tongue was trying to pull Demas into his game.

They got off their horses and were given some drink.

Within a half hour, a handful of others arrived with some of the audience from the collegium.

Gestas was not with them.

"What news?" asked Barabbas, as they gathered around the fire.

A burly man spoke up. "Jacob and Demetrius are dead, along with a few of the recruits. We brought these with us."

Barabbas looked over at the dozen or so recruits. "Congratulations men, whether you like it or not...," he looked at Demas, "you are now a part of the Zealot insurrection."

Demas ignored it. Let him think what he liked. He asked, "What about Gestas? Is he coming?"

The burly one looked fearfully at Barabbas. "Gestas was captured."

Demas' heart stopped beating. He became short of breath.

"Will he give us up?" another one asked.

Demas looked closely at Barabbas to see how he would respond. Would he have to kill this influential leader?

Barabbas said, "No. Gestas is true. But we must free him to afford these Kittim no opportunity." He looked straight at Demas. "What do you say, Demas? Will you join us in liberating your brother and ours?"

CHAPTER 5

Demas, Barabbas and eight other bandits hid in the shadows of moonlight. They looked up at the stone citadel where Gestas was imprisoned under Roman guard. Its imposing presence discouraged even Demas. It was a massive tower building of stone, six or more stories high, and no telling how deep. Four heavily armed and alert legionaries guarded the entrance. This was not going to be easy.

"If only we had an insider," said Demas. "Someone who could help us without being discovered."

Barabbas whispered, "I am taking care of that. Daniel will be here shortly with help."

"What kind of help?" asked Demas.

"Wait and see."

Demas shook his head. He always had to maintain control, this one. "We can't scale the walls. They have a mobile sentry. Our only chance would be to enter through the sewage system."

The others rolled their eyes. They did not relish the idea of sloshing through stinking filthy human waste-filled waters. The thought alone made one of them gag.

"Half of us can enter up through the latrine. The other half could strike from outside as a diversion. They would never expect it."

"And we would never forget it," said the one who gagged.

Suddenly the sound of a soldier approaching drew them back into the shadows. His legionary uniform with squeaky leather body armor, and clinking metal plates on chainmail gave him away long before he could see them.

It was a centurion. The transverse red crest or brush on the helmet indicated his rank at a distance.

A centurion? thought Demas. *What is a centurion doing out here? Did someone report us? would there be a guard with him?*

Demas grabbed his dagger, ready to lunge. The goal would be to kill quickly before he could make a sound.

The centurion stopped. He looked into the corner where the men where hiding.

Demas prepared to jump the Roman and cut his throat, when the soldier whispered, "Barabbas?"

Barabbas stepped out and gestured for the others to follow. "It's okay. This is Daniel."

Demas said, "You have a legionary contact?"

"Well, no actually. Daniel is one of the actors at the theater with Gestas. This is one of their costumes from the plays."

"Excellent," said Demas. "Take it off."

Demas approached the citadel entrance in the centurion outfit shoving a chained Barabbas in front of him as a fake prisoner. The legionary armor was authentic, since their playmaster believed in using the real thing. It was all quite uncomfortable and heavy. He wondered how anyone could fight effectively weighed down by all this armor. And he could already feel it strafing his arms underneath.

They stopped by the four guards at the entrance and saluted.

Demas said, "I caught another Jewish insurgent." Barabbas kept his head down to avoid recognition. His shackles were held closed by a tiny string that he could snap open with one yank. He carried a dagger beneath his cloak.

One of the guards answered, "We have special orders, sir, not to allow any entry."

Right now, Demas was wishing he had his brother's acting skills. He could very well ruin this entire plan.

"Of course, soldier. And why is that?"

"Because of the importance of our prisoner. He is an insurgent."

Demas acted impatient with the soldier's ignorance. "Exactly. And who did I just tell you I have with me as prisoner, you moron? *Another insurgent.*"

"Sir, we were told to report anything like this directly to the Tribune." The Tribune was over the centurions and was usually an aristocrat on his way up the ladder of political power.

"Then report it, fool. And let me through. I don't have time for your incompetence."

"Yes, sir." The soldier jogged off to make his report.

Demas demanded, "Where is the other prisoner?"

The soldier straightened up. "The normal cells, sir."

Oh great, thought Demas. *If I have to ask where the normal cells are, he will surely find me out.*

He would just have to wing it and pretend he knew where he was going.

He pushed Barabbas past the guards and they entered the belly of the beast.

Demas had no idea where they were going.

They walked down a corridor and heard several soldiers on break playing dice. They passed that room and found themselves in a stairwell. The tower was about six floors tall and they were on the ground level.

Demas whispered, "What do you think, up or down?"

"Up," muttered Barabbas.

Demas pushed him to take the stairs down. It was a power play at a dangerous moment.

It was one flight to the bottom. The stairs opened up to a hallway that led up to a guard post with two more soldiers. Demas still could not be sure this was the right way, but the guards saw them now, and they could not step back into the stairwell without drawing suspicion. He had to move forward and look like he knew what he was doing.

Halfway down the hall, They passed the latrine on the right. Demas smiled to himself remembering the bandit who had gagged at the thought of it.

When they arrived at the guard post, Demas noticed the bars on the door.

"Legionaries," he said with as much assurance as he could muster, "I have another insurgent on orders from Tribune Gallus. Open up."

One of the guards, an older gruffy soldier, looked at him funny. He said, "Tribune Gallus is over in Pella. Do you have your papers, sir?"

Demas had thought Gallus was the local Tribune. Did he transfer or was his just visiting Pella?

"I expect more respect when you address your superior. Gallus had no time to write up papers. We are on the trail of more insurgents and I need to drop off this prisoner immediately."

Barabbas saw the gruffy one slowly place his hand on the hilt of his sword. The other guard did as well. Barabbas tightened, ready to spring.

The soldier said, "I am sorry, sir, I mean no disrespect. However, we are under orders of the Tribune."

They were interrupted by the sound of two soldiers arriving from the stairs. Evidently replacements. Fresh and armed.

Oh no, thought Demas. He turned back to the gruffy one, who was now smiling.

The Roman said, "Sir, Gallus is not the Tribune here. Caius is. But you would know that if you were a true centurion."

The soldiers both drew their weapons.

Barabbas moved with lightning speed. He snapped open his shackles. He pulled the dagger from the belt of one of the guards beside him and jammed it into the man's throat. The guard choked and dropped to the floor.

The gruff one swung immediately at Demas. Demas dodged the blade and drew his own.

The soldier yelled to the two men approaching Demas from the rear, "Soldiers! This centurion is an imposter!"

The other soldiers paused for a moment, surprised by what they just heard.

Barabbas drew the dead guard's sword and faced off against the gruff one.

Demas turned to face the others. For a moment, he was reminded of how he had been attacked by multiple beasts at once in the arena not many days ago. This time, he had help.

Inside the holding cell of the stone dungeon, Gestas woke from his sleep, roused by the commotion just outside the door. He heard swords clash. He saw a head hit the bars on the door window and slide down out of sight. He heard the gurgling cries of death beneath a swift sword.

He could only think one thing, *Demas*.

The sound of keys fumbling in the lock was followed by the dungeon door opening up to Barabbas and his brother.

Demas said, "We are getting you out of here."

Demas ran over to the cell door and opened it as Barabbas stood watch.

The brothers embraced. Demas handed Gestas a sword. "This is not the stage, Gestas. Strike with surety or we will not get out of here alive."

Demas led them out the door and through the hall over the four bodies of the dead soldiers.

Wait, thought Demas. *There are only three. I thought we got them all.*

The three of them bounded up the stairway and arrived at the walkway out of the building.

Demas whispered, "Hide your swords. You are my captives."

Gestas and Barabbas responded immediately.

The guards at the entrance had seen them and were watching them approach. They were fifty feet away.

Demas held onto Gestas by the gruff of the neck as if to pull him along in his charge. “We are under attack. I’m getting these two out of here.”

They were almost upon the exit when the wounded soldier Demas thought he had killed arrived limping with four more soldiers.

“That’s him!” yelled the wounded man. He collapsed to the ground. One of guards at the entrance sounded a ram’s horn.

Demas, Barabbas and Gestas turned around and ran back the way they had come.

At the end of the hall, they saw to their left an opening to a small courtyard, where ten other soldiers where bounding their way toward them.

They entered the stairway to climb to the top, but they heard another dozen soldiers above them on their way down.

Demas looked out and saw the eight bandits they had left outside the prison attacking the soldiers at the entrance.

But they could not go back into the fray. It would be a slaughter. “There is only one way,” said Barabbas. They bounded down the stairs back to the dungeon area.

They heard the soldiers exit the stairway into the hall, to fight the other bandits. Good. They were temporarily unnoticed.

They ran back towards the cell. Demas stripped off his centurion garb.

Gestas spit out, “It’s a dead end. We’ve run back into the bowels of hell.”

“Precisely, Gestas,” said Barabbas. “So that we can be shit out of here.” He pulled them to the latrine room, lined with toilet holes carved in wooden covers over a long ledge built for a dozen men to sit upon.

“We are going out the sewer system.”

They pulled off two toilet seats. Demas was down to his tunic. “Hold your nose.” They were using Demas’ plan after all, only in reverse.

They climbed into the portals and landed down in the sewage system, with a splash of filthy water.

Gestas exclaimed, “Disgusting.”

“It was your brother’s idea,” quipped Barabbas.

“I must say, Demas,” said Gestas. “You always were an asshole.”

Barabbas smirked.

“Very funny,” said Demas. “This way.”

By the time they arrived at the Zealot hideout, the waste had dried on them and was cracking off in pieces. They had stolen some horses and arrived shortly before the other brigands.

When the others arrived, they were two men short, with several wounded. "We lost Daniel and Micah," said the lead brigand.

"Get these men's wounds dressed," said Barabbas. The wounded were helped off their horses and brought inside the caves.

Barabbas turned to Demas and Gestas, surrounded by the men. "Well, Demas. What say you now of the cause?"

Demas could not say much. Barabbas had risked his own life to help rescue his brother. Two men of this band of brigands had given their lives in the venture.

"I thank you for your help. But I also know that Gestas was important to the secrecy of your plans and protection."

"True enough," said Barabbas. "But where else will you go? Who else will not give you up? You are both too famous to hide in cities."

Demas cursed himself for the truth of Barabbas' point. The brothers were both considered insurrectionists regardless of the facts, and they were both under the death sentence of sedition. They would never be able to return to their home. They could never have their lives back. If they tried to hide out in another city, it would only be a matter of time before they were recognized and captured.

They had no choice. They had to join Barabbas.

Demas protested, "We will carry our weight, but we will not kill innocents and we will not rob the rich."

"I like a man of principle," said Barabbas. "But I do believe your brother can speak for himself."

Barabbas looked to Gestas, whose eyes darted back and forth between his brother and this powerful leader.

"I am truly grateful for your rescue of me," said Gestas. "I owe you my life and allegiance. But I also stand by my brother."

Barabbas said to them both, "I respect your steadfastness of mind, and I trust you." He thought for a second, then concluded, "I trust you such, that I will ask you to go on a mission for me. Not as warriors, but as spies."

The brothers glanced at one another, wondering what they were getting into.

"Some time ago, I sent my closest ally, a man named Simon ben Josiah, to investigate stirrings around upper Galilee. There is an itinerant rabbi they call the Nazarene, who has gained a following. The rumors are that he speaks of a messianic kingdom and the visitation of Yahweh in judgment. I sent Simon to find out if the rumors were true and if this—rabbi—is with us or against us. I never heard from Simon again. It has been months."

"How do you know something is wrong?" asked Gestas.

"Simon was like a brother to me at Qumran. We left the Community together with one purpose. I owe him my life. And he owes me his."

Demas looked to Gestas again for agreement. They could communicate without words. "Where did you last hear of him?"

"Capernaum. It's where the Nazarene had lived for a time."

"We will find Simon for you," said Demas. "But first, we need to bathe. We stink like excrement." The men around laughed.

"Indeed we do," said Barabbas. "And if the Nazarene is for revolution, perhaps you might persuade him with your happy disposition to join our stinking party."

The men chuckled again and broke up to care for the camp and take their posts of watch. Gestas took some wine from a fellow bandit to quench his thirst before washing.

Barabbas pulled Demas aside.

"The rumor is this Nazarene shares my name, Jesus."

Demas nodded.

Barabbas added, "If he is against us and Simon has changed his allegiance, I want you to kill them both."

Demas looked reluctantly at his new leader.

"I am sure you can understand how serious it would be if your own brother betrayed you."

Demas would not answer him. What would it take to kill his own brother? What would he do if the only person he had left in all the world turned against him?

"Do not worry, Demas, this rabbi and his followers are not rich—or innocent."

CHAPTER 6

Simon ben Josiah could not believe what he had just seen. He had been staying at Simon Peter's home with Rabbi Jesus and his other disciples, and the Rabbi had just healed Peter's mother of a fever, when a Roman lord arrived to thank him for healing his servant of paralysis.

It was not the healings that he was astounded by. That was almost a daily occurrence with the Rabbi. Simon had seen epileptics calmed, fevers cooled, and even yesterday, a leper instantly cleansed. It seemed that every time they entered a new town, the Rabbi would cast out a dozen demons riled up by his presence, in addition to the dozens he would heal of sicknesses. This one had been healed remotely, without the Rabbi being in his presence.

It was not this miraculous healing that astonished Simon. It was who he had healed. The lord of the servant was a Roman centurion! Not merely a Gentile, but the armed oppressor of Israel!

Simon had been with Jesus for quite a while now, but the Rabbi was still a mystery to him. Simon had been sent by Barabbas to find out if the Nazarene was a fellow revolutionary, a self-proclaimed messiah, or something else. Simon's heart had been strangely moved by this stranger and he was still trying to figure him out.

But the Rabbi remained a mystery to him. The centurion had asked him to heal his servant and Jesus replied that he had not seen such great faith in all of Israel. That was shocking enough, to attribute such goodness to a filthy, unclean stranger to the covenant. But then he said that many such people would come to the feast of Abraham, Isaac, and Jacob in the kingdom of heaven, while the sons of the kingdom—in other words, *Israelites*—would be thrown into the outer darkness where there is weeping and gnashing of teeth.

As an Essene scribe at Qumran, Simon had spent his whole life in rituals of cleanness and separation. He had spent days with the Pharisees, the Sadducees and even amongst the Essenes themselves debating who were the true Jews of Israel and who were not. The existence of the monk community of Qumran, separated from the rest of Israel on the isolated shore of the

Dead Sea, was for this very reason. They had concluded that they alone were the only true remnant of Israel and all the rest were apostate frauds who would be thrown into that outer darkness of wailing and gnashing of teeth.

The Rabbi's condemnation of Israelites was all too acceptable to Simon. But then, to eat meals with sinners and harlots, to touch the unclean, and to embrace the godless Kittim was incomprehensible to Simon. It was like making the unclean clean and the clean unclean. It was like saying that God would adopt his enemies and disinherit his own children. The opposite of everything Simon had learned.

The centurion and his servant hugged the Rabbi in the presence of all the disciples. The centurion said, "Jesus, I can never repay you."

Jesus replied, "Your faith is enough. Now, stop extorting money from those beneath you, and be content with your wages."

Simon wondered, as all the disciples had wondered, that if Jesus was the Messiah long hoped for, why would he not call for this man to lay down his arms or join him in preparation for revolt against Rome? Did not the Scriptures say,

Yahweh said to me, "You are my Son;
today I have begotten you.
Ask of me, and I will make the nations your heritage,
and the ends of the earth your possession.
You shall break them with a rod of iron
and dash them in pieces like a potter's vessel.

And the scrolls of the Dead Sea Community confirmed a War of the Messiah against the Roman Kittim:

As it was said by Isaiah the Prophet, there shall come forth a shoot
from the stump of Jesse the Branch of David,
And they will enter into judgment with the Prince of the
Congregation,
But the Branch of David will kill him
And a Priest of Melchizedek will command the slain of the Kittim.

Simon could not forget the sermon Jesus had proclaimed on the mountain not many days ago. It haunted him. Roman law granted the right for a legionary to force any civilian to carry his supplies for him at least one mile. Rather than countering such an unjust law, Jesus said that they should carry the supplies an extra mile above and beyond their duty. He spoke of loving their enemies and praying for those who persecuted them. Local rabbis scoffed at him as he offended their interpretations of Torah, the Law of Yahweh.

So much of that sermon was offensive to Simon's own sense of holiness, and yet, there was something so right with this man. Simon was rethinking everything he had been taught in the Community. He was afraid of how the rabbi had affected him. He failed to return to Barabbas or even send a report, because he was drawn more to Jesus than Barabbas. If Jesus should prove to have hidden plans of revolution that opposed Barabbas, he was supposed to kill him. But Simon could never do such a thing. The Rabbi was the incarnation of Shalom, the peace of wholeness that he had sought for all his life. And it seemed to be a wholeness that worked against the division that was fomented by the revolutionaries.

But what was Jesus hiding? If he was Messiah, when would he rise up? Where was his army? He needed more time with him.

"Simon," said Jesus, breaking Simon's wandering thoughts.

"Yes, Rabbi?"

"I would like you to meet Gessius and his servant Joram."

Simon nodded uncomfortably. The centurion smiled.

"This is Simon the Zealot."

Jesus knew Simon's Zealot background and used the nickname to tease him.

Then, looking straight at Simon while talking to the Roman, Jesus said, "I think you two have more in common than you think."

Simon was thrown. What did he mean by that remark? A zealous Jew having anything in common with an aggressive Kittim? All this mixing of clean and unclean, Jew and Gentile confused him to no end.

Gessius spoke up. "I am sorry to say, my lord, that a large crowd has followed us."

Peter turned from looking out the window. "Oh no, not again," he complained. "Sometimes these crowds are suffocating." He looked at Jesus. "You are exhausted, Rabbi. There will be plenty more time tomorrow for you to cleanse and heal."

"I have an idea," said Jesus.

Outside Peter's house, the crowds were indeed suffocating. They filled the streets and back alleys, hundreds of them. Many were sick, looking for healing, others were simply miracle hunters looking for a spectacle. Jews may have disparaged the arena and its games, but they still loved their entertainment like anyone else, and miracles were truly entertaining. As some watched the door, a number of them crying out for help, others watched for any little movement that would indicate Jesus's presence.

Suddenly, the door of the home opened up, and the twelve disciples exited quickly, as if in a hurry. The whole group of them moved together so fast that people were not sure if they could see Jesus with them or not. But these were all his disciples, so they had to be protecting their master. The crowds followed them, yelling out and begging for healing and attention.

The disciples got down to the shoreline of the city and quickly entered their boat to take them across the lake. It was getting dark, so the people could not see the faces of the men clearly to determine whether or not Jesus was among them.

It was a diversion. Jesus had told his men to cross the Sea of Galilee and he would see them on the other side. While the crowds followed the group of disciples, Jesus stayed behind and snuck out of the house alone.

By the time the disciples cast off into the waters, the crowd had already begun to disperse back to their homes for the night. Their entertainment had left them.

Some of the children stayed to watch the boat glide away on the water as the sun was setting behind them. Calls for dinner drew them all back to their homes, except for one curious little eight-year old girl, Anna, who noticed something in the water. There was a swirling movement like that of a large fish just beneath the surface. It approached the land where she stood transfixed.

She drew her breath in a hush as she saw a large creature rise from the water. It looked human and female, but it was almost twice as big as any woman she ever saw. She was naked and her battle-maiden body glistened like bronze from the water. Was this a Shining One that she had heard of in her bedtime stories?

She wasn't afraid. She was mesmerized. She forgot to breathe.

The being saw her and tread the sand right up to her with a graceful smoothness that made her feel safe. She noticed the being's eyes were like that of a serpent, thin pupils in lapis lazuli blue eyes. Anna's head tilted skyward to look up at the charming shining woman that towered over her as a goddess.

Asherah reached down, placed her hand over the little girl's mouth, and snapped her neck.

She had just finished marking her enchantment spells in the bottom of the sea as a means to draw forth Leviathan, and she needed a human sacrifice to complete the ritual. A child was perfect. Innocent blood carried more weight in the world of spirit. Molech would have been happy for such opportunity. If he were here now, he would have asked for the remains so he could engage in his despicable acts with the corpse.

She had to hurry. She had little time.

•••••

Thunder rumbled in the night sky above the fishing boat that carried the twelve disciples across the Sea of Galilee. Lightning cracked. Simon could see one of the disciples leaned over the boat's side, retching into the waters in the pelting rain. Obviously not one of the fishermen. Earlier, the wind had whipped up as if from nowhere into a tempest that hindered their journey across the huge lake.

They had taken down the sail before it ripped off the mast. Now, everyone's attention focused on keeping the boat from capsizing. Water was filling the boat. Several tried desperately to bail it out.

Another lightning bolt lit up the sky. Someone screamed, "A phantom!"

Everyone turned to see a human figure walking toward the boat on the surface of the water about a hundred feet out. Who else but phantoms of dead ones could do such a thing?

Simon, however, had looked down when the lightning flashed and saw something below the boat that captured his attention. It looked like the scaled back of a huge fish a couple feet down into the murky water. But a second flash illuminated several heads stretching out on several necks.

Leviathan the sea dragon.

He had read about this monster in the Scriptures and in other ancient manuscripts from the Qumran library. It was the unstoppable monster of chaos. No human harpoon could pierce its hide. Leviathan was there when the Sons of God sang over creation. It was at the War of Gods and Men before the Flood. It was there at the Red Sea when Pharaoh attacked the Israelites. On earth there was not its like, a creature without fear. It was the king over all the sons of pride.

And right now, it was a couple feet below the waves, ready to rise up and crush their boat into splinters.

But it didn't. It didn't seem to swim or move. It was as if the sea dragon had been hypnotized into stillness. Then Simon could see it was Jesus who was walking upon its back, mere inches below the water.

That is when Simon heard the voice of Jesus calling to them from the water. "Take heart! It is me. Do not be afraid!"

The storm was subsiding and the waves had lessened. The rain became a drizzle.

Peter blurted out, “Lord, if it is you, command me to come to you on the water.”

Simon knew Peter was gutsy, but he was also a bit thoughtless. He obviously had not seen what was lurking in the dark waters.

Simon watched as Peter stepped out of the boat and onto the water. His eyes were fixed on Jesus, so he did not see the creature that he was walking upon below his feet in the darkness. Nobody did, except Simon.

The dragon was so huge that he must have created a walkway for Jesus to approach the boat. Did he ride the creature to this location as one would a trained pack animal? Simon saw Peter look down and when he did, he began to sink in the water, but then Jesus held out his hand, Peter grabbed it, and he rose back up.

The two of them walked back to the boat and got inside it.

As soon as they did, the wind stopped, the rains ceased, and Simon could see that the sea dragon was gone. How could he explain to the others what he knew? They had seen the miracles that Jesus performed. But would they be able to handle a vision into the spiritual reality he just experienced?

It became clear to Simon what had just happened. Jesus had shown mastery not merely over the storm, as Ba’al might, but over the forces of chaos. He tamed the untamable Leviathan. He walked upon its back as would a conqueror upon the neck of his defeated foe. When Yahweh had divided the Red Sea in the exodus, he crushed the heads of Leviathan. He pushed back the chaos of the waters to establish his covenantal order with Moses and the people of Israel. He created order out of the disorder of the cosmos, like creating the heavens and the earth. What was this amazing event but a sign of Jesus’s power to vanquish the chaos and establish a new covenantal order, a new heavens and earth? This rabbi was no mere human Messiah, he was a god-man.

CHAPTER 7

After the disciples had crossed the Sea of Galilee, they stayed near the town of Gergesa of the Gadarenes. The next day, some of the townspeople led Jesus and his followers up to a cliff where the tombs of the area lay. Graveyards were locations that caused uncleanness because of the corpses and death. To Simon, it was yet another violation of his heritage of ritual separation so necessary to holiness. To make matters worse, this area was part of Bashan, the place of the Serpent, the old kingdom of Og, last of the Rephaim. It had too many dark connections in his mind to allow him any peace of mind.

As they neared the tomb area just above the cliff wall, they passed a pig herder leading a herd of swine. The herder was a Jew who seemed ashamed when he saw Jesus. Simon knew it was because Jews were forbidden pork in their diet, so a Jew herding pigs was a particularly shameful act against their Torah.

Before they could go any further, two men jumped out from the rocks to block their way. They were naked from head to feet and unshaven, with long, ratted hair that made them look like animals. They both had shackles on their hands and wrists, one chained, the other broken clean.

Simon stepped near Jesus. He could smell their rank odor even from eight feet away. Then he saw why. They had smeared their bodies with excrement. Simon gagged.

The two men stood side by side, chests heaving like wolves ready to attack. Some of the disciples stepped back in fright, making sure they were behind the Rabbi.

Simon looked over at Jesus. The Rabbi was not afraid. But he was surprised and serious as he stared at the two men.

One of them cackled like a hyena. The other bellowed with the sound of a hundred voices laughing.

It chilled Simon to the bones. He now knew they were facing demoniacs. But he had never seen such a frightening presence in the possessed persons that Jesus had previously cast out in the villages. These two seemed different. It was as if something serious had changed in the air, in this spiritual war of the heavenlies. A small whirlwind encircled the two hairy demoniacs. Brush and leaves flew about, dust billowed up from the ground to create a small cloud. The eyes of the wild men had no whites. They were completely black, like the Abyss, and their stare burned into Simon's soul. He could tell the other disciples felt the same way.

The cackling devilish fiend held up his hands. Simon noticed they were still shackled. He snapped the thick chain as if it was nothing. These creatures were mighty. Simon doubted that the entire group of disciples could withstand their fury.

The monster gurgled out, "I adjure you by the Living God, do not torment us!" It was a common phrase of magical incantation, used by exorcists for the binding of spirits. It was followed by gibberish words that Simon recognized from the Greek magical papyrus texts he had read in his past study of magic. These two creatures knew that Jesus meant to bind them, and they were trying to reverse that curse back upon the Rabbi.

It had no effect.

Jesus said to them, "You will leave these men."

Suddenly, both of them screamed with the sound of a thousand furies, "NOOOOOOOOOOO!" They ran full speed at Jesus. Simon and the others stepped back in fear of the impact.

A moment before they hit Jesus, they stopped, as if they had collided with an invisible wall. They screeched again. The sound pierced Simon's ears. Everyone clapped their hands over their ears, except Jesus.

Jesus stood still and firm, staring right back into the dark pools of eyes.

The demoniacs looked frightened. As if they had seen a ghost. They spoke in unison, "What have you to do with us, Son of El Elyon?" El Elyon meant "the Most High God." It was the name that Ba'al had stolen for himself as the leader of the pantheon at Hermon.

"What is your name?" demanded Jesus.

Both of them jerked and twitched as if the spirits were losing control of their bodies.

They answered, "Legion."

Legion? thought Simon. *A legion was around six thousand armed forces. Could this be true? Could there be that many? Could they be lying spirits?*

Evidently, Jesus knew they were not. He raised his hands and the two demoniacs froze like puppets in the hands of a puppetmaster.

One of them screeched like a child, "Please, we beg of you, do not cast us into the Abyss!" The other finished his sentence, pointing at the herd of pigs that passed them by during their altercation. “Send us into that herd of swine. Please!”

Jesus kept his eyes on the two of them and prayed.

The two fell to the ground and flopped around like fish out of water trying to survive. What the disciples saw next took several minutes but seemed like an eternity, as each of the multitude of demons exited the two men’s bodies like a small increasing whirlwind of souls.

Finally, after the last of the demons had left their hosts, the whirlwind moved over to the herd of swine and engulfed the animals like a rushing wind. The pigs squealed with their possession and reacted by stampeding their way to the edge of the cliff. The herdsmen ran after their animals, only to see them launch off the cliff to their deaths in the waters below.

The herdsmen glared angrily at Jesus, and ran back down toward the city.

Peter said with amusement, “You just ruined their illegal business, Rabbi. I guess that puts them in a real bind.”

Simon added with disgust, “Jews selling swine. They should be flogged.”

Jesus gestured to the two men, now laying on the ground awakening from their unconsciousness. “Get them some clothes and water.” Some of the disciples did so as Jesus sat down on a rock.

He looked troubled. Simon asked him, “What is wrong, Rabbi?”

Jesus stared out into the void. “The Gates of Hades have been opened. The Nephilim have returned.”

A wave of understanding washed over Simon. *Of course*, he thought. *My obsession with separation and uncleanness blinded me to the spiritual truth.*

Peter asked, “What does that mean, Rabbi?”

Jesus remained silent and distant.

Simon tried to help out by explaining it to Peter and the others who listened. “The healings, the exorcisms. They are not mere tricks of magic power intended to invoke awe, like a circus spectacle. The lepers, the blind and the lame—and sinners—are all those who are not allowed in the Temple because of their uncleanness. They are cut off from the privilege of Yahweh’s holy presence by Torah. By casting out the uncleanness, Jesus is purifying the land and the people of Israel. He is preparing us for our inheritance.”

The disciples remembered when Jesus had read the prophet Isaiah in synagogue and proclaimed its fulfillment. But now it was beginning to make more sense to them.

The Spirit of Adonai Yahweh is upon me,
because Yahweh has anointed me Messiah
to bring good news to the poor;
he has sent me to bind up the brokenhearted,
to proclaim liberty to the captives,
and the opening of the prison to those who are bound;
to proclaim the year of Yahweh's favor.

"And what of the Nephilim?" asked Peter. "We have seen no giants since the days of King David."

Simon explained, "Demons are the spirits of the Nephilim. You will remember the readings in synagogue from the Scriptures that in the days of Noah, the fallen Sons of God mated with the daughters of men. Their unholy offspring were the Nephilim, giant hybrid bastards of angel and human essence. This unholy mixing of heaven and earth, was a violation of the separation of creation. But it was also the attempt to corrupt the human bloodline of the promised Messiah who would crush the head of the Serpent."

Peter interjected, "The Nephilim were killed in the Flood."

Simon nodded. "Yes, but their seed rose again to occupy the land of Canaan that was promised as Israel's inheritance by Yahweh. Joshua used the holy wars of Yahweh to cleanse the land from the evil filth of the Nephilim, whose descendants were the mighty Anakim and Rephaim. It was not until King David that they were fully subdued and wiped out."

Peter asked Jesus directly, "Well, then what do you mean that the Nephilim are back, Rabbi?"

Jesus sighed. "The god of this world, and his principalities and powers know that I am here. So they have awakened the spirits of the Nephilim to occupy the Land. The holy wars of Yahweh are renewed in the heavenlies."

Simon added for clarification, "Rabbi is cleansing the land for inheritance by Messiah."

"In the synagogue," said Jesus, "I did not quote the entire passage from Isaiah. I left out the last line."

"What was the line, Rabbi?" asked Peter.

Jesus said somberly, "To proclaim the day of vengeance of our God."

A silence swept over the men.

Simon felt sure that this was Jesus telling them to prepare for all-out war. So the War of the Sons of Light against the Sons of Darkness was here after all. Sometime soon, the weapons of their warfare would be revealed.

Still, Simon felt something was missing. They may have had crowds of interested listeners and gawking grateful healed. But that didn't constitute an army or even a regiment of reserve soldiers. Where would the gibborim come from, the mighty warriors?

All the disciples started talking at once. Suddenly, they were interrupted by a group of villagers from Gergesa arriving, led by the herdsmen.

"There he is!" one of the herdsmen shouted.

The crowd of fifty or so angry villagers arrived. A group of five Pharisees stepped out and pushed the herdsmen aside.

The lead Pharisee was an ugly, swine-looking corpulent man. Simon chuckled to himself, thinking that those pigs had more effect on the villagers than he had first realized.

The pig-faced one looked at the two men who had previously been possessed. Those men now sat at Jesus's feet, clothed and in their right minds. But the Pharisee was as angry as the crowd with him. He spat out, "Those two men were possessed by the power of Ba'alzebul, the prince of demons. No one but Ba'alzebul would have such power to cast them out!"

Simon smiled. These conniving, little Torah-breakers. They were coming up with ridiculous arguments to hide the fact that Jesus just ruined the taxable income of an illegitimate swine business in the town.

Jesus responded, "A kingdom divided against itself cannot stand. If the Accuser casts out the Accuser, he is divided against himself. How then can his kingdom stand?"

The Pharisees were dumbfounded. They had no answer. It made too much sense.

Jesus added, "But if it is by the finger of Yahweh that I cast out demons, then the Kingdom of God has come upon you."

Nice touch, thought Simon. "Finger of Yahweh" was a reference to the power that Moses used to bring the plagues, in contrast to the pathetic secret arts of the magicians of Pharaoh's court.

Jesus continued to confound them. "How can someone enter a strong man's house and plunder his goods, unless he first binds the strong man?"

The Pharisees remained flustered. The crowd from town became more agitated.

Jesus said, "I tell you the truth, I am binding the strong man, and I am plundering his house. But I warn you. When an unclean spirit goes out from a man, it passes through waterless places seeking rest, but finds none. Then it says, 'I will return to my house from which I came.' And when it comes, it finds the house empty, swept, and put in order. Then it goes and brings with it seven other spirits more evil than itself, and they enter and dwell there, and the last state of that person is worse than the first. So also will it be with this evil generation."

Simon was amazed. Jesus was making the demon-possessed clean, and declaring the clean to be demon possessed. Could it be that judgment was not reserved exclusively for the Gentiles but for all those Jews who rejected him as well? It was not the house of Belial that was divided. In fact, it was the house of Israel that was divided, with all their factions squabbling over who was the true Jew, while missing the Messiah right under their noses. Was Jesus predicting that the house of Israel was going to fall?

The crowd burst out shouting for Jesus and his disciples to leave their town.

Jesus let his disciples walk ahead of him. He turned back for a last look at the graveyard of tombs. He saw the shadow of Belial watching him from amongst the dead. But there was something different about him. His gangly body was partly twisted in distortion, and he had what appeared to be organic roots growing upon his face so as to muffle his voice. His binding had begun, and with each victory of Jesus over the principalities and powers, with each exorcism, he knew that binding would expand to hold back the Prince of the Power of the Air.

"Rabbi?"

Jesus was brought out of his thoughts by Peter and Simon.

Peter said, "Are you coming?"

Simon looked to where Jesus had been staring. He saw nothing, but he imagined what he could not see.

Jesus said, "I saw the Accuser fall like lightning from heaven. And he was bound so that he might deceive the nations no more. That the Gospel would go forth and draw all nations to Mount Zion."

Peter shook his head. Sometimes, Jesus sounded profound to the disciple, and sometimes he just sounded crazy.

CHAPTER 8

Marcus Lucius Longinus arrived at the prison in Scythopolis. His rank of centurion garnered him the attention of the entrance guard. He left his own guard of twenty outside the doors as he was introduced to the head of the prison, an optio, one rank below his own. The optio must have been intimidated by Longinus' presence because his hands trembled and his voice quivered.

"I have been commissioned by Pontius Pilate," Longinus told the nervous optio, "to ascertain the facts of the case and apprehend the seditious rebels who escaped. I expect a full accounting of what happened."

"Yes, sir," said the optio.

Longinus was tired of all this. He was forty years old, and felt like the last of a dying breed of quality officers in an army of sloppy, unprofessional morons. It was a wonder the Roman legions held the nations in their power. It was a wonder they maintained the order they did, with all the lazy irresponsible lawlessness he saw around him. It didn't help that these Jews were such a rebellious lot of ingrates. Longinus knew of several bands of fanatical Hebrew outlaws that just increased the chaos and mess. Unfortunately, because of Longinus' dedication to the law and to excellence, the prefect governor of the region, Pilate, called on him to clean up his messes, such as the one before him this moment.

The optio pointed out the front entrance. "Well, first off, they stormed the entrance with about a hundred armed outlaws."

"One hundred?" repeated Longinus. It didn't seem very feasible, considering how few dead soldiers there were: six, and two of the outlaws.

"Yes, sir. They tricked us by impersonating a centurion with a false Zealot prisoner." He reached down and held up the centurion costume. "We found these in the latrine below."

"Show me where," said Longinus.

The optio led him down the stairs and into the long hallway leading to the holding cell, where two guards stood sentry.

They stopped at the latrine.

The optio explained, "The centurion freed the prisoner and the three of them exited through the latrine toilets into the sewage system below."

"Did anyone follow them?"

"No, sir."

"Why not?"

"Well, sir. In all the confusion, and the fighting above...," the optio hesitated with shame.

"What, soldier? Speak up."

"Well, sir, we lost track of them. They killed the two holding cell guards and their replacements. And by the time we made our way down here from the fighting above, well, they were long gone."

Incompetents, thought Longinus. "Where is the holding cell?"

"This way."

The optio led him to the cell at the end of the hallway.

Longinus asked, "Tell me, soldier, by the time your sharpened sense of logic figured out how you had been duped, did the idea ever cross your little mind to record a description of the imposters? Or was that just too much to ask, what with all the fighting going on above."

The optio looked shamefully at the floor. "I did, sir. I will retrieve the drawing for you from the officer's quarters. We believe one of them was the prisoner's brother, a bestiarius from the arena."

"What a pleasant surprise, optio. You did one thing right. Open the door."

The guards opened the cell door. Inside were two prisoners in chains.

The optio said, "These were the two hoodwinked soldiers at the entrance."

Longinus said, "Take them out and flog them in the yard."

The two guards were tied to whipping posts in the center of the citadel yard. They were stripped completely naked in humiliation. Flogging was the prescribed punishment for dereliction of duty. These two guards allowed an imposter to get through to the cells and kidnap their prisoner. Death by bastinado was the normal procedure for such failure, but because one of the outlaws had impersonated a centurion, the soldiers were not culpable for the breach with their lives.

Longinus was more infuriated with the intruders. Impersonating a Roman officer was a high offense punishable by crucifixion. Of course, that was only the conclusion of the series of tortures the law had in store for those miscreants. Longinus was a man of law. As much as he hated criminals, he did not relish their suffering under punishment. What he cherished was justice. What he treasured was the harmony of balance restored by law and order. The punishment should fit the crime.

Two soldiers unfurled their whips. They began their application of thirty-six lashes each upon the disgraced guards. The scourge, which the Romans called the flagrum, was a long-handled whip that branched out into multiple leather thongs a total of five feet in length. At the end of each thong was a knot with an embedded piece of iron or glass. The sharp material would rip the flesh from the victim in streaks of bloody gore down their backs. The soldiers tried to remain silent to maintain their dignity as warriors, but the scourge ripped their cries out of them. The good news was that the six thongs counted for six lashes with each hit. Thus, they only required six actual hits by the enforcers.

Good news.

Pain was cathartic. Law was pure and impartial. Even those responsible for peacekeeping required chastisement when they failed in their duty. A lawless world was the quintessence of evil to Longinus. Unruly barbarians and savages killing and eating each other like the animals. But Caesar created order out of chaos. He brought stern but just rule into a primitive cosmos. Longinus could understand the barbarians on the eastern frontier. They were like undomesticated beasts in the wild. But these Jews and their restlessness under Pax Romana, the Peace of Rome, were simply without sense or reason. They had all the benefits of civilization and progress, yet their religion seemed so intolerant and easily offended by the rule of Roman law that provided that protection and abundance.

A splash of blood hit Longinus' cheek, bringing him back to the moment. He wiped his face. The lashes were almost completed. The soldier's backs looked like a bloody plowed field of pulpy flesh. He could see the white of a rib showing through one of their backs.

Another slap of the flagrum and one of the soldiers fell into unconsciousness with the pain.

"Sir," interrupted the optio from behind. "Here are the likenesses." He handed him three pieces of parchment. Longinus stared at them one by one, memorizing the features of the criminals' faces. The original captive was a handsome scoundrel.

"That is Gestas Semaras. An actor in the theater."

"No wonder," muttered Longinus. "An idle mind immersed in fantasy. An easy target for dissatisfaction and sedition."

He flipped to the next parchment.

"That is his brother, Demas. A bestiarius in the ring."

Longinus sighed with contempt. "Circus performers."

"Demas is quite famous," said the optio. He momentarily forgot his fear of Longinus as he called up his memory of Demas. "He recently conquered four wild beasts in the arena. I would not doubt if it was he who slew all four of the guards at the holding cell."

"Let us see how he fares with a real warrior, not animals and bumbling prison guards."

Longinus flipped to the last parchment containing the image of the fake prisoner that the fake centurion used for their façade. His eyes opened wide. His breath faltered. The long wavy black hair, the unshaven wide jaw, and that scar down the cheek.

"Barabbas," muttered Longinus.

"Who?"

Longinus ignored the fool. He also didn't notice the half-dead soldiers, finished with their punishment, being dragged away to the healing ward.

This revelation of Barabbas' activities changed everything for Longinus. His annoyance with this case just turned into renewed hope. He had been trying to track down this brigand leader for some time now. Barabbas had first begun by robbing Herodian transports and attacking small Roman outposts with his growing band of outlaws. Longinus had hunted him, and the trail had gone cold. But it had just returned to the centurion with a flaming vengeance.

Longinus said, "Show me the home of these entertainers."

Longinus left his century of a hundred legionaries in their camp outside the city as he went to examine the premises of the Semaras estate. It was a large village house near the edge of the city which the brother "entertainers" had inherited from their deceased adoptive parents. The couple had adopted the boys after the destruction of Sepphoris years ago. At least, that was what Longinus got out of their servant Micah, who had been left without knowledge of the brothers' whereabouts.

The actor's room reflected vanity with its many mirrors and over-abundance of clothes.

Longinus asked the servant, "What of his social life?"

Micah replied, "He had not been in the company of much society in recent months."

"Why not?"

"He had sought marriage with a Herodian princess and was spurned. He seemed quite angry and began to visit secret meetings in the evening."

"What did he talk about after returning from the meetings?"

"The injustice of the Herodian ruling class and the right of the Jewish commoner to live under their god without oppressive taxes."

Longinus shook his head. *The fool. This actor could not be more predictable in his vainglory and self-interest.* His involvement in revolution was nothing more than the jealousy of being jilted by the upper class to which he groveled and whored himself.

"Where is the other brother's quarters?"

"On the other side of the villa."

Micah took him there.

The first thing Longinus noticed was the sparseness with which this one lived, in contrast with his soft and indulgent sibling. A bare bed, with minimal changes of clothes and various weapons lining the room. No decoration, no vanity. This one was dangerous. He didn't care what the world offered him. As a bestiarius, he no doubt made good money in the arena, but he evidently did not care to spend it on himself.

Micah answered Longinus' thoughts without knowing it. "He gave most of his wages to charity."

So, he killed for the thrill of killing. Little concern for his own safety.

Longinus asked, "Did he have a lover?"

"His wife died several years ago."

Now Longinus knew his prey as well as he knew himself. He too had lost his wife in the midst of his long years away from home in the service of Caesar. He knew the darkness of hopelessness and despair.

He concluded that it was time to visit Herod Antipas, the tetrarch over Galilee. Antipas had captured the troublemaker Essene, called John the Baptizer, who had caused a ruckus about a coming Messiah king and the sins of the Herodians. Perhaps this Baptizer was connected to Barabbas and his anti-Herodian conspirators, the Semaras brothers. Perhaps Antipas had information on the whereabouts of one of those brothers, the actor, who sought to infiltrate Herod's circle.

CHAPTER 9

Demas and Gestas had grown out their beards and disguised themselves as traveling day laborers. It allowed them the flexibility to travel and the anonymity of poverty.

They arrived in Capernaum in search of the Nazarene because they had learned it was the headquarters for his Galilean ministry. It was also a bustling center of commerce at the crossroads between Damascus in the north-east and Caesarea Maritima on the coast, along with a large fishing community on the shore of the Sea of Galilee. Such high economic and merchant activity made it dangerous for the brothers. They might be spotted by travelers. Worse yet, a detachment of Roman soldiers was quartered in the city because it was a Roman tax polling station. It was the worst town in Galilee for these wanted outlaws, but it was their only bet. They had to find Simon ben Josiah, and he was with the Nazarene. They could only hope that word of their escape from Scythopolis had not made it here so that the Romans would not be on the lookout for them.

They came upon a town gathering with a local centurion upon the dais in the marketplace. He was in mid-speech when the brothers arrived at the back of the crowd. His voice carried over the crowd with conviction. "Their leader has a scar across his left cheek down to his chin. They may be all three together or have split apart to avoid detection as one or two together." He lifted up a couple drawings. "Please come forward afterward and take a look at these images drawn of the suspects. If you see anyone suspicious or any travelers without purpose in our town, report them to my station."

The brothers looked at each other in alarm. Then Demas saw a Roman soldier at the edge of the crowd watching them with interest. It unnerved him.

Gestas muttered to the person next to him, an old fisherman, "These revolutionaries will bring the Roman fist down upon us and ruin our country." The best way to avoid suspicion was to join the crowd and blend in.

The old fisherman shot back, "Gessius will not be harsh on us. He helped build our synagogue, and I even heard his servant was healed by the Nazarene at Simon Peter's home."

Gestas filled with hope. Gessius was apparently the centurion up front who also resided in the city. And now they knew where to find information about the Nazarene. But where was the home of this Simon Peter?

"Which Simon Peter?" repeated Gestas. It was a common enough name.

"The fisherman," said the old man.

Demas' nervous look back at the soldier drew the Roman's attention. The suspicious legionary started to move through the crowd toward them. Everyone began leaving or moving up front to see the drawings of the outlaws. Demas grabbed Gestas and whispered, "We have to go."

He pulled his brother away and into the moving masses.

They dodged out of the crowd into an alleyway. Demas told Gestas about their follower. His brother breathed a sigh of relief at having evaded the suspicious Roman.

They turned a corner and stopped dead in their tracks. The Roman soldier stood ten feet away, looking straight at them.

"Halt! You two there."

They played calm. The legionary spoke as he approached them. "I do not recognize you as locals. What are you doing here?"

Gestas took the lead with his superior acting skills. "We are day laborers. Here to help with the fishing."

"When did you arrive in the town?"

Gestas said, "Over a week ago."

The soldier thought a moment. "Oh, did you help out with that big dragnet haul?"

"Yes," said Gestas. "We were contacted by Simon Peter. We were just on our way to his home."

"You were?" said the soldier.

Gestas and Demas nodded their heads. The soldier quickly withdrew his sword and thrust it up to Gestas' throat. "Well, now that would be odd, considering Simon Peter lives beside the synagogue in the opposite direction of which you are going."

Demas tensed up. He began calculating in his mind, searching for his moment to make a move.

"I can explain" said Gestas.

"I am sure you can, liar," said the soldier. "And you will also have to explain why you helped at the dragnet haul that never happened."

Gestas sighed and closed his eyes with failure. Caught red-handed.

"Who are you two, and why are you here?"

Gestas recovered quickly, "We told you, we are day laborers. We were working in Bethsaida and our wages were withheld. So, we beat up our employer. I am sorry for lying, but we were afraid of being found out. We never stole from him, that is the honest truth, sir. We worked for three days straight and the man never paid us our lawful wages."

The soldier stared at Gestas trying to figure out if he was lying again.

"You two are coming with me to the centurion station."

Demas was about to make his move, but his brother beat him to the punch.

Gestas stepped inward to the chest of the soldier, grabbed his sword arm and flipped him into the dust, removing the sword from his twisted hand. Gestas spun around and thrust the sword into the soldier's throat. The Roman couldn't scream out. He just gurgled through his blood and died.

Demas was amazed at Gestas' skill. Gestas looked up at him and said, "I learned the move for the Hercules play. Done it a thousand times. Change your mind about acting?"

Demas replied, "Let's get this body out of here and go find that synagogue."

After depositing the body in a pile of garbage, Demas and Gestas went to the southeast corner of the city where they could see the synagogue towering above the smaller homes around it. Right next to it was a large villa that had Simon Peter's name inscribed on the outside. They knocked on the door and a young man with a hair lip answered it.

The brothers were a bit thrown by the unsightly birth deformity. Gestas was about to speak, but this time Demas surprised him. "We are here for Jesus of Nazareth."

Gestas gave him a side glance, trying to hide his surprise in front of the stranger.

The young man spoke with a lisp through his hair lip, "Pleathe come in. You are late. The dithcuthon already thtarted."

Demas whispered to Gestas, "You are not the only one who can act."

They followed the young man through a large north court and into a meeting room filled with about sixty of the locals. The curtains were drawn over the windows to keep their meeting clandestine.

They looked around the group for Simon or the Nazarene, but could not see anyone who matched the descriptions they had been given.

A middle-aged man stood with one arm held tightly around what seemed to be his wife and the other around his twelve-year old daughter.

From his dress, it was apparent he was a synagogue ruler. He was mid-story, speaking with a hushed tone. "While I was pleading with him, a messenger came and said, 'Do not trouble the rabbi any further.'" He choked up. "'Your daughter is dead.'"

The ruler looked down at his daughter, obviously alive now, and kissed her head with adoration. He continued. "But Jesus told me, 'Do not fear. Only believe.' I led him with Peter, James and John to my house. There was already much weeping and wailing by the crowd. And then he said, 'Why are you making such a commotion?'" This time the man choked up with amusement. "'The child is not dead, but sleeping.'"

Demas listened intently.

Gestas looked around the room, intrigued by the mixture of upper and lower classes that were here. He had never seen such a thing. This synagogue elder was surrounded by fishermen and other plebeians, including what looked like a harlot. But he also saw several other ruling class leaders. What could bring together in secret such divergent classes of people who would not otherwise be seen together in public?

The man continued. "So Jesus put them all outside, and took me and Mary," he looked down at his wife and hugged her, "and several others of you." He looked around the room at several people. "You were there. You saw it." They nodded their heads. "He took Rebecca's hand and said, 'Little girl, I say to you, arise.'"

The man stopped. He choked up again, and could barely continue. But he pushed through. "And Rebecca got up. Jesus brought her back to us."

The brothers heard a peppering of "hallelujahs" from the people in the crowded room. One said, "Yahweh saves!" followed by amens. "Yahweh saves" was the meaning of the name Yeshua, which was Jesus's Hebrew name.

Demas felt weird. He was in a secret religious cult surrounded by members under a spell. They actually thought the Nazarene raised this little girl from the dead? She had obviously been so sick as to appear dead. But these poor fools had convinced themselves that the Nazarene was some kind of a god. The words of Aeschylus rang through Demas' mind like a whisper, "Once a man dies and the earth drinks up his blood, there is no resurrection."

An elderly lady stood. She appeared to be the matron of the household. She said, "Thank you for your testimony, Jairus. And I thank you all for coming to my home to share with us how your lives have been dramatically impacted by Jesus of Nazareth. As you all know, he healed me of a fever, so that I could serve his disciples dinner for my son-in-law Peter." A smattering of suppressed laughter brought some light into the dark seriousness of the room.

A centurion appeared in the doorway with two soldiers behind him. A hush of surprise washed over the crowd.

Demas and Gestas grabbed the hilts of their swords beneath their cloaks. It was the centurion from the marketplace. He had tracked them down. Did they walk into a Roman trap?

Peter's mother-in-law spoke up, "Many of you know Gessius and how Jesus healed his servant, Joram."

The centurion added, "With only his words—and from a distance."

Murmurings of approval covered the brothers' startled exchange of glances. They remembered what the stranger in the crowd had told them about the centurion, the information that had brought them to this house in the first place. Would he recognize their faces from the drawings? They tried to keep their heads low.

The old woman looked around the room. "And Jesus cast demons out of several of you."

"I was blind and mute by a demon," said a man, who was obviously seeing clearly and speaking freely.

Demas thought, *A demon or your own captivating fears and madness?*

Peter's mother-in-law added, "And there were those tormented by long maladies." She pointed at a middle-aged woman. "Sarah, you had an issue of blood for twelve years."

Sarah spoke out, "Yes! I simply touched his garment and I was made well."

Peter's mother-in-law continued, looking at two men in the corner. "And Josiah and Daniel. We all know you were blind until a week ago." More amens where whispered.

Demas could see the two men were obviously not blind, but were quite normal. He began to feel suffocated by the delusions of this maddening crowd. He wanted to leave.

Gestas, on the other hand, was amazed by it all. The stories sounded like the fantastic legends he would act out in his pantomime plays. But these were real stories. The people claimed to be eyewitnesses or actual recipients of the miracles. They couldn't all be lying, could they?

Both brothers wanted to leave before the centurion recognized them.

The woman continued, "Let us now pray for the ministry of Jesus and the disciples in the district of Tyre and Sidon."

The brothers looked at each other. They knew their next destination. They bowed their heads, thankful that it would keep their faces from visibility.

After the prayer, the brothers mulled about, trying to avoid the gaze of the centurion, looking for their opportunity to slip away. The centurion did not seem to notice them. Apparently, the drawings were crude enough and different enough from their newly bearded faces to avoid detection.

They saw some people leaving and used the opportunity to join them without drawing attention.

"Brothers," came a voice from behind them. It was the centurion.

They were discovered. They turned to look, ready to draw their weapons and kill who they must to survive.

The centurion surprised them. "The blessing of Messiah be upon you."

Demas went blank. Gestas was quick. He replied, "And also upon you, brother."

Gestas pushed the stunned Demas out the door.

Once they left the house, Gestas whispered to Demas, "Amazing. They consider each other family. Roman, Pharisee and pleb."

Demas muttered, "A Roman soldier looking for *our* Jewish Messiah? What is this madness?"

Gestas responded, "Apparently, they believe the Nazarene *is* the Messiah."

Demas countered, "The Nazarene is dangerous. He has the ability to bewitch entire crowds."

Gestas protested, "All these people could not be under the same spell. They have lived and worked with each other all their lives. They could not get away with such lies."

"With such magic tricks," said Demas.

They found their horses and untied them, walking them through the side streets toward the northern end of town.

Gestas said, "So you believe he is merely a magician?"

Demas evaded him, "Do you believe he is the Messiah?"

"I do not know what I believe at this point, Demas. But feeding five thousand people with four loaves and two fish is no magic trick. That is a miracle."

"Five thousand people is a crowd large enough to hide the presence of secreted food stores."

"No magician can heal a man born blind, or a lifelong paralytic and then forgive his sins."

"*Claim* to forgive his sins. And why did he not heal the boy that we met with the hair lip? Is that not spectacular enough for his reputation?"

Gestas sighed. "Some people will just find any excuse *not* to believe."

Demas smirked. "And some people will just find any excuse *to* believe."

They got on their horses at the edge of town and galloped off to their new destination, the Phoenician city of Tyre on the sea.

CHAPTER 10

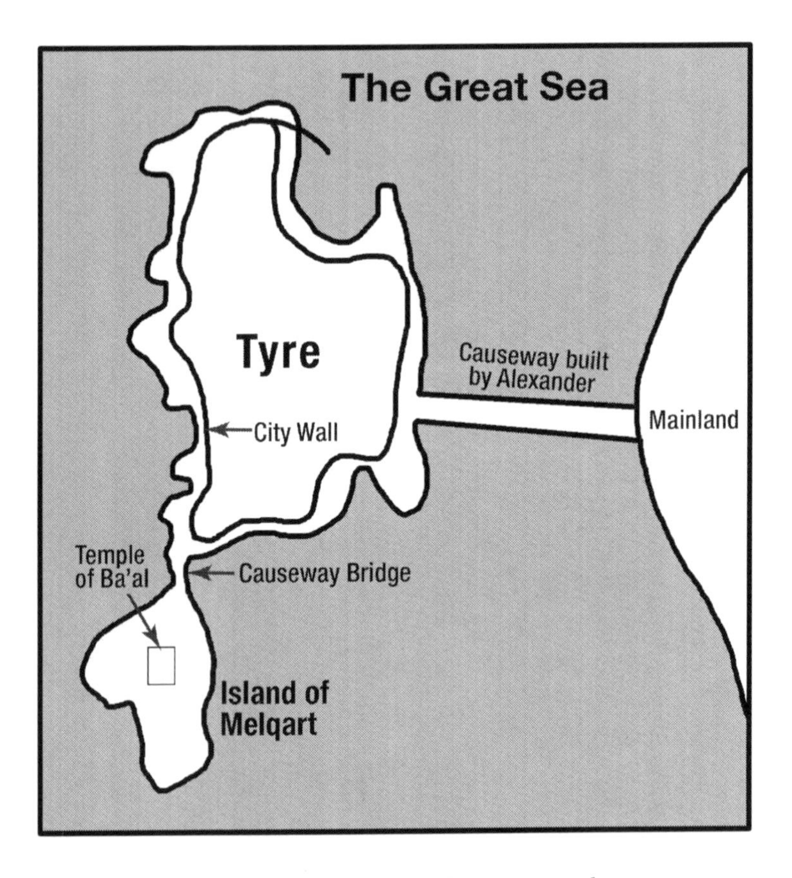

Elohim has taken his place in the divine council;
in the midst of the gods he holds judgment:
"How long will you judge unjustly
and show partiality to the wicked?
Give justice to the weak and the fatherless;
maintain the right of the afflicted and the destitute.
Rescue the weak and the needy;
deliver them from the hand of the wicked."

They have neither knowledge nor understanding,
they walk about in darkness;
all the foundations of the earth are shaken.
I said, "You are gods,
sons of the Most High, all of you;
nevertheless, like men you shall die,
and fall like any prince."
Arise, O Elohim, judge the earth;
for you shall inherit all the nations!

— A Psalm of Asaph

Simon the Zealot mused over the text that Jesus had explained to the disciples before he left them to visit the southern island of Melqart that was part of the island port city of Tyre. The twelve were familiar with the words of the Second Book of the Law of Moses about the principalities and powers that ruled over and through the nations. At Babel, Yahweh separated the seventy idolatrous nations who had sought to make a name for themselves and become as gods. He placed them under the authority of the remaining seventy fallen Sons of God.

When El Elyon the Most High gave to the nations their inheritance,
when he divided mankind,
he fixed the borders of the peoples
according to the number of the Sons of God.
But Yahweh's portion is his people,
Jacob his allotted heritage.

These gods of the people were given the responsibility of administering justice. But they were corrupt, every single one, in their rebellion against Yahweh's justice. And the nations followed them in their defiance and abominations. On earth as it is in heaven.

The gods took pleasure in ruling wickedly and fought for dominance of the earth. Thus, Yahweh Elohim was visiting the earth to judge them and take away their inheritance. The principalities of the nations would fall in unity with their human princes, as they did in the time of Daniel's vision.

Peter had asked when the legions of heavenly host would join them, and Jesus said, "When you see the Son of Man seated at the right hand of power, coming on the clouds of heaven." That made everyone more confused.

"Coming on the clouds" was a common poetic phrase that indicated an earthly judgment of cities or nations. *On earth as it is in heaven.* Canaanites had used the term "cloud-rider" of their god, Ba'al. But Ezekiel had used it of Yahweh when he judged Egypt, Nahum used it of Yahweh when he judged Nineveh, and Isaiah had used it when Yahweh judged Edom and even Israel.

Simon, being learned in the scrolls from Qumran, asked Jesus if he was referring to the prophecy of Joel that had yet to be fulfilled.

Blow a trumpet in Zion;
sound an alarm on my holy mountain!
Let all the inhabitants of the land tremble,
for the Day of the Lord is coming; it is near,
A day of darkness and gloom,
a day of clouds and thick darkness.

Jesus simply said, "Yes," but offered no more. It drove the curious scribe up a stone wall. He wanted answers. He wanted to know the plan. But Jesus seemed to want it kept hidden. What kind of Messiah keeps such things hidden? The only thing Simon could figure was that somewhere, maybe in heaven, an army of heavenly host was preparing for a surprise assault. And why not? A single angel of Yahweh killed one hundred and eighty-five thousand Assyrians in the days of King Hezekiah. Elisha's servant had his eyes opened into the heavenlies to see a mountain full of heavenly host on horses and chariots of fire surrounding the evil Syrians.

But how would Messiah gather the Sons of Light together for their war against the Sons of Darkness? The War Scroll from the Community said that Edom, Moab, Ammon, Amalek, and Philistia would join the Roman Kittim as the army of Belial against the true sons of Israel exiled in the desert—in other words, the Essenes—but that "the great hand of God shall overcome Belial and all the angels of his dominion, and all the men of his forces shall be destroyed forever." The way Jesus was violating all the principles of holiness and separation, if he *was* Messiah, he certainly didn't fit the Community's definition in the scrolls.

A Canaanite woman had come before Jesus in this very city of Tyre, pleading for him to cast out a demon from her daughter. Jesus told her that his ministry was to the lost sheep of the House of Israel, not to the Gentiles who were like unclean dogs to Jews. Yet, after she told him that even the dogs got scraps of food from the master's table, he cast out the demon as she originally requested.

The Community would never have accepted such a thing.

But was he the Messiah of the Pharisees or Sadducees either? The Jews had been waiting for Yahweh to come and free them ever since their exile in Babylon. Though they were back in their Promised Land, they were still under the principality and power of Rome, the god of this world, Belial. *On earth as it is in heaven.* They were still slaves in spiritual exile waiting for their promised deliverance. Yahweh had gone silent on them for four hundred years since their last prophet Malachi.

Malachi had foretold that Elijah would return before the great and dreadful Day of the Lord. But Jesus had then told them that John the Baptizer was Elijah preparing the way. He had spiritualized the prophecy that they thought was literal. But the Baptizer was now in prison at the fortress of that treacherous fox, Herod Antipas. It seemed to get more confusing the more any of their questions were answered.

So much of their Scriptures was poetic and figurative language, like Jesus's parables about the kingdom of heaven. When Simon asked him why he spoke in parables, he quoted Isaiah about how the people's hearts were dulled and their eyes blinded by their own sin. So Yahweh would keep the secrets of the kingdom of heaven from everyone except those who repented. How much more of their hope and understanding was darkened by such hidden language from Yahweh?

Simon's curiosity burned within him. Jesus had ostensibly taken the disciples to this island to get away and get some rest from all the crowds in Galilee and Judea. But Simon knew there was more to this trip than a vacation getaway to a Gentile port city of wickedness. The Master had already cast out a dozen demons, in addition to the Canaanite child, as if he were preparing for something bigger. Simon suspected Jesus was here to take down the gods of Tyre: Ba'al, Asherah and Molech.

Those heavenly principalities and their little island fortress had an important spiritual history. Tyre was an island, in the shape of Ba'al's war mace, just off the coast. Centuries earlier, Alexander the Great had conquered the island stronghold by building an artificial land bridge from the mainland to the island, where his forces could cross and besiege the city.

Legend had it that Alexander heard there was a temple of Melqart on the island. The Jews called Melqart Ba'al, but the Greeks called him Hercules. Alexander wanted to sacrifice to Hercules at the temple of Ba'al, but the king would not allow it. So Alexander besieged the city's walls, slaughtered the army of Tyre, subjugated the king, enslaved its people, and got his sacrifice at the temple of Ba'al at the end of it.

But this island and her sister city, Sidon, just twenty-five miles north up the coast, had a far more dark and fascinating spiritual significance than mere Greek imperial expansion. The gods of the Phoenicians, Ba'al, Asherah and Molech, constituted a trinity of wickedness that shadowed Israel through much of her history. The Seed of Abraham never seemed to fully eradicate this Seed of the Serpent from their land. These gods seemed to have their talons dug deep into the soul of the nation.

Molech was a despicable deity with an evil taste for little children. As the original abomination of the Ammonites, Molech's human sacrifice required passing their sons and daughters through the fire. He eventually settled in the valley of Hinnom where Solomon had acquiesced and built him a high place. The Phoenicians had adopted his ways into their multicultural pantheon.

Ba'al had risen to become the most high god of the Canaanite pantheon, and the Phoenicians worshipped power, so they had embraced him eagerly. Asherah was known in Phoenicia as Asherah of Tyre, goddess of the Sidonians. "Sidonian" had become the generic name for the Phoenicians along the coast from Byblos and Ugarit above Sidon all the way down to Tyre.

The downfall of the northern tribes of Israel began in the days of the divided monarchy. King Ahab of Israel had married Jezebel, the daughter of the king of Tyre for political and economic gain. Jezebel built temples to Ba'al and Asherah all throughout the land and persecuted the prophets Elijah and Elisha. The righteous Jehu had killed Jezebel and Ahab's line and destroyed the Asherim and temples of Ba'al. But the talons of idolatry were never fully released from the soul of Israel.

Tyre and her rulers became a symbol of recalcitrant evil in Israel, warranting a curse by the prophet Ezekiel that reflected the very essence of Adam's original sin that led to the Fall and to Babel's pride.

> *The word of the Lord came to me:*
> *"Son of man, say to the prince of Tyre, Thus says the Lord:*
> *"Because your heart is proud,*
> *and you have said, 'I am a god,*
> *I sit in the seat of the gods,*
> *in the heart of the seas,'*

yet you are but a man, and no god,
though you make your heart like the heart of a god—

Some scribes and rabbis recently had begun to interpret the Prince of Tyre as an analogy with the Shining One, Nachash, in the Garden. Simon saw in it a mockery of Ba'al's elevation to the throne of the Most High that results in the casting of the king to the ground or underworld.

"Thus says Yahweh Elohim:
"You were the signet of perfection,
full of wisdom and perfect in beauty.
You were in Eden, the garden of Elohim;
every precious stone was your covering...
From the day you were created,
I placed you with the cherub on the holy mountain of Elohim;
in the midst of the stones of fire you walked.
You were blameless in your ways
from the day you were created,
till unrighteousness was found in you.
In the abundance of your trade
you were filled with violence in your midst, and you sinned;
so I cast you as a profane thing from the mountain of Elohim,
The cherub has led you out,
from the midst of the stones of fire.
Your heart was proud because of your beauty;
you corrupted your wisdom for the sake of your splendor.
I cast you to the ground;
and I turned you to ashes on the earth
in the sight of all who saw you.
All who know you among the peoples
are appalled at you;
you have come to a dreadful end
and shall be no more forever."

Simon knew that the subjugation of Tyre was important because the gods Ba'al, Asherah and Molech would have to be bound and judged as part of the reclamation of the Promised Land for Messiah's inheritance. But Jesus was not letting them in on his clandestine activities.

Jesus left his disciples on the north area of the island near the Sidonian harbor for the evening. He walked the mile down to the southern harbor. The stone walls of the fortress city towered overhead. They acted as fortification against both armies and sea storms.

He reached the causeway bridge to the smaller Island of Melqart. This peninsula was only a third the size of the main island and had no fortification walls. The Tyrians considered it sacred space. They built a Temple of Ba'al upon the high place of Asherah in the center of the peninsula.

At the gateway of the bridge, Jesus met seven cloaked figures who were not very good at hiding the fact that they were paladin warriors, with strange looking armor beneath their covering cloaks.

They were the archangels, Mikael, Gabriel, Uriel, Raphael, Saraqael, Raguel, and Remiel. It would take an extremely serious and difficult task for these seven mightiest of heavenly warriors to meet together like this.

They walked across the large stone bridge to the peninsula.

Jesus asked Mikael, "What did you find at Sapan?" Mount Sapan, the cosmic mountain, stood some two hundred miles far north of Tyre. Generations ago, Ba'al had built his palace headquarters there with the construction help of Kothar-wa-Hasis and the political lobbying of Asherah. The archangels had journeyed to the sacred mountain, fought Ba'al, bound him into the molten liquid earth, and destroyed his palace. They had never anticipated that the earth would vomit him back out in the volcanic eruption of Thera, and launch his return to the pantheon in the days of King David.

Mikael answered Jesus, "Ba'al's palace is still in ruins as we left it. He has never returned. And we could not find the Tablet of Destinies."

"Then it must be here," said Jesus. "He relocated to Tyre with Asherah and has been here ever since."

The Tablet of Destinies had a long tortured history that led back to antediluvian days. In ancient Sumer, the Tablet contained the universal decrees of heaven and earth, including godship, kingship, war, sex, and music, as well as magic, sorceries and occultic wisdom. Guardianship of the tablets had become a mark of favor in the pantheon of gods. It represented the sovereignty of the divine council. The hands that possessed it were the hands of the patron deity of the ruling city. The ancient yearly Akitu festival would climax with the presentation of the Tablet of Destinies by the holder who would lead the gods in deciding the fates of earthly rulers for the coming year. Ba'al had been the latest in a long line of guardians to hold the Tablet in safekeeping. Jesus intended to wrest it from his grip.

"Don't look, now," said Uriel, "But we have a spy following us."

The others had already spotted the dark figure hiding behind a pillar of the bridge, watching them.

"It's Simon ben Josiah," said Jesus. "He has been following me since I left the disciples by the northern harbor. He's zealous. Reads too many scrolls. Unquenchable curiosity. Leave him be."

"He could get hurt," said Mikael.

"Not if you do your job," said Jesus. "Uriel, why don't you watch over him for me."

"Jeeeesuuuus," whined Uriel. "Why always me?"

Gabriel teased, "Because you're small enough not to intimidate a human."

Uriel was the smallest angel of the lot, a full foot smaller than most. But he made up for it with his wits and will power. No one could match his double swords in speed or technique or his mighty tongue. "But Gabriel, you are more homely and plain looking, so you won't scare him either."

Jesus said, "Uriel, stop whining. Did I not have you watch over Noah?"

"Well, yes, but…"

"Was he not the first of my chosen line to protect?"

"Yes." Uriel felt like a scolded teenager. "But he was a grump at first. You have to admit."

Jesus said, "The greatest among you shall be your servant."

Gabriel added, "Unless you become like a little child—with the emphasis on little—and child."

Jesus said, "Shut up, Gabriel."

They now stood before the temple of Ba'al. It was a huge stone architectural wonder with exquisite Phoenician craftsmanship. The entrance was flanked by two huge pillars, one of gold, the other of emerald, shining brilliantly even at night. It reminded Jesus of the two pillars of Solomon's temple, crafted by the Phoenicians as well, and named Jachin and Boaz. These pillars should be named Resheph and Qeteb, after the demon gods of plague and pestilence.

Jesus suddenly stopped, as if aware of a presence. He looked out to sea. It was a clear night with a near full moon. Nothing approached on the horizon. Nothing visible. He said, "On second thought, I will stay with Simon."

Uriel grinned with the hope of a hungry warrior.

"Instead, Uriel, I want you to find the Tablet of Destinies."

Uriel gave a snide look at a pouting Gabriel. Like a couple of children these two were.

Jesus was not afraid of facing the gods. They could not touch him. But human operatives of the enemy could. Uriel wondered what portent the Son of Man foresaw. Were the priests of Ba'al and Asherah sworn to kill him?

Jesus said, "Molech is in his valley of Gehenna at Jerusalem. Ba'al and Asherah await us here."

"Archangels," said Mikael, their leader, "let us go bind us some gods."

Jesus said, "Gabriel, Uriel."

They stopped before leaving.

"Remember, you are fighting the enemy, not each other."

He gave them a smile. They both said simultaneously with a sense of shame, "Yes, Lord."

Jesus watched them spread out into the darkness as they approached the high place.

A strange ethereal noise, sounding like a bull in agony, rose from the Temple of Ba'al.

Jesus closed his eyes and prayed to the Father with the pain of what he knew was happening.

He wiped the tears from his cheek, turned around, and whispered up the stairs, "Simon. Come on out. I won't hurt you."

Simon stepped out from behind the pillar at the top of the stairs like an embarrassed urchin caught with his hand in the honey jar.

Jesus made his way back up the steps of the causeway bridge.

"I am sorry, Rabbi," said Simon.

Jesus said to him, "I think it is time I explain to you what the Community of Qumran failed to understand."

• • • • •

Ba'al and Asherah had indeed been awaiting the inevitable confrontation that now descended upon them. They were ready for it. They had completed a mass sacrifice of ten children in the belly of the Brazen Bull just moments before the angels had approached the temple.

The Brazen Bull was a large, cast bronze image of a life-sized bull, the symbol of the Canaanite high god El, and his calf-son, Ba'al. The device had been imported from Carthage by the Phoenicians. It had a hollow center with a hinged latch that would allow the insertion of a human locked into the belly. Fires below the bull would then roast the victim alive inside the beast. A special bronze acoustic apparatus caught the sounds of the dying victims and projected them through the throat and mouth of the brazen statue, creating the strange bull-like sounds that Jesus and the archangels had heard upon their approach.

Human sacrifice empowered the gods with the spiritual life source of their victims. Ba'al and Asherah were full of strength and ready to strike. They stood in battle stance in the large marble sanctuary surrounded by pillars. Asherah had a live python wrapped around her body armor like a living protector. She prided herself on her fusion of fashion with fury. She readied her battle shield and gripped her sword tightly. The python licked the air, smelling the presence of approaching intruders.

Ba'al needed no shield. His favorite battle dress was a mere loin cloth with leather belt. His musculature was so massive it could frighten an archangel. His preferred weapons were the mace and battle net. But this evening, he held a huge battle hammer in his hands. He had used this very one in the war with Ashtart at the Battle of Nine Kings outside Sodom in the days of Abraham. No angelic armor could withstand its crushing force.

The Brazen Bull had been removed to the back room of the holy place. The fires of a tophet were stoked high in the circular fire pit at the head of the sanctuary, before the massive bronze image of a seated humanoid Ba'al. His head was that of a bull, his arms outstretched before him. This tophet was another form of sacrifice where the victim would be placed in the arms of the image and would roll off into the flames to be consumed for atonement. Ba'al stood on one side of the image, Asherah on the other.

The temple priests and prostitutes would be useless in this supernatural battle, so the gods cleared them all out.

Ba'al and Asherah stood defiantly behind their incense censers that filled the room with a smoky haze of opiate intended to slow down their enemies and obscure their vision.

Seven determined and focused spiritual warriors entered the sanctuary like cloaked wraiths of doom. They whipped off their cloaks to reveal full battle regalia underneath. Their cloaks floated to the marble floor at their feet.

Uriel muttered, "The stench is disgusting."

Gabriel retorted, "I think that's the intent, Uriel."

Uriel said, "I'm going to have to wash the smell out of my clothes after this."

A deep voice bellowed as if from all around them, "Do not be so quick to assume victory, archangel."

Mikael nodded to the others. They spread out before approaching the altar at the front. But before they could move forward, a large muscular being emerged from the smoke.

The archangels took defensive stances.

Ba'al raised his huge battle hammer overhead with all his might and slammed it down onto the marble floor of the temple.

An earthquake convulsed the temple and island. Pillars shook. Loose marble fell from overhead. A huge opening cracked the floor and split the temple, separating angels from gods with a chasm that now belched up churning water from the sea.

The angels fell to the floor with the impact.

Mikael was the first to figure it out. He yelled, "We have mere minutes! Archangels, attack!"

When Ba'al had used his thunder hammer to crack the earth on land near Sodom, it had the effect of inducing an earthquake of immense magnitude. Mikael realized that the use of that hammer on this island created an earthquake that displaced the ocean floor below. There was one titanic effect from such a cause: a tsunami.

The water on the shoreline of Tyre drew back out toward the sea, enlarging the shoreline by hundreds of feet. The water was being sucked away into the ocean. It would only last minutes. A mile or so off shore, all that displaced water now headed back toward the island in the form of a ten foot high tidal wave with the unstoppable speed of over a hundred miles an hour.

The angels had little time to achieve their goal, the capture of the gods. They each had an armband made of white, thread-thin indestructible Cherubim hair to be used as a binding. It was the only thing that could hold these monsters in order to capture them and imprison them in Tartarus, the lowest region of Sheol.

But the gods would not be bound easily.

Suddenly, the python flew through the air from behind the angels, thrown by Asherah hiding in the shadows of the pillars.

It hit Remiel and wrapped around him like a bolo tourniquet, squeezing the life out of him. He dropped his sword. Angels could not die, but they could be incapacitated.

The others turned to face Asherah. Two of them, Raguel and Saraqael, engaged the battle maiden. She lashed out with mad fury, throwing them off their footing. She was fighting for her eternity. Her shield stopped the strikes of her foes. She pushed them backward, toward the crevice.

Mikael, Uriel, Raphael, and Gabriel leapt over the ten foot chasm to chase their muscle-bound quarry. Ba'al had pulled back into the murky haze. Uriel slipped away for his appointed task to steal the Tablet of Destinies.

Raguel and Saraqael pushed back at Asherah. They could not help the entwined Remiel, struggling to get his hands free from his serpent entrapment.

Uriel circled behind the back of the towering image of Ba'al. The Tablet was almost certainly hidden in a secret compartment of the idol. But where? His hunch was confirmed when a cadre of sacred priests attacked him with spears. They were pathetically easy targets to take down. He wanted to keep one alive to find out where the compartment was.

Mikael, Raphael, and Gabriel pulled down the censers. The stands crashed to the floor, extinguishing the incense and its ability to veil the movements of their enemy. They moved cautiously, in search of the hidden Ba'al.

Gabriel shouted out, "Come out, you coward, and face your destiny like a Son of God."

Mikael looked out through the thinning haze and pillars, and saw the ten foot wall of water almost upon the island. It wasn't huge, but it was big enough to wash over the entire small rock with its wave.

Raguel and Saraqael rushed Asherah and wrestled her to the ground in a grappling match of titans. Asherah was powerful, but she was not a good match for the two archangels who now dragged her to the crevice. They pulled her kicking, flailing form past the pieces of a chopped-up python. Remiel was now free. He joined them, with a line of Cherubim hair ready to bind her.

Gabriel had made an error when he called out his insult to the storm god. It gave their hidden foe a pinpoint for their location. Before they could spread out, a huge battle net burst out of the last of the smoky haze and enveloped them like a spider web.

All three angels struggled to free themselves from the tangled snare.

The gargantuan Ba'al broke through the fading mist with his battle mace. He pummeled the archangels with furious rage.

Behind the large idol, Uriel gripped the neck of a high priest in his hands.

Raguel, Saraqael and Remiel had Asherah in position to bind her and plunge her into the crevice that lead to the Abyss below.

Out by the causeway, a horn blew, alerting the Tyrians of the impending deluge about to hit their walls. Jesus and Simon ran back up the stairs and headed for the gate that was already almost closed.

The tsunami hit the small island and blanketed the surrounding buildings with tons of crushing seawater. The main island's walls held firm against the tide. The inhabitants within remained safe.

Jesus and Simon did not make it back to the gate in time. They were locked out on the causeway bridge, thirty feet above the water, but in the path of the wave. Simon said, "A miracle might be appropriate right now." The bridge shook with the force of the water hitting it. But it held strong and the wave was not high enough to reach them.

The wall of water hit the temple structure smashing much of it to pieces. Pillars came crashing down around the combatants.

The three angels binding Asherah had just plunged into the crevice when the water filled it in.

The three netted angels could not untangle themselves before they were swept away in the flood of seawater.

Ba'al rode the wave like a shark surfing just below the crest. He was on his way to the mainland. He had escaped his binding by mere moments.

The statue of Ba'al was buried in the rubble of the collapsing marble—with Uriel beneath it.

Then, just as quickly as the water had devastated the island, it was gone. The receding waters drained back into the ocean, along with the decimated ruins and bodies of the few inhabitants of the sacred isle.

Jesus and Simon ran back down the stairs and waded through the rubble and debris left in the wake of the tsunami.

Simon complained, "My lord, you calmed the storm on the sea of Galilee. Why did you not stop this wave?"

Jesus said, "I have my reasons for why I allow these things. You just follow me."

They approached the marble ruins that had been the temple and sought for any sign of life.

There was none to be found.

Finally, a figure crawled out of a pile of rock. He was bruised and battered, but he was free.

It was Uriel. He limped up to Jesus and Simon. He handed Jesus a stone tablet the size of a large wineskin. He coughed up some water and said, "The Tablet of Destinies. Do I not deliver?"

Jesus asked, "What happened to the others?"

"Asherah is on her way to Tartarus. But Ba'al got away. He netted Mikael, Gabriel and Raphael like a school of tuna. They were washed inland somewhere."

Jesus replied, "Uriel, I do not want you crowing over Gabriel. Do you have ears to hear?"

Uriel mumbled downcast. "Yes, Adonai."

"We have to get on the road as soon as possible," said Jesus. "We have to catch up with Ba'al."

Simon looked at him curiously. "You know where he is going?"

"I have a good idea," replied Jesus.

CHAPTER 11

Longinus followed Herod Antipas through the dressing room of the extravagant palatial bathhouse of the Herodian fortress of Machaerus. The black and white mosaic floor annoyed him with its dizzying effect.

"Come on, Longinus, join me," said Antipas.

"Not today," said Longinus. He kept his toga and sandals on, as Antipas stripped naked and led him into the tepidarium to receive a royal rub down.

"Suit yourself, centurion."

The indulgence of the royal class disgusted Longinus. Their lazy, leisurely excess resulted in the fat, weak bodies like that of Antipas before him. He wouldn't want to be caught dead joining in on such aristocratic decadence.

Antipas lay on a table. A masseuse rubbed him down with body oils and perfume ointments more suitable for his effeminate appearance than for the masculine leader he should be. The metaphor that came to Longinus' mind was that of a worm.

Longinus had to wait for the rigorous pat down of the fleshy worm to finish before Antipas could talk.

Antipas got up from the table and they continued on into the caldarium, or steam room, with Longinus dutifully following.

Antipas touched the steaming waters of a personal bath. He whimpered. "Ow, that is scalding hot."

Longinus thought this was the limit of pain and suffering that such soft-bodied, weak-minded royalty had to endure. He thought, *I would like to see you last two minutes in the desert heat of a Roman march, you subhuman slug.*

Still, Longinus was thankful he was in his lighter toga. The steam room was heated from below by hot water pipes that would have caused heat exhaustion, had he been wearing his full officer's uniform.

Antipas lowered himself into the steaming liquid and finally said, "What is it you want to know that is so important to Pilate?"

"He has commissioned me to track down some insurrectionists caught in seditious acts against Caesar."

Antipas groaned, "Another uprising? Jewish rebels are like cockroaches. You stomp them out, but they keep breeding and returning. Those cursed sons of Judas the Galilean, James and Simon, are still running around the hill country, causing me great pains."

Longinus said, "One of the brigands that I am trying to find, I understand, was a well-known actor in Scythopolis, a Gestas Semaras. Do you know of him?"

"The name is familiar."

"He ingratiated himself with some of your family, and sought to burrow his way into the aristocracy through marriage."

"I do remember something of that. My wife, Herodias had me ban the marriage."

Pathetic cuckold, thought Longinus. *Manipulated by his controlling bitch wife*. Longinus said, "What can you tell me?"

"Nothing that will be of help to you, I am sure. But Herodias can tell you everything about it. She revels in such court intrigue and romance."

Longinus wiped sweat from his brow. "I understand you have a prisoner, here. John the Baptizer?"

"Ah yes, the Baptizer. Let me tell you about that son of a whore. Talk about troublemaking brigands! He has quite a following. And while he is a fiery prophet, he preaches no armed revolution, so I cannot just kill the little insect. He would become a martyr."

Longinus asked, "Why have you imprisoned him, then?"

"Oh, he was causing quite an uproar by spreading his self-righteous moralizing about my marriage to Herodias. The Jewish law forbids marrying the wife of one's brother as incest. Herodias is the wife of my brother, so I am sure you can see *that* was not good for political gravitas in my kingdom."

Kingdom. The little twat was a prince of the tetrarchy of Galilee, not a king. He used kingship of himself as a means of self-flattery.

Antipas kept spewing. "Now, I do not know what to do with the Baptizer. If I kill him, I make a martyr and may cause an uprising. If I let him go, he will return to spreading his poison of political dissent that may still lead to an uprising."

"I would like to talk with him," said Longinus. "I want to see if he has any connection with the Zealots that my outlaws seem to be a part of."

"Zealots," complained Antipas. "Like I said, back like cockroaches."

Longinus thought, *Like Herods*.

"I tell you what," said Antipas. "Today is my birthday, and I have a feast prepared. Why don't you join me as my guest? Herodias can fill you in on all the gossip you want to know about your actor outlaw. You can visit the Baptizer in his cell afterward."

"I cannot afford delay on my quest. I would prefer…."

"Nonsense," interrupted Antipas. "You need to eat. It will not hurt you to rest before your long journey back to Galilee. Please accept my offer as a form of gratitude to Caesar."

Longinus sighed. This lazy, soaking worm was insufferable. But Longinus did have a grueling two-day journey back from this palace on the eastern shore of the Dead Sea.

"I insist," said the worm.

Longinus felt uncomfortable amidst the excess of conspicuous consumption that marked the feast in Herod's palatial banquet hall. Like all of Herod's rebuilt structures, this desert palace was Greco-Roman in style and lay atop a sixteen hundred foot tall rocky prominence, five miles east of the northern tip of the Dead Sea. The banquet hall sported a mosaic floor and purple curtains from Tyre. The food set before them was lavish in display and forbidden by Jewish standards—from roasted boar to shell fish to other, rich, exotic foods prohibited by their Torah. Antipas had no sense of honor or discipline. Of course, such taboos were nonsensical to Longinus. But for Antipas to so defy his own cultural codes of conduct just meant the hypocrite could not be trusted on any level, even by Romans.

Yet, he simply carried on the legacy of his royal family from the past hundred years. A legacy of lies, intrigue and betrayal. The taboo marriage of Antipas was only the beginning of his incestuous interests. For the moment, Longinus had to endure an erotic "dance of the seven veils" performed by Antipas' own step-daughter by Herodias, a young girl named Salomé. She appeared barely of marrying age. She writhed and wriggled like a nubile seductive serpent. She stripped off her seven veils one by one to the music until she was stark naked before the tetrarch and his company. Antipas watched her with lascivious eyes and clapping hands.

Longinus conversed with Herodias, to try to avoid the disgusting sight, but he found Herodias engaged in her own lascivious flirtations—with Longinus. These people had no limits to their debauchery.

He whispered to Herodias, "Did you know anything of the actor's political entanglements?" He was referring to Gestas Semaras.

"Not before we cut him off. But if it is entanglements you are interested in, I am sure I can provide some satisfaction."

He ignored her advances. He wanted facts. He needed something more. Some piece of information that might lead him to the actor's whereabouts.

"What do you know of the criminal Jesus Barabbas?"

"Well, I did have a servant spy on Gestas for a short time afterward as a precaution of protection for the princess. He followed the actor to some caves southwest of Scythopolis."

Longinus' ears perked up. "May I speak to this servant?"

She smiled at him. "Such manners. Are you so proper in all areas of your life?" Longinus could see her breathing rate increase and her eyes turn into those of a bitch in heat. "Or do you have that little forbidden part of you, hidden from your lawful discipline, where you unleash yourself?"

He tried to dodge her advances. "You and I both know, there are some laws whose violation leads to execution for both parties involved."

His intent had the opposite effect on her. "That sounds titillating. After the feast, I will personally bring you to him."

This hound will not let up. Longinus knew where she really wanted to bring him: to her bedchamber. He had no desire to be pulled into such a trap.

The music ended. The filthy dance was over and the naked girl bowed to the tetrarch. When the applause died down, Antipas stood and made a proclamation that made Longinus lose even what little respect he had for the ruler.

"Magnificent!" shouted Antipas. "Absolutely magnificent! Whatever you ask of me, I will give to you."

The girl looked confused. She wasn't sure she heard him correctly.

"I mean it, child. Ask me for whatever you wish, and I will give it to you, up to half of my kingdom!"

A hush went over the crowd. Then scandalous whispering broke out.

Antipas swaggered. He was drunk. And he was also clearly aroused. Longinus thought the foolish pervert should have stayed sitting down. He considered reporting Antipas to Caesar, because Herod, as a client ruler, offered what he had no legal right to do.

Salomé looked over at Herodias, who finally took her attention off of Longinus. At first, she was angry, jealous that this moron whom she had coddled, stroked and flattered, was now giving her daughter what she herself deserved. She said to Antipas, "My lord, you cannot be serious."

"Who are you to say I am not?" crowed Antipas. "I am king here, and I have the power." He stumbled backward a step.

Herodias' anger then turned to realization. She immediately gestured for Salomé to follow her out of the room. Salomé obeyed. The crowd whisperings grew louder, as gossip exploded over the outrageous proposition of the king.

"Longinus!" The call came from the tipsy Antipas, who was about to fall over. "You look like you need to have some fun. Celebrate! I demand it for my birthday!"

He leaned over a pail held by a servant and stuck his finger in his mouth. He gagged and then vomited into the pail. More disgusting decadence to Longinus. Royalty would often purge their meals in this way so they could keep eating.

Antipas finished gagging. His servant wiped his mouth with a kerchief and handed him a goblet of wine. Antipas rinsed his mouth with the wine, gargled and spit it into the pail. The servant left him.

Antipas moved over to the centurion, and noticed an absence. "Where is Herodias?" He smiled devilishly, "What have you done with my wife, Longinus?" He looked around with the façade of being secretive, and semi-whispered, "Just make sure the body is cold before reporting it." He grinned and slapped the officer on the back with a "Ha!"

Longinus knew this would not end well.

Antipas stopped and said, "I am hungry. Let us eat!"

The returning entrance of the young Salomé into the banquet room, newly clothed, snared the attention of Antipas. The girl was followed by Herodias, who reclaimed her place at the banquet table. Salomé floated up to the staring tetrarch and bowed low to the ground before him. She wore a flowing, embroidered gown, Antipas's favorite.

"My step-father and king, I have carefully considered your offer."

Antipas looked over at Longinus with surprise. He saw Herodias return to her seat.

"And what is your wish, my wonderful step-daughter?"

Longinus knew that Antipas was regretting his offer to this little twat. But he also realized that the returning Herodias had obviously used her daughter as a proxy, to get what she wanted. He only prayed to Mithras it had nothing to do with Longinus himself.

Salomé raised herself up and with pretentiousness announced, "I want you to give me the head of John the Baptist on a platter."

The company around Antipas all fell silent. Longinus could see the shock in Antipas' face, and the subtle smirk on Herodias' lips.

Of course, he thought. *I should have guessed it. This treacherous bitch was getting revenge on the one who challenged her moral behavior. No doubt how she will deal with me, if I do not get out of here tonight.*

Longinus got up and knelt down by Antipas, who mused to him, "I do not want to kill the Baptizer, but I should be glad she did not ask for something injurious to my actual kingship." Antipas turned back to the girl and said, "Granted, my precious one."

Longinus whispered in Antipas' ear. "You must let me see him before he is executed. It is for the procurator, remember."

"Of course," said Antipas. "You may do so, but quickly. I received a report that Caesar has sent Vitellius of Syria to meet with the Parthian king's envoy up north. I have to leave immediately in the morning to join them."

Longinus followed the guards down to the cell where the Baptizer was being held. He gestured for the guards to wait for him at the door until he was through with his interrogation.

When the door slammed shut, John looked up from his sitting position against the wall amidst a pile of straw, his only comfort. He was bedraggled and starved. His long, bushy beard made him look like a madman.

Longinus placed a plate of bread and fruit with a cup of wine at John's feet. The mad prophet ignored it.

"I am Marcus Lucius Longinus, envoy of Pontius Pilate, the procurator of Galilee."

"I know who that criminal is," croaked the Baptizer.

Longinus watched him with eagle eyes. "I can help you. If you will but help me."

John said nothing in response.

Longinus continued, "I understand you are the one to prepare the way for this 'Messiah' of yours. A new King of the Jews."

The Baptizer threw an intense stare at him. Longinus was taken aback. It felt as if he was looking into his soul. Longinus was a battle hardened soldier, who had stood before Caesar as before a god. But he had never had such an experience as this. This simple madman's stare frightened him, cut to his soul.

Longinus asked, "Is this an armed revolt? Does it have anything to do with the bandit leader, Barabbas?"

John's solemn glare turned into a smile. He shook his head with disdain. "I know nothing of Barabbas. I anointed Jesus bar Joseph as Messiah. And as for his kingdom, well…." He paused. "The blind receive their sight, the lame walk, lepers are cleansed, and the deaf hear, the dead are raised up, the poor have good news preached to them. And blessed is the one who is not offended by him."

Longinus hated prophets. They always spoke in obscure, poetic references rather than straight talk. Even those in his own religion of Mithraism, the religion of the Roman legions. So much more could be accomplished in this world if people would but be clear in their speech and intentions.

"This Jesus, he is a sorcerer? A magician?"

John ignored the question. "Tell me, centurion, I can see you are upright, a man of law." A chill went through Longinus' spine. *How did he know?*

"Will such law save your soul?"

"What do you mean?"

"You are a man of integrity. You believe in directness and you hate deception. But have you ever lied?"

Longinus did not know where this was going, so he balked at answering him.

"Even once? In your entire life?"

Still no answer from the Stoic Longinus.

John said, "Take for instance your claim to be able to 'help me'."

That statement shot through Longinus like a javelin of truth. How could he know such things?

"Of course I have lied. Everyone lies. I am human."

"So, it is human to lie. But is it right?"

It was strange, the influence this strange prophet had on breaking down the barriers.

"No, it is not right."

"Have you ever taken anything that was not yours?"

In this, Longinus was unlike most other officers and soldiers of the legions. He did not skim from war booty, he did not charge extra taxes for his own purse. But alas, he was not always so.

"When I was young, I was a delinquent and an ingrate. I had to learn the value of ownership, responsibility and integrity."

The Baptizer gave him a nod of acknowledgement. "No doubt you have met the Herods. Does their sexual depravity disgust you?"

Longinus knew this was the accusation that had gotten this madman in trouble. He would not defend this Jew, no matter how much he may have agreed with him.

The Baptizer asked him as one might ask a child, "Have *you* ever lusted after a woman?"

Such questions were ridiculous. He answered, “Lust is the natural order of mankind. But character is destiny.” Longinus had read Heraclitus as well as the Stoics. But his character was in his discipline.

“So you have *not* lusted after women.”

“I have. But *you* are not here to interrogate *me*, Baptizer.”

“Forgive me,” said John, “I plead for your indulgence. For you know I have but little time left.”

Another chill went through Longinus’ bones. How did this flea-bitten beggar know of such hidden royal decisions? He sighed with contempt and waved his hand. “Go ahead.”

“Well, in answer to your question about Jesus; where others say we must not commit adultery, he says, that if we even look at woman with lust, we have committed adultery in our heart.”

Ridiculous, thought Longinus. *Such petty scruples and semantics*.

The Baptizer kept going, “You have been employed to bring murderers to justice.”

Longinus was thinking of how this was not leading him to his target, Barabbas and the two brigands.

“Well, Jesus said that everyone who is angry with his brother or hates him will meet their justice in the fires of Gehenna.”

Longinus protested such insanity, “I love my fellow Roman, but my enemies, I hate.”

John replied, “Jesus said to love your enemies and pray for those who persecute you. For loving those who love you,” he paused again for ironic emphasis, “is no better than what Romans do.” John broke out in a devious grin. “I was just praying for Herod Antipas when you arrived, but now I see I should pray for you as well.”

“Stop this foolishness, Baptizer. You are correct. You do not have much time. So what is your point?”

John said, “Well, centurion, you pride yourself on your righteousness. Yet you have just admitted to me that you are a lying, thieving, murderous adulterer of the heart, and you will one day stand before your Creator to face judgment for all the deeds you have done. A holy god who allows no evil, no matter how small, in his presence. Will the Law save you then? Or will it condemn you?”

“You Jews and your god,” grumbled Longinus. “I have seen your elaborate sacrifices in the temple from the Antonia.” The Antonia was a Roman fortress built along the northern wall of the Jerusalem Temple in order to allow the Romans to keep an eye on Jewish religious activities.

"This is why Jesus came," said John. "Atonement. Behold, the Lamb of God who takes away the sins of the world. Even the sins of repentant Roman centurions."

"I am through with your nonsense, Baptizer. If this Messiah of yours has no other secret plan than meekness, mercy, and poverty of spirit, then I fail to see how his followers think they can stand up to the might and power of Rome. You would have a better chance with the Zealots."

And he was about to hunt down those seditious rebels and crush their hopes and dreams as well. He got up to leave.

"Centurion."

Longinus turned.

"You will never find what you are looking for. I pray it finds you."

More gibberish, thought Longinus. He rapped on the door and two guards opened it to let him out. They stayed inside and approached the Baptizer.

Longinus turned to watch them through the barred window. *What did the Baptizer mean, I would never find what I am looking for? Did he mean Barabbas and the brothers? Or was he using that cynical trick of double meaning for his spiritual longing?* It bothered Longinus. There was something about this madman prophet and his meekly Messiah that Longinus could not get out of his mind.

He watched the guards carrying in a platter with a display of lettuce, vegetables and fruit. But this was not another offer of food for the prisoner.

One of the Guards shackled the Baptizer's hands behind him. The other got behind him and pulled out a long dagger.

Longinus swallowed. He knew what came next. He had been there when Herodias commanded the guards. She hated this harmless Baptizer with such venom that she wanted him to suffer, to really suffer. So instead of using the standard swift blade of the executioner's axe or broadsword, this guard used a simple dagger to manually saw through the poor soul's neck, throat and vertebrae.

It was a heinous, wicked act of cowards, and it confirmed to Longinus that he would not even return to the palace. He would set out immediately for his century out in the desert and leave for Galilee.

For the first time in his life as a soldier, he could not watch. He had overseen atrocities of every kind; the horrors of war, the slaughter of innocent men, women and children, the evisceration of barbarians, the crucifixion of criminals. But for some reason he could not comprehend, this simple, cruel beheading made him sick to his stomach.

These Herodians deserve the fires of Gehenna, he thought. But he felt almost as if he was party to it as well.

And what of me?

He walked away before he could see the climax of bizarre evil: placing the Baptist's head on the platter of fruit and vegetables.

He tried to push the haunting experience with the Baptizer and his horrifying demise out of his mind. He set his sights on his next target: the outlaws' hideout just outside of Scythopolis.

CHAPTER 12

Eleazar ben Shemuel shifted uncomfortably in his shackles. They were a bit too small for his wrists and ankles. They were made for normal prisoners. Eleazar was not normal. A Jew by birth, he had grown up in the remnant of exiled Jews still residing in Babylon. But as a giant, over ten feet tall, he was ostracized by his own people and so had led a band of outlaws in the Parthian empire east of the Euphrates River. He was currently a captive of the Parthian king Artabanus III, awaiting his transfer as a gift to Caesar.

Eleazar was the product of his Jewish mother having been raped by a Philistine Rephaim from Gath. Out of shame, she traveled from Judea to the Israelite community in Babylon. When he had his growth spurt at the age of five, she took him into the wilderness to raise him. She had told him many stories from the Torah of her people. But she had carefully left out the story of his own cursed background. It wasn't until he had come of age and joined a band of outlaws that he learned of his true heritage.

A captured caravan had produced various scrolls on their way to the monastery of Qumran. The literature was Mesopotamian, Canaanite and Jewish holy writ. To the other bandits, these were worthless. But to Eleazar, they were a treasure trove of knowledge that filled in his own incomplete storyline. Eleazar promptly read through the Tanakh, or Hebrew Scriptures, with an increasing anger and hatred for the god of those Scriptures, Yahweh Elohim, and his minions of evil.

He had learned of the curse on the Serpent in the Garden. How Yahweh had promised a war between the Seed of the Serpent, and the Seed of Eve, that would rage through history until a messiah king would crush the head of that Serpent.

He had learned of the origin of his identity as a giant in the primeval Nephilim of antediluvian days. Sons of God from Yahweh's divine council had come to earth and mated with the daughters of men. This unholy mixing of Yahweh's separated creation order earned them the name Seed of the Serpent. They were the minions of the gods who brought great violence and wickedness upon the earth. There was a rebellion of giants called the Titanomachy and War on Eden called the Gigantomachy. They were both uprisings led by Nephilim against Yahweh. Yahweh had regretted that he had made man on the earth and sent the Great Deluge. But he saved a man, Noah, and his family because Noah was uncorrupted by Nephilim blood and was righteous before Yahweh.

The Nephilim bloodline survived the Flood and most of them migrated to the land of Canaan, where they became the mighty giant clans of the Amalekites, Amorites, Emim, Zuzim, and Rephaim. The giants were nearly wiped out again in the war campaign of the Four Kings of Mesopotamia led by Chederlaomer in the days of Abraham.

Over the next four hundred years, they repopulated and filled the land of Canaan, with the Anakim becoming the mightiest of all giant clans. Their leaders, Ahiman, Sheshai, and Talmai, each ruled with a giant iron fist throughout the Cisjordan in the west, while the giant warrior king, Og of Bashan reigned over the Transjordan in the East.

Around this time, the Hebrews left four hundred years of slavery to Egypt behind in an exodus. They came to the land of Canaan to claim it as their inheritance. Their warrior general, Joshua led them to wipe out all the Rephaim and Anakim in the land in holy Wars of Yahweh to cleanse the land of their enemy. It was a penultimate climax to the War of the Seed.

But Joshua had left some Rephaim in the coastal cities of the Philistines. Those giants once again reproduced, and by the time of the monarchy of Israel, they had become a military cult dedicated to assassinating the Messiah King of Israel. They were called "The Sons of Rapha," and they were led by a Philistine champion, a Rephaim giant, Goliath of Gath.

Eleazar had learned how the Israelite David rose up and slew the Philistine Goliath with a simple stone. He read that David became the Messiah king, and wiped out the last of the giants in the Valley of the Rephaim. As was always the case, some had survived, but they were not a very fertile people group. As time went on, the Rephaim giants had almost completely died out, save a few remnants scattered throughout the earth. Eleazar had heard that there were some that had escaped the Wars of Yahweh by taking ships to the far west. Just where they ended up, he did not know.

The story read to the titan Eleazar as if they were Chronicles of the Nephilim. These giants were his own kin. Goliath was his forefather. He was the Seed of the Serpent. But he never asked to be, which angered him even more. He was just as mad at the gods who birthed him as he was at the god Yahweh who cursed him. His bitterness had boiled over in him. He lashed out at everyone and every power and authority. He even rebelled against the Persian god Ahura Mazda in Parthia.

He actually attacked the divinity in the midst of an uprising and fought with him in battle. Of course he was bested and captured by the god, but Ahura Mazda was so impressed with the bravado of the Rapha, that he decided to spare him. Giants and humans did not attempt such a thing since primeval days. Archangels were the evenly matched opponents of deity. But Eleazar showed real skill when he fought Ahura Mazda. It seemed to the Persian god like a waste to destroy such a specimen. It would be better to put him on display as entertainment. Thus Eleazar's current predicament of captivity.

Eleazar was awakened from his sleep by a group of twenty Parthian soldiers. They could never be too cautious in guarding their titanic prisoner. He was chained from his neck to his hands to his feet. They marched him across a bridge on the Euphrates river in the northern regions of the Parthian empire of Mesopotamia. This was the very bridge that Vitellius of Syria met in concert with Artabanus to negotiate peace between Rome and Parthia.

Those two powers had been in conflict for decades. The recent years of Pax Romana had brought a temporary cessation of hostilities and the cautious interchanges of diplomacy such as this very one occurring across the Euphrates.

Eleazar saw his destination, a large festive tent across the river that leaked music and loud celebration. The captive giant had to hobble slowly on his chained feet through the cold, windy evening. It felt humiliating. He looked for an opportunity to escape or strike back at his captors. He saw none.

He ducked down to go through the low entrance to the tent. As he stood back up, the festive crowd inside went silent. All eyes had turned upon him. His twenty guards surrounded him and led the way through a parted crowd, up to the front table of the tent. Naked female dancers stopped and moved out of the way.

Eleazar's head gently brushed the top of the tent. He was used to it. Up front were two portable kingly thrones of equal height that held Vitellius and Artabanus, reposing with chalices of drink. Their advisors sat clustered around them.

Vitellius' eyes went wide when he saw the giant. The Roman legionaries around him tightened their stances and pulled in closer to their general in protection.

A portly blob of a man stood next to the Syrian ruler's throne. Eleazar could see by his robes he was some kind of Jewish royalty. His soft, pale flesh reminded Eleazar of a grub worm.

The Parthian king's son, Darius, stood beside Artabanus. He was about twenty years old and looked quite glum.

Artabanus spoke out, "In addition to my son, I offer this creature as a gift to Tiberius Caesar."

Eleazar realized the reason for Darius' gloom. The boy was going to go live in Rome as a gesture of diplomacy between the empires.

Vitellius said, "Where did you find him? I thought the Rephaim had all died out."

"They are a rare breed these days," said Artabanus. "This one is quite the fighter. Believe it or not, he is a Jew. One of the lawless brigands around the Babylonian region."

Eleazar noticed the grub worm step out in the light to get a closer look at him. It was Herod Antipas.

Artabanus continued, "Jews are the most stubborn of animals. Near impossible to tame. They are obsessed with prophecies of a coming warrior king, a new "deliverer" who they think will overthrow the powers of the earth. Thanks to your prophet Daniel who infected our Magi centuries ago."

Eleazar saw the Parthian king look at the grub and say, "But then, I take it, Antipas, that you Herods are all too familiar with such rebellion and its religious babble."

Antipas replied, "Indeed. It seems the only thing our many factions of outlaws have in common is their certitude of a living Messiah somewhere in the midst of Judea or Galilee."

"Really?" said Artabanus. "Are there any prospects?"

The discussion piqued Eleazar's attention. *Living Messiah?* That would be the Seed of Eve who was prophesied to crush the Seed of the Serpent. That would be Eleazar's arch enemy, his ultimate foe.

Antipas said, "It is difficult to say. We are hunting down the brigand leaders. I don't see any of them having sufficient forces to be of major concern to Rome." He paused. "There is one curious fellow though. I imprisoned and executed a prophet who, according to his fanatical followers, was Elijah come back from heaven. He claimed to have anointed this one fellow, a Nazarene, itinerant rabbi. Claimed he was the Son of God. That he would inherit the earth."

Eleazar immediately remembered a prophecy, he could not remember from where, that said of Messiah, "He shall be called a Nazarene." He was also well acquainted with the Davidic Psalm that spoke of Yahweh having a unique Son.

> *"You are my Son; today I have begotten you.*
> *Ask of me, and I will make the nations your inheritance,*
> *and the ends of the earth your possession.*
> *You shall break them with a rod of iron*
> *and dash them in pieces like a potter's vessel."*

"A Nazarene?" said Artabanus. "Can anything of importance come from Nazareth, a town of such insignificance?"

Antipas said, "Oh, it is more unreasonable than that, my lord. The prophet, the one whose head I removed, he said this Nazarene was born in Bethlehem, an even more worthless backwater town."

Eleazar shuddered. He knew all the prophecies. He had studied them. That small town cut out virtually all claimants to Messiah.

> *But you, O Bethlehem Ephrathah,*
> *who are too little to be among the clans of Judah,*
> *from you shall come forth for me*
> *one who is to be ruler in Israel,*
> *whose coming forth is from of old,*
> *from ancient days.*

Artabanus chuckled. "It seems this Jewish god is playing a joke on your so-called liberators."

Vitellius had nothing to add to this annoying exchange. He couldn't wait until he could get back to his tent and get to sleep. But such banter was good diplomacy, so he tolerated it.

Antipas said, "The Jews love their mythic connections. The Son of God, a Son of David, the original Messiah king of Israel."

Eleazer knew all too well about the promised Son of David.

> *"Behold, the days are coming, declares Yahweh,*
> *when I will raise up for David a righteous Branch,*
> *and he shall reign as king and deal wisely,*
> *and shall execute justice and righteousness in the land.*

"A son of Zeus!" said an amused Artabanus.

"You jest," said Antipas, "But you are more in on the joke than you realize."

Antipas wanted to ingratiate himself with the foreign ruler. He kept the amusement going like a master of chorus in a Greek play.

"Rumors have been spreading that this Nazarene was born of a virgin!"

Artabanus outright laughed. "Ah ha! I was right! How entertaining. He is trying to cast himself as born of divine human copulation, like your own hero, Vitellius, what is his name again?"

"Hercules."

"Bravo! Hercules reborn!"

But the virgin birth was no rumor or legend. Eleazar knew of the prophet Isaiah speaking seven hundred years before their own time.

> *Therefore the Lord himself will give you a sign. Behold, the virgin shall conceive and bear a son, and shall call his name Immanuel.*

"Immanuel" meant "God with us."

"But here is the biggest joke of all," said Antipas. "The man is a favorite of peasants and plebs. He has no armed forces, and he tells his followers to love their enemies. He is about the *only* one who would turn down the crown if everyone made him king!"

Artabanus clapped with glee. "Wonderful! Wonderful! It sounds like a comedy worthy of Aristophanes." Artabanus prided himself on knowing the culture of his Greco-Roman opponents.

Antipas said, "That is not a bad idea, my lord. I will commission it and have it dedicated to your lordship."

Eleazar was not amused. A Nazarene, born of a virgin, in the town of Bethlehem, from the tribe of Judah, a Son of David. It did not matter what these chortling fools thought, the odds on fulfilling those prophecies alone were only possible for one man: Messiah. Artabanus was right about the prophet Daniel's influence. The story of King Nebuchadnezzar II and his dream of a mighty statue of kingdoms to come was fresh on the minds of all Jews in the region. The dream image had foretold the kingdoms of Greece, Media-Persia, and now, Rome. But what was of more interest to Eleazar was the stone that was cut from the mountain of God without human hands. It hit the last kingdom of the statue and broke them all to pieces.

> *And in the days of those kings the God of heaven will set up a kingdom that shall never be destroyed. It shall break in pieces all these kingdoms and bring them to an end, and it shall stand forever. But the stone that struck the image became a great mountain and filled the whole earth.*

That stone was Messiah, the Seed of Eve, the Seed of Abraham. And the time had arrived for the visitation of God. Eleazar knelt down to one knee, cleared his throat, to get their attention, and said, "My lord Antipas, may I ask what the name of this Nazarene is?"

"Oh yes," said Antipas, "I nearly forgot. It is Yeshua. Jesus in Greek." Yeshua meant "Yahweh saves." Antipas turned curious. "But what is of your concern, captive?" He gave a side glance with a smirk to Artabanus. "Did you want to join him?"

Artabanus and his surrounding officers guffawed. Even Vitellius smiled at the remark.

"No, my lord," said Eleazar. "I want to kill him."

The laughter went dead.

Artabanus said, "Well, giant, you certainly know how to kill the fun around here. I am glad I am getting rid of you."

The officers brightened up a bit at the sarcasm.

Vitellius finally spoke up. He wanted to finish this juvenile bantering. "There will be no more killing for you, giant, until you reach Rome. There you can amuse Caesar and the masses with your warrior skills in the arena."

Vitellius got up from his throne. "We leave for Antioch in the morning. From there, we ship to Rome. I bid you goodnight, King Artabanus."

•••••

After several days' march, Vitellius' forces were halfway to the city of Antioch on the coast of Phoenicia. They camped for rest outside Berea, the largest city in Syria. Vitellius had with him a cohort of just under five hundred men. A third of them were in the city on reprieve. A third of them were on duty in camp. Herod Antipas had taken the King's Highway back to his home in Galilee.

Eleazar knew they were two hundred miles due north of Baal-Hermon and the northernmost city of the Palestinian provinces, Caesarea Philippi. He knew Hermon was the cosmic mountain of the gods located in the land of Bashan, the place of the Serpent. If he could escape and make his way to that sacred place, he could find intelligence on the Nazarene's whereabouts and strike with all his fury and revenge on the Messianic Seed.

After dinner, every night, he was locked up in the prison wagon, a traveling cage on wheels pulled by a team of horses. It was a cramped jail that he couldn't even stretch out in to sleep. The Romans had freed him from his leg restraints to enable his ability to march with them during the day. They didn't bother to replace the leg chains at night, only his hand shackles. After all, he wasn't being marched to his death, only to Rome, where he might actually have a career, become famous, and make a lot of money; something he had not been too successful at in his Parthian rebellion.

But Eleazar didn't care about fame or money.

He made his move in the early evening hours after dinner. Security was lax, attention was spare. There was but one guard on duty at the wagon. Eleazar looked around the wagon. They were at the edge of camp, and no one was around.

Eleazar called out quietly in a scratchy voice, "Legionary. May I have some water, please?"

The guard, an older soldier with one eye lost from a battle wound, stepped over to the wagon. He stayed just outside the reach of Eleazar's long arms and handed a water skin to the giant using a stick for extension.

Eleazar took the skin and drank deeply.

"What is your name?"

The soldier did not respond. He knew not to interact with such wily creatures as captive giants.

Eleazar finished. "Thank you, my friend."

The soldier growled, "I am not your friend, freak."

Eleazar held the skin back out through the bars. He tried to hang it on the stick, but it slipped and fell to the ground by the wheel of the wagon.

"I am sorry," said Eleazar.

The soldier was too wise for such tricks. And too wary to say anything. He glared at Eleazar, who knew what he was supposed to do.

He turned slowly around with his back to the soldier so he could not see him. He got a second look back into camp. Still no one was near them. Many were eating their meals.

Something the old soldier did not know was that giants had preternatural senses. Eleazar could see a centipede crawling at a hundred feet and hear its myriad legs moving at fifty feet.

He heard the steps of the solider in the dirt, and then his chain mail shuffle as he bent down.

Eleazar spun around and reached through the cage bars as far as he could, barely catching the old soldier by the scruff of his neck. He yanked his head into the wheel. The soldier still had his helmet on, so it made a loud clanking sound. It was enough force to stun the old codger.

Eleazar pulled him up to the bars by his throat. The soldier was dizzy. He couldn't yell out, because his throat was clutched in the vise grip of the giant. He choked for air.

Eleazar whispered to him, "If you had been a bit more cordial, I might have let you live."

Eleazar then squeezed his hand and crushed the soldier's larynx. His other hand held up the Roman as he ripped out his esophagus.

He pulled the keys from the soldier's belt. Then he dropped the body to the ground.

As he turned to open his door, he noticed some soldiers had been alerted by the sounds of struggle.

Curses, thought Eleazar. *I will have to fight my way out.*

He fumbled with the keys, trying to get the door open before the soldiers could arrive. There were a dozen of them.

Too late. A soldier reached the cage, wielding his gladius. Eleazar pulled his hands back inside, just avoiding the blade as it clanged against the iron where his hands had been.

The keys were still in the lock. What the soldier didn't know was that the lock had been opened.

Eleazar kicked the door open, knocking the soldier and a newly arrived one to the ground, unconscious.

Ten other warriors came rushing up behind the first two.

The giant was fortunate. None of them had sounded the alarm. They were all responding immediately, to quench a threat before it could get out of control.

They were too late.

Eleazar's armor and weapons were stored beneath the wagon in anticipation of his use in the Roman games. He pulled them out just as the guards reached him.

Eleazar's sword cut the first unlucky arrival in half with one swing. He knew he only had seconds before he would be overwhelmed. He would most likely be tortured for his attempted escape, castrated and sodomized with a lance. These could all be done without spoiling his fighting ability for Caesar.

He had to make sure this would not be a foiled attempt at escape.

He cut down four others in a flurry of swings.

One of them had a shield up. Eleazar kicked him in the shield and sent him flying through the air like a catapult, bringing down two others.

The other three he skewered with his javelin.

But the fight drew attention in the camp. Others gathered for an offensive. One sounded a horn.

Eleazar picked up his sack of armor, sheathed his sword and bolted into the darkness of night before anyone could see which way he went.

Some cavalry would chase him. But he could run as fast as a horse. He also shared the endurance of one.

He began his two hundred mile journey south to Caesarea Philippi, and the Gates of Hades.

CHAPTER 13

Demas and Gestas stopped from their journey to set up camp and eat a meal. It was already late in the day. They had traversed the mountain passes of the Kadesh mountain area north of Capernaum, and were now on the highway that linked Tyre on the coast with Caesarea Philippi and Damascus in the east. It was a well-traveled route for commercial trade between the three influential cities. They were on their way west toward Tyre, to track down Jesus and his band of disciples that in all likelihood included Simon the Zealot.

The sound of an approaching company made Demas run ahead and reconnoiter, to see if it was anything important. If the approachers were questionable, the brothers would hide in the bush.

Demas waved to Gestas that it was all right. When he reached his brother, he said, "I think it is them."

"The Nazarene?" asked Gestas.

Demas nodded. "And his followers. About a hundred of them. They look like fishermen, farmers and the like. Harmless."

"They must be returning from Tyre to Galilee."

"Well then," said Demas, "so are we."

The brothers decided to pretend to keep their camp and appear to be surprised by the arrival of the company. They would play their day laborer identities and ask to travel with them back to Galilee.

When the traveling group appeared on the near stretch of the road, Gestas unexpectedly ran out to meet them. He called out, "Fellow Jews! Greetings! We have been traveling from Capernaum in search of Jesus bar Joseph, the one they call Messiah. Do you know where we can find him?"

The disciples appeared on edge. A couple of them stood protectively in front of a bearded man.

Demas' stomach dropped. What was he doing? This was *not* the plan. Demas was not good at improvising like his brother was. He felt sick.

The group had stopped. One of them, which Gestas suspected was Peter, spoke out, "Why do you seek him?"

Gestas pointed back to Demas and said, "My brother and I had heard stories of miracles, healings, and exorcisms."

Oh great, thought Demas. *He is not going to pretend at all? What in the world is he doing?*

Gestas kept talking as Demas walked toward him. "I think he could be Messiah, but my brother here has his doubts."

Now, Demas looked at him with true shock. "Brother!"

Suddenly, the shielded man stepped out from the group of travelers. He wore a traveling robe, a clean, trimmed beard and haircut, and penetrating eyes. Gestas actually felt a peace come over him just from looking at the man. It was strange.

The man smiled and said, "Welcome, Demas and Gestas. There is plenty of room for both of you. Even with your doubts."

Demas whispered, "How did he know our names?"

Gestas shrugged.

The man spoke, "I am Jesus whom you seek. We are on our way to Caesarea Philippi. You are welcome to join us. We will camp here with you for the night."

"Thank you, Jesus!" Gestas blurted out. They returned to their fire as the traveling company unpacked and settled down.

Demas whispered to him, "Why in Hades did you do that?"

Gestas said, "I figured it would be easier if we just play a version of ourselves. Especially since you cannot act very well."

"Why don't you just tell them that we are also looking for Simon, to consider killing him along with Jesus?"

"Hush, brother. It will be much easier for us to be more direct. I actually am quite fascinated by this rabbi. And you can continue to play your own ornery self, so what is there to complain about?"

Gestas smiled. Demas frowned back. They sat down in the lengthening shadows to finish eating their meal.

Demas whispered again, "How did he know our names?"

"How would I know?"

Jesus called out again, "Gestas, Demas! Please join us with your meal."

The brothers ate by the fire with Jesus' followers, and discovered which one was Simon when they were introduced to the main disciples. The best that Demas could determine was that there seemed to be three who were especially close to Jesus; Peter, James, and John. Then there were about ten others who were the next closest to them. The rest were more distant from the inner circle but followers nonetheless. Demas was amazed to see that six of them were women. It was not a usual thing in this patriarchal culture for women to be traveling disciples. He wondered if they were priestesses of Asherah or some other goddess.

Gestas asked the group if there were any who could explain to him and his skeptical brother more clearly the Scriptures and their references to Messiah. It was a clever ploy to get close to Simon, seemingly by chance. They had known of Simon's scribal background from Qumran through Barabbas. So it was no surprise that their plan worked perfectly. Simon volunteered to help them.

They finished up their food and drink as some prepared for sleep. Gestas said to Simon, "Where do you come from?"

"Originally, Qumran," answered Simon. "I was an Essene. We were sure we were the true remnant of Israel in a land of hypocrites and frauds. We were waiting for the End of Days. But I rejected their ways and joined a band of Zealots in the desert."

Barabbas, thought Demas.

"We wanted to do something about the Roman occupation of our land, instead of just talking and fighting amongst ourselves as to who was the true Jew or not."

"How did you end up here?" asked Demas.

"Well, we had heard about Jesus. His signs and wonders. About John the Baptizer and his proclamation of Jesus as Messiah. But we wanted to know if he would be an ally of ours or an enemy. So I was sent to find out."

Gestas could not believe how truthful Simon was being with them. Why would anyone be so honest? Why would he feel he had nothing to hide?

"What did you conclude?" asked Gestas.

"Jesus is Messiah," said Simon.

"Will you return to the Zealots?" asked Demas. "Or are they your enemy?"

Simon turned somber and said, "I will let you decide that for yourself."

The brothers would not get the easy answer they wanted. Demas said, "If he is Messiah, then why does he lead no armies?"

Simon spoke in a lower tone as if sharing a secret. "If you had seen what I have seen, you would understand."

"What did you see?" said Demas.

"I cannot say. But I can tell you that if you go with us to Caesarea Philippi, you will see for yourself."

"What is there?" asked Gestas.

"You shall see," whispered Simon.

The brothers had heard of the place. But they had always thought it was a legend. Was it really what the rumors and tales said it was?

Seven travelers in cloaks arrived at the rear fire, sixty feet away. They caught everyone's attention. Jesus met the seven apart from the group of disciples, as if he were familiar with them. Demas knew disguised warriors when he saw them. They must be bodyguards of some kind. This would make their task of killing Jesus a near impossible one. He still wasn't sure if it was even worth killing this Simon either. What kind of competition could this peaceful rabbi be to Barabbas, anyway?

Gestas was thinking along the same lines as his brother. He felt there was something they were not seeing. Maybe it would be helpful for them to wait and see what happened at Caesarea Philippi before deciding to risk their lives with their task of assassination.

Gestas said, "May I ask you a personal question, Simon?"

Simon nodded eagerly.

"Do you think that maybe all this talk of 'turning the other cheek,' and 'loving your enemies' may be a necessary smoke screen to allow Messiah to gather enough forces and release a secret cache of arms?"

Simon looked perplexed. "You may be right, Gestas. I have thought much about his storytelling. He teaches using parables to obscure their meaning from those who are against him. He told us so himself. And if you consider them closely, you find they all have violent ends as judgment in the age of Messiah. For instance, his parable of the weeds describes the true sons of the kingdom separated from the wicked false sons who are intended for the flames of purging; the parable of the dragnet has fishermen separating fish, the righteous from the evil, who are thrown into a furnace of fire. He told a parable of virgins awaiting the bridegroom, and another wedding story only to end in tragedy as certain invitees are rejected and judged; a parable about separating sheep and goats leads to eternal life for sheep and eternal destruction for the goats. I could go on, but you see my concern. He does seem to indicate that the end of this age and the inauguration of the age of Messiah results in as much destruction as it does redemption and atonement. And the separation unto judgment is led in all of the parables by his angels."

Gestas watched the seven strangers as he said to Simon, "Do you think he will lead an army of Yahweh's heavenly host against Rome?"

Demas stared at his brother with surprise.

Simon responded, "It is possible, from what I have seen."

Gestas said, "What have you seen?"

"I told you. I cannot explain." Simon looked up and saw Jesus with his stranger guardians waving him over to them. "I will be right back."

As he walked over to Jesus and the seven, he realized that the angels had all regathered sometime after the tsunami incident.

After Simon left, Demas whispered to Gestas, "Are you play-acting or are you starting to believe this fanaticism?"

They watched Simon talking with Jesus and the seven guardians. The strangers glanced back at them from afar.

"Do not be so pig-headed, Demas. Consider this, if this Jesus is more powerful than Barabbas, whose side would you want to be on if war does break out?"

Demas would not say. "All the same, I say we kill Simon in his sleep and slip back to Galilee. We can tell Barabbas the truth. The rabbi is unapproachable, protected by disguised warriors."

CHAPTER 14

A fat, burly Jew and his young helper walked their mounts up the trail a few miles outside of Scythopolis in the hill country. It was the middle of the night. They led a small train of four pack animals carrying a large amount of supplies. The burly one turned back for a view of the city from his vantage point. He looked out upon the rich, fertile Jordan valley to the east with the River flowing south. To the west over the ridge was the more barren Esdralon Valley. He had to catch his breath before they could continue to their destination quite a bit further up the ridge: a series of hidden caves where their comrades were encamped.

His heart nearly stopped when three Roman legionaries stepped out of the bush. He turned to call for his helper to leave, but he ran into three other legionaries right behind him, swords at the throat of the young man. He froze in fear.

A centurion walked up to the burly one, the obvious leader, and asked him, "And where might you two be going in such a hurry, Zealots?"

The centurion was Longinus.

•••••

Four Zealot lookouts planted around the mountain ridge surveyed the land around them. It was the last watch of the night as the sun rose over the Jordan valley to the east. They had spotted a century of a hundred legionaries marching south along the foothills beneath them. This was a common occurrence, as Rome rotated forces between Jerusalem and the Decapolis regularly through this very route.

Roman scouts ambushed all the lookouts and slit their throats. This gave the century of soldiers about an hour to make their way up the mountain pass, before they might be discovered by the Zealots.

There were more of the outlaws sleeping in the caves than there were legionaries ascending upon them, one hundred and fifty or so. Though the Romans were not able to completely surprise the Zealots, they surrounded the Jews, so that none could escape and were forced to fight.

The Zealots had awakened with barely enough time to suit up with arms. They had been well-trained by Barabbas and managed to kill a dozen legionaries. But they were not the superior trained and synchronized armed forces of Longinus. The Zealots eventually succumbed to the Romans with a third of their men dead.

Not all the Zealot warriors were there. A small band of fifty, led by their leader Barabbas, had gone on a mission known only to the band for security reasons. A delegated messenger escaped during the fighting to warn the sortie operation not to return.

All this, Longinus had pulled from a handful of the captured Zealots whose backs he had ripped open to the bone with a scourge.

These Jews are amazing fanatics, thought Longinus as he oversaw the crucifixion of the rest of the hundred surviving Zealots. *Their dedication is quite admirable.* He kept hearing them recite the slogan, “No king but God,” a direct affront to Caesar’s imperial lordship.

The victims were stripped naked and lined up along the path to the mountain hideout as a warning to those who might consider using these caves as another den of thieves. It took the entire day just to cut down trees, create the crosses in “X” and “T” shapes, dig their holes for elevation, and then hang all hundred of the rebels onto their posts. With hands outstretched on the crossbeams, wrists were nailed to the posts with long thin spikes into the wood. To save on nails some were tied tightly with rope. Feet were nailed through the heels or ankles on each side of the vertical post. Again, to save on nails, many had their feet overlapped with bent knees and nailed with one nail through both feet.

Longinus became lost in thought to the rhythmic pounding of hammers on nails, followed by the screams of pain and cries for mercy that filled the mountainside. *All this for the promise of a deliverer.*

Some of the Zealot soldiers had even claimed to believe Barabbas was the Messiah. *What was it with these Jews? They have been slaves most of their history, and finally, they are delivered by a benevolent god, Caesar, and given special privileges to maintain their petty rules and rituals. What more do they want?*

The crucified outlaws, once hanged naked on their crosses, were elevated under the hot sun. It would not be the nailing of their wrists and heels that would kill them, or even the dehydration in the boiling hot sun. Rather, it would be the weight of their own weakened bodies that would put pressure on the lungs and suffocate them. Longinus did not have much time. He had an outlaw Zealot leader to hunt down. In order to speed up the suffocation process, soldiers broke the legs of the victims with bone-crunching clubs. The weakened cries from already half-dead lungs followed those assaults. Crucifixion was a cruel punishment used to inspire terror in insurrectionists and dissuade rebellion against Caesar, the god-man.

As an officer in the army, Longinus participated in the imperial cult of Caesar. The great general, Julius Caesar had been divinized after his death through the act of apotheosis, the posthumous declaration of divinity by the state. The divine Julius had been validated by his successor, Augustus, who cited a bright comet in the sky seen by many during the funeral games.

Though Tiberius was the current emperor, it was the previous one, Augustus, who was the first real savior to Rome and to Longinus. Augustus' mother had claimed his father was the god Apollo who copulated with her in the form of a wise snake. Into a world of turmoil and disarray, Augustus had brought *Pax Romana*, the Peace of Rome. His title was printed on coins, "Emperor Caesar Augustus, Son of God, Savior."

Longinus walked curiously along the path, looking up at the bleeding, sweating, groaning forms of the Zealots baking in the sun and dying their slow deaths. He mused, *What a waste of lives, pursuing the impossible against all odds.* For millennia, the Jews had been looking for their king, who would bring order from disorder, put an end to war, and restore all things. Did not Caesar perform these feats? These followers of the Nazarene that the Baptizer spoke of claimed the "Good News" of a new age with the birth of their savior, god manifest, who would be the hope of all the world. But was not Caesar all of these things and more? Though the Jews often appealed to ancient prophecies, it seemed to Longinus that they had simply taken all the language about the Roman god-man, Caesar, and applied it to their Messiah as a gesture of defiance.

Longinus had memorized one of the proclamations from the Provincial Assembly of Asia that sounded quite similar to the Jews' own scriptures:

> The most divine Caesar, we should consider equal to the Beginning of all things: for when everything was falling into disorder and tending toward dissolution, he restored it once more and gave to the whole world a new aura; Caesar, the beginning of life and vitality. Augustus, whom Providence filled with strength for the welfare of men, and who being sent to us and our descendants as Savior, has put an end to war and has set all things in order; and, having become god manifest, Caesar has fulfilled all the hopes of earlier times in surpassing

> all the benefactors who preceded him, and whereas, finally, the birthday of the god Augustus has been for the whole world the beginning of the Gospel of Good News concerning him, therefore let a new era begin from his birth.

Why did these Jews not consider Caesar as the fulfillment of their own prophecies? What did this promised Messiah offer these poor dying fools that Caesar could not? Elysium? A happy heaven in their martyrdom? He was certainly no worthy opponent of Caesar, if these were his warriors.

Longinus remembered how years earlier, his ruthless troublemaking prefect, Pontius Pilate, had brought the ensigns of Caesar into the holy city of Jerusalem. The Jews were so intolerant of Caesar's image, that their protest made it to the ears of Tiberius. But when Pilate arranged to have them all surrounded and killed by a legion, he was stopped in his tracks. Instead of rioting or defending themselves, the Jews had all, to a man, bowed low in the dirt and offered their necks for martyrdom. Pilate knew it would not benefit him politically to engage in such wanton slaughter of peaceful citizenry, so he took the ensign standards out of the city. But Pilate was never one to be outmaneuvered, so he continued looking for opportunities to aggravate these "desert rats," as he called them. Longinus' assignment was important to providing Pilate with advance knowledge of any plans for revolution.

Still, the tragic absurdity of it all made Longinus wonder if he was missing something. He decided to spare one of the Zealots who was a scribe, in order to learn more about their holy books and therein, their intended strategy. Despite all the social unrest, he did not think the Jews were anywhere near the organized or armed capabilities of true effectual revolution. Was there a piece to this puzzle that was eluding him? He would need to find this Barabbas and the two circus brothers. He would torture it out of them. But where were they?

It came to him that if there was any merit to these claims of Barabbas considering himself to be the Messiah, then a certain predictability would follow. Historically, whenever these Jews congregated with grievances, there was trouble. Their yearly Passover feast was approaching soon. It commemorated their exodus from slavery in Egypt, a perceived analogy of their submission to Rome. With the increasing unrest, it would seem a perfect time to rise up in revolt.

And the perfect place would be Jerusalem. They made their pilgrimage for the feast to Jerusalem, the location of their holy temple, and the "City of

David," their original Messiah king. Would it not make most sense for the "Son of David," as they called him, to claim his throne and capture first their holy city, from there, to launch a rebellion against Caesar?

He would travel to Jerusalem and wait for this criminal usurper, this serpent, to raise his head, so that Longinus could strike it off before the rebel could make his move.

He knew that wherever he found this pretended Messiah, Barabbas, he would find the escaped outlaw brothers, Demas and Gestas.

CHAPTER 15

On the way to Caesarea Philippi, Simon befriended the day laborers, Demas and Gestas. They asked many questions and seemed interested in Simon's own reasoning for his change of mind about Jesus. He was pleased with their interest, but could not help but wonder if they had ulterior motives. When the rabbi entertained questions from the larger group, Gestas seemed most focused in his own questions about the armies of the heavenly host and their part in the end of the age. Demas seemed interested in employment as a bodyguard with his fighting skills. But Jesus told him that now was not the time for such needs.

Winter came on, so their traveling had slowed a bit, with cool days and very cold nights around campfires. After Simon saw Jesus meet with the archangels in disguise that one evening, they left immediately the next day. Back on the causeway of Tyre, Jesus had told Simon about the binding and imprisonment of Asherah. Evidently, the archangels had made it into the crevice of the Abyss, moments before the tidal wave had washed over the island of Melqart. The three archons, Remiel, Raguel and Saraqael had bound her and dragged her down to Tartarus.

The trio had met up with the other four and were now on the road, conversing with Jesus about their next plans. What those plans were, Simon had no idea, but he finally understood the larger picture they were all participating in. Jesus was binding the principalities and powers over the land, and his next target was at Caesarea Philippi.

The city was at the mid-point of the highway between Tyre on the coast and Damascus in the northwest. It was nestled in the foothills of Baal-Hermon in a fertile area of trees and lush vegetation, between the waters of the Jordan coming out of Dan to the west and Panias Springs that flowed through the city. Twenty-five miles to the south, the Sea of Galilee and its surrounding cities of Capernaum, Bethsaida and Tiberius were all within reasonable distance for common travel and economic activity. Caesarea Philippi was a multicultural nexus of ethnicity as well, with a thoroughly mixed population of Semites, Greeks and Romans from all over the empire.

As they approached the city, the group of traveling disciples could see the large Augusteum like a shining white beacon on a hill in the center of the city. This Greco-Roman temple had been built by Phillip, the reigning tetrarch of the area for the last twenty-five years. He had it erected years before to honor the imperial cult of Augustus Caesar. Made of bright, white marble and graced with Corinthian style columns, this open-air temple embodied the worship of the emperor in conjunction with Roma, the personification of the Roman state. The rest of the architecture of the city was also Hellenized by Herod's building programs. The veritable procession of sculpted images of gods like Zeus, Hermes, Apollo, Echo and Nemesis made Simon sick to his stomach. He detested images. He tried to envision himself as part of an army occupying this spiritual stronghold of demonic habitation.

Jesus held up his hands and stopped the traveling company. "I am taking the twelve with me into the city. But I want the rest of you to pitch camp further up the river outside Panias. We will meet you later."

The traveling group of Jesus' followers continued on toward Panias, while Jesus turned up the road with his twelve disciples. Demas and Gestas stayed behind as the larger group headed toward the sacred grotto. The brothers looked at each other. They didn't have to say anything. They knew they were going to spy on the twelve to see what happened. They waited until the disciples had disappeared up the pathway into the city, and returned to follow Jesus at a safe distance.

As the twelve entered the large marketplace, Simon discovered they had arrived in the middle of the city's yearly pagan festival, Lupercalia. The city had originally been named Panias in honor of the satyr goat god of nature, Pan. The festival remained from ancient days. It consisted of celebration and ritual, one of which was currently in progress. The disciples had to move aside with the crowds that lined the street.

A sacrifice of goats had been made at the sanctuary of Pan, near where the disciples were setting up camp. Two young men, called *luperci*, stripped naked like the faun Pan, took strips of skin from the sacrifice, and smeared their foreheads with the blood of the victim. They then ran down the hill into the city and used the bloody strips of skin to slap women who lined the streets. The women had offered themselves for fertility to the god. Later, there would be games and competitions, as well as music and drama, all part of the celebration. But the religious rites of this festival had an additional purpose: to ward off evil spirits.

Simon knew that such pagan activities produced the opposite effect, they opened the entire city up to evil spirits. He now understood Jesus's timing for their arrival. This was a spiritual war, and he was invading the enemy's territory to call them out and face them down.

And the enemy discovered Messiah's presence in their midst.

Behind the corner of an alleyway, Demas and Gestas watched Jesus and the disciples. The brothers saw residents of the city that were standing around or near the visitors begin to tremble violently. The people could not control themselves. They fell to the ground howling and screaming as if in torment. But the voices were not their own, for the cries had an eerie, otherworldly presence to them. Evil spirits possessed the people. There were a dozen or more of the spirits, all belching out blasphemies and curses.

The young man closest to Jesus flapped on the ground so violently that he appeared to be a blur to those around him. Jesus laid his hand on the poor soul. The young man stopped moving. A terrible wail filled the air as the demon left his body.

Jesus turned to his disciples. "Join me, now! Cast them out."

Simon took a deep breath. Earlier in their journeys, Jesus had given authority to the twelve to heal sicknesses and cast out demons. They had split up for a while to visit towns separately and exercise their new gift. It had amazed them all, and they had come back together to share their experiences. That practice had prepared them for this. Simon suspected there was more to come.

All twelve of the disciples began casting out demons from those near them, in the power and authority of Jesus. The crowds moved away in fright. The celebration had been interrupted.

The crowd ran away in droves. Hundreds of them. They seemed frightened to death by what they saw.

Simon knew where they were running to: Pan's cave on the outskirts of the city. He knelt beside a young girl on the ground spitting up foam and speaking what sounded like magical incantations in foreign tongues.

Demas and Gestas watched it all from their shadowed corner near the disciples. It was pandemonium all around them. They didn't know what to do. They had never seen anything like it before. No amount of monstrous beasts, real or play-acted, could prepare the brothers for what they were seeing. What bothered Gestas most was that he felt strangely attracted to the afflicted girl that Simon was attending to.

Simon laid his hands on the babbling girl. Suddenly, she stopped and looked past Simon with her black-orbed eyes. He followed her gaze to see Demas and Gestas hiding by the alleyway. Her head tilted at an unnatural angle. With a diabolical grin, she spoke out in an unearthly voice to Demas and Gestas in the distance, "You want to lick me, don't you, actor? And you, bestiarius, you want to thrust your sword through my belly. Do it! Come, set me free! Slit my throat and pierce my dead body. Sssssssssss!"

Demas and Gestas froze in fear. How did this spirit know their hearts? How did it know that Gestas was in bondage to his lust and Demas to his violence? This—thing—was more frightening than any animal Demas had faced in the arena.

They stepped back into the shadows, but could not hide from the penetrating blackened gaze of the demon-possessed little girl.

She writhed on the ground like a serpent, trying to move toward the two of them in the alley.

She hissed to Simon, "Let me enter into them."

"No!" commanded Simon.

The brothers turned and ran as fast as they could to get away from there.

Simon yelled at the girl, "I cast you out in the name of Jesus the Messiah. Be gone, wicked spirit!" The demon left her quivering body with a howl, and she went limp.

Peter, James, John, and the other disciples moved about casting out the evil spirits as they were taught to do.

There must have been twenty to thirty demons. By the time the disciples finished exorcising them, the entire square had cleared out.

Jesus looked outside the city just to the east where a cliff was visible, rising up a couple hundred feet in the air. It was the destination of the fleeing demoniacs: the sacred grotto of Pan.

Jesus turned to the disciples and said, "Men, it is time to storm the Gates of Hades." He brushed himself off and walked out of the marketplace toward the eastern outskirts of town. The twelve followed.

The rest of the townspeople were happy to be rid of the strangers. The visitors had caused such a commotion with their arrival in the square that they had ruined the festivities for that day. The people just wanted to forget what they saw, get back to their celebration, and then go home to finish their daily chores.

•••••

Simon followed Jesus with the rest of the twelve, walking straight through the Cardo Maximus, the main thoroughfare that stretched through the city end to end, lined with Greek columns. Their progress felt like a victorious triumphal march with everyone watching fearfully from the sidelines. But Simon knew it was more like a gauntlet, for they were about to enter the stronghold of the enemy.

Panias, the sacred grotto of Pan, lay just two hundred yards up the low incline at the base of the red rock bluffs. Across the river, a short distance from the grotto, Simon could see the traveling disciples setting up camp and the staring faces of Demas and Gestas, watching from their safe distance. He smiled to himself. He would have to explain to the brothers later the bizarre occurrence they had just run away from.

The twelve with Jesus arrived at the sacred pool, about a hundred yards wide. At its origin, another fifty yards ahead of them, the Springs of Panias gushed out of the Cave of Pan, a large mouth in the red cliff towering a hundred feet over the temple district. A temple of Pan, altars, tombs, and other architecture carved into the very rock, housed a thousand eyes watching Jesus approach them. Inhuman eyes.

Jesus held his hand up to the disciples. "Wait here."

They stopped.

Jesus walked on. From his position, Simon saw what looked like a high priestess step out of the temple. He could barely see in the waning light, but she wore an elaborate headdress and flowing purple robes.

She saw Jesus, turned, and led her entourage of nymphs back into the cave. She was not going to face down her challenger.

The sun was already setting and the long shadows played over the grounds like phantoms. A chill grew in the air.

Simon wrapped his cloak tighter. He couldn't tell if the shiver that went down his spine was from the temperature or the eerie, developing scene before him.

The priestess stopped at the mouth of the cave. She raised her arms, and an ugly unearthly howl came out of her, as if from the very depths of Sheol. The acoustics of the grotto were astounding. Every sound was amplified.

Then she disappeared inside the cave.

Jesus walked up to the temple area.

Simon saw people appear from inside buildings and tombs, from behind trees, rocks and architecture. They were the local residents, but they were not acting normally. They walked with slight jerks and twitches, stumbling toward Jesus. Some could be heard squealing like swine and making guttural animal sounds. Demoniacs. Hundreds of them. Descending the slope like slow, crouching predators upon their prey, the Son of God.

Peter yelled out, "Jesus!" He and the disciples moved to help.

Jesus snapped his palm back at them to stop.

He was fifty yards away from the disciples, right inside the temple district of the ravine.

The demoniacs staggered out of their hiding places toward Jesus.

He now looked up into heaven with hands held out in vulnerability.

Simon could feel, if not hear, the sounds of a thousand spirits whispering foul words and vile thoughts in the air.

The possessed drew nearer and nearer to Jesus, hundreds of them encircling him.

In all his experience with exorcism, Simon had never seen so many demoniacs in one location. He remembered the legion of spirits in the two men of the Gadarenes. But this was a significant segment of the population of an entire city. Jesus had warned them of this location. It was called the Gates of Hades for a reason. It had some kind of access to the underworld. Equally significant was the fact that this sacred space stood at the foot of the mountain range of Hermon, the cosmic mount of assembly of the gods. Simon had read the Book of Enoch, and the Book of Giants at Qumran. He knew of the fall of the Watcher gods at this very mountain before the Flood. This was the heart of evil in the land of Bashan, the place of the Serpent.

As their ranks closed in, Simon could see that the solid crowd of hundreds of possessed creatures had stopped its advance within a few yards of Jesus. Those behind tried to push forward, but the line would not move. It was as if an invisible barrier held them from advancing upon him. There was no way out for Jesus, and no way in for them.

They swayed as if under a spell. A cacophony of growls and screeches peppered the crowd, making Simon think of a pack of devilish hyenas held at bay with spiritual leashes.

Jesus lowered his arms.

The entire massive crowd of demoniacs fell to the ground, unconscious, downed by a spiritual wave of power. A gust of wind drew up out of the fallen bodies and became a whirlwind around Jesus. Dust and debris flew around him.

The whirlwind then sucked away from Jesus into the large cave opening, and everything went silent. Dead silent.

When the individuals in the crowd began to move, they were disoriented, as if they were waking from a sleepwalking trance. Simon knew that Jesus had engaged in a mass exorcism of the entire crowd. This location was truly a bastion of demonic power. But Jesus had neutered the forces of evil that guarded it.

What would be next? What was in the cave? Did the Nephilim spirits merely regroup inside for a second offensive?

Jesus waved for the disciples to come to him. Simon followed Peter in the lead.

When they reached Jesus, the crowd thinned. People found their way home, and others thanked Jesus.

Demas and Gestas had led a small group from the camp on the other side of the river up to the temple district. They stood behind the disciples.

Jesus said to those around him, "Who do people say that the Son of Man is?"

Peter blurted out, "Some say John the Baptist come back from the dead."

John spoke up, "Some say you are Elijah from heaven."

Simon added, "It seems the masses have imagined you being the return of just about every prophet from our Scriptures."

Jesus looked around at them with a somber face. "But who do you say that I am?"

The disciples glanced at each other sheepishly. As usual, Peter was the first to respond.

"You are the Messiah, the Son of the living God."

Jesus smiled. "Blessed are you, Simon bar Jonah. For flesh and blood has not revealed this to you, but my Father who is in heaven."

Peter beamed with a proud smirk.

Jesus turned completely away from them and looked out upon the mountain range looming beyond them several miles away.

He glanced at Peter. "You are a rock, Peter."

Simon could see Peter wasn't sure what to think of the statement. His name in Greek meant stone. But did Jesus mean he was rock solid? Simon thought it would be more appropriate to mean rock head.

Jesus pointed to the twin peaks of Baal-Hermon and gestured downward from them to the sacred cave they now stood before, drawing a line of connection. "From primeval days, this cosmic mountain and its gates has been a stronghold of evil on this earth. Yet, I say to you, upon *this* rock, I will build my church. And the Gates of Hades shall not prevail against it."

He thought for a moment, then looked back at the disciples again. "To you, I will give the keys of the kingdom of heaven. Whatever you bind on earth shall be bound in heaven, and whatever you loose on earth shall be loosed in heaven."

Another pause and he said, "Tell no one here that I am Messiah."

At the back of the crowd, Demas and Gestas looked at each other with confusion. They had no idea what he was saying to them. Magic binding? Don't tell anyone? What kind of Messiah is a secret Messiah? This rabbi was too enigmatic.

Jesus looked back at the cave, then up at the mountain and recited a Psalm of David.

"O mountain of God, mountain of Bashan;
O many-peaked mountain, mountain of Bashan!
Why do you look with hatred, O many-peaked mountain,
at the mount that Elohim desired for his abode,
yes, where Yahweh will dwell forever?
The chariots of God are twice ten thousand,
thousands upon thousands;
the Lord is among them; Sinai is now in the sanctuary.
You ascended on high,
leading a host of captives in your train
and receiving gifts among men,
even among the rebellious, that Yahweh Elohim may dwell there.
But God will strike the heads of his enemies,
the hairy Seirim crown of him who walks in his guilty ways.
Yahweh said,
"I will bring them back from Bashan,
I will bring them back from the depths of the sea."

Simon swallowed hard. He looked with trepidation over at the cave entrance. "Rabbi, where are you going?"

After an uncomfortable silence, Jesus finally said, "Back to camp," and he turned and walked away.

The disciples caught up with him on the path along the other side of the river. Demas and Gestas overheard Jesus explaining to them, "We must prepare to go to Jerusalem soon. It will be a time of great suffering for me."

"What do you mean?" asked Peter.

"I will be killed there. But the twelve of you should not despair. This was ordained and spoken of in the prophets. But on the third day, I will be raised."

Peter pulled him aside as the others continued. Simon waited for them, close enough to overhear the rest of their discussion.

Peter said with agitation, "Far be it from you, Lord. This shall never happen to you. Do not the Scriptures say Messiah will reign at the right hand of Yahweh until he has made his enemies your footstool?"

Jesus turned angry toward him. "Get behind me, Accuser. You are a hindrance to me. For you are not setting your mind on the things of God, but on the things of man."

Jesus strode away, leaving Peter in shock, crestfallen. A moment before, Jesus had given him the keys of the kingdom, and now the Master was rebuking him as a satanic adversary.

Simon could not help but sympathize with Peter. He too was confused about how suffering and death could fit in with a Messiah as conquering king. Peter had not twisted Scripture. So where was all this leading?

Yahweh says to my Lord Adonai:
"Sit at my right hand,
until I make your enemies your footstool."
Yahweh sends forth from Zion
your mighty scepter.
Rule in the midst of your enemies!
Yahweh is at your right hand;
he will shatter kings on the day of his wrath.
He will execute judgment among the nations,
filling them with corpses.
A Psalm of David

Back at the camp, Peter sat, sullen, by himself at one of the fires. The chill in the air had gotten biting cold.

Demas and Gestas drew close to their fire with Simon. They asked the scribe to explain to them the disturbing events of that day.

Gestas asked Simon, "The demon in that girl you exorcised, how did it know our hearts?"

Simon said, "The power of demons lies in the sins of mankind. Unconfessed or unatoned sin is the weapon that a spirit uses against its host and its enemies."

The implication was obvious to each of the brothers. *They needed atonement.*

Demas thought, *Why do I need atonement? Rome is the evil that has raped our land, enslaved our people, and stolen everything from me. I am the victim, not the perpetrator. I am fighting for righteousness.*

Gestas asked, "And what was all that Jesus said about the keys of the kingdom and the binding magic?"

Simon smiled. "It is not magic. Jesus is binding the unclean spirits of this land by the finger of Yahweh, to make it holy. It is the spiritual consummation of *herem*, the Holy Wars of Yahweh from the time of Joshua. Jesus is binding the principalities and powers to prepare the land for Messiah. Remember the Lord's prayer for his kingdom to come on earth as it is in heaven?"

The brothers nodded their heads. It was a universal notion in their world since primordial days that the heavens were connected to the earth. The saying went, "As above, so below." From Baal-Hermon, to Babylon, to Assyria, to Israel, temples were cosmic mountains that connected the heavens above with the earth and underworld below. As Asaph, the Israelite psalmist wrote, "He built his sanctuary like the high heavens, like the earth, which he has founded forever." The earthly temple was a synchronized replica of the heavenly temple.

So too were the divine rulers linked to their earthly counterparts. When kingdoms rose and fell, their heavenly princes rose and fell with them. Battles on earth involved battles in heaven.

Simon continued, "At Babel, the seventy nations were given as an inheritance to the seventy Sons of God who rebelled. These were the gods of the nations. Messiah has come to reclaim their inheritance as Yahweh's own. As he binds the spiritual powers, he makes way for the kingdom of heaven to grow like a mustard seed on the earth. It starts the tiniest of seeds, but grows to become the biggest tree in the garden. When sin is bound on earth, it is bound in heaven. This is the Good News of atonement for sins."

This is madness, thought Demas. Heaven, Hades, angels and demons. All that was real to him was what he experienced here and now in this world of flesh, blood and dirt. Yes, he had seen some fantastic things in these past days. But men had always interpreted life through this heavenly vision, in order to invest the chance events of history with meaning and purpose. Otherwise, how else could they live with the victory of wicked nations over Israel? How else could they justify the gratuitous suffering of the innocent? The meaningless loss of parents in an armed uprising? The senseless murder of a wife by occupying forces? Hopes of an afterlife were self-delusions to avoid facing the permanent force of chaos over life.

Gestas was not as skeptical as Demas. He probed for more answers. "What did Jesus mean by his recitation of the mountain of Bashan?"

Simon looked solemnly out into the darkness. He recited some of it again, "'O mountain of God, O many-peaked mountain of Bashan. The mount that Elohim desired for his abode.'" He looked directly at Demas and Gestas. "The phrase, 'twice ten thousand, thousands of thousands' refers to the heavenly host of Elohim's divine council. They are his holy ones, Sons of God who did not rebel." The brothers knew that "host" was a military term for a king's army of warriors.

"Sinai was Yahweh's holy mountain in the Exodus, until Mount Zion with its temple in Jerusalem became the holy mountain." Simon's eyes narrowed as he spoke. "This area is known for the Seirim, the sons of hairy Esau. It is an original dwelling place of satyrs, goat demons of Azazel. Pan is the last of the satyrs and the guardian of Gaia, the Mother Earth Goddess."

It was all coming together for Gestas. He tried to finish Simon's thought. "So Hermon is the cosmic mountain in opposition to Yahweh? And Jesus is going to strike down the 'hairy crown' of Pan, storm the Gates of Hades, and occupy this cosmic mountain as his own?"

Simon nodded in agreement, and added, "And he will ascend on high with his train of captives, as any military conqueror would in a Triumphal Procession."

"Grandiose claims for a man without a single soldier amongst his wild-eyed fanatics," said Demas skeptically.

Gestas looked at his brother angrily. "After all we've seen, you are still unimpressed?"

Demas didn't want to get into it. "I'm going to sleep." He got up and left them for his tent.

CHAPTER 16

In the middle of the night, the campfires were almost out. All was quiet around the camp of disciples. Demas quietly slipped out of his tent, and spotted Simon wrapped in his blanket near his fire. Several others lay around the smoldering coals, but they were sound asleep. One of them snored quietly.

Demas moved like a panther over to the prone form of Simon. He crouched down to look at the scribe's peaceful, sleeping face. Demas hated that peace. Simon was a fool, content in his own ignorance of the pain of others. True believers had that ability to block out reality that did not fit with their picture of the world. Demas knew he could not return to Barabbas without any blood on his hands. It would make him appear weak and vulnerable to attack. He had to kill at least one of his targets.

Demas placed a dagger up to Simon's sleeping throat. He would kill this traitor, then tell his brother, which would force him to leave with Demas to go back to the Zealot hideout.

A sound caught his attention, from a few fires away. He saw what looked like Jesus in the moonlight, coming out of his tent. Demas immediately laid on the ground and feigned sleep, with his eyes watching the rabbi.

He saw seven figures dissolve out of the trees to meet Jesus. Demas remembered those seven. They were the warriors he had previously spied on the road to Caesarea Philippi. Demas thought it strange that they had traveled with them to the city, but then, a day earlier, had disappeared, leaving the rabbi unprotected as he entered the city.

Now they were back. And they led Jesus away from the camp toward the Cave of Pan.

Jesus led his seven guardians to the cave entrance. He stopped and said in a low hush, "Now, Uriel and Gabriel, I want you two to promise that you will not bicker or compete on this mission. I need your full attention."

The angels looked at Jesus guiltily.

"Do I have your promise?"

"Yes," sighed Gabriel. "Yes," added Uriel.

"Good. Now, give each other a kiss of fellowship."

"Jesus," whined Uriel.

"Do not 'Jesus' me. Kiss your brother in arms."

The angels reluctantly grabbed wrists, then kissed each cheek as was their custom.

Jesus turned back to the cave, took a deep breath, and said, "Get ready for all Hades to break loose."

He led them into the dark, wide cavernous mouth of death.

It was pitch black. But the archangels could see just as well as in the light with their preternatural sight. Being human, Jesus was not so equipped. He stumbled on some rocks. Mikael, his guardian, took his hand and led him gingerly into the blackness.

They had gone some distance in, when they saw torchlight around a large golden image. As they approached it, Jesus could see more clearly whose image it was.

"Azazel," he said with bitterness.

The twenty foot statue loomed over them. Jesus saw his goat-like hairy legs with hooves, and his muscular human torso covered with the fine scales of a serpentine Shining One. Along with Semjaza, he had led the original rebellion of the Sons of God from heaven. Though he was bound in Tartarus, his powers were still felt throughout history, in the worship given him by foolish idolaters seeking power. The wilderness was called "the wilderness of Azazel" and it embodied the chaos of disorder as much as Leviathan had embodied the chaos of the sea. Jesus was here for Azazel's successors.

He took the torch and moved on.

The company could hear the sound of slithering and hissing at the edges of the cave as they walked on. They kept their eyes ahead as they approached the next source of light.

A series of torches surrounded the curved opening of a large pit, the opening of the Abyss.

The high priestess from earlier stood on the opposite side of the pit, before an entourage of twelve nymphs, all seductively alluring in translucent gowns and jewelry.

The priestess wore a headdress of gems on her raven black hair. Her purple robe, made from the finest of Phoenician silks, flowed behind her like a spirit. Her eyes were large, deep brown and hypnotic. Her beauty was beguiling. When she spoke, her voice sounded like seven voices blended into one bewitching unity.

"Welcome to the Gates of Hades, Son of God," she said. "And your ass-kissing suck-upssss."

Her "esses" slid through the air like the serpents that wrapped around her arms and neck.

Jesus stared her down.

She faltered and visibly shivered, but regained her composure and approached him.

"What is your name, woman?"

"I am the Ob of Paniassss."

She opened her robe and dropped it to the floor, leaving her completely naked before Jesus and the angels.

"You would not attack an unarmed, naked woman, would you, Son of God?" Her voice turned from vulnerable to sexual. "Or would you like to?"

Jesus kept looking her in the eye. Compassion flowed from his gaze, not judgment.

It shook her to the core.

He said, "You are a woman created in the image of Yahweh and you have a name."

"I am the Ob of Panias. I belong to Pan."

"You belong to Yahweh," said Jesus. He reached out and touched her head.

She froze. Her eyes went wide with terror. She began to tremble. The serpents slid off her body in a self-protective move.

Her head tilted back and her mouth opened wider than humanly possible. A black swarm of flies issued from her mouth as if from her very soul.

Uriel thought flies a most disgusting creature and quite apropos for demonic entities.

This was only beginning.

She fell to the ground in convulsions.

Jesus said, "That is one of you. There are six more. Come out of her, foul spirits."

A piercing, shrieking howl bellowed from deep within her and echoed throughout the cave. Uriel winced at the high pitch. He had sensitive ears. Another demon left her.

Jesus reached over and placed her robe back over her to cover her dignity. She shivered, as if freezing like ice.

The angels heard a noise and turned. Behind them stood two eight foot tall gods, Ba'al and Pan. The warriors moved to shield Jesus, who remained kneeling beside the quivering Ob.

Ba'al carried his mace, and Pan, a dagger in each hand.

Ba'al said, "We meet again, godlickers."

Uriel quipped, "But no running like a chicken this time, Lord Lettucehead."

Ba'al was the god of storm and vegetation. The insult was Uriel's witty way of getting under the deity's scaly skin.

"And no Asherah to give up, either," added Gabriel. "Does the goat here know how you betray your allies?"

Pan gave a surprised glance at Ba'al.

Ba'al said, "We cannot touch the Son of God. But our human puppets can."

The angels glanced behind them. The dozen nymphs approached Jesus, with their eyes black as the Abyss and serpentine fangs ready to bite.

Mikael and Raphael stepped in front of them to protect Jesus.

Uriel, Gabriel, Remiel, Saraqael and Raguel faced the gods.

Ba'al gave a war cry and launched into the three angels nearest him with furious swinging. They blocked with their weapons. But he was strong, very strong. He pushed them off balance.

Behind them, The Ob vomited a stream of black bile. The third entity left her.

She became drenched in sweat as if being roasted in flames. Another scream pierced everyone's ears, as the fourth left its host.

Uriel faltered at the noise. He was off guard.

Ba'al's mace hit him broadside in the head, crushing his skull and launching him to the side in a heap. Angels could not die, they were heavenly flesh, that healed supernaturally. But even heavenly flesh could feel pain and be temporarily impaired. Uriel was out of commission for the moment.

"Big mistake, god of broccoli," yelled Gabriel. "Nobody hurts my little buddy without paying my price!" It was heartfelt if not a bit condescending toward his comrade angel. Gabriel launched into his own relentless fury of strokes, driving Ba'al back. Remiel joined him.

Pan used his blades lightning fast to block and attack the swords of the other two angels.

Mikael hacked off the head of one nymph, and Raphael impaled another before the ten others leapt onto the two archons in a demonic pile up.

The Ob now flopped around like a piranha out of water gasping for life as another spirit was exorcised.

A howl announced the sixth entity to leave her. Jesus continued praying on his knees.

Pan saw an opening. He ran from the two angels on him, crossed behind the two fighting Ba'al. As he ran past, he slashed the backs of those angels.

Gabriel dropped to his hands and knees. The blow stunned Remiel.

Ba'al's mace pummeled Remiel into the ground.

Ba'al turned to face the two others.

Mikael and Raphael, burst their way out of the vampiric nymphs and cut them to pieces.

Jesus laid his hands in prayer on the Ob to wrest the final spirit from her body. She choked and gagged. She couldn't breathe.

Her neck tilted back inhumanly. The demon, in the form of a black python, slithered out of her throat, and away into the darkness.

Jesus collapsed to the floor, drenched in sweat.

The two angels had forced Ba'al toward the edge of the pitch black pit. The warrior god would not go easily. He pushed them back.

And just when the situation could not get any worse, it did.

From behind them, a ten and a half foot tall giant emerged from the darkness in Parthian armor, wielding a sword and shield.

Eleazar ben Shemuel fixed his eyes on Jesus. He knew his prey. He had much time to strategize during his two hundred mile journey from Berea up north. He had much time to plan his revenge on the Seed of Abraham that had wiped out the Seed of the Serpent over the past millennia. He wanted vengeance.

Before he could attack, a whip snapped around from behind him. It latched onto his face, and took out one of his eyes with its iron cracker tip.

He screamed in pain and turned to face his attacker.

Demas ben Samaras stood there defiantly, wielding his whip with dangerous accuracy. "Come on, you beast, I've taken down bigger brutes than you." He snapped again. The giant held up his shield to block it.

Jesus shouted, "Demas, no! This is not your fight!"

Demas pulled back on his attack. He couldn't believe what he heard.

The giant turned to face Jesus, who now stood before him, looking up into his good eye. The other one was gone, and in its place a bloody gaping hole of ripped flesh.

Eleazar froze. Something in the look of his prey burned into his heart. His entire life flooded his soul, and he felt the weight of his thoroughly depraved life upon him. *What sorcery was this? How comes this puny Jew by such power? What is happening to me?*

Before he knew it, Eleazar dropped his shield. He was on his knees. The Nazarene was now eye-level with him. Eleazar could easily reach out his hand and crush the vulnerable human's skull. But he could not move his arms. He could only stare into the face of the rabbi.

Jesus whispered to the giant, "You were brought here for a reason."

Eleazar thought, *Brought? I came here of my own accord to kill.*

Jesus looked up at Demas with scolding eyes.

He doesn't want my help? thought Demas. *He is under attack and he doesn't want my help? Fine. I won't risk my life for such a fool. Let him fight his own fights.*

Demas turned and left the cave.

Jesus placed his hand on Eleazar's bad eye. The giant jerked back. But Jesus would not let go.

Eleazar felt a strange numbness spread out from his wounded eye socket over his entire head. The pain faded.

Jesus pulled back his hand, and Eleazar could see through both eyes again. He had both his eyes!

His hands reached up and felt his face. He had been healed by this god-man. And he suddenly knew why he was brought here.

He fell to the ground at his feet in worship.

During this entire exchange, the gods had continued their battle by the edge of the Abyss. Raguel and Saraqael ran after a fleeing Pan, while Raphael and Gabriel fought a desperate Ba'al, battling for his eternity.

Ba'al forced the angels up against the wall. His back was turned toward Mikael, who saw his opportunity. The archangel grabbed some Cherubim hair from his arm band, ran and leapt onto Ba'al's back, choking him with the indestructible binding.

Ba'al spun around, trying to grab his assailant, as the other two angels backed off.

Ba'al got a handful of Mikael's cloak and flipped him around onto the ground. They were at the very rim of the precipice. He picked up Mikael by his throat with a sickly grin, and moved to drop him into the Abyss.

Mikael latched onto Ba'al's arms. He would not be so easily disposed of. But Ba'al was the most formidable deity the archangels had faced. And since their previous encounter he had grown even stronger. These three were not going to take this deity down. They needed an edge, something to tip the scales in their favor.

That edge came in the form of a speeding ten foot-tall battering ram named Eleazar, a giant unafraid of brawling with the gods, and about the only one with enough mass to throw the god off balance. He hit Ba'al from behind. The three of them launched out into darkness.

The mortal giant would not survive the fall. He was after all, half human. As they fell down the impossibly deep crevice, Eleazar had time to consider the providential purpose of his presence here at the Gates of Hades. He had fought with gods and men in distant lands, killed hundreds of enemies, escaped captivity in pursuit of revenge, only to be supernaturally redeemed by the god he had hated. And all of it was so that Yahweh could use him in a single important event to capture an enemy of God. Of all the glory and fame that Eleazar had sought for in his life, it was all a pile of steaming excrement compared to the surpassing value of meeting Jesus and being used for this solitary event of spiritual significance. He considered it an honor to sacrifice himself on behalf of such a worthy cause.

Mikael maneuvered to gain advantage over the god as they fell. The last time the angels had taken down the deity, was in his Mount Sapan palace. In that case, the other angels had tackled Ba'al in a similar way, by knocking him off a cliff into a river of fiery magma in the earth.

This time he would land in the waters of the Abyss as opposed to the molten flames of lava. But this time, it would be permanent, because the waters of the Abyss led to Hades and Tartarus, where Mikael would leave the Watcher god bound until judgment.

Finally, after what seemed like an eternity of falling through the darkness, the three warriors hit the black waters of the Abyss, killing the giant.

Mikael already had Ba'al bound with the Cherubim hair as they sank into the depths.

Back up at the cliff ledge, the violence had ceased. A silence now filled the cavern.

The Ob opened her eyes with shock. She sat up, pulled her robe to cover herself more, as if she was a modest woman. She was herself again.

The woman looked into Jesus's eyes and she knew everything. She knew that he knew everything about her. She knew he was her savior, and that he had cast out seven demons from her.

She began to cry and crawled over to him to kiss his feet. His hands stopped her and pulled her face up to his level.

"What is your name, woman?"

"Mary," she said.

"Where are you originally from?"

"I grew up in Magdala."

"Well, Mary Magdalene," he said, "I have need for someone of your gratitude in our little community. My disciples seem to think they are entitled to everything."

He smiled. She smiled back at him, and hugged him again.

The angels came up to Jesus carrying Gabriel and Uriel.

Raphael said, "Mikael is on his way to Tartarus with Ba'al."

Saraqael and Raguel approached from out of the black. Saraqael said, "Pan got away. He is a slippery scoundrel, that one."

Mary smiled broadly. "I know where he went."

They looked to her for more.

She said, "He went to Gaia, the Mother Earth Goddess."

Gabriel said, "Well, isn't that convenient. That old gnarly tree was next on our list. We can kill two gods with one battle axe." He still had his wit through his wounds.

Uriel croaked through his migraine headache. "Wrong, Gabriel. Three gods."

They all remembered that the Earth Goddess carried within her tangled roots of evil another demoness long worthy of punishment.

Gabriel gave a lighthearted laugh, "Well, Uriel, I do defer. You have bested me verbally while suffering a worse handicap."

They both looked to Jesus for approval and they got it in the form of a very subtle smirk of acceptance.

Uriel was not done. "Jesus, would you say that 'little buddy' remark from Gabriel constituted a putdown?"

"That was a term of affection," complained Gabriel.

Jesus broke into a broad smile. "Do not start again, or I won't bring you to find Gaia."

The two angels groaned simultaneously through their pains.

Uriel said, "Our tongues will heal as quick as our wounds."

Jesus smiled.

Mary said to Jesus, "I know where she hides."

CHAPTER 17

Gestas awoke to sounds outside his tent. He peeked out into the night to see Demas taking down his tent.

"Brother," whispered Gestas, "it is still the night watch. What are you doing?"

"Pack your gear. We're returning to Galilee."

Demas got out of his tent into the freezing cold night. "What do you mean returning? We haven't finished our reconnaissance."

Demas stopped and glared at Gestas. "Gestas, we have enough intelligence on these people. They think they are following Messiah, but they are uneducated farmers, fishermen and women. They are too small in size, they have no army, and they have no will to fight. They are no threat to Barabbas."

"But what about Jesus?"

"He is involved with black magic of some very dangerous kind that I do not want to have anything to do with. He is a leader, a powerful sorcerer even, but no warrior king. He speaks in veiled language and other nonsense of a heavenly kingdom. He is more of a madman than a prophet."

Gestas turned somber and whispered lower, "What about our orders?"

Demas looked at Simon's sleeping form by the coals. "I'm not going to kill Simon. He has already castrated himself with his theological delusions. And I sure as Hades am not able to kill Jesus. His bodyguards are mighty warriors like I have never seen. They are gibborim." Gibborim was an ancient word that was used first of the giants and then of human warriors who fought with the skill and achievement of giants.

Gestas looked quizzically at him. "But they left the other day." He looked over to Jesus's tent area then back to Demas. "Have you seen them return?"

Demas sighed. "Yes. But I do not believe Jesus wants us to fight. He is no threat to Barabbas. And he is doomed."

Gestas glanced back again at Jesus's area, then to Panias beyond. He narrowed his eyes at Demas. "Did you go to Panias this evening when I was asleep?"

Demas ignored the question. "I am done here. I'm leaving with or without you." He turned back and finished his packing.

Demas was not a good bluffer. Gestas knew Demas must have gone to the sacred grotto and seen something that was causing him to make haste in leaving. The grotto had an eerie morning haze moving in from the sacred pool. The sun was just beginning to rise on the horizon. He could see no movement in the temple district.

What did Demas see that would cause such an extreme reaction?

"Wait up, Demas. You're not leaving me behind, brother."

•••••

Mary led Jesus and the six angels through a secret tunnel that led out into a small forested area. A short hike through the woods brought them to a new ravine some distance away from Panias. The terrain didn't look familiar in the morning light. They turned into a side ravine, walked some way into it, and felt as if they were in another world. The canyon opened up and they stopped at the sight before them.

"Gaia," said Jesus.

A huge tree stood in the middle of the valley, hundreds of feet in diameter and stretching into the sky high above them.

The ground around it was dry, cracked, and without life. Everything was dead. The tree appeared to be drawing the very life out of the soil, transforming it into the desert of death like the encroaching desert in the east.

Mary knew that Pan was hiding somewhere in the tangled knot of roots along with a very dangerous demoness, one she knew all too well. Mary had visited the goddess Gaia many times. She had secret passageways in the folds of her bark that led down into her bowels below the soil.

Mary watched the six archangels, minus Mikael, disappear into those folds in pursuit of the gods and their demonic helpers.

She felt the dirt below her feet move as if something was tunneling its way toward the tree and the angels. Something very big. Another devilish beast she was all too familiar with.

"Jesus," she said. "do not let them go. They are walking into a trap."

"It is all right, Mary. They know what they are doing."

The archangels were well acquainted with the Mother Earth Goddess and her protective parasites. Her evil was ancient. Before the Flood, she had resided in the land now called Arabia. It had been a vast fertile continent in antediluvian days. But Gaia sucked the soul out of the environment and turned it into a lifeless desert. She had the ability to manifest herself between heaven and earth, unseen by mortal eyes from a distance behind a veil of illusion. The area around her was like being in a world between worlds. It was there, but not there. Before the Flood, Enoch and his band of giant killers had encountered her within a *Shaitan*, a supernatural sandstorm.

After the Flood, the great King Gilgamesh and his companion Enkidu had cut down the great tree with their mighty axes. But Gaia's seed always finds new earth and she had planted herself in these foothills of the sacred mountain of Baal-Hermon. Protected in the shadow of the assembly of gods, by the cult of Pan and the idol worship of the tribe of Dan nearby, Gaia flourished.

A deep sorrow came over Mary for all the child sacrifices she presided over at the base of this monstrosity. The deaths of the innocent gave Gaia life and sustenance, and enslaved women to the illusion of empowerment. The goddess feasted on the flesh and blood of the offering of their wombs. They believed that somehow they were helping their community and saving Mother Earth in giving up their offspring. And every human offered up was absorbed into the tree. When she was up close to it, Mary could see in the grain of the wood the twisted agonized forms of the sacrificial victims melded into the bark so as to become one with it. She had formerly believed that this tree of death was the Tree of Life.

But this was not the only false narrative that had held her in its grip of deceit for so many years.

Lilith, the guardian mistress of Mother Earth, had enchanted all her followers with the story that she was the original wife of Adam, spurned by her abusive, controlling husband because of her independence, forced to flee his oppressive domination to protect her two hellions, Lili and Lilitu. That patriarchal dictator Adam then took a second wife, Eve, who was deluded into accepting her subordinate position as barefoot slave and breeder.

Freed from her demons, Mary now knew it was all a malicious lie, an inversion of the truth. She had worshipped a self-serving idol, deluded by her own willing lust for power. She thought she had been pursuing equality with man, to be just like them. But she now realized she had merely been defying her Creator. She broke down into tears and fell to her knees in the dirt.

Jesus knelt down beside her and comforted her.

She cried, "What have I done? What have I become? I am a monster."

"Mary," whispered Jesus, "you are forgiven."

A wave of peace came over her like nothing she had ever felt before. In the cave, she had experienced release. But now she felt the tendrils of healing gently digging deeper into her, like a new tree planting its roots into her heart, the true Tree of Life.

But there was so much darkness in her. It was as if her soul was stuck in deep sludge.

She looked up at him and thought, *How could this be? How could I be cleansed from so vile a heart and life?*

As if he heard her thoughts, he said, "Let us go. It is time you were baptized, so you can finally believe what is already true of you."

"But what about Gaia? What about the angels?"

Jesus looked over at the colossal tree, a good hundred feet away from them.

He said to her, "I have two baptisms I perform. Water and fire." He looked up into the heavens.

Mary saw a column of fire pour out from the sky onto the mighty tree and engulf it in flames. She heard the crackling sounds of burning timber, felt the wave of hot air blow over her. As it burned, she thought she heard the spiritual piercing shrieks with wailing and gnashing of teeth. It felt more inside her head than from the tree, which she knew was the source of the pain. She understood at that moment that the baptism of water was salvation and the baptism of fire was judgment.

Jesus led her out of the canyon, back to the camp.

Mary said, "I definitely want the water."

Jesus smiled. "The water you will have." He paused, then added, "Just don't tell James and John about the fire from heaven. They'll be envious."

"What will become of the gods?" she asked.

"The roots and tunnels of Gaia lead down to Hades. The angels will drag them down to Tartarus and bind them with the others."

She blurted out what she had just realized. "You are dispossessing the gods from the land."

He looked at her as they walked through the forest. She was smarter than the disciples. He had plans for this special one.

"Yes. But don't be too hasty to discount Gaia. She is a weed. She will be back in latter days to spread her cancerous roots throughout the earth, not merely in Israel."

"How many more gods are there to dispossess?"

"Not many. But these bindings of principalities are not my sole purpose."

"What do you mean?"

"First, I must defeat the powers, then I purchase redemption. But you will be the first to figure it out, I can tell you that much."

The sun was now in the mid-morning sky as they broke out of the forest on the way to their camp.

CHAPTER 18

Uriel's head still ached from the battering he took in the cave. But he was healing, as were Gabriel and the others. They would not be at their full strength by the time they found their adversaries in this labyrinth of tangled roots. He prayed for their speedy recovery.

They had found an entrance in the massive folds of bark on the gnarly base of the gargantuan Gaia. They now made their way downward through constricting tunnels, surrounded on all sides by the twisted roots. They were following the path that Enoch and his fellow giant-killers had taken in antediluvian days, when they were almost enchanted by the black wood magic of Lilith. She had kidnapped Methuselah's pregnant wife Edna to perform a ritual sacrifice on an altar in the deep below.

That very sanctuary was the archangels' destination. They figured they would find the demonic beings hiding there absorbing strength. They were strongest in their temples of abomination.

Enoch and Methuselah had rescued Edna, but they lost the child through miscarriage. They were forever haunted by their error of judgment. They were rescued from the soul-eating tree by the Thamudi people of the desert.

This time, the angels needed no rescue. They were not going to leave the way they came. They were going to keep going downward and drag these devils, kicking and screaming, into the very depths of Tartarus.

It would not be easy. The entire organism was enchanted with evil.

Uriel stopped to see the images of the tortured souls embedded within the very grain of the tree roots. He noticed that they moved ever so slightly in their grimaces and pain, like a silent slow moving sculpture of agony. They were souls of the damned captured in a living prison.

He moved to catch back up with the others making their way through the maze of cursed wood that reminded Uriel of the coils of intertwined serpents.

He said with a sing song voice, "Lilith and Paaaaan. Come out, come out, wherever you are."

Gabriel stopped to look at him. "Must you?"

"What?"

"A time like this is no place for jesting."

"Would you rather I carry a sourpuss like you?"

Uriel walked past Gabriel with a smirk.

Gabriel rolled his eyes.

Then he noticed movement to his left. He could have sworn he had seen the movement of a split tongue that would match the serpentine feel of this slithering tunnel.

He kept his sword at the ready and stooped down to look into the dark recesses of the wall. Did he really see…?

In a split second, two sliver-pupiled eyes opened and a huge snake head, half the size of Gabriel's body, struck at him.

Gabriel's lightning fast reflexes kicked in. He barely dodged the monstrous fangs that brushed by him.

The momentum knocked him to the floor with a thud. He lost his grip on his sword.

The huge serpent had missed him, but it kept moving. It erupted out of its hiding place and wrapped itself around the angel's body with preternatural speed. Gabriel dodged the bite, but he wasn't ready for the coils that now gripped his entire body in a death grip. They squeezed the air out of his lungs so he could not call for help. He only got out a piece of whimpered warning. "Nin–"

In his mind, he heard the serpent talking to him telepathically with its slithering accent. *Yesssss. Ningishzida am I. And you are mine.*

Ningishzida was the ancient serpent guardian of the demonic tree of which the prophet Isaiah had written,

Yes, the night monster, Lilith, will settle there
And will find herself a resting place.
The tree serpent will make its nest and lay eggs there,
And it will hatch and gather them under its protection.

The fact was, Enoch's companions had killed Ningishzida, and then so did Gilgamesh and Enkidu—because each offspring took on the identity as the new Ningishzida, the guardian.

This latest incarnate guardian squeezed the final breath out of its prey and protracted its fangs. It sank them deep into Gabriel's shoulder. A human would have died from the venom. Gabriel sank into a coma.

The serpent knew it could not eat its prey, because that would slow it down for the fight. So it released the body and slithered back into the roots of darkness.

Uriel noticed that Gabriel had not followed him. He turned back in search of his annoying companion.

He found him lying on the ground.

"Archangels!" he yelled. He whipped his two swords around, preparing for a new attack.

It did not come.

He bent down to examine his comrade. He found the bite mark and knew immediately what had happened.

When the others arrived, he said, "Ningishzida."

Raphael said, "That infernal serpent."

Uriel sheathed his swords and gently picked up Gabriel in his arms. He whispered to the comatose angel, "I am sorry for my reckless frivolity, brother. I should have been here for you." He turned to the others. "I will carry him."

They continued onward through the maze of roots, down ever deeper.

The air became filled with the constant hissing sound of a serpent. "Sssssssssssssssssssssssss." It came from everywhere and from nowhere. It would make a human break down in madness, but the angels were not easily affected by black magic. They continued on.

Uriel was affected by the limits of his flesh, heavenly though it was. Carrying Gabriel slowed him down, and kept him from being able to access his swords should he need them in an attack.

The ubiquitous hissing sound also masked the almost imperceptible slithering of the large serpent behind him.

Ningishzida had planned for exactly this. To hamper them with hindrances and hunt them down, one by one, the weakest to the strongest. And right now, this smallest of the group was easy prey.

Uriel could not hear the monster approach, but his preternatural senses warned him—moments too late. He tried to set Gabriel down to draw his swords, but the serpent had already launched at him. It clamped down on his back, injecting the same poison into him that had taken down Gabriel.

Uriel collapsed.

The others discovered them lying in a heap in the middle of the passageway.

"We must carry them," said Remiel.

He and Saraqael bent down to pick them up.

"No," said Raphael.

They stopped.

His face was grim, but set like flint. "We must leave them."

"We do not leave our comrades behind," said Remiel.

"This time, we must," said Raphael.

The others began to understand his point.

"The serpent wants us to carry them, because it makes us easy prey. That is why he is not eating them. We leave them here. When they heal, they will find their way out."

"Through a pile of burning timbers above," complained Remiel. They could feel the increasing heat above them of the fire from heaven.

"We are only four, now," said Raphael. "We cannot afford to lose any more. We must leave them behind."

The angels looked at each other with solemn recognition. They knew Raphael was right. And they knew he was the most torn by his decision, because he had been through much with these two over the millennia, especially in the days of Enoch.

Remiel said, "Then let us get on with it."

Saraqael said, "As Uriel would say, let us bind some bitch goddesses and their goat."

The angels kept their weapons at the ready and continued on down the pathway toward their destination. Now they went with even greater determination.

Raphael, Saraqael, Remiel, and Raguel were deep into the heart of the earth when they arrived at the sanctuary. The constricted passageway opened up to a cavern a hundred feet wide and about fifty feet high. A tremor rattled the ground under their feet and they lost their balance. Remiel fell against a large root. He jumped back.

"Ow, the roots are hot," he blurted out.

They looked closely and saw some very subtle flames were already starting up on thinner roots like kindling.

Raphael said, "The fire above is descending. We haven't much time."

They broke out into the sanctuary, with arms presented. Two had shields, two did not.

But no one was there.

They looked around. In the torchlight, they could see that the walls were plastered with the skull and bones of thousands of infants. They were the dead sacrificed on the altar at the center of the sanctuary. Unlike the bark and roots above, these bones did not meld into the wood, but rather retained their white calcium constituency. It was a deliberate ornamentation.

On that altar in the middle lay the body of a young girl sacrificed to the goddess moments before their arrival. Her blood still flowed from her stained white garment down the altar stone to the floor. Her hand hung dead, swaying after dropping from her side.

The gods would be empowered by this bloodletting. It was their source of strength.

Another tremor rattled the sanctuary. Bones fell from the ceiling. Flames appeared high above as the judgment descended upon them.

The sound of scraping claws made them focus their sights behind the altar, where they saw two hyenas scrambling to hide in the darkness.

Raphael immediately knew it was a diversion. He yelled, "Behind us!"

They turned.

Two arrows came flying at them from behind. Saraqael was able to get his shield up in time to block one of the missiles.

Raguel had no shield. He tried to dodge, but he was a moment too slow. An arrow lodged itself in his left shoulder. He cried out.

The sound of a cackling hyena laugh echoed through the chamber from behind the altar.

Remiel stood in front of Raguel to protect him with the shield. Raguel raced behind the altar to nurse his wound.

Pan and Lilith were nowhere to be seen. They were attacking from the shadows.

The angels backed up into a tight circle.

Behind the altar, Raguel saw three hyenas cowering in the darkness. He swung his sword to scatter them. Scavengers of flesh. Disgusting.

He winced as he broke the arrow. He prepared to push the arrow outward through the wound, when everyone's attention was taken by a little girl coming out of the darkness.

She was dressed in a white garment like the one the victim on the altar wore. She was pale and fragile looking, the second precious innocent whose sacrifice they evidently had interrupted with their arrival.

She trembled with fright and called out in a frail voice as she stumbled toward the closest angel, Remiel. "Help me, help me, please. I don't want to die."

Remiel moved his shield to receive the little girl and draw her behind him.

Two things happened simultaneously. One, the little girl turned out to be a little boy dressed as a little girl. He turned into a demonic fury with fangs and blood red eyes. He leapt onto Remiel's back and bit him deeply in the neck.

Second, the child victim on the altar suddenly rose up with her own crimson eyes and vicious fangs. She grabbed the wounded Raguel, biting down hard on his carotid vein.

Remiel spun around trying to get the thing off his back. It would not release its fanged bite. Remiel became dizzy. He blurted out, "Black magic!"

The entire sanctuary was a pit of black magic and occultic powers of hell.

Raguel had already dropped to the floor, unconscious. His little creature scurried off like a scavenger into the darkness.

Flames burst out on the ceiling above, as a second wave attack broadsided them.

Pan and Lilith came at Raphael and Saraqael. The cloven-hoofed satyr wielded his double long daggers against Raphael. Lilith commandeered a scimitar, a curved sword blade of bygone eras. But that was not the only strange thing about her.

It disarmed Saraqael to see this beautiful raven-haired siren, in her long flowing robes, fighting with the fluidity of a Karabu warrior.

He thought, *What lethal beauty.*

Karabu was the fighting technique the Cherubim of the Garden had developed in millennia past to protect Eden itself. It was more a dance than a muscular force. Some of the enemy had taken up the fighting style in order to match the archangels. Lilith was evidently one of them.

Saraqael did everything he could to match her leaping, flipping, twisting and jumping. He dodged a large burning timber that fell to the floor from above.

Remiel managed to grab the little vampiric creature off his back and threw her against the wall. She hit with a sickening crunch as half the bones in her body were broken.

He heard the feint echo of a hyena howl in his fading consciousness. Then a strange thing happened. The thing got up on all fours. Its legs were broken backward, its neck sagged from a snapped spine, and its elbows were bent at awkward angles. But it was still alive. It scurried away like some kind of human crab.

Remiel tried to make sense of it, but he fell to his knees, under the deep spell of the poison.

Through his blurry vision, he saw a huge black head, a serpent's head watching him from the dark corner. He thought, *Ningishzida.* Everything went black.

Pan was a god of nature, and the angels were on his turf. So when Raphael had backed up against a wall, Pan whistled and a hundred roots reached out and grabbed Raphael, wrapping around him like manacles. Hot manacles.

Saraqael did not understand why his nemesis Lilith was not faltering. He had managed to cut her multiple times in their exchange, but she appeared unfazed. How much longer could he go if she could not be wounded? But how was that even possible? Even divine beings could be wounded.

Howls continued to echo through the chamber as the gods fought onward.

Raphael's sword arm was free, but he was being squeezed by the burning roots around him. He would cut through some of them and return to his fighting, but then more would grab him. And more of them were on fire, singeing his skin through his leather armor.

Saraqael was tiring. Lilith got one good cut on his arm. He felt the burning slash. It was just enough for her to get an advantage over him.

The demon children tried to attack Raphael like wild dogs, as he held off the raging Pan. It was a losing battle.

The fire above them had become an inferno, burning furiously down the walls.

Saraqael's weakened condition kept him from seeing another burning timber fall on him from above. It hit him in a burst of flames and knocked him to the floor. Lilith raised her sword high to cut him in half.

Out of the darkness, two javelins whizzed through the air and hit two hyenas at the back of the room. They howled in dying pain. A third javelin hit the third hyena in the head. It was dead instantly.

At the same time, piercing shrieks came from Lilith and the two feminine siblings. The demon children dropped dead to the floor.

Lilith suddenly manifested all the wounds that Saraqael had managed to inflict upon her which had previously not shown at all. They overwhelmed her and she dropped to the floor in a quivering heap of cuts, bleeding profusely.

Saraqael looked to the sanctuary entrance. Gabriel and Uriel entered the chamber and drew their swords. Their brothers had healed and come to their rescue.

Gabriel dispatched Pan in moments, as Raphael cut himself free from the enchanted, flaming roots.

The angels bound the god with Cherubim hair.

Saraqael pressed a hand over his wound and rose. "Am I glad to see you two." Behind Saraqael the huge, black serpent slithered out of the darkness. It rose up to chomp him from behind.

Before it could launch at its prey, two swords criss-crossed themselves and cut off the head of the titanic snake. It dropped to the floor at Uriel's feet.

"You are very welcome," said Uriel as he tied up Lilith with Cherubim bonds. "But I do believe Gabriel and I are owed an explanation and apology for being unceremoniously ditched to burn up in the flames."

Saraqael said, "Talk to Raphael. Executive decision."

Raphael complained, "You all agreed with me."

"Raphael," said Gabriel.

Raphael continued, "We prioritized the mission as Yahweh told us to." Remiel and Raguel groggily pushed themselves up from the floor.

"Raphael."

"I didn't know the flames would burn this deep."

"Raphael!"

Raphael turned to Gabriel, who was looking at him with a big grin.

"We're teasing you. It's only a joke."

Uriel added, "Of course you did the right thing, you lunkhead. We would have left you behind as well." Raphael frowned.

Gabriel glanced upward. "Angels! Move!"

The fiery ceiling above them finally gave way. It began to cave in on them.

They found a last burst of energy to drag their wounded selves and the bound gods into the tunnel.

The ceiling collapsed into the sanctuary like a crashing fiery furnace, burning everything in its wake.

The angels and their prisoners landed inside the tunnel in a pile of arms and legs, as a wave of scorching air blew over them, singeing hair and skin.

Raphael looked at Gabriel and Uriel. "You two and your silly bantering. Now I know why Jesus is fed up with it. It's going to get us trapped one day."

"But we did save you, Raphael," said Uriel with a grin.

Gabriel added, "That's got to count for something, don't you think?"

Raphael sighed.

Everyone got up and brushed themselves off.

A thought hit Raphael. "How did you know the weakness of Lilith and her demon spawn?"

Gabriel said, "Enoch and Methuselah ran into them in their day. The hyenas were daemon avatars. Animal spirits that accompany the gods and carry their vital force within them. That is why you could not vanquish them without killing their daemon."

Saraqael complained, "Why did you not inform us of such an important detail?"

"I am sorry," replied Gabriel. "It had slipped my mind."

"For a couple of millennia," griped Saraqael.

Uriel jumped in, "Saraqael, if you remember those days, we were all a bit consumed with more pressing matters, like the War on Eden."

Gabriel said, "I was going to tell everyone right before Ningishzida took me out."

Uriel said, "We better stop gabbing and get these gods to their destination, or our bantering just may get us trapped."

The six of them, wounded and exhausted, carried the gods down to Tartarus.

CHAPTER 19

"Jesus! Jesus!" Mary Magdalene could see him across the camp. But several men kept her and her female guests from getting any closer. One of them was Peter.

"I am sorry, but the rabbi is busy and we cannot allow everyone who wants to see him to take up his time. Least of all, women."

"But I was with the Lord in the Cave of Pan. Ask him. I am Mary Magdalene."

Peter's eyes went wider. He hadn't recognized the Ob without her exotic make up and priestess outfit. This Mary was dressed in plain clothes, though the women with her were not. They were aristocracy of some kind, and quite Greek in their dress.

"All the more reason," he said. "A woman of your background and reputation has no business with the rabbi."

From behind Peter came the words, "On the contrary, Peter, she has much business with me."

Peter and the men turned to see Jesus behind them with Simon.

Peter stepped over to him and whispered, "But rabbi, she is the Ob priestess. She is no doubt full of demons."

Jesus whispered to him, "Seven. She actually had seven demons. I already cast them out."

Peter said, "But, women? What business can we have with them?"

Jesus said, "We are about to find out." He leaned in. "Peter, I think you had better reevaluate your low opinion of women in the kingdom of God. They are your fellow heirs of eternal life. You had better get used to their valuable contributions. They may be subordinate to you in their roles, but they are going to share equally with you in your inheritance."

Peter stood dumbfounded and chastised. Jesus looked at Mary, who was staring wide-eyed at Simon. Jesus leaned over to Simon. "And you had better change your monkish views as well, Simon. I think she has an interest in you."

Simon had been staring back at Mary with wonder. He turned red with embarrassment.

Jesus drew closer to the women and said with affection. "Greetings, Mary."

"Greetings, Rabbi. I want you to meet some other women who may be able to help fund your ministry." She pointed to an older woman with graying hair but a bright smile. "This is Susanna, a seller of fabrics. She is a widow. I told her all about you. She has known me for many years."

Susanna said, "Thank you for what you've done with Mary."

Jesus placed his hand empathetically on her shoulder and said softly, "I am sorry about your husband. How long has it been?"

Susanna suddenly teared up. She could barely get out, "Four years."

"You loved him deeply."

She couldn't say anything without bursting into tears, so she just nodded her head.

Jesus pulled her close and hugged her.

Peter looked uncomfortable. Such affection in public was not appropriate. People could get the wrong idea.

Jesus pulled away from Susanna and looked at the other woman. "And who is your other friend?"

"Joanna." Mary then lowered her voice with a quick look around. "She is the wife of Chuza, Herod Antipas' steward."

Jesus's brow raised with interest. Peter and Simon looked around to see if they were being watched.

Joanna said, "I know you must be wary of me. But I assure you, I have been following your travels and teachings, and I believe you are Messiah."

Peter looked around again to see who was watching them. "She has spies."

Simon added, "Antipas killed John the Baptizer."

She tried to allay their fears, "Herod does not know of my interests. My own husband does not know. I've told no one, and my servants are believers in you as well."

"He *is* contagious," said Simon. He noticed that Mary chuckled at his remark.

Joanna said, "I agree with Jesus. Herod is a vixen." Vixen was a female fox, which was an insulting political reference to the manipulation of Herod by his own wife.

Simon elbowed Peter and said to him teasingly, "She has attentive spies."

Another chuckle from Mary, another lifted smile from Simon.

Joanna said, "I have money, earmarked for charity, that I have put aside to help you and your disciples. Pay for food, lodgings, fresh clothes."

"I will need a donkey when we get to Jerusalem," said Jesus thoughtfully.

"I can buy you fifty donkeys."

"Well, Peter," said Jesus. "Do you know of any men who will provide as much?"

Peter felt like a scolded child. "No, Rabbi."

Jesus said, "We are certainly in need of finances."

Peter muttered, "I think Judas is pilfering from the treasury."

Jesus said, "Nevertheless, I see no reason to reject the help of such beautiful and resourceful women."

Jesus reached out and hugged Joanna. Another moment of discomfort for Peter.

Simon thought of another comment. "What a funny irony to have Herod on the one hand hunting you, and on the other, funding you."

He immediately looked to Mary to see her reaction. She giggled.

Simon felt on top of the world.

Jesus turned sober. "Peter, get James and John. We are going up Mount Hermon."

Simon gulped. Whatever had happened inside that cave, the incident at the Gates of Hades was a breach of the walls. But how could four unarmed commoners make an assault on the stronghold of evil itself?

CHAPTER 20

Longinus waited patiently for Pilate to arrive at the Chamber of Hewn Stone, adjacent to the Court of Priests inside the Temple area in Jerusalem. He had made the trek down to Jerusalem from Galilee in pursuit of his revolutionary Zealots. He had requested that Pilate call a Sanhedrin meeting to address the question of Messiah.

The Sanhedrin of Jerusalem consisted of seventy or so of the city's elders and leaders, who acted as a supreme judicial court and a political diplomatic link to the Roman governor. As guardians of the public order, they were invested with the authority to try, convict and sentence criminal cases, with one exception: capital crimes. Only Rome had the authority to execute. But even then, Rome often relied upon the Sanhedrin's legal process before receiving convicted felons for execution.

Longinus could make out two major factions that vied for control of the Sanhedrin council, Sadducees and Pharisees. Sadducees were mostly the rich aristocracy, while the Pharisees had popular support. In the current scenario, the Sadducees seemed to dominate the proceedings with their numbers.

Since Pilate was late, the chattering and small talk had evolved into a full-blown debate between the factions.

These Jews love to argue, thought Longinus as he observed the group from his seat at the pillared entrance. The Chamber of Hewn Stone was a fairly large, open area in a high-ceilinged room that gave him the impression of loftiness toward heaven, despite the very earthy and emotionally charged argumentation unfolding before him.

He was glad for it. He was glad to get a glimpse into the way they thought and saw the world. Anything to help him figure out the mindset of a rebellious people who seemed to inspire so much trouble for themselves.

They mostly sat around the outer edge of the room with polygonal walls which created a circular structure. At the forefront of the room was a head seat, that looked very much to Longinus like a royal throne, with its framed arch and red curtains displayed behind it. This was the seat of the High Priest, who was currently Caiaphas, a bootlicker of Herod, under Pilate's direction.

Longinus detested this despicable monkey, not in spite of Caiaphas' intimate relationship with Pilate, but because of it. The fat and luxury-loving sycophant was an ally of Rome, due to informing on his fellow Jews and keeping them in line. But Longinus still detested anyone who betrayed their own people. He had more respect for the Zealot lunatics and their fanaticism than for subtle serpentine traitors like Caiaphas.

It was Caiaphas who led the current heated debate about some theological difference that seemed quite unimportant to Longinus. It seemed to be one that had a long history to it.

Ridiculous, he thought.

Caiaphas said, "Order! Order! You will please refrain from interruption!" The noisiness calmed down. "Now, Annas, you were trying to say?"

"I am saying that these so-called signs and wonders of Jesus raising a little girl and the man, Lazarus, from the dead are unsubstantiated rumors and legends. There is no resurrection and there is no afterlife spoken of in the Scriptures. Pharisees draw their arguments from non-Scriptural sources and traditions, which we Sadducees simply do not recognize as authoritative. We alone stand on the Word of our God."

Annas had a snooty arrogance to him.

Another gray-haired gentleman spoke up. Longinus had heard that he was Joseph of Arimathea, another wealthy man, but a Pharisee.

Joseph said, "My brother Annas sounds more like a pagan Greek than a Hebrew." Some scattered laughs peppered the crowd. Longinus shook his head with contempt.

"Not only does the prophet Daniel clearly speak of a general resurrection of the dead, but Isaiah and our beloved David reveal it to be so. May I quote from the *Scriptures* that Annas and his Sadducees so proudly claim to be the sole beneficiaries of? A Psalm of David: 'For you will not abandon my soul to Sheol, or let your holy one see corruption.' And the prophet Isaiah, who, I may remind my illustrious opponents, wrote *Scripture*, said of a Suffering Servant, and I quote,

> *'But he was pierced for our transgressions;*
> *he was crushed for our iniquities...*
> *And they made his grave with the wicked...*
> *Yet, when his soul makes an offering for guilt,*
> *he shall see his offspring; he shall prolong his days;*
> *the will of the LORD shall prosper in his hand.'"*

Annas responded quickly, "My colleague Joseph is taking Scripture out of context. David was speaking metaphorically, and Isaiah's Suffering Servant is Israel, not Messiah."

A voice interrupted their debate. "I can see my tardiness has inspired you to discuss the matter of Messiah in my absence."

Pilate paused at the entrance of the chamber, with his personal guard. Everyone stood in respect.

Longinus saluted Pilate and whispered, "Prefect, sir, their quibbling and bickering only now touched on the subject. You know how they can get carried away."

"Do I ever." Pilate looked back around at the council. "You may be seated."

They took their seats.

Pilate paraded to the center of the room, the center of attention. He snapped his fingers for Longinus to join him.

Pilate looked at Caiaphas and said, "Beside me is Marcus Lucius Longinus. I have tasked him with tracking down some particularly egregious Jewish rebels. One of them goes by the name of Jesus Barabbas. Do you have any intelligence on him?"

Caiaphas said, "No, my prefect."

"And what of his comrades, the brothers Demas and Gestas Samaras?"

"No, my prefect."

"What good are you to me, Caiaphas, if you don't keep on top of your own people, and their rebel leaders?"

"Your eminence," said Caiaphas, "we have told you everything we know of Amram and Tholomy, as well as the sons of Judas the Galilean. Is Barabbas the leader of the cave-dwellers of Galilee?"

Pilate nodded to Longinus, who replied to the high priest, "Yes. They are considered a separate splinter group of the Zealots."

Pilate threw out with a laugh, "Yet another 'splinter group.' I swear, Caiaphas, if this increases, you may find Caesar himself coming to crush these brigands and the entire nation with them. Then you might take it all a bit more seriously. Would you prefer Caesar take his place in your Temple as god?"

The whole crowd erupted in shock and muttering at the blasphemy. Pilate's previous incident of placing Caesar's standards in the temple was blasphemous enough and still fresh on their minds. The thought of Caesar's personal presence was too much to consider.

Pilate shouted, "QUIET!" They quieted down.

He said, "And what of this other Jesus, the Nazarene? I heard you mention signs and wonders. Do any believe him to be your Messiah?"

"He is nothing, governor," said Caiaphas. "They are parlor tricks, and his followers are fishermen and plebs. He speaks nothing of violent overthrow. Merely peculiarities of our laws."

Pilate looked to Longinus for response, who nodded in agreement.

Pilate said, "I have no more patience for this tripe. If any of these men, be they Barabbas, Amram, Tholomy or even this patsy, the Nazarene, if any of them enter Jerusalem, I want you to immediately alert Longinus, who is now stationed in the Antonia fortress. Am I understood?"

"Yes, my lord," said Caiaphas.

"Let us go, Longinus." Pilate turned and left the room with Longinus in tow.

Outside the room, as Pilate and his soldiers marched away, Longinus stayed behind and hid just around the corner of the open entrance. He wanted to hear what these sniveling little Jews would say behind their backs.

After a few moments of rumbling discontent, Longinus heard Caiaphas command everybody, "Settle down!"

As they settled, he then heard Annas say, "Why did you downplay the Nazarene? You know his influence is on the rise. And the signs and wonders are not being discounted as 'parlor tricks.' They are spreading like wildfire. You heard what the prefect said, if this rebellion keeps up, Rome will come and take away both our place and our nation."

Caiaphas' voice again, "Annas, you know nothing at all. We need to be in control of the information. We let the Jesus movement gain momentum, and the next time he arrives in Jerusalem, he will be significant enough to become our scapegoat, and we the loyal Roman subjects who will in turn be trusted. And with trust comes power."

In the silence, Longinus imagined Annas with his mouth open in surprise. Yes, the high priest had actually had an original thought in his head, utterly self-serving thought it may be.

Caiaphas concluded, "It is better that one man should die for the people, not that the whole nation should perish."

Interesting, thought Longinus. *That crafty Caiaphas is scheming to place all the unrest symbolically upon the back of the Nazarene and away from the rest of the Jews. How easily the vermin gives up his own. A pity the high priest doesn't know anything about Demas and Gestas. I would have them by now. Well, regardless. They will eventually come to Jerusalem, and when they do, I will be waiting for them.*

CHAPTER 21

Simon and Mary made their way up Mount Hermon. It got colder as they ascended. Mary pulled her cloak tighter around her. Simon saw her motion.

"Would you like my outer cloak?"

"No, Simon. You need it or you'll freeze to death."

He gestured up the hill to the four figures they were following at a safe distance. "Well, you can just call up to Jesus and he will thaw me out."

Mary giggled. She couldn't believe that she felt like a teenage girl around this scribe. He made her laugh. He was so smart. He could quote her Scriptures that fed her hunger for Yahweh's Word.

"Wait," he said.

She looked up to see the figures had stopped to enter a small wooded area. They were not yet past the tree line, thank Yahweh. That would be too barren of foliage to hide, and far too cold to survive. It had already begun to snow lightly on them.

They were following Jesus, Peter, James, and John on their way up the mountain on a mysterious mission. Jesus did not say what for. Only that he would take his three closest friends with him.

Simon and Mary longed to be in the inner circle. They had both come from backgrounds where they previously were in the inner circle. Their curiosity got the better of them. They conspired to sneak up after the four hikers and spy on them.

They moved around some boulders and stayed close to the brush, in case they needed to duck out of sight.

Simon continued to explain to Mary as they climbed. "David's Psalm says that the principalities and powers of heaven and earth would take counsel together to stand against Yahweh and against his Messiah. But,

Yahweh will speak to them in his wrath,
and terrify them in his fury, saying,
"As for me, I have set my King
on Zion, my holy mountain."

I will tell of the decree:
The LORD said to me, "You are my Son;
today I have begotten you.

"When Jesus was baptized in the Jordan by the prophet John, he was given the kingship of Yahweh's holy mountain, Zion. Now, Mount Sinai was Yahweh's first cosmic mountain of habitation. But with the building of the Temple in Jerusalem, it is now Mount Zion. But this mountain we climb, Hermon, is the cosmic mountain of the Watcher gods, the mountain of Bashan."

She said, "Bashan is the place of the Serpent." She knew more about this world around her than he realized.

"Yes," he said. "It is like a battle between two cosmic mountains. That is why the Psalm says,

"O many-peaked mountain, mountain of Bashan!
Why do you look with hatred, O many-peaked mountain,
at the mount that Elohim desired for his abode,
yes, where Yahweh will dwell forever?
The chariots of Elohim are twice ten thousand,
thousands upon thousands...
Elohim will strike the heads of his enemies."

Mary stopped walking. They were almost to the forested area. She looked fearful. "Do you mean that we are walking into the midst of a battle of gods and angels?"

"Well, it's too late now. We're here."

Mary turned and began to tromp back down the mountain.

"Mary, wait." Simon scurried to catch up to her. He held her arm to stop her.

"Listen. I didn't tell you the next part of the Psalm. It prophesies, 'You ascended on high, leading a host of captives, in your train.'"

She said, "A triumphal procession."

"Yes. The king parades his conquered foes behind him in victory. If Jesus is the Messiah as we believe, then yes, he will face off against the principalities and powers over the nations. But he will conquer them, and ascend to heaven with them bound behind him."

"What if you are wrong?"

"Then we won't be in the midst of a supernatural battle."

She sighed. "That's hardly comforting."

They had already come too far. "Let's go."

He led her back to the forest and they tread softly through the brush to find where the four men had gone.

•••••

Deep in the heart of Mount Hermon, a desperate assembly of the gods met in council. The cavern was aflame with the fiery light of over sixty Shining Ones. Their bronze and beryl-like skin flashed with raging emotions of fear and anger. Huge stalagmites and stalactites filled the cave with millennia of their crystalized formations that reflected those flashing lights. It created a lighting spectacle not unlike a rapidly exploding nebulae of stars.

Molech, the underworld god, and infamous abomination of the Ammonites, squinted in the brightness. His eyes had become sensitive, along with his pale, calloused skin, from spending so much of his time underground. He led the major complaint with his scratchy, fearful voice. "Jesus is ascending the mountain at this very moment. This is it. This is Armageddon!"

Belial presided over the assembly. He kept judiciously silent, as he listened to the debate.

Zeus said, "He is coming with three of his weak and foolish disciples. It looks more like a diplomatic mission for cease fire than a declaration of war."

"Declaration of war?" replied Molech. "Easy for you to say, gallivanting around on your distant decadent homeland of Greece. Jesus has been exorcising demons and diseases throughout Judea and Galilee, He has compromised the Gates of Hades, and he has taken out the gods Dagon, Asherah, Ba'al, Lilith, Pan, and even Gaia! I alone am left of the gods of Canaan!"

Resheph and Qeteb, the twin gods of pestilence and plague, protested. "You are not the only god left in the pantheon, Molech," said Resheph. Qeteb added, "And Dagon was betrayed by Ba'al and Asherah long before Jesus arrived."

"Is this a council of morons?" said Molech. "The Seed of Eve, the Seed of Abraham, is coming up *our holy mountain.* And I am listening to fools quibbling over petty details of insignificance! Don't just sit there! Say something, Belial."

Belial finally spoke up. "The mole god is correct. The Nazarene has been deliberately understated in order to fool us."

Molech felt smugly vindicated, though simultaneously insulted by the derogatory mole reference. But it was classic Belial.

"I have sent some spirits to spy on Jesus. If they have an army of the heavenly host approaching, they will alert us. In the meantime, we must arm ourselves and prepare for battle."

•••••

Simon and Mary found Jesus and the three disciples in a clearing. Peter, James and John were talking amongst themselves, while Jesus knelt and prayed a short space away.

Simon and Mary crouched, trying to get a good look from their hideaway in the brush. A twig snapped beneath Mary's foot.

They froze.

The disciples looked their way.

Peter began to walk toward them.

Mary and Simon cringed in fear of discovery.

Before Peter could discover the little spies, Jesus stood where he was and lifted his hands to heaven.

A beam of intense light burst from heaven above and bathed him in its brightness.

Peter turned back around. He and the other two ran to Jesus.

They could not believe their eyes at the sight before them.

Jesus transformed. His face shone like the sun, and his clothes became white as light.

Mary looked to Simon, whispering, "What is happening?"

"Shhh."

She turned back to see the disciples on their knees.

Now two other figures appeared with Jesus. The two shone brightly like the sun and they conversed with Jesus.

Mary heard Peter say with excitement, "Lord, I am glad we are here. If you wish, I will make three tents, one for you, one for Moses, and one for Elijah."

Mary whispered to Simon, "That is Moses and Elijah?"

"Shhhh."

The disciples looked up into a bright cloud that had appeared over them. They heard a voice say, "This is my beloved Son, with whom I am well pleased. Listen to him."

The disciples fell to their faces on the ground, terrified.

The brightness emanating from Jesus became so intense, Simon and Mary had to shield their eyes. It felt as if their very souls were exposed and naked.

When they looked again, Moses and Elijah were gone. Jesus was alone with the three. They saw him wave in the direction of the woods behind him. It was as if he were dismissing unseen visitors. Were there others spying on him?

Jesus helped the disciples up. He looked about again to make sure there were no more of the unseen visitors that he had dismissed. Simon and Mary could hear him say to his three companions, "The Son of Man will be delivered into the hands of men. They will kill him, but he will be raised on the third day."

The disciples were visibly shaken. Peter wept. Jesus led them out of the clearing. Simon and Mary heard him say, "Let us return to camp. Tell no one about this vision until the Son of Man is raised from the dead."

Suddenly, Jesus stopped, turned and faced the brush where Simon and Mary were hiding. They ducked down further. They heard him call out, "And that means you two as well! Tell no one." He winked with a smile and turned back to the disciples.

Simon and Mary looked at each other astonished. How did he know?

The four men left the woods and two little spies behind.

Their breathing labored. Mary's eyes were as big as the moon.

She said, "He knew we were here. Who were the other spies he dismissed? Watchers?"

Simon wasn't listening. "This is amazing, Mary. Truly amazing."

"What was it?"

• • • • •

The evil spirits returned to Belial inside the mountain. He stared with a dire face into the blackened ooze of the Abyss that filled the large lake inside their sanctuary. Small flames of fire flitted across the surface of it.

The sixty plus other gods gathered around their leader like a bodyguard of Watchers, swords drawn, javelins and maces held tight. Would they fight this day?

Belial said, still staring into the oblivion, "It is worse than I thought."

Molech whined, "Are the heavenly host approaching?"

"No. He transfigured."

"Glorification," said Molech. "Is that not a call to battle?"

"He is not attacking us on our turf. He is challenging us to his."

"It is almost upon us," said Belial. "All gods, prepare for war."

•••••

Simon explained to Mary as they made their way back down the mountain. He was breathless.

"Moses spent so much time face to face with Yahweh, that his own face began to transfigure and shine like the sun. He had to pull a cloak over himself because the Israelites could not stand before the brightness of holiness. The direct presence of Yahweh changes one's very being from human to divine."

"Moses was made into a god?"

"Like a Son of God. *Bene ha Elohim*. But it was only a foretaste, because it would fade with time."

Mary was putting it together. "So, Sons of God are the holy ones who surround Yahweh Elohim's throne chariot, and they are myriad."

"Ten thousands upon ten thousands. They are the divine ones who administered the Law of Yahweh at Sinai. They are direct creations of Yahweh, and because they are in his presence, they shine with holiness."

"So that is why they are called 'Shining Ones'."

"Yes."

"So Jesus is both a Son of Man and a Son of God?"

"The unique Son of God. The only one of his kind. What we saw was a living apotheosis, the declaration of his divinity. Yahweh in the flesh, the second Power in heaven."

Mary knew what apotheosis was from her understanding of how Augustus was supposedly divinized after his death.

He said, "Jesus is the fulfillment of the Law and the Prophets."

"Is that why Moses and Elijah were with him?"

"The giver of the Law, and the father of Prophets. But that is not all. Jesus told us to keep his secret."

"That didn't make sense to me. That he would die and raise from the dead in three days."

"It is the Messianic secret, kept hidden from the principalities and the powers. And yet it was in plain sight all along."

"What do you mean?"

"Jesus told us that no sign shall be given this generation of ours except the sign of Jonah. He said that just as Jonah was three days and three nights in the belly of the great fish, so will the Son of Man be three days and three nights in the heart of the earth. I remember reading a revelation from the angel Gabriel that was recorded on stone and stored in the library at Qumran."

"What did it say?"

He quoted it by heart. He could never forget it.

"By three days you shall know that, thus said Yahweh of Hosts, the god of Israel,
the evil has been broken by righteousness…
Behold, all the nations gather against Jerusalem…
In just a little while, I will shake the heavens and the earth…
My servant David, ask of Ephraim for a sign…
By three days, live, I Gabriel, command you, prince of princes.

"It fits together with the prophet Daniel. The breaking of evil by righteousness is Daniel's Messiah Prince ending sin through atonement and bringing in everlasting righteousness. The shaking of the heavens and earth is the establishment of a new covenant. 'My servant David' is a reference to Messiah, whose sign of power is resurrection after three days. He is the Lord of lords and the Prince of princes."

"Wait, slow down," said Mary. "You are losing me with all your scribal talk."

Simon stopped to catch his breath and give her a smile. "The battle of the gods of the nations with Messiah will be in Jerusalem."

CHAPTER 22

Demas and Gestas stood, sickened before the sight of the vile atrocity. One hundred of their comrades crucified, dead, and rotting in the hot afternoon sun on the pathway to the Zealot mountain hideout. The stench was unbearable. Gestas didn't even try to shoo away vultures feeding off the flesh. There were too many of them. The victims had been there for a week by now, and were half eaten and covered with maggots and worms. Some bones had already fallen to the ground where they were picked clean by carnivores of the desert. It was such an ignoble death, deliberately calculated by the Romans to defile the religious beliefs of their enemies, who sought the honorable means of burial for their dead.

The brothers had made their way back to the caves, just southwest of Scythopolis, in search of Barabbas. They could not find him amidst the dead, so they hoped he had gotten away. Simon had told them where his monastic community was located, of which both he and Barabbas had originally been members. They suspected Barabbas would return to that hideout in safety to plan his next moves.

•••••

It took them several days to travel fifty miles south to the Qumran community on the northwestern edge of the Dead Sea. It rested on a broad plateau beside the body of salt water made infamous by the judgment on Sodom and the cities of the plain on the opposite southeastern edge. It was a self-reliant village protected by walls, more for privacy than security, and housed several hundred sectarians in a brotherhood that maintained their own agricultural plots and animal herds for sustenance. Their main concerns were contemplative solitude, austerity, the pursuit of holiness, and the maintenance of the wisdom of the ages. A scriptorium provided for the practice of copying manuscripts, and their scrolls were kept dry and cool in various libraries in caves of the surrounding desert bluffs.

Part of their obsession with holiness was multiple baptisms for ritual cleanness. Demas and Gestas dipped themselves into one of the many baptisteries around the village. It was a requirement in order to even enter the village and participate in any social interaction with the members.

The brothers walked naked down the steps into the small, enclosed pool and washed. When they exited, they were shaved of facial hair and given some simple tunics and cloaks more applicable to peaceful contemplation than the warrior garb they had arrived in. Their weapons were packed away for the duration of their stay.

At last, they were brought to a large meeting room, where they were greeted by Barabbas and fifty of his men, also clothed in the community's apparel and clean shaven. Gestas thought it was a great disguise to avoid being recognized by any Romans snooping around in search of wanted Zealots to imprison.

Barabbas smiled and opened his arms wide. "Demas and Gestas Samaras. My two theatrical performers. Welcome to my new hideout. David hid in the Engedi, not too far from here, when he fled the wrath of Saul. I follow in his steps for my own strategy of victory."

Follow in his steps? thought Demas. Simon the Zealot had explained to the brothers that the Messiah would be a "Son of David" following in the footsteps of his forerunner, the original anointed messiah king of Israel. Was Barabbas claiming his identity as Messiah?

Barabbas said, "It has been too long, and you have much to tell me, I dare hope. Let us share a meal."

They sat on mats around the floor with simple food for nourishment. Bread, figs and vegetables from their gardens and plots, along with olive oil and wine from their own presses.

The brothers had shared their sorrow over the loss of their comrades to the Romans.

"I was out raiding a Herodian palace over the Jordan with these fifty men, when they were ambushed."

Barabbas put his arm around the young man next to him, a brooding intense lad, who looked always scowling and always distrusting.

"Eleazar ben Dinai here, escaped and alerted us. He has become my right hand these days."

Barabbas took a deep drink of wine and said, "So, my brothers, what news have you for me about the missing scribe, Simon bar Josiah?"

Demas looked at Gestas. Gestas spoke first. "We will not lie to you, Barabbas. We found Simon alive on the way to Caesarea Philippi, and a follower of the Nazarene."

Barabbas' festive face turned suddenly dour. "Did you kill them?"

Gestas hesitated. Demas offered, "No."

Eleazar ben Dinai nodded and six Zealots sitting beside the two brothers grabbed them. They didn't fight back because they expected it.

They were bound tight with ropes.

Barabbas stopped eating and wiped his hands with a towel. He leaned forward and clenched his teeth in anger. "Why did you return to me with such betrayal, knowing that you will hang?"

Gestas swallowed. But Demas was not afraid. He still didn't care whether he lived or died. But he would try to protect his brother. "Because you needed to know, and we knew you would agree with our assessment."

Barabbas raised his brow in feigned surprise at the challenge. "And what is your assessment?"

"The Nazarene seems to have power to sway the masses with delusion, make them believe his magic tricks. He speaks of the visitation of Yahweh, the Day of the Lord and coming judgment. But he does not tolerate violence, and prepares no arms."

"Does he claim to be Messiah?"

Demas said, "Yes and no. He gives many hints that it is so. But he will not come out and claim it in public."

Barabbas was not comforted by the assurance. He still appeared agitated. "And what of Simon?"

"He did not speak a single ill word of you when we were with him. He does not seem to be against you."

Gestas added, "Jesus teaches, 'He that is not against you is for you.' I heard him say that if anyone wanted to be his disciple, they must deny themselves, pick up their cross, and follow him."

"What are you trying to say?" said Barabbas, still bothered.

"Crucifixion is for insurrectionists. Jesus may be a secret Zealot."

Demas added, "We do not think the Nazarene is your competitor or your enemy. And we believe he has a secret army hidden somewhere until the right moment for them to rise up against Rome."

"Where is this army? I have heard not even a rumor of any forces other than the scattered bands of Amram, Tholomy and the sons of Judas."

Gestas jumped in with a bit too much enthusiasm. "Some believe it is an army of angels, Yahweh's heavenly host. To bring judgment."

Barabbas looked at him as if he were a madman. "You believe such nonsense?"

"No," said Demas, covering for his brother.

Eleazar jumped in, "Is that what the Nazarene claims?"

"Well, not explicitly," said Gestas. "But the point is that whatever he means, he has the charisma to make the crowds believe him. And that is a necessary component of any good uprising. A believing mob."

Barabbas continued to think about it. Eleazar said, "Where is the Nazarene now? What are his plans?"

Gestas said, "We believe he is on his way to Jerusalem."

Barabbas said, "I am on my way to Jerusalem. How can you say he is not my competitor, if we both plan to deliver Zion?"

Now Demas and Gestas knew Barabbas was deluded into believing he was the Messiah. Eleazar was no doubt considered his Elijah.

Demas said, "But you only have fifty men. That is no longer a large enough force for an uprising."

Barabbas smirked. "But it is enough for an assassination that is carefully orchestrated to cause an uprising."

"How so?" said Demas.

"The Passover is arriving. Thousands of Jews will be filling the holy city with their devotion to Yahweh *and* their hatred for Rome. But so too will the Herods be there. If we can assassinate the high priest and Herod, we would bring enough chaos to turn the mob mad with vengeance."

Gestas said, "But how will you gain the support of the crowds if you Jews murder your own leaders, Herodian or not?"

Eleazar answered, "We will nail it on the Romans somehow."

Demas brightened with a plan. "That is why you don't want the Nazarene dead. If he does have a hidden force of arms, then their uprising combined with yours will become an earthquake that begins with Jerusalem and rolls out through all of Judea and the Galilee. But if this Jesus is a fraud, then all his followers will no doubt move over to you as deliverer, and you can execute the Nazarene at your will after you take the crown from Antipas."

Gestas was proud of how inventive his simple warrior brother had become with his impromptu acting. He had encouraged the messianic aspirations of Barabbas without the cheap tactic of flattery.

Gestas threw in, "And I know exactly how we can nail this on the Romans and get away with it."

Barabbas smiled, looked to Eleazar for approval, and said, "Well, it looks like you two have just saved your lives from hanging."

Barabbas thought privately that he would still have to kill this Jesus afterward, to consolidate his own power and authority as Messiah over Israel.

CHAPTER 23

Molech looked up at the walls of Jerusalem from the base of his *tophet,* his burning place in the Valley of Hinnom on the western side of the holy city. He was proud of all he had accomplished in Israel over the millennia as the god of the underworld. He was sick and tired of being picked on and mocked by the other gods for his taste in little children. As if their abominations were any better. Did they not know that he was born this way from the very hand of Yahweh? He simply followed his desires as all of them did, so what right did they have to judge and condemn him? Ashtart, the goddess of sex and war, who tread through rivers of blood and bizarre sexual perversity had the gall to call him detestable. Ba'al, the most high bully and mightiest ego of the pantheon, treated him like a retarded child. Dagon, that fish of the Philistines, didn't let him build any temples in Philistia. And that bitch Asherah ignored him, even though her Phoenician people had a distinct liking for his practices. All of these divinities scoffed, spurned and spit on him from their arrogant lofty high places of privilege and bigotry.

And yet all of them, every single one of them, were gone. Bound in their pride in Tartarus by the archangels. Molech alone was left. He had played his game with craftiness and savvy. He had survived them all. The fools. *Now, I spit on you.* He hocked with his throat to gather a clump of mucus, saliva and worms, and spit on the ground as if on their graves. He lifted his chin with pride of status and took in a deep whiff of the pleasant scent of child sacrifice now burning on his altar.

On my "low place," he mused to himself with a smile. The altars of the gods were usually called high places, being situated on mountains or other artificial elevations in order to connect them with the heavens. In his case, sacrifices were made in the lowest parts of valleys, in order to connect with the underworld. His servants had even placed piping from the altars that would direct the blood into the recesses of the rocks to filter down to his abode. An added benefit was that the southern portion of Gehenna opened up to meet the Valley of the Rephaim, where the last of the giants were wiped out by the messiah king, David.

It made Molech grin to think how the fate of the Rephaim connected to the fate of the gods who were bound in the deepest part of Sheol. Those pompous blowhards who bullied Molech had finally received their comeuppance.

Molech's signature achievement was his tophet altars where worshippers "passed their children through the fire." They were usually bronze statues of himself with a bull's head, seated with outstretched arms to place the child over the flames. It was so bold and brilliant that Ba'al had stolen his idea and used it for his own altars. The muscle-bound brute didn't have an original thought in his puny little skull.

Molech made himself invisible to his worshippers, as the Watcher gods typically did in these latter days. In primeval days, the days of Noah, they had walked amongst men and engaged in the open. It was almost as if the growth of knowledge and technology had the deleterious effect on humans of blinding them more and more to the spiritual world around them. It was just as well. The gods could achieve things through hiding that they could not through visible means.

Molech achieved much as the underdog among deities, which was worthy of his pride. He had managed to burrow his home into the Valley of Hinnom, called Gehenna, right under the walls of the holy city itself. What other god came as close? Asherah had seduced her way into the high places of the Israelites with her Asherim, or wooden cult objects, and teraphim, which were little statues of her depicted as the consort of Yahweh. "Yahweh and his Asherah" was the phrase. Ba'al gained much ground through the vices of the Tyrian princess Jezebel who had been married to King Ahab of Israel. She instituted Ba'al worship in Israel, with a temple and altar in the capital city of Samaria, a worship that had plagued the fanatical Jewish priesthood for generations. The northernmost tribe of Dan, near Panias, never freed themselves from the grip of Ba'al's golden calf worship ever since the early days of the divided monarchy.

But Molech, he had wormed his way right into the heart of Israel even with his so-called detestable practice. Ha. Several kings of both Judah and Israel certainly enjoyed his "detestable practice," without complaint. Ahaz and Manasseh were his favorites. They made their own sons to pass through the fire. Manasseh, one of the longest reigning kings of Judah, had been so effectively won over to Molech that the Jews were exiled to Babylon as a punishment for his misdeeds. Because of that exile, they had lost their Book of the Covenant that had contained the very words and instructions of Yahweh.

He was proud of that victory. What other god had such a resumé of achievement?

And they call me the "mole god." Pftah. If it weren't for that self-righteous godlicking prig, King Josiah, after the exile, I'd be sitting on Yahweh's throne right now in the heights of the north, above the very stars of god.

Josiah had found the lost Book of the Covenant and instituted massive moral, legal and cultic reforms. That evil, scheming iconoclast tore down all the high places, the statues of Ba'al, the Asherim, and idols of all the host of heaven. He defiled Molech's own main tophet at the confluence of the Kidron and Hinnom valleys. He spread the bones of the dead over the valley to make it ritually unclean for sacrifices. It was a great setback for Molech. The prophet Jeremiah had even pronounced Gehenna as a "Valley of Slaughter" for the Day of Vengeance.

Thanks to Molech's fires of sacrifice, combined with Josiah's desecration, Gehenna had become known to the Jews as a metaphor for fiery judgment, a reference to the destruction of the wicked. *So be it,* he thought. *I can turn that fear and revulsion toward my benefit.*

His worshippers were now few and not as bold. They hid in the crags of the rocks and engaged in their abominations in the dark, as opposed to the good old days when they did it in broad daylight. But it was still a foothold, a talon into the heart of Israel. And thanks to Belial's Rome, the Jews were not allowed to punish "idolaters," as they called them. They could shun them socially, but they could not harm them as they could under the Mosaic law of oppression. Those hateful, bigoted worshippers of one god, were forced to be more tolerant and inclusive in their treatment of other deities and their sincere believers. One day, they would also get back to allowing pedophilia love and the beautiful acts of passing their children through the fire.

Then Molech could breathe free and reign again.

Molech's breathing suddenly constricted, as if a boa were tightening around his neck. He saw two figures on the walls of the city, looking back down at him. Even from this distance, he knew who they were.

Archangels.

He shivered. He looked nervously around the valley. There. Down the northern part of the Hinnom, he could see two more figures approaching on horseback.

To the south, two more. Coming his way.

The two on the walls had disappeared. They would be at the city gates in seconds.

He spun around to see a seventh wraith high above him on the ridge.

He was surrounded. Seven archangels. There was only one reason why they would be here.

But he had been preparing. He was not going to let that happen. He was going to gi --.

He was suddenly tackled to the ground by the angel from above. The attacker had moved down from the perilous height with surprising speed.

Mikael wrestled with Molech to get control. This was the strongest of the archangels. Molech would not ordinarily have much of a chance. But the god had just received sacrifice and was stronger at the moment than Mikael could be.

Molech kicked Mikael off him and launched him into the air.

The angel hit the bronze statue of Molech with a clang. The large eight foot tall metallic image fell to its side. The remains of the sacrifice scattered to the ground. Mikael shook himself out of his dizziness, to see the deity escaping into the rocky crag of a cave entrance.

He picked himself up and ran after the coward.

Mikael saw a large stone rolling across the entrance from inside some special groove. He only had a second or two before the stone completed its roll, blocking off the hunter from his prey. He dove and made it through the opening, just as the huge stone slammed shut. He was locked inside the cave with his nemesis. By the time the other angels arrived and moved the stone, Molech would be long gone. Mikael had to go it alone. He bolted off into the darkness of the underground tunnel.

Molech had the advantage. This was his turf and his dwelling. He had spent much of his time over the millennia below the surface, which made his skin pale white and his eyes unable to see well when up above on the surface. But down below, he was the god of the underworld. He could see better than even Mikael's preternatural night vision.

Mikael didn't know what he was running into down here.

He arrived at a fork in the small tunnel. He looked at the dirt and could see that his adversary had gone to the right. Mikael followed.

The tunnels were quite small, only big enough for the bulky eight foot deity to move, with little leeway. For Mikael, there was more room because he was smaller, but not by much.

He stopped again. Another split. But this time, three options. He took the middle way.

Mikael figured that by now, his comrade archangels would have moved the stone away and were on their way to join him.

He felt his pathway was circling back. When he saw another crossroads, he realized what he was now inside: a maze. The mole god had burrowed out a complex labyrinth of tunnels that seemed to Mikael a web of confusion. The rock was harder and the dust sparser, making it even more difficult for Mikael to follow his prey's foot prints. About the only thing he could follow now was the creature's stench.

He heard the sound of footsteps in the dark, not far from him. He picked up his pace, trying not to make as much noise as the clumsy brute was making.

He turned a corner and saw the deity jump down into an opening in the rocky floor. When he reached it, he saw it was an opening that led deeper still, to a lower level.

He heard the voices of his comrades in the distance, shouting for him. He decided he would take this one time to give some direction, even though it would also warn Molech. But he needed his comrades.

He shouted, "Down here, Angels! There's an opening to a deeper level!" Then he jumped.

He landed twenty feet below. Before him, a new opening to a new maze of tunnels. He thought, *This has been one busy little mole*. He followed the smell. His opponent now knew how close he was.

Mikael turned another corner and saw the god waiting for him, before bolting down a pathway.

Mikael responded instinctively to the sight of the fleeing divinity. It wasn't until he was almost upon the pathway that it registered in his mind that he was being led into a trap. He slid to a stop.

It was too late. He heard the sound of a release being tripped and rocks shifting.

Above him. A triggered cave-in crushed him beneath a ton of rock. He was completely immobilized. He could not get to his weapons. He could only see through a thin crevice of some rocks as Molech walked up to him, laughed and spit at him, before disappearing deeper into the network of twisting tunnels.

Within minutes, the other angels followed the sound of the collapsed tunnel and found Mikael's location. They were able to dislodge enough of the rock and pull his broken body from the rubble.

He had been severely crushed.

Gabriel held him. "I can bring him back to the surface to heal."

Raphael said, “That leaves five. We can split up and try to surround the mole. He can’t hide here forever.”

They heard the sound of a howl.

“Dire wolves,” said Uriel. “We can’t chase him here forever.”

Dire wolves were vicious, fanged black hounds of hell almost as tall as a man.

Raphael said, “He must have bred them down here. There could be dozens.”

“Or hundreds,” said Uriel.

The angels could kill dozens of the wolves. But hundreds was another matter altogether. Several of them had almost been overwhelmed by a hundred dire wolves in the days of the giant King Arba, while rescuing Abraham and Sarah from the clutches of the Anakim in Kiriath-arba. They were rescued by a hundred archers. But they didn’t have a hundred archers down in this dungeon of dread darkness.

“Take Mikael to safety,” said Uriel. “The rest of you draw the wolves back up to the surface.”

They looked at Uriel with fear.

Gabriel said, “No, Uriel. We can do this together.”

Uriel grasped the leather harness of the special weapon strapped to his back. “I must do this alone.”

They all knew what it meant. Uriel had the most sensitive senses. He was the best tracker of all of them.

Gabriel protested more, “I will not let you.”

“You have no choice.”

They heard the sound of wolves getting closer.

“And I have no time to quibble with you, Gabriel. Leave — all of you. Draw them after you.”

Gabriel teared up. What Uriel was going to do was akin to suicide for humans.

Raphael said, “He’s right.”

They agreed silently.

Gabriel went and grasped his friend in a bear hug that he didn’t seem to want to let go. “My brother.”

“Stop your pouting, Gabriel. It’s only until the judgment.”

Gabriel pulled away with an angry look in his face. It softened, and he said with a smirk, “You will finally outdo me, little friend.”

Uriel gave him a dirty look. *Little friend.* There was still time to tease.

“I outdid you a long time ago,” said Uriel with a grin.

Gabriel added, "But there is still Armageddon. You don't know what I might be capable of."

Uriel said, "Go. We'll have all eternity to debate that."

They turned to leave. But their delay had lost them time.

The underworld dire wolves were upon them. Fifty glowing eyes locked on them, approaching slowly, ready to pounce.

There was only enough room to fight against one or two wolves at a time through the narrow passages. Gabriel stood at the back, carrying the broken form of Mikael, who was starting to heal, but not able to fight yet. The other four approached the wolves in single file.

They would hack their way through the assailants one by one and climb over their dead bodies to the exit.

Uriel launched into the darkness after Molech. He wasn't hard to follow. Uriel's olfactory senses were highly attuned to the deity's rancid odor. Unfortunately, he was too attuned. Uriel gagged. *Revolting*, he thought. But he kept moving on, cautiously prepared for more snares. He had to give the other angels enough time to fight their way through the wolves to the surface before he could achieve his intended goal.

The angels killed their way through the twenty-five dire wolves, one and two at a time, with sword, axe and arrow. It was not without its cost of exhaustion. Could they take on hundreds?

When they reached the end of the slaughter, they saw another hundred glowing eyes racing their way from several other passages.

The archangels ran toward the surface.

Uriel knew he was near his quarry. Or was it the other way around? He couldn't help it. He had to make a crack.

"Molech, you really need to take a bath. You smell something foul."

To his surprise, a voice echoed back from one of the tunnels. "I will give you a bath in my excrement, godlicker."

Uriel went down the tunnel toward the sound.

The archangels reached the twenty foot ledge they had taken to get down to this level.

Raphael said, "The wolves will not be able to climb this. They will turn back toward Uriel."

Gabriel let Mikael hang on his back and began the ascent. "Uriel will do his job. Just climb. We don't have much time."

Three of them climbed. Remiel and Saraqael faced the wolves that had reached them first and cut them down.

But the wolves kept coming.

Remiel shouted out, "I wish I had Uriel's signature move right now!"

He was referring to Uriel's special skill in handling two swords.

Remiel jumped up a good ten feet and reached his hand down.

Saraqael was barely able to keep back the onslaught of chomping wolves. How could he stop to make the climb?

"Saraqael, come on!"

Saraqael slashed and stabbed. The bodies piled up. If he stopped, he would get pulled down into their fangs and claws.

Finally, the bodies were so high, it took a moment for the next wolf to climb over to jump at the angel.

Saraqael spun and threw the sword at the beast, piercing it. He turned to leap upward.

The next wolf jumped over the mountain of flesh.

Saraqael grabbed Remiel's hand.

Before Remiel could pull him out of harm's way, the lone wolf jumped and latched its teeth on the angel's ankle.

Saraqael yelled in pain.

More wolves came through the opening.

Saraqael pulled a dagger from his belt. He reached down and sliced the wolf's spinal column.

The creature yelped, released its bite and fell to the ground on top of the other wolves just below.

Saraqael scrambled up out of the jumping reach of the dire wolves. The angels looked down at the monsters now gathering below.

It didn't take the intelligent creatures very long to understand their predicament. One of them howled. The wolves turned their sights away to find a more achievable prey.

"Uriel," whimpered Gabriel, looking down the precipice with Mikael safely at his side.

Uriel entered what appeared to be a sanctuary of some kind. It wasn't huge, just a hundred foot square stone cavern. He saw Molech at the other side. He glanced up to make sure there was no net or trap above him. Nothing.

Without even thinking, he threw his javelin at the deity.

It caught the god before he could exit the subterranean den. Molech cried out. But then he stepped aside, and a file of dire wolves padded their way past him into the den.

Uriel heard the sound of snarling growls behind him. He glanced back and saw other wolves filing in.

He drew his two swords and prayed a prayer to Yahweh.

The wolves surrounded him, maybe sixty or so. Others waited outside in the tunnels.

Their eyes glowed green. Their teeth showed through their snarls. They prepared to spring upon the angel and bury him in a pile of claws and fangs.

They began to pounce.

Uriel engaged in his signature move that the other angels had been so envious of. He held his swords out like windmill blades and twirled around with blinding speed. He became a kind of fan of death that sliced up his enemies as fast as they could approach him. Within seconds he had cut them all down.

When he stopped, he lost his balance from dizziness.

The next batch of wolves made their way in.

Molech disappeared down the tunnel, behind the next line of wolves protecting him.

This was it. Uriel had Molech in his sights. He had all he needed.

He dropped his swords to the ground with a clang and reached behind him to pull out the weapon he had strapped to his back.

It was the hammer of Ba'al. The weapon the god had used successfully to escape their grasp at Tyre. He had left it behind in the tsunami wave. Uriel had brought it with him for this very purpose.

The wolves were piling in, preparing a new attack.

Uriel screamed with all his might.

He raised the hammer high and struck the ground at his feet. Not once, but twice. He needed this to be a thorough burial.

A violent earthquake rumbled outward from the epicenter and shook every creature to the ground in its wake.

The cavern collapsed upon Uriel and the wolves.

The tunnel where Molech was escaping caved in upon him and his wolven servants.

The complete complex of tunnels collapsed under the massive weight of the shifting earth.

This had been Uriel's plan all along. If they could not catch the slippery worm to bind him in Tartarus, they would simply bury him under billions of tons of immovable rock, which was almost as secure as the prison of Sheol.

Molech would never see the sun again to engage in perversion with humanity. But the price that the archangel had to pay to achieve this prison was to sacrifice himself in order to do so.

He too would be imprisoned in the rock, until the final judgment. At that time, Yahweh would raise all from the earth unto the glories of heaven or the fires of Gehenna. One thing was for sure, Gehenna would no longer be a valley of Molech's power, but a symbol of the valley of Yahweh's judgment to come.

Uriel would spend the rest of his days entombed alive in that prison of rock, praying to Yahweh until the final day. He had made the ultimate sacrifice to help pave the way for Messiah's own restoration of Israel and drawing in of the nations.

CHAPTER 24

Jesus and his followers were upon the ridge of Gehenna looking down at Jerusalem when the earthquake occurred. It seemed to be quite deep in the earth, but it rattled the area for miles around.

When the tremor stopped, Jesus brought the crowd over to look down upon the valley and the walls of the city. At about four miles in circumference, Jerusalem sheltered a populace of about eighty thousand. But during Passover like this, more than a million pilgrims came from all over the land to participate in the festival, so the surrounding environs hosted many camps of visitors. A hundred or so people had come from the city to hear Jesus, because of his reputation, including a group of Pharisees and scribes.

He spent some time telling them parables that enraged the religious leaders and confused the common folk. Tomorrow, they would enter the city.

Simon was visibly disturbed. He stayed sitting at the butte's edge after everyone else returned to their camp. Mary Magdalene approached him.

"Simon, are you well?"

"No."

"What is wrong?" She sat on the rock beside him, looking out onto the valley. It was quite barren and ugly. As if life could not grow there. They could see a destroyed altar to Molech below them, pushed over on its side, the fire long died out.

He said, "Do you remember the Scripture Jesus read in the last synagogue we had visited in Bethany?"

"Yes. The prophet Jeremiah." It had only been a couple days earlier.

Simon quoted what he could remember, "'Behold, days are coming, declares Yahweh, when this place shall no more be called Tophet, or the Valley of the Son of Hinnom, but the Valley of Slaughter. And in this place I will make void the plans of Judah and Jerusalem, and will cause their people to fall by the sword before their enemies.'"

She asked him, "That was about the destruction of Jerusalem by the Babylonians when they took them into exile, right?"

Simon stared out into the void. "The prophet said their bodies would be food for the scavengers of heaven and earth. That the inhabitants of the city would turn to cannibalism. And then he said that Yahweh would make Jerusalem like a Tophet."

She said, "It must have been a horrible time to be alive."

He said, "Have you noticed that Jesus's parables and stories are increasingly sounding very similar to that previous destruction of Jerusalem?"

"In what ways?"

"The parables he just taught on this very overlook of Gehenna carried the same message." He concluded, "As if Jerusalem will be destroyed again."

She said, "I have always assumed his words were about the judgment of the nations."

He protested, "But he seems to be prophesying that our people will reject his kingship, rather than accept it. And they will be judged just like a pagan nation."

"How could that be?" she asked. "He has always said that he has come to minister to Israel."

"Yes. But remember the tenants in the parable? They kept rejecting the landlord's plea to bring him the fruit of the vineyard. And when the landlord sent his son, they killed him too. They wanted to steal his inheritance."

"So, the son in the story is Jesus, and the tenants are his people, Israel?" Her voice was thoughtful.

He nodded. "Do you remember what Jesus said the landlord would do to the tenants?"

She nodded. "He would put those miserable wretches to a miserable death and let out the vineyard to other tenants."

He said, "And then he told the Pharisees and chief priests and their followers to their faces that the Kingdom of God would be taken away from them and given to a people producing its fruits."

"The only people other than the people of God are the Gentiles. But he said his ministry was to Israel."

He shook his head, puzzling it out. "What if his ministry is to bring judgment upon Israel so that salvation would be open to all who believed him, including the Gentiles?"

She stared at him. Could it be true? Would they have the guts to ask Jesus about such a thing? What if they were wrong?

He said, "Jesus is the stone that Israel's leaders and her people, the builders, rejected. But that stone will be the cornerstone of God's new temple and holy city. And he will crush all those he falls upon."

"Those who reject him?"

"Yes. Days of Vengeance for those who would not recognize the day of Yahweh's visitation."

"But the Jewish nation will reject her own Messiah?"

He dared not say. It would be a heresy to suggest such things. But it was perfectly consistent with the prophets. Isaiah, Jeremiah, Ezekiel, Malachai, they had all spoken of Israel's repeated spiritual adultery with the gods of Canaan, and their abominations. Could the Day of the Lord spoken of in Joel be a Day of the Lord against Israel? Was their march to Jerusalem a march to destruction?

• • • • •

Longinus looked down upon the Jerusalem temple area from the fortress Antonia, connected to the northwest corner wall of the temple mount. The Antonia was about five hundred feet square with four corner towers. It housed a Roman garrison that watched over the temple activities. The Jews despised the Romans for this invasion of their religious privacy, but they had no choice in the matter. Tiberius Caesar wanted oversight of all their activities, especially the ones they considered more important than Caesar.

Within the week, the Jews would be celebrating their Passover sacrifice, a symbol of their exodus out of slavery in Egypt. Longinus knew they equated Rome with Egypt and Babylon and every other force that had ruled over them or occupied their land. So, in a way, even this festival and its cultic rituals were an expression of contempt for Rome. Tensions were high; tempers flared, and rioting mobs were a constant threat in this volatile environment. And this year brought with it the added insurrectionists and their contagious madness of Messiah expectation. The Roman forces were on high alert.

The entire temple complex was over a thousand feet long and just under a thousand feet wide. The largest area, the outer court, or Court of the Gentiles, was open to all, both Jew and Gentile alike. It had marble flooring and was lined all around by porticos. Here animals were sold for sacrifices, like a marketplace, and worshippers could congregate or wait in line for their sacrifices. Upon closer approach to the Temple itself, in the center of the temple area, a screen with an engraved sign warned Gentiles not to proceed upon pain of death. Like every temple in the world, the closer one got to the inner sanctum or Holy of Holies in the temple, the more sacred the space became, and the fewer who were allowed to go further.

The Temple itself had several courts of increasing holiness as well. Though Longinus could see inside these walls from his highest tower perch, no Roman could ever set foot in them. First, there was the Court of Women shaped much like a cross. It amused Longinus to find such a reflection of their instrument of death in the Jews' structure of supposed life. This was about two hundred feet square, and evidently, women could go no further than this court, though all worshippers brought their animal sacrifices here. On Passover, one lamb would be chosen without blemish, to substitute for a group of twenty or so Jews, usually an extended family.

They would then bring the lamb into the next smallest court, the Court of Priests. This was where the animals were cut and bled and burned on the large horned altar of unhewn stones that stood before the Temple, while a chorus of priests played their instruments and sang hymns of praise to the deity. A bronze laver stood nearby for what appeared to be cleansings. The Temple façade stood a hundred and fifty feet high behind the altar, with its golden roof visible from anywhere on the entire temple mount.

Inside was the holy place, a huge candelabra, some incense stands, and then the curtained Holy of Holies where the Ark of Covenant housed their god Yahweh. Or at least that is all Longinus had been told by his rabbi informant. One day, he would like to gut the entire edifice and burn it to the ground, just to show these Jews that Caesar was a superior god. If anyone might actually do such a thing, it would be Pilate, who had already incensed the Jews with his past offensive behaviors. He liked to provoke them.

Of course, Longinus had his own religion of the Imperial Cult and Mithras, but these people seemed to have an elaborate system of myth that was quite impressive to him. He had learned much about it from his informant. The intolerant exclusivity of their deity and his dogma seemed to create an inability to tolerate each other. It resulted in a multitude of factions squabbling over who were the "true remnant" of followers of the Law. Such diversity made it more difficult to keep tabs on them, because their leadership was so decentralized even within the Sanhedrin.

He had received intelligence from his spies about one of those factions approaching the Shushan Gate on the east end of the Temple, where it led out to the Kidron Valley below. Longinus made his way over to Solomon's portico that stood atop the eastern walls, to look down upon the arriving company. Pilate had appointed his century as part of a cohort of five hundred troops ordered to station themselves discreetly behind the pillars surrounding the Court of Gentiles. If this Nazarene attempted to start any kind of trouble, he would be apprehended and brought immediately to detention in the Antonia through the underground tunnel connecting the Roman fortress to the temple area.

Longinus met his rabbi informant and looked down the wall to see the Nazarene arrive with his company of a few hundred followers, gawkers, and miracle seekers. The sight of it made him laugh. The Nazarene approached the city and temple as a king might for a triumphal entry into a subdued city.

The rabbi whispered to him, "This is the gate through which the red heifer is brought for sacrifice outside the camp as a special sin offering. It is also the exit for the journey of the scapegoat for Azazel."

"Scapegoat?" asked Longinus.

"Yes. On our most holy Day of Atonement, one goat is sacrificed for the people and another has the sins of Israel placed upon it, to be led into the wilderness to be consumed into chaos. It carries away our sins."

Childish, thought Longinus.

The entrance up to the gate was covered with arches that led toward the Mount of Olives. Hundreds of Jews lined the paved way waving palm branches and even laying down their cloaks as an expression of submission to the Nazarene.

The rabbi said, "This is interesting."

"What?" said Longinus.

"This was the very same ritual that the citizens of Jerusalem performed upon the arrival of King David when he conquered Jerusalem a thousand years ago. Listen to their shouting."

Longinus could hear them crying out, "Hosanna to the Son of David! Blessed is he who comes in the name of Yahweh! Hosanna in the highest!"

Longinus looked at the rabbi for confirmation.

He nodded. Messianic.

The centurion whistled to the commander of the cohort. The Nazarene was approaching. The soldiers stood ready in the shadows of the pillars.

It was a joke. The Jew had no armed accompaniment, not even bodyguards. And instead of riding a horse in any kind of warrior gear, he was riding a pathetic donkey, and pulling a colt behind him.

A donkey? If Longinus didn't know better, he'd say this was a mockery of the Imperial triumphal entry—an inversion of power into weakness. What fool would engage in such theatrical self-deprecation? It was more like the satirical entry of a jester than the arrival of Messiah.

Unless, of course, it was just another Jewish tactic of subversion. Longinus suspected that there was some kind of tie to Barabbas the Zealot. Maybe Barabbas led the army that would rise up from its hiding amongst the people.

Longinus had to be ready.

Demas and Gestas wore their disguises of commoners down in the crowds receiving Jesus. Barabbas watched from the portico below the roof where Longinus observed. To the hiding Zealot warriors, this was a disheartening sight. It seemed the opposite of a triumphant arrival.

Demas thought, *Was it a diversionary tactic?*

Since the Nazarene knew the Romans would be more than prepared to receive an insurrectionist with force of arms, Demas figured Jesus still kept any of his secret forces hidden for the right moment.

Gestas hoped that Jesus really had an army of heavenly hosts ready to burst the veil of heaven and earth.

As Jesus left the temple mount on his way back to Bethany a couple miles away, another spy watched him from the Mount of Olives: the prince of Rome, Belial, the Accuser. The deities of Canaan had all failed and been imprisoned in the underworld by the angels of Yahweh. Jesus had dispossessed them from their inheritance. Belial had counseled the other Watcher gods to return to their inherited territories, because if they were to all show up in Jerusalem to battle, then so would the minions of Yahweh's heavenly host. No, this had to be a properly executed assassination. All through history, the Seed of the Serpent had sought to extinguish the Seed of Eve that led to the Seed of Abraham, Messiah. Enoch, Noah, Abraham, Rahab, David. But they had failed over and over again.

If I want something done right, thought a disgusted Belial, *I simply have to do it myself.*

As god of this world, Belial was too legally protected to be captured and imprisoned like the others. But ever since the temptation in the desert, he kept his distance, putting forth the other gods, playing the game board with caution.

The stakes had risen. He was being slowly strangled by a spiritual binding that increased its grip on him like a boa constrictor, as the spirits of the Nephilim were cast out of the land. He was losing his grip on the nations. He knew his time had arrived. He must now lead the fight.

CHAPTER 25

The next day, Demas and Gestas followed Jesus and his group as he returned to the Temple. They didn't want to be noticed by Simon or any of the followers who had gotten to know them up at Caesarea Philippi, so they wore their hoods up and kept their distance. They were spies for Barabbas.

The Sanhedrin had assigned a group of scribes and Pharisees to follow Jesus, in order to keep an eye on his activities and teaching, especially in the temple precinct. Jesus, followed by his disciples, critics, and spies, walked up the broad stairs of the main southern Huldah Gates that led up into the outer court. They passed through the ceilinged Royal Stoa on the way into the court. The columned area was packed with sellers and moneychangers that overflowed into the outer court.

Jesus stepped out onto the marble terrace. All around them, the sounds of marketplace buying and selling filled the morning air. Animals squawked and grunted, baa-ed and bellowed. Worshippers would purchase their animals for sacrifice here and bring them up to the Temple. Because of the distance from which many Jews had traveled, they would have to exchange their currency in order to pay the Temple tax with the standard Tyrian shekel. It was a hive of business, religious business.

Simon and Mary followed behind Jesus and his closest disciples. They saw Jesus stop and look around the cacophony of noises and the bustling of activities. He moved over to a pen of sheep and oxen. He pulled some ropes together to make a handmade whip. He opened the pen and used the whip to drive the animals out of their confinement. They squealed and poured out into the temple area, creating havoc. Jesus snapped his whip to drive them toward the Huldah Gates from which they entered.

The owner of the sheep began yelling at him and cursing him. Jesus pushed him aside and walked up to those selling pigeons for the poor to sacrifice. He crashed open the cages and a flurry of birds escaped into the air. Some women screamed.

Some of the men approached to stop him, but Jesus snapped his homemade whip at them to keep them at bay. Then he snapped at those trying to enter the temple area with vessels in their hands.

The disciples all stood frozen in their tracks, not knowing what to do. They had never seen him act like this before. They didn't know how to respond.

Had he become delirious with rage because of the ineffectiveness of his teaching? But he had caused an uproar amidst the ruling class already. He had the attention of the authorities. Maybe it had not been enough for him. Maybe he wanted more.

Demas thought he could teach the Nazarene a trick or two about using a whip. He and Gestas noticed the Roman soldiers standing by, watching, doing nothing. They were actually smiling amongst themselves. To them, this was the harmless tomfoolery of a madman Jew. Something for their entertainment, not restraint.

The next thing he did shocked them all.

Jesus walked right up to the tables of the moneychangers and started overturning their tables. Coins went flying everywhere. The men shouted curses.

Jesus shouted back in a voice that outdid his opponents' anger.

"IT IS WRITTEN, MY HOUSE SHALL BE CALLED A HOUSE OF PRAYER FOR ALL THE NATIONS. BUT YOU HAVE MADE IT A CAVE OF BANDITS!"

People cleared away from Jesus. He stood there alone with heaving chest and wild eyes, his hair a tattered mess about his face.

Demas and Gestas looked at each other. They both knew at that moment that this fool was no leader of an insurrection or army of warriors. He was a frustrated backwoods madman with delusions of grandeur who had fooled enough people with his confused babblings and magic tricks, but whose real impotency was now on display before the world.

The fact that he had condemned the temple itself as a "cave of bandits," the very identity of the Zealots, clearly meant he had no sympathies for their cause. They left to report to Barabbas that they should move ahead with their own plans.

The scribes and Pharisees had enough temerity to speak up and complain to Jesus. One of them stepped forward and said angrily, “You are not the only one here who knows the Scriptures, Rabbi. You quote the prophet Isaiah and you act out this prophecy of yours like Jeremiah acted out his prophecies. But Jeremiah stood in the divine council of Yahweh. By what authority do you perform this theatrical prediction?”

Jesus responded, “I will tell you by what authority I do this if you first tell me if the baptism of John was from heaven or from man?”

Simon and Mary overheard the Pharisees discussing amongst themselves. Jesus had them on the horns of a dilemma. If they said, “from heaven,” then he would say, “Why did you not believe him?” And if they said, “from man,” then the people would stone them because they believed John was a prophet. The lead Pharisee said, “We do not know where it came from.”

Jesus retorted with contemptuous spite, “Then neither will I tell you by what authority I do these things.”

Another scribe shouted out, “What sign then do you show us for doing these things?”

Jesus looked about and said through clenched teeth, “Destroy this temple and in three days, I will raise it up.”

The religious authorities looked at one another, surprised at the absurdity. One of the scribes called out, “It has taken forty-six years to build this temple, and you will raise it up in three days?”

Jesus shook his head and said nothing.

Another scribe reached down and picked up a denarius from the ground. Simon could see that this one had penetrating, skeptical eyes. He lacked the shock and offense of the others. The scribe noticed some Herodians had gathered around and smirked with satisfaction. He said with a sarcastic tone, “Jesus we know that you are true, and teach the way of Yahweh truthfully. You do not care about anyone’s opinion, for you are not swayed by outward appearances or status.”

Simon scowled. This one reeked with diabolical intentions.

The scribe continued, “Tell us, then, what you think. Is it lawful to pay taxes to Caesar or not?”

The attempt to trap him did not intimidate Jesus. He said, “Why do you put me to the test, you hypocrites?” Voices of shock and offense went through the gathering crowd of religious leaders.

“Show me the coin for the tax.”

The scribe tossed the coin at Jesus. He caught it, still glaring at the scribe with angry eyes. There was something about the scribe that seemed inhuman, as if he was a creature impersonating a man. Simon knew that creature was trying to trap Jesus into defying Caesar, which was tantamount to treason, and therefore worthy of death.

Jesus slowly approached the scribe, while continuing to stare into his eyes. He raised the coin as he moved, showing it to everyone. "Whose likeness and inscription is this?"

Someone shouted out, "Caesar!"

Another said, "Our king!"

Simon and Mary saw that the Roman soldiers had moved closer to listen in, ready to respond to any call for uprising.

Jesus now stood face to face with the scribe. Simon saw the deviant step back just a little, as if in deference.

Jesus spoke to the crowd, while still glaring at the scribe. "Therefore, render to Caesar the things that are Caesar's and to God, the things that are God's." And he tossed the coin away. The crowd murmured. The soldiers looked at one another with uncertainty. Nothing illegal about that. What could they do?

Simon heard Jesus whisper to the scribe, "Leave, Belial."

The scribe turned in anger and trampled out toward the gates.

Jesus looked around at the accumulation of religious authorities. He said, "Woe to you, scribes and Pharisees, hypocrites and actors! You are like whitewashed tombs, which outwardly appear beautiful, but within are full of dead men's bones and all uncleanness. So, you outwardly appear righteous to others, but within you are full of hypocrisy and the lawlessness of Belial."

The religious authorities around him began to rumble with anger and even shout curses. But Jesus kept going. He pronounced woes upon their pettiness in keeping detailed religious rituals while negating the weightier things of the Law of God, such as justice and mercy and faithfulness.

Someone yelled out, "We have the Law and Prophets!"

"Yes," replied Jesus. "And you are sons of those who murdered the prophets. Fill up then the measure of your fathers! You vipers, you Seed of the Serpent! How are you to escape being sentenced to Gehenna?"

Some of the authorities were so vexed, they left in a huff. Only the hecklers remained. "You blaspheme!" yelled one.

Jesus continued unabated. "I send you prophets and wise men and scribes, some of whom you kill and crucify, and others you flog and persecute. And because of this, upon you may come all the righteous blood shed on earth, from the blood of righteous Abel to the blood of Zechariah, whom you murdered between the sanctuary and the altar. Truly, I say to you, all these things will come upon this very generation."

By this point, the scribes and Pharisees had left. Only stragglers and onlookers remained. The disciples had cowered around the pillars, trying not to be noticed.

Then Simon and Mary saw Jesus cry. Mary moved to comfort him, but Simon held her back.

Jesus cried out, "O Jerusalem, Jerusalem, the city that kills the prophets and stones those who are sent to her! How often would I have gathered your children together as a hen gathers her brood under her wings. But you were not willing. See, your house is left to you desolate!" He gestured all around him to the temple area.

Now, even the Romans were leaving this madman to his meaningless babbling.

"For I tell you, you will not see me again, until you say, 'Blessed is he who comes in the name of Yahweh!"

He finally stopped. He wiped his eyes of tears, and began to walk toward the eastern Shushan Gate.

The disciples followed tenuously. They felt like cowards. They had not moved to support their lord, because they were too shocked and frightened by his words.

Mary turned to Simon and said, "What did he mean by this display? The scribes said he was acting like a prophet. What did that mean?"

Simon explained to her as they followed through the Court of the Gentiles toward the east exit. "The prophet Jeremiah performed many of his prophecies as dramas before the people. Jesus was not trying to fix the problem of temple corruption by throwing over tables and releasing animals. He is but one man. What he was doing was similar to Jeremiah. He was prophesying through dramatic display."

"What kind of prophesy?"

Simon whispered it to her, "The destruction of the Temple."

She looked at him with shock. "But the Temple is the heart and soul of our religion. It is the means of atonement for sin. Why would Yahweh want to destroy the Temple?"

"To build a new one, pure and undefiled."

She tried to follow, "The one he said he would build in three days?"

"Mary, he was referring to his own body with that statement. The temple of his body."

She could not quite put it all together. Questions were filling her mind like the cacophony of noise around them.

"What did the scribes mean by a prophet standing in the divine council?"

"The authority of the prophets derives from their being called into Yahweh's throne room before the holy Sons of God. It is like a heavenly court. And the prophets are the prosecutors of Yahweh's spiritual lawsuits. If you haven't stood in the divine council, you do not have the authority of a prophet of Yahweh."

"Has Jesus ever stood before the divine council?"

"He is *one of* the divine council. The unique one-of-a-kind Son of God, uncreated. Remember how he refers to himself as the 'Son of Man?'"

"Yes. How can he be a Son of Man, *and* the Son of God?"

"Because he is both. Daniel the prophet had a heavenly vision of the Son of Man ascending on the clouds to the very right hand of Yahweh, the Ancient of Days. The right hand of Yahweh is the place of his omnipotent power. The Son of God is the second Yahweh in heaven."

Simon then quoted the prophet from memory,

"'And to him was given dominion
and glory and a kingdom,
that all peoples, nations, and languages
should serve him;
his dominion is an everlasting dominion,
which shall not pass away,
and his kingdom one
that shall not be destroyed.'"

Simon was clearly bothered by the ramifications.

He said, "Jesus is prosecuting a heavenly lawsuit against Israel."

CHAPTER 26

Longinus with thirty other Legionary officers finished a chant of the greatness of Mithras as "sol invictus," the unconquered sun. They filled the benches of the small rectangular Mithras temple and shrine. It was a vaulted subterranean chamber just outside the Antonia, created for their secret new religion. Pontius Pilate led the group by virtue of being the senior member of the gathering. The membership consisted mostly of Roman army officers, from legates to tribunes and centurions and even some lower level ranks like optios. As a religion of privilege, they kept their activities mostly secret, including the initiation rites each must undergo to join.

Pilate elevated a chalice of wine and a bone of bull's meat and said, "This is the flesh and blood of our god, Mithras the mighty. Let us eat and become one with the power."

The officers ate their meal on a long table the length of the cave. Above them, the vaulted ceiling had the stars of heaven engraved in its arch. The temple was, like all temples, a representation of the cosmos. The centerpiece of that cosmos was a large stone relief of the god Mithras in human form, engaged in tauroctony, the slaying of the sacred bull. Mithras held the nose of the bull with his left hand and pierced him with a sword in his right. The signs of the zodiac encircled the engraving, along with several scenes from the myth of Mithras: his birth from a cosmic rock encircled by the Serpent of wisdom; and a feast of the Bull's flesh called the "Banquet of the Sun," which they now re-enacted.

Longinus felt refreshed by his involvement in the ritual feast, its rules, its orderly regulations. Down here, he could have the peace of focus, away from the noise and pungent smells in the Semitic "holy city," with its massive influx of traveling Jews from every corner of the earth. The only holy city to him was the eternal city, Rome, with its classic architecture of perfection and heavenly beauty. These backwater Jews and their primitive tribal culture seemed to create nothing of lasting permanence beyond its singular temple complex, and even *that* displayed Greco-Roman influence and Phoenician design. The only beautiful things in this Mediterranean garbage dump were its Roman structures, the Hippodrome, the theater, and Herod's palace, all built by Herod, the Roman sympathizer.

Longinus sighed. He just wanted to find his seditious bandits, crucify them and get back to leading his century in battles for the Empire.

After they finished the meal, censers were lit with an incense of special intoxicating herbs. The aroma gave the initiates an inebriated high. They laughed and joked through the smoky haze, but eventually stumbled out of the sanctuary to return behind the walls of the Antonia.

After the initiates left, Longinus stayed behind alone, for contemplation. The misty haze still hung in the enclosed underground temple.

He closed his eyes and prayed to Mithras for help to find his criminals. A voice interrupted his prayer.

"Longinus."

He stopped and looked up. Before him, in the hanging mist, stood a being eight feet tall, with glimmering bronze skin.

Longinus froze. He murmured, "Mithras?"

It did not answer him. He felt the terrible greatness of the being. It was rather skeletal and androgynous looking, unlike the masculine muscular features he expected of the warrior god. But it was frightening still. Longinus had never been very spiritual in his leanings. He performed Mithraic cult acts more out of obedience to his military order than out of actual belief.

But now everything he believed had been stood on its head.

"Who are you, my lord?"

"The principality of Rome. Chief of the gods."

"Jupiter?"

The being said, "Think of me as you will. I know of your commission, Longinus. That you seek Barabbas and his Zealot criminals. I have heard your prayers."

Longinus whispered, "My lord and god."

The principality said, "I am here to help you find them."

•••••

Before Jesus could make his way through the crowds of the outer court to the Shushan Gate of the temple, he was stopped in Solomon's colonnade. A group of about twenty Pharisees blocked his way.

One of them shouted out, "If you are the Messiah, tell us plainly!"

The disciples gathered near him.

He said to his accusers, "I told you and you do not believe. The works that I do in my Father's name bear witness to me. But you do not believe because you are not among my sheep. My sheep hear my voice and I know them, and they follow me. I give them eternal life and they will never perish, and no one will snatch them out of my hand."

Another countered, "Who are you to claim such greatness?"

"My Father, who has given them to me, is greater than all, and no one is able to snatch them out of the Father's hand. I and the Father are one."

The members in the group looked at each other in agreement. They drew stones out of their sacks. They had obviously prepared for this in advance. The leader, a scrawny, tall man, said to his comrades, "You heard him. Blasphemy! He makes himself out to be God!"

The disciples drew near. Peter, James, and John stepped in front of Jesus to take the stones for him if needed.

Jesus moved them apart so that he could look the scrawny leader in the eye. Then he spoke to the entire group of them.

"Is it not written in your Law, 'I said you are gods?' If he called them gods to whom the word of God came—and Scripture cannot be broken—do you say of him whom the Father consecrated and sent into the world, 'You are blaspheming,' because I said, 'I am the Son of God'?"

It flustered the accusers. They could not answer.

Simon whispered to Mary, "That is what we spoke of earlier. Jesus is one of the divine council."

Simon didn't have the time to explain that the Psalm Jesus quoted also described Yahweh's judgment upon the other gods of the nations for their usurpation of justice.

Jesus said to the Pharisees, "What do you think about the Messiah? Whose son is he?"

The scrawny one spoke up again. "The son of David!"

"How is it then," said Jesus, "that David, in the Spirit, calls him Lord, saying. 'The Lord says to my Lord, 'sit at my right hand, until I put all your enemies under your feet''? If David calls him Lord, how is he his son?"

The Pharisees stood perplexed. They muttered to one another, but could not give an answer.

Simon whispered to Mary, "He is saying that Messiah must be more than a man. He transcends David. He is David's god."

Mary understood the language of conquest as well. A triumphant king's foot on the neck of his enemies was total victory and dominance. Jesus was claiming full authority over the powers. But when? When would he make good on this promise? Where were his armies?

A Sadducee pushed his way forward in the crowd. He made way for a group of Sadducees behind him. He was an elder who carried himself with much pride. He called out, "Rabbi, I have a question about resurrection!"

Simon grumbled, "Will these competitions never end?" The Sadducees always seemed to want to start a fight over resurrection, since they detested the belief.

The proud one said, "Now, Moses said, 'If a man dies having no children, his brother must marry the widow and raise up offspring for his brother.' Am I misinformed?"

"No," said Jesus.

Simon could not stand the mocking contempt of the questioner. He knew it was only mere moments before the Sadducee would turn into an accuser, like all the others.

"Well, you see then," said the proud man, "I have a problem. Because I know this family who had seven brothers. The first married and died, having no offspring. So he left his wife to his brother. Then that second died and gave her to the third."

Simon saw it coming.

"So too, all seven of the brothers died, handing off the woman as their wife. Ultimately the woman died as well. So, in the resurrection, of the seven brothers, whose wife will she be? For they all had her as their wife."

He ended with a sarcastic smile, assuring himself of catching Jesus in a trap.

But Jesus said, "You are wrong, because you know neither the Scriptures nor the power of God. For in the resurrection, they neither marry nor are given in marriage, for there is no marriage in heaven."

Now Simon had the joy of seeing the Sadducee accusers stumped.

Jesus added, "And as for the resurrection of the dead, have you not read what was said to you by God?"

He was turning the sarcasm back on his accusers. Delightful.

"'I am the god of Abraham, and the god of Isaac, and the god of Jacob.' He is not the god of the dead, but of the living."

Jesus then walked straight through them.

They parted with stunned faces.

The disciples quickly followed after Jesus.

Mary turned her head and stuck her tongue out at the Sadducees and Pharisees as she passed.

CHAPTER 27

Gestas stepped out onto the proscenium arch of the large Roman theater. He looked up into the three tiers of audience seats called the *cavea*. Unlike the more gradual inclines of the Grecian theater built on the hills of his native Scythopolis, this one in the city of Jerusalem had to maximize its use of minimum space. So it towered three stories upward with steep seating.

The auditorium was empty at the moment. Gestas closed his eyes and imagined it filled to capacity with patrons. He could hear the music and chorus singing praises in the orchestra below him.

He was Hercules, and they worshipped him as he accomplished his twelve labors ending in the underworld of Hades. He re-enacted once again his victory over the three-headed hound of hell, Cerberus. He could hear in his mind the resounding applause of his many performances.

He missed the theater and its glory. Strangely though, he also remembered that it seemed that the more praise and worship he received, the more he needed just to feel significant, to feel loved. A poor reception of one of his performances brought on deep depression and anxiety, sometimes even suicidal thoughts. Now, that was all gone. He was no longer the center of attention, but rather a part of something bigger than himself, something that would outlast him. He was part of changing the world, relieving suffering, and bringing hope to his fellow Jews for deliverance. The armed robbery of the rich who oppressed the common folk was simply an inconvenient necessity in order to finance their moral cause. Sometimes, you had to do evil in order to achieve the greater good.

"Gestas, what are you doing?" a voice came from behind him.

He turned to see Demas opening the curtain. Behind his brother a dozen other men carried piles of costume clothing. They were stealing Roman soldier costumes for their plan, an adaptation of the one used to free him from the Roman prison.

"We have to get out of here now. If we get caught, our whole strategy will be undone."

Because of the Passover feast, there would be no performances for another week in the holy city. The theft would not be discovered until after the uprising.

Gestas said, "Do you ever miss the arena? The glory?"

Demas's face stilled with memory. "Not so much."

Gestas looked surprised. Demas explained, "That's where you and I differ. You did it to live. I did it to die."

"But if you *had* died, it would have been glorious, would it have not?"

Demas thought a bit. "I suppose there is a certain—glory—in the thrill. It was in the face of death that I felt most fully alive. It has been pain that has made me appreciate life. But in the end, we are all dead."

"And forgotten," added Gestas.

"We may die with this gamble," said Demas. "And if captured—"

"I *know* what the punishment for sedition is." The fate of their comrades in the Galilean caves was still stark in their memory.

"It's already too late," said Demas. "We might as well try something bold, if not mad."

"But what if we succeed? What if Messiah really does show up? What if Barabbas is—"

Demas put up his hand to stop him. "Don't, Gestas. All our lives we have been abandoned. We have had to make our own way. No one will show up at the last minute. No one will save us, but ourselves."

Gestas stared out into the barren theater, the setting sun causing deep shadows to move over the stone.

He grinned darkly. "Let us take our bows—for an encore performance."

•••••

Simon sat with Mary Magdalene on the Mount of Olives, overlooking the Temple. It was the end of the day. The setting sun created a reddish-orange backdrop glow to the city.

They were about a hundred feet higher than the Temple walls and the crest of the hill was several thousand feet away. Jesus had recently finished his sermon on the destruction of the holy city and its temple. The meaning that Simon had been figuring out by implication, Jesus had finally said explicitly. For all of his teaching on love, mercy, and atonement in the Kingdom of God, this prophecy had deeply bothered all the disciples.

As they looked out upon the wonderful stones and noble buildings of the temple mount, Jesus had shocked them all. He had said that there would not be one stone of the Temple that would not be thrown down. Complete desolation. It would be the end of the world for them.

When asked when it would all happen, the sign of his coming as Messiah, and the end of the old age, Jesus had responded that all the things he was about to tell them would come upon their own generation—within the next forty years.

He said that the Pax Romana they currently lived under would be unsettled with many wars and rumors of wars. It was hard to believe for most of them, because the might and power of Rome seemed so invincible. But it did coincide with Daniel's prophecy of the Messianic stone that would crush the last kingdom after Greece, the statue's feet of iron and clay, the empire of Rome.

There were many false prophets, false messiahs, and much persecution to come for the true remnant of believers. They had already seen some of them. The lawlessness of the sons of Belial would increase. But the good news of the kingdom would be proclaimed throughout the entire Roman empire, the whole world to them, before the end would come.

Simon had explained to Mary that the "end of the age" was the end of the old covenant embodied in the sacrifices of the holy Temple. When Yahweh made a covenant with Moses, it was like the creation of the cosmos of the heavens and the earth.

You divided the sea by your might;
you broke the heads of the sea monsters on the waters.
You crushed the heads of Leviathan;
you gave him as food for the creatures of the wilderness.
You split open springs and brooks;
you dried up ever-flowing streams.
Yours is the day, yours also the night;
you have established the heavenly lights and the sun.
You have fixed all the boundaries of the earth.
A Maskil of Asaph

When that covenant was ended, it would be the end of the cosmos, and a new heavens and earth would commence. A new covenant that the prophet Jeremiah had promised and the prophet Haggai warned with poetic flourish.

For thus says the LORD of hosts: Yet once more, in a little while, I will shake the heavens and the earth and the sea and

> *the dry land. And I will shake all nations, so that the treasures of all nations shall come in, and I will fill this house with glory, says the LORD of hosts.*

They were living in the last days of the old covenant. Messiah would bring the Day of the Lord and change everything forever.

Jesus had warned them of the great tribulation to come, when the "abomination of desolation"—the Roman armies with their eagle standards—would surround the holy city and trample the Temple underfoot.

Mary asked Simon, "When will they come?"

Simon replied, "So far, the Romans have been able to crush the various uprisings of individual bandit leaders like Judas of Galilee, Athronges, Simon of Herod. But if the others still alive and on the loose could be unified behind a central figure, that kind of revolt would bring—."

"Armageddon," she whispered.

He nodded. "The sun darkening, stars falling from the dome of the sky, and the shaking of the powers of heaven is the Scriptural language for the removal of earthly rulers and their heavenly powers over them. The dispossession of the land and the disinheritance of the gods by the New Covenant of Messiah."

She had already been familiar with the poetry of gods coming on clouds in Canaanite scripture. Ba'al was described as the great Cloud Rider, the most high god, bringing judgment. So when Jesus had used the same language of himself coming on the clouds, he was claiming to bring Yahweh's hand of judgment upon Israel, who had rejected him. He would use the armies of Rome as an axe in his hand. Isaiah had said the same of the Assyrians. Mary said, "So the sign of the Son of Man's judgment on the tribes of the Promised Land is the destruction of the temple."

He added, "Which ends the Old Covenant and its shadows of atonement, and replaces it with the New Covenant."

She scrunched her face in confusion. "You have told me that Daniel says the Messiah will put an end to sacrifice and offering. But how?"

"I do not know, Mary. He won't tell us."

"It must be a secret to us so that it will be a secret to his enemies as well."

Simon nodded in agreement.

Mary remembered that Jesus had told them all that the Son of Man would suffer and be rejected by this generation. That he would be killed and on the third day raised. She wondered if the disciples were missing it in their understanding of Messiah. They had assumed all along that Messiah would be an earthly conqueror. What other kind of deliverer could there be for such oppression under Rome? They could not conceive of suffering as a means of victory. That was why Peter had rebuked Jesus for saying so at Caesarea Philippi. But she remembered Jesus had then called him "Accuser" to his face. And she remembered Simon telling her of the words of John the Baptizer at Jesus's baptism, "Behold, the lamb of God, who takes away the sins of the world."

What if Yahweh's anointed servant would suffer rather than attack? What if Messiah himself would replace the sacrifice with his own suffering? A human sacrifice of Yahweh's own son? She shuddered at the heresy. She would speak of it to no one.

CHAPTER 28

The feast of Passover officially began in the afternoon of the fourteenth day of the month of Nissan, the beginning of spring. The disciples James and John carried their Paschal lamb in the long lines of worshippers. They were led in large groups from the outer Court of Gentiles through the Gate Beautiful into the inner Court of Women in the Temple. Each of them had lambs that would substitute for companies of ten to twenty people each.

Then, a group of thirty were allowed through the Nicanor Gate into the Court of Priests. The massive gates closed behind them. In their turn, James held the lamb while John cut its throat with a knife. A trio of priests drew a threefold blast from their silver trumpets with every slaying of a lamb.

Other priests then caught the blood in golden and silver bowls, which were passed up to the priest at the large stone altar. He jerked each bowl at the base of the altar in one splash.

Behind them, a chorus of priests led in a solemn hymn of praise to Yahweh, with the presenters singing in response.

The Levites sang, “Hallelujah!”

The people responded, Hallelujah!”

“When Israel went out of Egypt!”

“When Israel went out of Egypt!”

“The house of Jacob from a people of strange language.”

“Save now, I beseech thee, Yahweh.”

“Blessed is he that comes in the name of Yahweh!”

The sacrificial lambs were hung up while other priests flayed them, cut out the entrails, and separated the fat. They placed the fat in a dish, salted it and threw it on the fire of the altar for burnt offering.

When the sacrifice was complete, James and John took the lamb back with them for the Passover feast with Jesus and the disciples.

As they left, the next section of worshippers were let in with their lambs. The process began all over again, until the entire nation had participated.

James and John left the Temple and made their way to the Shushan Gate to return to the Mount of Olives. They passed by a large, staged platform with several royal seats, guarded by a company of twenty Roman soldiers and heralded by three Levitical priests. Any minute, the tetrarchs Antipas and Philip, accompanied by the high priest Caiaphas and the Roman prefect Pilate, would arrive to take their seats in oversight of the early day's activities. It was official business. It bored them all, but it had to be done for a show of participation. Pilate would be there to oversee the sacrifice made on behalf of Caesar.

But the leaders were late.

A group of ten priests approached the dais.

The three priests already at the platform were Barabbas, Demas and Gestas in stolen disguise. The twenty Roman soldiers, their Zealots in Roman costume, with other Zealots hidden in the crowd.

Barabbas leaned in to Demas and muttered below his breath, "The Herods and Pilate should have been here an hour ago."

Demas whispered back, eyes focused on the arriving priests, "They are going to recognize us as imposters. We'll be discovered."

Barabbas muttered to his soldiers, "Follow my lead."

The priests were almost upon them.

Demas looked around. The hustle and bustle of the crowd paid no attention to them. Could they get away if they had to?

The priests stopped before Barabbas, Demas and Gestas and began to give their matter of fact report. The lead, an obvious neophyte, said, "Have you not received the order? Pilate and the Herods are not coming."

"We are new to the ranks, brother," said Barabbas.

The neophyte looked at them curiously. "I am new. I do not remember you in the classes." His eyes narrowed, then widened as his suspicion increased.

Barabbas turned to the Soldiers around the display. "We've been betrayed. Kill these priests!"

The faux soldiers responded immediately. They were in tune with their leader.

The priests could not believe what they heard. They froze like ten frightened lambs.

It made the slaughter that much quicker and easier.

The blades of the soldiers sliced, hacked and severed the priests into a gruesome bloodbath, like lambs on an altar.

Passersby screamed in shock.

It drew attention to the platform.

Barabbas jumped up and yelled to the crowd with all his lungs, "THE ROMANS HAVE KILLED OUR PRIESTS!"

Twenty other men of Barabbas' gang rushed out of the crowd and pretended to kill the soldiers. They thrust their swords safely by the sides of their disguised comrades. They faked slashes to bring about false vengeance on the Romans. They had given the crowds something to react to.

Barabbas continued, "SONS OF ABRAHAM, WE HAVE BEEN ATTACKED BY THE ROMAN FORCES OF CAESAR IN OUR MOST HOLY PLACE! WE MUST RISE UP AND FIGHT BACK! TO ARMS! TO ARMS!"

The crowds edged away from the scene of bloodshed. They could not see that it was all an act, a false flag intended to incite a riot.

And riot was beginning to stir.

"FIND ALL ROMANS AND SLAUGHTER THEM IN THE NAME OF YAHWEH!"

The Zealots raised their swords and shouted a war cry in support. All the crowd could see was a bloodbath and their trusted Jewish priests calling upon them to fight.

Shouts in the crowd agitated more. "NO KING BUT GOD! NO KING BUT GOD!"

Shouts of agreement could be heard. Anger grew. They were becoming a mob.

Pent up fury and hatred for their oppressors began to spill out of the souls of the masses. Demas began to think that maybe they could get this plan going after all.

Suddenly, a thousand Roman soldiers stepped out in military unison from all around the temple porticos of pillars. They were in fighting formation, surrounding the masses with shield and lance, ready to put down the riot.

The gates to the underground tunnel connecting the Antonia burst open and a cavalry of fifty men on horseback, led by Pontius Pilate, entered the outer Court of Gentiles.

Antipas, Caiaphas and Longinus were with him. The high priest blew a shofar trumpet, normally used as a call to worship. The rage and unity of the crowd began to dissolve.

A hundred legionaries surrounded Barabbas, the Zealots and the "dead" faux soldiers. Some of the pseudo-corpses stood up in fear.

Barabbas and the two brothers stood in shock on the dais. They had been betrayed. But by who?

Pilate gestured up above them on the roof of the portico.

Barabbas saw a contingent of archers, with arrows nocked and aimed at them. They wouldn't stand a chance. He nodded to the other Zealots. They dropped their weapons.

The mob that had only moments before begun to build into murderous rage, were now tamed and open-mouthed with curiosity.

Antipas turned and yelled to the crowd, " I AM HEROD ANTIPAS, KING OF GALILEE AND PEREA! THERE IS NO REVOLT! RETURN TO YOUR ACTIVITIES!"

Pilate rolled his eyes, thinking, *Grandstanding twat, using the title of king again instead of tetrarch.*

Barabbas gritted his teeth in anger. *Outplayed with my own game.*

A group of soldiers grabbed the three counterfeit priests and brought them up to Pilate on his horse. Their coverings were torn from their heads. Their hands shackled behind their backs.

Pilate looked back at Longinus, who nodded.

Pilate made a hand gesture to the soldiers surrounding the fifty Zealot captives. They backed up.

Demas could see what was going to happen.

Barabbas screamed, "NOOOOOOOOOOO!"

The guards held him back.

Pilate yelled, "RELEASE!"

From up above, the archers released their arrows and pierced every one of the Zealots with lethal missiles. They went down in a rainstorm of wood and bronze. All of them fell dead, the fake legionaries with them.

All of them, save one, who was still hidden in the shadows of a column in the portico. Eleazar ben Dinai. Barabbas had appointed his most trusted right hand to continue the movement should they fail. He disappeared into the masses of the faithful. But he would never forget his fallen comrades, nor their horrible ambush of death.

Barabbas and Gestas wept.

Demas stood stone-faced. They got the easy way out.

Longinus said to them, "Jesus Barabbas, Demas and Gestas Samaras, you are under arrest for murder, sedition and insurrection."

Pilate said, "To the Antonia with them."

•••••

Belial walked through the streets of Jerusalem, freely and unseen. He was proud of the fact that he could do as he pleased within what was supposed to be the holy city. And why? Because the people of Israel had so thoroughly rejected Yahweh for so long with their layers of idolatry and self-salvation that they hardened themselves to the living God. It made them open to him. Like a prostitute, Israelites had fornicated with the gods of Canaan for so long, they no longer knew what love of their husband Yahweh was. Their many factions fought over the works of Torah, yet here was Messiah in their very midst, and none of them even recognized him.

He licked his lips. How delicious. Except for that despicable remnant of true believers. If it weren't for them, he would be dancing on the grave of God. But they were few, and manageable for Belial. As long as he had his useful idiots involved, he had power to create chaos and chicanery. And Belial had a specific useful idiot in mind, embedded within the very heart of Yahweh's own foundational remnant. He may yet dance on that grave.

Belial had been working this one for quite a while. Iscariot, the son of perdition. He virtually owned the man. Though he was considered one of the twelve disciples of Jesus, and trusted with the privilege of the money purse, Judas Iscariot pilfered from it every chance he could get.

He was the perfect counterfeit, someone who couldn't believe fully in anything, so he half committed to everything out of pure survival instinct. Waiting to side with the winners. Judas was not a man of great sins, but of many little ones. It was the little ones that primed a soul for useful service to Belial.

Because Belial was a member of the original divine council, he had heavenly flesh. It had transcendent properties that earthly flesh did not have. He was immortal and could move between the heavenly and the earthly realms. But he could also eat physical food as angels could, and even procreate with human women, as the original fallen Sons of God in the days of Noah. But unlike the spirits of the Nephilim, he was not pure spirit in search of a body. He already had a body, so he could not inhabit a human the way a demon could.

One thing he could do was to enter a human through their consciousness. He could manipulate them from a distance like puppets. By projecting his mind into the mind of a willing "bag of bones" as he called such fools, he could steer them any way he wished. Fine. Let them think they were "free," that they had complete autonomy from all other sources of influence or control outside of themselves. Let them think they were the ultimate arbiters of their decisions and destinies, masters of their fate, captains of their souls. That gave him even more control because they no longer trusted Yahweh, but rather their own will to power. His nemesis said it well, they were all slaves of sin. Belial was their master.

Yahweh has mercy on whom he has mercy and compassion on whom he has compassion. Well, I have malice on whom I have malice and contempt on whom I have contempt.

He turned down an alley and stood outside the home of a certain man, where the disciples had all gathered for their disgusting Passover meal. He gazed in the window and saw all thirteen of them laid out on their mats before the meal. Jesus had broken bread and gave thanks to Yahweh. Then he said, "This is my body, which is given for you. Do this in remembrance of me." He passed it around and the disciples ate the bread in unity.

Then Jesus took a cup of wine and held it up saying, "Drink of it, all of you, for this is my blood of the new covenant, which is poured out for many for the forgiveness of sins."

A ringing started in Belial's ears. He turned away with grinding teeth and clenched fists. Jesus was establishing a sacrament. Belial hated sacraments. He detested them with all his being. They were incarnate means of grace. Acts of spiritual warfare. The ringing grew to a piercing level that seemed it would make his head explode. It drove him mad with anger.

This was it. It was now or never. He looked back in upon the gathering, found his prey, focused his consciousness, and entered Iscariot.

CHAPTER 29

Barabbas awoke to the sound of a contingent of soldiers entering the dungeon area. He was in a prison cell in the Antonia. He saw Gestas and Demas already awake in a separate cell across the way.

The centurion walked up to the bars and spoke. "I am to take you to the palace on the other side of the city."

Barabbas said, "You are the one who has been hunting us since we broke out from the Scythopolis prison."

"Yes. I serve the orders of the prefect."

The guards shackled Barabbas' hands and feet.

"Impressive," said Barabbas.

"Disappointing," said Longinus, looking him up and down.

"I outfoxed you for some time."

Longinus raised his brow. It was a good point.

Barabbas asked, "How did you find out about our plan? Who betrayed us?"

"No one betrayed you."

"Then how did you know?"

"I remembered your dirty little trick back in Scythopolis impersonating a centurion." He didn't have the temerity to admit that Mithras, or Jupiter, or whoever it was, had visited him and told him of their plans. It was all a blur of memory to him now. He had even begun to question whether he had actually had the divine encounter.

Barabbas nodded. Of course. He stared defiantly into Longinus' eyes and said, "No king but God. No god but God."

"Guards, take him away."

Barabbas was taken to the upper city on the northwest side. He looked up into the beautiful Greco-Roman stone edifice of Herod's fortress. A large crowd of agitated Sanhedrin leaders and public onlookers had gathered at the entrance of the praetorium, Pilate's headquarters. The guards took Barabbas into the praetorium through the tower gates on the north side of the complex to avoid the unruly crowd.

He was thrown into the holding cell inside the praetorium. He could see flogging poles in the courtyard and winced at his fate.

Longinus left him, returning to the Antonia.

A group of Herodian guards escorted a prisoner from the far end of the yard toward the holding cell. Barabbas could see it was the Nazarene. Herod Antipas followed them in and Pilate met them from the exit.

The guards pushed Jesus into the cell with Barabbas. Herod dismissed them. The Nazarene wore a purple royal robe, an obvious mockery of his Messianic claims. Barabbas could see he had a black eye and bruising from being roughed up by the soldiers already.

Pilate and Antipas stood at the cell door.

Antipas sighed and said, "He won't speak to me, the little rodent."

Pilate said, "Well, my dear Antipas, it appears we finally have something in common. I like the robe. Clever."

Antipas said, "All these years, I wanted to find the man. Interrogate him. At one point, I even feared he might be the prophet John back from the dead. Only to find out he's just another pathetic clown seeking attention."

He looked over at Jesus, in the corner wiping blood from his nose. "Well, how do you like the attention, clown?"

Antipas turned back to Pilate. "I humbly thank you, my prefect, for including me in on this deliberation."

"Well, he is a Galilean," said Pilate. "I owe you that much."

Antipas looked at him, surprised. Antipas had been the one to complain to Caesar when Pilate put the standards inside the Temple. Antipas saw this as his first chance to mend his relationship with the prefect for political interests. He said, "I find him—incorrigible and seditious."

Pilate said with a smile, "All you Jews are incorrigible."

Antipas smiled in deference. No argument there.

Pilate sobered. "The city is in an uproar, and over what? Another one of dozens of fools who claim to be your deliverer. I don't find guilt in him. You Jews and your doctrinal disputes. You want to kill each other over petty differences of interpretation of your sacred texts. So he claims to be 'the Son of God.' What do I care for such insanity? He doesn't even have the temerity to defend himself. At least Barabbas over there actually committed a crime worthy of death."

Antipas offered, "There is the custom of Passover release."

Pilate looked at him with renewed interest. "Yes, there is. I almost forgot. That should be interesting."

Every year during the feast, Pilate would release a single prisoner by recommendation of the crowd. It was his twisted version of displaying godlike mercy.

Antipas said, "I want you to know that whatever you decide, you will have the full support of the Herodian leadership behind you. Now, if you please, I have a pressing matter back in my palace to attend to."

Antipas bowed and left Pilate alone with the two prisoners.

Pilate said, "Nazarene." Jesus looked at him. He gestured with his finger for the Jew to come close to the bars.

Jesus coughed, held his bruised rib, and stumbled over to the bars.

Pilate said, "Do you know my wife has had dreams about you? She tells me to have nothing to do with you."

Jesus said nothing.

Pilate said, "I am going to ask you one last time, are you the King of the Jews?"

Jesus finally spoke up. "Do you say this of your own accord, or did others say it to you about me?"

"He speaks. Finally. Am I a Jew? Your own nation and the chief priests have delivered you over to me. What have you done?"

Pilate felt the look the Nazarene gave him was one of pity. He felt anger arise in him. He shook it off. He would not let such a worthless plebeian affect his countenance.

Jesus said, "My kingdom is not of this world. If my kingdom were of this world, my servants would have been fighting on my behalf."

"Ah, so you are a king?"

"You say that I am a king. For this purpose I was born and for this purpose I have come into the world—to bear witness to the truth. And everyone who is of the truth listens to my voice."

Pilate chuckled. "Well, you certainly do have visions of grandeur, don't you." He peered at the weak and frail-looking prisoner, barely able to stay standing. "You speak of truth. What is truth? Listen to my voice and I will tell you what is truth." He stepped close to the bars and whispered, "Power is truth."

Pilate turned and walked back out to the crowd in the streets.

Barabbas stared at the Nazarene as he grunted and found another place to sit on the floor.

Barabbas mused, "The Passover release. You may be freed yet."

"Azazel," said the Nazarene.

"What did you say?"

"Azazel. It is a ritual that occurs on the Day of Atonement. Two goats are brought before the high priest. He lays his hands on one of them, and transfers all the sins of the people onto it. They then lead the goat out into the wilderness of Azazel, the place of chaos outside the holy city. The desert of Belial."

"What happens to it?"

"The chaos consumes it. The other goat is for Yahweh. It is sacrificed as a sin offering."

The sounds of the crowd outside grew increasingly agitated.

Roman soldiers entered the praetorium and opened up the cell. They brought the two prisoners through the yard and out onto the outer porch of the entrance where Pilate awaited them.

The crowd yelled smears and curses as Barabbas and Jesus were presented before Pilate.

Pilate quieted down the crowd, and then spoke, "I have two Jesuses before you. Whom do you want me to release for you, Jesus who is called Barabbas, or Jesus who is called Messiah?"

Barabbas thought, *Two goats of the same name. Who is the true Son of the Father?*

The crowd yelled in a cacophony of yells and screams. The name most clearly heard was Barabbas.

Barabbas heard Pilate mumble to himself, "Damned fools."

He raised his voice again, "Tell me again, which of the two do you want me to release for you?"

Someone started a chant that drowned out any other meager voices for Jesus in the crowd. "Bar-abbas, Bar-abbas, Bar-abbas!"

Barabbas could not believe it. He was going to be set free. They were choosing him over the peaceful lamb of the Nazarene. He couldn't help but smile. He felt his heart beat out of his chest and his breathing increase. He was going to go free. He was going to go free.

Pilate waved them to be quiet. He shook his head with disgust. "Then what shall I do with Jesus, who is called the King of the Jews?"

A strong dominant voice bellowed, "We have no king but Caesar!" The crowd cheered. Others shouted in agreement, "No king but Caesar!"

Now Barabbas soured. These idiots who were releasing him over the Nazarene were chanting the very opposite of his own slogan, "No king but God." It was against everything he had lived and fought for. He was being championed by blasphemers. He felt sick to his stomach. *What does that make me?*

Barabbas thought of how Pilate had mused about truth, back at the holding cell. But the mob didn't care about truth. They would worship Caesar as quickly and as easily as they would revolt against him. What was Barabbas even fighting for? A pack of cannibals who would eat their own? A nation of traitors?

A new chant started, "Crucify him! Crucify him! Crucify him!"

Pilate whistled. A contingent of fifty soldiers came out from behind him and lined up along the porch in armed readiness. The crowd pulled back in fear, and quieted down.

Pilate nodded and one of the servants brought forth a bowl of water. He reached in and ceremonially washed his hands. He turned back to the crowd and said, "I am innocent of this man's blood. See to it yourselves."

He turned to the guard and said, "Release Barabbas."

A guard released the shackles from Barabbas' hands and feet.

A dominant voice in the crowd yelled, "His blood be on us and on our children!"

Barabbas thought, *It will be, you fools. It will be.*

Pilate told him, "You may go." He turned to the guards beside Jesus. "Scourge him and hand him over."

Barabbas stepped down the steps in uncertainty. He turned to look back. He saw them drag Jesus back into the praetorium for scourging. He knew the serious pain and damage that the whip did to the body. The image that came to him was of the Passover lamb, an innocent, silent, peaceful creature being tethered to a post and slaughtered.

CHAPTER 30

The sharp iron tip of the scourge hit his back and pulled, ripping off flesh and blood. He yelped in pain and pulled on the ropes that tied him to the flogging post. He was completely naked in humiliation. This was only the beginning of a long day of pain ahead of him. He hoped he would have the endurance.

Demas looked over at his brother Gestas, also tied up to a post in the yard of the Antonia. Their backs were shredded from the scourge. Demas didn't know if he could take any more. Ironically, the thought occurred to him what a bad aim his soldier was with the whip. Demas could have been far more effective.

Not that it mattered. He was delirious with pain. He saw the soldier over his brother pull back for another crack, when a voice penetrated the air like a god. "Enough! Get these men their crossbars and walk them to the hill."

He recognized the voice as belonging to Longinus the centurion, their hound of hell.

He felt hands untying the ropes around his wrists. He saw that his brother was barely conscious.

Soldiers brought a wooden crossbar for each prisoner. They placed them on their bloodied shoulders to carry. The brothers both winced in pain.

"Get a move on," said one of the soldiers. He pushed Gestas forward and they began their journey to the crucifixion posts waiting for them up on the hill, three hundred feet away from the fortress.

Demas marched out of the gates and down the Tyropoean Valley with his brother by his side. The centurion Longinus led them on his horse. The impatient soldier pushed them along. Every step was a jarring pain with the weight of the wood upon their torn flesh. But Demas had faced greater feats of daring in the arena. He had felt the claw of the bear, the teeth of the lion, and the madness of the hyena before. He was determined to make it without fainting from blood loss or pain.

Gestas was determined to keep up with his brother. He had been overshadowed by Demas' fortitude his entire life. Now, in the face of death, Gestas wanted to match him. As if they were entering the stage, and they would perform this final act like heroes—together.

Gestas imagined himself as Hercules performing a labor. The mental game gave him a second wind. He pictured himself with mighty bulging muscles on his way to meet Cerberus at the Gates of Hades. He managed a small laugh at himself

"Shut your mouth, bandit!" came the voice of the impatient soldier. He slapped the actor's back with a horse whip. Gestas grimaced in pain.

Demas wanted to throw down his crossbar, pull that pig to the ground, and strangle him.

Longinus looked back from his mount and said, "Leave them be, soldier."

Strange, thought Demas. *As ruthless as this centurion is, he goes no further than the law. He seems quite—just.*

Longinus was tired. He had been hunting these criminals and their leader for too long. He had immersed himself in their thinking and religion in order to understand his enemy. But something had happened in the process. The zeal of these Jews had gotten to him. At first, he could not understand why they refused to submit to Caesar. Why did they seek autonomy, when they were worse off without the civilized culture and iron protection of Rome? Did they prefer to grovel in the mud and stone with their simplistic religion of a bachelor god? But when he was visited by the god, Zeus, or whoever it was, he could not get it out of his mind that he was merely the pawn of a much greater game being played out by the powers. For the first time in his life, he felt used. Manipulated. Was this what the Jews felt in their longing for a deliverer? Is this what their "Son of God" was supposed to do, free them from the control of principalities and powers? Why then had their "messiah" failed? Or was he just another one of the many pretenders to the throne of this "King of the Jews?"

They arrived at the top of the hill, Golgotha, Place of the Skull. There was a figure ahead of them, being hoisted upon his cross, his hands already nailed to the crossbar. The Nazarene.

The wood was taken from the criminals. They were slammed down on the ground, their hands held tightly, as a soldier pounded vicious Roman nails into their wrists and into the crossbar. They screamed in pain.

Longinus had presided over thousands of crucifixions. He had even performed some of them as a young legionary. He had become hardened to the pounding, to the cries for mercy. Why then was he troubled so? He saw the naked humiliation of the Nazarene, moaning in agony above him, and he suddenly felt a betrayer of the law and justice he had sought to uphold.

What happened next to Demas was all a blur. He faded in and out of consciousness as they hoisted him up on his crossbar. Another explosion of stinging pain in his heels as they were nailed on each side of the vertical post.

He looked over and saw his brother, hanging yards away to his left, and in between them was Jesus. They were all three naked and beaten bloody. Jesus had a crown of thorns on his head, an obvious mockery of the sign nailed above him. It had several languages on it, but Demas strained his neck to see it. He could read the Aramaic that said, "King of the Jews."

Below him, Demas saw soldiers rolling dice for ownership of the royal robe they must have taken off the poor soul. The centurion stood apart, not partaking.

> *They stare and gloat over me;*
> *they divide my garments among them,*
> *and for my clothing they cast lots.*
> *But you, O Yahweh, do not be far off!*

Demas looked down at the crowd standing around. They all seemed to be here for Jesus. Hundreds of them. Morbid onlookers, crying women, mocking scribes and Pharisees.

> *O you my help, come quickly to my aid!*
> *Deliver my soul from the sword,*
> *my precious life from the power of the dog!*
> *Save me from the mouth of the lion!*

Demas barely made out Jesus's words, mumbled through pain. "Father, forgive them. They know not what they do."

Forgive them? Who could possibly forgive them?

Then Demas caught Barabbas in the crowd. He was staring up at Jesus with eyes of horror. He wiped tears from his face and pushed his way through the crowd to escape.

Demas knew at that moment what Barabbas had seen. Because he had seen it too. This innocent man who was hanging next to him, was the very incarnation of forgiveness and mercy. The opposite of everything that Barabbas, the revolution and his Zealots, were—what Demas and his brother were. They cried for justice but produced chaos. They proclaimed "No king but God," but worshipped Belial. Demas had sought revenge on Rome, the Beast that murdered his love, and he had become the Beast.

This was one single, solitary, righteous man, and all the world was evil.

He had no form or majesty that we should look at him,
and no beauty that we should desire him.
He was despised and rejected by men;
a man of sorrows, and acquainted with grief;
and as one from whom men hide their faces
he was despised, and we esteemed him not.

Gestas's attention was caught by Jesus saying through his own pain, something about taking care of his mother. Gestas looked down and saw Mary Magdalene standing with Simon the Zealot, Jesus's mother and the disciple John. Gestas noticed that they were the only male disciples with the liver to show up. All the others had run away from the trouble like scattered sheep. They had betrayed their rabbi after three years of following him.

Pathetic cowards, he thought to himself. *For a pathetic leader. I should have killed Simon after all.*

Hecklers in the crowd hurled curses at Jesus. Scribes mocked him. "He saved others, he cannot save himself!"

"If you are Messiah, king of Israel, come down from the cross and we will believe!"

"You said you would destroy the Temple and rebuild it in three days. Ha!"

They were right, thought Gestas. He remembered the time he had spent around Jesus. All the teachings about the Kingdom of God, the rule and judgment of the Messiah. Jesus had made them believe that he would launch the War of the Sons of Light against the Sons of Darkness. He made them believe that he was going to call down an army of Yahweh's heavenly host, to destroy the enemies of God and put all things right. How did it all come to this? The false hope. The lies. How did he ever for a moment believe that this weak worm of a man beside him was a deliverer? How did he allow himself to be fooled? There were no heavenly armies coming to rescue them.

He spit out at Jesus, "Are you not the Messiah?! Then prove it! Save yourself and us!"

Demas shouted back through his own physical and psychic pain, "Do you not fear God, brother? We are receiving the justice we deserve for our deeds. But this man has done nothing wrong!"

Gestas sought to spare his energy. He chose not to respond, only to mumble to himself, "You are no brother of mine."

Demas cried out, "Jesus, remember me when you come into your kingdom!" He cried as he had never cried since he lost his beloved wife so long ago. He felt the stinging salt of his tears flowing down his opened flesh—a baptism of suffering.

Jesus raised his head and glanced at Demas. "Truly, this day I say to you, you will be with me in Paradise."

Gestas heard the exchange. He burned with a rage as strong as his wounds. *There is no Paradise. There is no Messiah. There is only death.*

Though it was midday, about the sixth hour, the sky suddenly rolled up like a scroll and all around went dark. Women screamed. Some people fled in fear of impending doom.

• • • • •

Barabbas stumbled through the desert just above Gehenna, the Valley of Hinnom. He had wandered out past some stationed Roman troops and now tread along the precipice of the valley. He couldn't think straight. He was haunted by the sight of the Nazarene on the cross. Barabbas knew it was he who deserved to be up on that instrument of torture, not the innocent Nazarene. Barabbas had fancied himself a deliverer, trying to act like King David. He had come to believe his own lies.

The voice in his head was not his own. *You fraud. You phony. You are no hero. Look what you've done. You are guilty as hell, and yet you walk free, while the innocent Nazarene suffers. You should be up on that cross, but instead you took the easy way out. You coward.*

Barabbas looked around. He saw a figure standing at a distance from him. It looked taller than human. It wore a hood. But he knew it was staring at him. Sending him its thoughts. Or was he going mad?

The sky above him suddenly went dark. It became like night, while it was actually mid-day. Was this a sign? He could barely see where he was walking.

Yes, this is a sign, you fool. It's a sign that you should be in darkness. You should end it all. Be a man and take upon yourself the just punishment you wormed your way out of.

Barabbas shook his head, trying to get the voice out. He heard a ringing start in his ears, ever so low. It increased. It became intense. Painful.

The voice continued. *Just do it. Stop waiting around for some kind of atonement. There is none for you. There is only darkness. You have lived a lie and there is no redemption for what you've done. Just end it all. Just step off that ledge.*

He looked down into the valley. He could not see much because of the darkness. But it was high, maybe a hundred feet or more with jagged rocks below.

The ringing stopped. The voice turned soft and gentle. *One step and the pain will stop. Forever.*

The thought of Azazel came to Barabbas. What the Nazarene had said.

He turned to see the shadowy cloaked figure closer now.

Azazel.

It raised its hand and pointed at him.

Azazel.

Was this the angel of death?

Jump. Jump. Jump. Jump. Jump.

Barabbas jumped into Gehenna.

•••••

On his way back to Golgotha, Belial stopped by the body of Iscariot, hanging from a tree in a deserted field outside the city. It had been there for hours already, still undiscovered. He could smell the rot like perfume in his nostrils. There were no maggots yet. That would take another day or so. The eggs were only now gestating. But what had happened with delicious irony was that the branch that held the rope around the betrayer's neck had eventually broken under the weight of the body. It fell to the ground and Iscariot's bowels split open.

Belial bent down and licked up some of the blood and excrement that had leaked out. The rancid decay was the bread of life to him, the blood like wine, his own sacrament, a sacrificial offering. The betrayer had become so overwhelmed with guilt that he returned the blood money to the Sanhedrin for handing them Jesus. But rather than repenting, as that pond scum Peter did for his betrayal, Judas took upon himself the price of his own actions. *Ah, to pay for one's sins. The ultimate delusion*. There is only one price for such pride: perdition.

•••••

The darkness had been over the land for almost three hours. Mary Magdalene huddled with Simon, Jesus's mother, Joanna, Susanna, Mary, the mother of James, and others, praying to Yahweh. Most of the gawkers, mockers and scoffers had given up interest. The centurion had remained to maintain order with a group of soldiers, and ensure the penalty was fully carried out.

The onlookers had felt an evil presence arrive with the clouds and grow with intensity over the hours. Mary knew this presence well from her past life. She whispered to a knowing Simon, "Demons."

He nodded. Hordes of demons. They were the bulls of Bashan, from the Place of the Serpent, spoken of by the Scriptures, and expounded to her by Simon. It was as if every evil spirit from every corner of the land gathered together for their final offensive. Because of her spiritual sensitivity to this realm, she could see them.

Simon knew of them from the Scriptures.

Many bulls encompass me;
strong bulls of Bashan surround me;
they open wide their mouths at me,
like a ravening and roaring lion.
I am poured out like water,
and all my bones are out of joint;
my heart is like wax;
it is melted within my breast;
my strength is dried up like a potsherd,
and my tongue sticks to my jaws;
you lay me in the dust of death.
For dogs encompass me;
a company of evildoers encircles me;
they have pierced my hands and feet—
I can count all my bones—

But where are the heavenly host? thought Simon. Jesus had said in the Garden of Gethsemane that he had twelve legions of angels at his beck and call. Surely, Jesus was holding back until the most significant moment to call them down and bring in his glorious kingdom. But that moment was becoming later and later, and now it looked dangerously late for such a rescue. *Where are the angels of God?*

It was about the ninth hour of the day, as best as Mary could determine without the sun visible behind the curtain of darkness.

The men on the crosses were labored in their breathing now. Their lungs were being suffocated as their legs grew too weak to hold themselves up.

The sound of Jesus crying out drew everyone's attention. He yelled in Aramaic, "My God, My God, why have you forsaken me?"

The name for God in that language was "Eloi." Some had misheard him and said, "He is calling Elijah!"

In you our fathers trusted;
they trusted, and you delivered them.
To you they cried and were rescued;
in you they trusted and were not put to shame.
But I am a worm and not a man,
scorned by mankind and despised by the people.
All who see me mock me;
they make mouths at me; they wag their heads;
"He trusts in the LORD; let him deliver him;
let him rescue him, for he delights in him!"

A scraggly looking dwarf brought a long hyssop branch up to the foot of the cross of Jesus. It had a sponge dipped in sour wine at its end. No one could tell if the dwarf was a male or female. It was only a few feet high. Mary was unnerved, because she saw its true nature hidden behind a cloak of enchantment that others could not. The creature looked at her and grinned a toothy smile. It felt like a lion baring its teeth. She prayed harder.

The scraggly dwarf held the wine up to Jesus's mouth. Jesus looked down at him and saw him for what he really was, the eight foot tall serpentine Belial, almost eye level with him. His breathing was like a snake's hiss. His eyes were reptilian pupils of cold-blooded malevolence. He spoke in a voice that everyone else heard as the dwarf's almost childish pitch. "Let us see whether Elijah will come to take him down."

He grinned, looking up at Jesus and for his ears only, whispered, "Lick up, Messssiah. You have losssst."

The dwarf walked away and left the crowd, laughing.

All we like sheep have gone astray;
we have turned—every one—to his own way;
and the LORD has laid on him
the iniquity of us all.
He was oppressed, and he was afflicted,
yet he opened not his mouth;
like a lamb that is led to the slaughter,
and like a sheep that before its shearers is silent,
so he opened not his mouth.

Demas tried desperately to draw breath. He wheezed and moaned. He was losing consciousness again. He knew his end was near. He felt himself in a haze, not sure of where he was.

He was brought out of his stupor by the sound of Jesus's voice crying out again, "Father, into your hands I commit my spirit!"

Demas jerked his head over to see Jesus mouth the words weakly, "It is finished." He bowed his head and breathed his last.

Surely he has borne our griefs
and carried our sorrows;
yet we esteemed him stricken,
smitten by God, and afflicted.
But he was pierced for our transgressions;
he was crushed for our iniquities;
upon him was the chastisement that brought us peace,
and with his wounds we are healed.

At that same moment, Mary Magdalene saw a spiritual rush of wind around them like a tornado, sucking the evil spirits around them down into the earth, through the rocks and into the Abyss. She looked around her. Simon had not seen it. Nor the other women.

No one else had seen it.

Longinus saw the women at the cross begin to wail. They knew their beloved rabbi was dead. Longinus felt a chill go through his body like a shock of lightning.

The earth began to quake.

Longinus widened his stance to keep sure footing. The ground shook around them. The crosses swayed. Everyone heard the sound of the earth shifting and grinding below them. Some screamed for Yahweh's help.

Longinus had never experienced such a confluence of signs over a single person in his entire life. He had heard of the legend of the comet, that shone for seven days over the Victory Games in honor of Julius Caesar's death. Octavian claimed to have seen a rainbow halo around the sun in a clear sky after the death of Julius. Those signs verified the deification of Julius, his apotheosis. Augustus, who called himself "the Son of God," was allegedly witnessed by an ex-praetor as being received into heaven as divinity at his death. But what had disturbed Longinus most, was the legend of the prophecy that Augustus himself had been given by the Pythian Oracle at Delphi. She had foretold,

> *"In token of judgment, the earth shall drip with sweat.*
> *A king destined to rule forever will arrive from heaven,*
> *present in mortal flesh, in order to judge the world."*

That king, Augustus was told, was not him, but someone else to come. Augustus had claimed to be the Son of God. The line of Caesars was to be the continuation of that divine identity. Longinus had misplaced his faith in a delusion of grandeur. Caesar was not the Son of God and savior. He was not divine. He played divine to secure his power upon the prejudices of the people. Longinus had been a fool. He had followed a demonic delusion.

When the rumbling had finally stopped, Longinus looked up at the body of Jesus and said, "Truly, *this man* was the Son of God."

Then the words of the Baptizer returned to him, from that cold, dark cell in the dungeon of Herod miles away. *You will never find what you are looking for. I pray it finds you.* Longinus had been found.

•••••

Deep underground, a half mile away from Golgotha, the earth had shifted and a crevice opened up that led to the surface a thousand feet above. With that titanic movement, an opening broke and the archangel Uriel could breathe fresh air again. He crawled out from within the trapping rock, and made his way up the precipitous climb, out of his earthly prison.

"Thank you, my lord, Yahweh," he prayed. "I certainly don't deserve such kindness. I vow to be nicer to Gabriel when I see him."

•••••

No human saw what happened in the Temple. It would only be discovered later.

The veil that shielded the Holy of Holies and kept Yahweh's throne separated from the world began to tear down from top to bottom. The sound of the ripping drew priests from all over the inner temple to see what had happened. They withdrew in shock.

The veil was a handbreadth thick, so this was not caused by the earthquake. It was the hand of God.

What was Yahweh doing? Why would he tear down the barrier between the sacred and the profane? Why would he expose to all what was only allowed to the high priest on a single Day of Atonement?

•••••

The bodies of the crucified normally hung for days until they died and had their corpses picked clean by scavengers. But the Jews had asked Pilate to kill them quickly and take them down, because it would be sacrilege to have them up during the Sabbath. Longinus had been given the orders to break the criminals' legs so they could no longer hold themselves up, and would finish their slow suffocation to death in minutes.

Two soldiers went up to Demas and Gestas. When Demas felt the first club on his leg, he heard the crunch of broken bone. He whimpered as a jet of pain shocked his entire body. Another clubbing, more lightning searing pain, and his other leg went limp. He sank and felt his lungs struggling desperately to suck air.

He saw his brother with the same injuries, gasping for the same air.

Their time had come.

In his last moments of life, through dizzied blurred eyes, he saw Longinus approached Jesus with a javelin.

Longinus didn't need to break the legs of the Nazarene. He was already dead.

Yahweh protects all his bones,
not one of them will be broken.

But the centurion had to make sure for legal reasons, so he raised his javelin and lanced Jesus's side. A sympathetic pain slashed Longinus' heart. He felt as if he lanced himself.

Separated blood and water poured out from the body and ran down the stomach and legs. The god-man was dead.

Longinus knew that he could raise his sword against the Jews no more.

Demas saw that Gestas was dead.

As Demas slipped into oblivion, he looked up and thought he saw, surrounding them at a distance, a myriad of heavenly host on chariots of fire.

He bowed his head and breathed his last.

•••••

The blood from Jesus poured down his body and onto the wood. It continued to drip down onto the rocks that held up the cross, and then into the hole where the post was stuck.

It continued to make its way, slowly through the crevices, driven by supernatural intent, until it finally pooled on an artifact deep in the soil of Golgotha, buried a millennium before by King David. The skull of Goliath from Gath, Seed of the Serpent.

By oppression and judgment he was taken away;
and as for his generation, who considered
that he was cut off out of the land of the living,
stricken for the transgression of my people?
although he had done no violence,
and there was no deceit in his mouth.
Yet it was the will of the LORD to crush him;
he has put him to grief;
when his soul makes an offering for guilt,
he shall see his offspring; he shall prolong his days;
the will of the LORD shall prosper in his hand.
Out of the anguish of his soul he shall see and be satisfied;
by his knowledge shall the righteous one, my servant,
make many to be accounted righteous,
and he shall bear their iniquities.

Therefore I will divide him a portion with the many,
and he shall divide the spoil with the strong,
because he poured out his soul to death
and was numbered with the transgressors;
yet he bore the sin of many,
and makes intercession for the transgressors.

CHAPTER 31

Darkness.

Demas opened his eyes with a gasp. What had happened to the pain? His legs no longer felt broken. He felt no crucifixion wounds in his hands and feet. His tongue and lips were no longer parched and cracked. He no longer felt pain.

He looked at his hands and legs. They appeared to be there, but were more like emanations of moving light than physical flesh and blood.

He was dead.

He looked around him. He was on a tall mountain, surrounded by a land of darkness. He didn't know how, but he could see despite the darkness. Did he now have "spiritual" eyes?

Below him on the southwest base of the mountain was a huge valley that burned with fire. Its yawning gulf beckoned like the mouth of a dragon, hungry for flesh.

Beyond the valley was desert wasteland. Above him was strangest of all. The sky was low-hanging rock in some places, and a ceiling of water in others. It was as if an ocean of water was upside down on the cavern roof of an upside down world. He knew those must be the waters of the Abyss.

The mountain he was on broke through a rock ceiling above that no doubt went up into the overworld.

So this was Hades.

His observations were interrupted by the arrival of Jesus from out of a cave opening. He too looked similar to his earthly body, but without his crucifixion wounds, and with an emanating light that gave him an ethereal presence. It was as if he were both there and not there at the same moment.

Jesus carried a giant skull in one hand and a strange tool in the other. He dropped the skull to the ground. Demas noticed that it had blood drizzled over it. Jesus then stomped on it, crushing it to pieces. Demas thought that a normal bare foot would have broken itself on the giant skull. These spiritual bodies must have interesting properties.

Jesus said, "I have been waiting to do that for a long time."

"Whose is it?"

"It's a long story." Jesus looked out into the distance. "But then again, we have a long trip ahead of us, so I will tell you, once we get going."

Demas smiled, "So this isn't the Paradise you promised me."

Jesus returned his grin. "Not yet."

"Where are we going?"

"You'll see." Jesus handed the strange object to Demas. He took it and examined it. It was a sword handle that ended in a worn leather sheath. But it wasn't a long sword scabbard. It looked more like a square bulky case, as if the sword handle had a large hammer head at the end of it. Demas opened the sheath and drew the handle out. A long, ten foot flexible blade unfurled out onto the ground. It looked like a long dragon tongue made of solid yet liquid metal.

Jesus said, "It's a whip sword. My ancestor Lamech nicknamed it 'Rahab' after the sea dragon of chaos. For obvious reasons."

Demas moved the deadly blade around, mesmerized by its fluid serpentine movements. "How is it I can wield an earthly object down here?"

"It was forged by the archangel Gabriel with heavenly metal on the primordial Mount Sahand."

"The Garden of Eden?" asked Demas.

"Yes. It was passed down through the hands of mighty Karabu warriors who fought the Seed of the Serpent through history. Lamech, Shem, Caleb ben Jephunneh, Ittai the Gittite. Now it is yours."

Demas stopped his examination of the blade. He looked up darkly at Jesus. "If I need a weapon, that can only mean...."

"You will only need it if you leave my side. Go ahead. Try it."

Demas said, "I am a little out of practice."

He looked around and noticed that there were trees and bushes around them. But instead of being rooted downward into the ground, it was their ugly barren and tangled roots that sprouted *out* of the ground. As if they were planted upside down in this upside down netherworld.

He stretched out the whip sword, spotted a target branch, and let loose a stinging crack. The large branch severed like a blade of wheat beneath a scythe. Demas smiled.

"I like it."

Demas rolled up the blade and returned it to its sheath that he belted around his waist. "Will I be needing this against Cerberus, the three-headed hound of hell?"

Jesus smiled. "You have been reading too much Greek mythology."

"No River Styx or the boatman Chabon?"

Jesus shook his head no.

"No Elysian fields?"

"No Elysian fields. No temple of Pluto or Hades. Nothing pleasant in this Land of No Return." Then Jesus added, "And I am not Hercules." They shared a laugh. "There are some rivers here, and there is Tartarus. But it's not what you think."

"Well, what is it then?"

Jesus paused for a moment, apparently deciding what to tell Demas. Then he said, "You are familiar with the spiritual concept 'As above, so below?'"

Demas replied, "Of course." *As above, so below* was the saying that expressed the understanding of the nature of the cosmos in all cultures of the world. Heaven and earth were spiritually united. Yahweh's temple and throne was in the waters above the heavens. Directly below it, in the center of the earth, was the Temple and the ark, his earthly throne. Sacrifices below were satisfied above. But also, the gods of the nations were so connected to their allotted territories that when nations fought battles on earth, the principalities and powers over the nations also fought in the heavenlies. Gentile pagans worshipped the host of heaven in place of Yahweh, granting sovereignty to signs in the heavens that Yahweh alone deserved. But the spiritual truth remained: On earth as it is in heaven.

Jesus said, "In a way, the same principle holds true for the underworld. The map of this world reflects the sacred map of the world above. Right now, we are on Mount Zion, the center of the earth, and the center of Hades."

Demas looked above him and imagined Golgotha, where they had just recently died.

"Where is my brother?" He was afraid to look at Jesus.

"Gestas chose his destiny as you chose yours."

Demas' eyes welled up with tears of regret. "I lived as depraved a life as he. I do not deserve to be with you any more than he does."

Jesus was beside him with an understanding hand of compassion on his shoulder. "You are right, Demas. You do not deserve what you have received."

Demas looked into Jesus's eyes. They were like flames of fire penetrating his very being with a burning, cleansing brightness.

Demas's knees buckled and he found a rock to sit down upon as tears now flowed from his eyes.

He sputtered, "But why me? Why me, Lord?"

All his life he had said those words as accusations against a God who had seemed to unfairly take everything from him; his parents, his love, his hope. Now, he realized he had deserved nothing. Now, he felt as if he was being unfairly favored.

Was this grace? Was this the mystery of God's election? Yahweh had chosen Israel, not because of her righteousness, but for his own reasons and purposes. Jacob he loved, Esau he hated.

Demas he loved, Gestas he hated?

Jesus said softly to him, "I will have mercy on whom I have mercy, and I will have compassion on whom I have compassion."

Jesus did not have to explain himself. Demas knew that he was not the only sinner on earth. Everyone stood guilty in their sins before a holy and just Creator. The sacrifices that atoned for sins in the temple were only temporary coverings. The blood of bulls and goats could not take away sins. Even the high priest needed to sacrifice for his own sins. The earthly temple and all its cult was a mere shadow of the more perfect heavenly temple that had to be entered into by a perfect and sinless high priest.

But time and again, he had been warned that not everyone would follow Messiah and join the Kingdom of Heaven. And what else could be in store for those who would reject the atonement of Yahweh and his Son?

Jesus looked out onto the valley of fire. "That is Gehenna, where the worm does not die, and the fire is not quenched. It is the 'Valley of Slaughter' where Yahweh pours out his wrath upon his enemies. Even now, the fires are preparing for the Day of the Lord that is soon to come."

He turned to the east. All Demas could see was blackness. Jesus said, "To the far east, beyond the ends of the earth and the waters of the Abyss, in the midst of *tohu wabohu*, is Tartarus."

Demas knew this land of chaos and disorder was where the disobedient angels were imprisoned. Jesus looked to the south and waved his hand. Demas could see the darkness part, as if by a vision, and he could see a distant ridge of mountains that ascended into the rocky ceiling above. There were seven of them, and they all sparkled of precious gemstones. The middle mountain was the largest and its top was on fire.

Jesus said, "That is Sinai, the mountain of fire, the original throne of Yahweh.

He turned to the north and waved his hand again. Again, Demas could see in the distance, as if by vision, a tall mountain that reached up to heaven.

Storm and clouds surrounded it. Jesus said, "That is Mount Hermon, the celestial storehouse. It is at the source of the rivers."

Demas thought of Jesus's statement so long ago, when he was with him at Panias: "Upon this rock, I will build my church." It would be a new Eden.

"Is that where we are going?"

"No." Jesus turned to the west. Miles beyond the fires of Gehenna, Demas now saw a tall mountain shrouded in darkness and silence. "That is where we are going. The Mountain of the Dead."

Jesus began to walk down toward the north side of the mountain. Demas ran to catch up.

Jesus said, "We must travel north a bit to get around the cursed valley. One of the rivers will take us the rest of the way to the mountain in the west."

CHAPTER 32

They had been traveling for some time through the barren desert wasteland. Jesus explained to Demas that time did not pass the same way down here as it did in the world above. What had seemed like a day down here in the underworld, was mere minutes in the overworld. In the previous age, it had been the reverse. A day down in Hades could be a hundred up on earth. But Demas was with the Son of God, and he was transforming the very fabric of reality with his mission. He told Demas he would ultimately defeat the power of death, but until then, he had merely slowed it down.

Despite this advantage, Jesus told him, they only had three days above to accomplish his mission down here. For just what, he didn't tell Demas. But he knew they had a long way to travel to get to his destination, the Mountain of the Dead.

Demas also noticed that though he was a spiritual body, he could still oddly feel the sense of thirst. Jesus told him he would soon have that thirst quenched. It was the longing in the soul for Yahweh, for redemption, for resurrection.

Yahweh had created humanity to be ensouled beings, creatures of undivided flesh and spirit. He had breathed into their bodies, his *nephesh*, his very breath of life. In death, the separation of that life from the human body was not the release of the spirit from the prison-house of crude flesh, as the Greeks believed, but rather, the unnatural tearing of a veil or tapestry of interwoven being. The same body that returned to dust in its mortality would one day be regenerated, and given back its breath of life, because Yahweh valued his creation. Whatever this world of the dead was, it was only a temporary holding place, while the earthly bodies slept in their graves, until they were resurrected in glory.

Something had caught Demas' eyes on the horizon. Movement. He had stopped to stare out into the distance. He could barely see through the darkness with his spiritual vision, but he could see enough to know that what he saw was human forms. Hundreds of them. Staggering and stumbling into each other like blinded creatures. No, wait. Thousands of them. And they were coming his way. Dark shadowy denizens. He noticed that Jesus had kept moving and was far ahead. He could see the unnatural glow that Jesus's transfigured body gave off in the darkness. He remembered the phrase "Light of the World," and chuckled. He figured that must be what these shades were being drawn toward.

He was so curious, he didn't even think to call out to Jesus. He saw the ground moving beneath his feet. He bent down to look at it. Was the ground alive in some way?

A hand burst from the dirt and grabbed his ankle. He stood up in shock. But the hand had grasped him tightly. He fell to his rump in the dirt.

More hands and arms and legs burst out of the ground. Then heads and bodies began to pull themselves out like the living dead.

He noticed that they looked like hideous corpses as well. Their bodies were desecrated rotting skin. Their faces were human, but lacking eyes. The only thing on their faces were huge mouths full of chomping teeth. They were grinding and gnashing as if desperately hungry.

Demas suddenly noticed that his own body had lost most of its light. He was beginning to look like these walking, grasping corpses.

He blurted out, "Jesus!"

He turned, only to find his path blocked by more of the chomping zombies, wandering in their confused state.

"JESUS!"

He couldn't see Jesus, but he heard his distant voice. "You have a sword! Use it!"

He remembered the whip sword he had been given. Rahab. He pulled it out and snapped it at the closest shades. It cut arms and legs off, but it didn't stop them. One of them was cut in half at the torso, and Demas could see what was animating them. The entire body cavity was full of worms instead of organs and flesh. It was as if the worms worked together collectively to make the shade act as a unified singular creature.

The worm does not die.

He noticed that cutting off heads seemed to stop them the best. So he swung Rahab around and snapped off heads all around him. He began to clear a pathway back to Jesus. He noticed that the infernal creatures could find their dismembered body parts and place them back together to become a moving entity again.

What horror is this? he thought, as he found his way forward, swinging and snapping and cutting dozens of shades into body parts.

By the time he made it to Jesus, he noticed that the shades had backed off. They could find their way to the light of Jesus, but they could not get closer to him than a hundred feet. It was like a hidden veil that kept them back, an invisible fortress wall. They surrounded the pair in a vast circle, and more of them crushed around.

Demas stumbled, but found his footing as he came near Jesus.

"I told you not to get too far from me," said Jesus.

Demas looked all around. The wailing and gnashing of teeth began to drive him mad. He tried to hold his ears. It didn't help.

Jesus pulled him along and explained to him, "When the dead first arrive, they become reduced to what you see now, ravenously hungry and thirsty for atonement. They are allowed to wander in this state for some time until they are taken to the Mountain of the Dead."

Demas looked at him with fear. "Isn't that where we are going?"

Jesus smiled. "Don't worry. As I said, just stay close to me, and you won't become one of them."

Demas became really worried. He thought, *I could become one of them?*

He resolved to never wander away from Jesus again. These shades were as drawn to the Son of God and his redemptive light as Demas was. And he was dying of thirst like one of them.

The shades created an animated circle around Jesus, that followed them as they moved.

Demas saw some strange phantom-like creatures arrive and begin to pull away the shades one by one. The creatures looked human in shape, but with leopard faces, and boar-like tusks in their mouths. Their eyes were blood and their hair was long and flowing like a woman's. They carried scourges in their hands that wrapped around the shades to pull them away. Soul catchers.

"Demas," said Jesus.

Demas turned to see they had arrived at a river's edge. A river of fire.

With a myriad of shades at their back, they had nowhere to go.

The mass of shades surrounding them was thinned out by the divine soul catchers. But there were still so many of them that Demas had to speak up. "I heard you walked on water. But it looks to me that if you can't turn that into walking on fire, we won't make your deadline of three days down here."

"I can do better than that," said Jesus.

He walked over to the river of fire and held up his hands.

Demas looked at the circle of shades around them, chomping mouths, famished souls. Some were snatched away by the frightening looking leopard beings.

When he looked back, he saw an amazing sight. The river of fire was separating where Jesus stood. A wall of cooled magma built up on both sides, holding back the fiery slag as a pathway formed across the divide.

"Holy Moses," exclaimed Demas.

Jesus smiled. It was, after all, like Moses and the parting of the Red Sea.

"Let's go," said Jesus. He led Demas across on cool, dry rock.

When they reached the other side, the cooled rock broke down and the magma returned to its flowing river course.

They left the yawning, groping, blinded shades on the other side.

Demas' thirst did not abate.

After a short while, they came to another river. This one was the opposite of the river of fire. It was a river of living waters that emanated bright light.

By now, Demas was so thirsty, he couldn't help himself. He looked at Jesus, who said, "Go ahead" with a smile.

Demas ran and dove into the river, head first. He took huge gulps of it into his mouth. It was a surge of life that reinvigorated him with hope and peace. He looked to the north and could see Mount Hermon, the source of all the rivers in this area flowing south and west. Both fire and life came from the same source. Somehow it all made sense to him now, as he could think more clearly. He had become so consumed with thirst, he was beginning to feel like one of the shades in desperate search of satiation. This was the river of living water, cut off from the dead so they could not quench their thirst.

Jesus had joined him in the river. But he wasn't drinking. He had moved into the middle of the waters. He gestured for Demas to join him, and the current took them both south.

It wasn't long on their floating trek before Demas saw the destination of the river. Before them was the towering, dark Mountain of the Dead. It looked so dreary and silent to Demas. But it enchanted him. He stared at it until Jesus told him, "Get ready to go underground."

Demas could see that they were fast approaching a huge waterfall, not far from the mountain. He became fearful.

Jesus laughed and said, "Fear not, Demas! You are already dead."

Demas realized what he meant as they plummeted down the vast waterfall into an underground tunnel. The walls tightened and the current pulled them along even faster now. It was actually quite fun. The light of the water illuminated their pathway of smooth, rock-hard walls. In darkness, you feared what you could not see. Light had a way of penetrating the darkness with a sense of safety. Everything was laid bare before it. This river was the sole source of life-giving refreshment in the otherwise dark and dreary underworld. It was cut off from the shades, but it was taking them somewhere right now, and Demas was no longer afraid or concerned.

An overwhelming sense of peace had come over him. He knew it was the water. This living water.

After going downward for a while, he finally felt the current sucking them upward.

Within moments, Demas and Jesus burst out of an underground fountain in a vast cavern. The water continued onward, but the two of them swam over to the shoreline and pulled themselves out. They walked over to the edge of the cavern.

They stood on the precipice of a vast chasm and looked down. Far below them flowed the river of fire they had previously crossed up-stream. It was wide enough to fill the bottom of the chasm with its flaming magma.

Demas looked across the distance. He could barely see the other side lined with a myriad of souls, moaning and crying out. But there was no sound. They were engulfed in silence. He knew what it was they wanted. The water.

"We are beneath the Mountain of the Dead," said Jesus. "Over there are the hollow places for the unrighteous. They thirst for a mere drop of this water on their tongues."

The living water, thought Demas. Then he said, "Where are *we*?"

Jesus turned. Demas followed his gaze to see a line of souls behind them. These were not thirsty, famished shades, but peaceful, patient souls.

"Abraham's Bosom," said Jesus.

Demas saw the men who approached them now. There were many of them. He realized that these were the saints of primeval days and of the age before Messiah. Jesus said their names as the leaders approached him with looks of wonder and joy. They had been drinking from the living waters in this place as a means of satiating them in their wait for Messiah.

Father Abraham and the incomparable Sarah; the earthy and old Methuselah and his beautiful Edna; Lamech and Betenos; their son, Noah, and Emzara; Moses, Joshua and Caleb; Othniel, Rahab, Abigail; King David and his mighty men, Benaiah, the brothers Joab and Abishai, Sibbecai, Elhanon, Ittai, Jonathan the Hawk, and so many more. All the righteous dead who died in faith before the coming of Messiah and his triumphal entry.

Wait a second, thought Demas. Messiah was to conquer death and the grave. He was to achieve victory over the principalities and powers of the nations. But he hadn't done that yet.

Demas blurted out, "Jesus, are we here for the resurrection and the final judgment?"

Jesus stopped hugging those around him. "Not quite, Demas. But your intuition is right. I have unfinished business. That is why we came here. I need some of your help."

CHAPTER 33

Mary Magdalene, a woman named Salomé, and Mary, the mother of James, approached the tomb of their beloved Jesus. It was early morning on the first day after the Sabbath, and they had brought spices to anoint the body of their crucified rabbi. Because he had been crucified just before the Sabbath, they did not have the time to anoint him before their day of holy rest.

Mary was lost in her thoughts and had fallen behind the other two by some yards. She dreaded seeing the body of Jesus. He had become everything to her; savior, redeemer, Son of God. But such an undignified death had more than crushed her hopes. It humiliated them and mocked her to her face.

All the disciples had fled like sheep without a shepherd when he was struck down. *The cowards.* Now they were in hiding for fear of being counted revolutionaries against Rome.

Revolutionaries? Ridiculous. Jesus preached peace and never lifted a finger in defiance of any authority. He was zealous for Yahweh's name, but he was no Zealot. Yet he died a Zealot's death for insurrection. The injustice of it all burned in her breast.

Suddenly, she remembered there was a big stone rolled over the entrance of the tomb. Three women would not have the strength to move that huge rock.

She blurted out to the others ahead of her. "Who are we going to get to move the stone? That is a huge stone they rolled over the tomb."

No answer came.

"Mary? Salomé?"

She saw the other women standing up on the ridge.

"Did you not hear me? I said who are we going to get to move the–"

She froze in her tracks. The two women stared at the tomb just ahead.

The stone had been rolled away.

The tomb's entrance was wide open.

Mary said, "It is too early. Who could have beat us here?"

They walked over to the tomb entrance and peeked inside. Salomé shrieked and stepped backward in shock. Mary was in the way. She fell to the ground.

"What? What did you see?"

Mary got up and pushed Salomé aside to enter the tomb.

Inside, the body of Jesus was gone. But across from where they had lain his body, were two men dressed in dazzling white robes.

Mary pulled back in fear. After all she had seen in her life as an Ob; demons and ghosts, the siyyim and iyyim of Azazel, they were not as frightening as these two men in white. She could see things in the spiritual realm, and they had an aura of power about them. Frightening power.

One of them said, "Do not be afraid, for I know that you seek Jesus who was crucified. He is not here, for he has risen, just as he said."

The other two women now stood beside Mary, gawking at the scary intruders. They looked over at the empty ledge. Jesus was gone.

Mary couldn't understand it. She couldn't understand why these men would move the body of their beloved Jesus. It didn't make sense to her.

The other man said, "Go quickly and tell his disciples that he has risen from the dead. He is going to Galilee. You will find him there."

•••••

Demas awoke in darkness with a hard cough. He felt different, heavier. He could feel the flesh of his body again, along with its little aches and pains. He felt a stinging sensation all over his body. He was laying down with a blanket of weight upon him.

A blanket of dirt.

He couldn't breathe.

He panicked. *I've been buried.*

He struggled to get his hands free in order to claw his way out.

Somehow, he managed to get one hand out of the ground. Thank Yahweh, it was a shallow grave.

He felt another hand grab his. It pulled him up and out of the dirt.

He gasped for air. The cool air inflated his lungs.

I am alive.

The bright light of day burned his eyes. He had been in the dark so long. He covered his squinting eyes with his arm.

Then the stinging on his flesh became intolerable. He noticed his body covered with white chalky powder. Lime. He desperately wiped the burning substance off his face and arms and legs.

Lime was used by the Romans in mass graves of corpses to speed up the decomposition of the flesh and cover the smell of decay.

Demas had after all been crucified as an insurrectionist. He didn't deserve a proper dignified burial.

He took another deep breath.

"Makes you appreciate life more, doesn't it?"

Demas looked up at Jesus, standing before him. They were no longer in Hades. They were on earth. Jesus had crucifixion wounds on his hands and feet. But he seemed unfazed by them. Demas looked at his hands. They had been healed. His entire body had been healed. The decayed flesh restored.

He looked back into the dirt. He saw the rotting body of his brother, Gestas, that had been beneath him. The flesh was dead gray and purple. His face peered out from the dirt, half-eaten by maggots and worms. The stench of the dead now overcame Demas. But worse, the reality of his unrepentant brother somewhere now wandering in Hades as a miserable shade in darkness and silence.

He knelt down and wretched. He had nothing to vomit because he had no food in his stomach.

Jesus placed his hand lovingly on Demas' shoulder.

Demas's eyes had adjusted to the light. He looked up at Jesus. "You resurrected me. Why?"

"You are not the only one."

"What do you mean?"

"Those saints you met in Hades. I've raised some of them as well. They are all finding their way to Jerusalem from their graves. I want you to go there and meet them."

"What do you want me to do?"

"Tell them I want to meet in Bashan, north of Galilee in a fortnight."

"Why?"

Jesus handed him the familiar leather case with whip sword, Rahab, returned from Hades.

"I'm claiming my inheritance."

•••••

Peter and John ran up to the sepulcher of Jesus. Behind them, Mary and the other women followed. They had gone back into Jerusalem and told the disciples about the empty tomb. Most of the eleven did not believe the women. Mary was known for her fantastic stories of angels and demons and spiritual visions.

Peter and John thought that this time was different.

They entered the tomb to find the body of Jesus gone. On the ledge where he had lain were the linen body wrappings. The head covering had been neatly folded and placed on the ledge.

Peter's mind was swirling with conspiracy. *Did the Romans take the body? No. That would make him a martyr, and surely enflame the very revolt they were trying to suppress.*

Who could have done this?

Peter picked up the shroud that had been laid upon the body. He held it up.

"John, look at this."

In the light from the entrance, they could see a transfigured image burned into the shroud. It was the image of Jesus.

Peter said, "How could such a thing happen?"

John said, "What *has* happened?"

They left the sepulcher and faced down the women.

Peter said, "Mary, you say the stone was already rolled away when you arrived?"

"Yes."

"And you saw no one carrying the body away?"

"No. There was only two angels sitting inside the tomb."

"Angels." He said it with doubt.

"Angels." She was sure of it. The other women were not.

"How do you know they were angels?"

"They had the aura of angels."

"The aura of angels." Still not believing.

"They said Jesus had risen and we were to meet him in Galilee."

"Why Galilee? Why not Jerusalem?"

"You will have to ask him that question. I don't know."

Peter said. "Well, let us go back to the city and confer with the other disciples."

"Why don't you believe me?" she said.

Peter said, "It's not that I don't believe you, Mary. It just seems strange to me that if Jesus had truly risen from the dead, why would he not have shown himself to the men?"

"Maybe he couldn't find the men because they had all run away in fear."

"Mary, that is not fair."

"It is true."

"Let us go back to the city and confer with the others."

Peter and John left. The other women followed them. Salomé tried to pull Mary along, but Mary refused to leave. She began to weep. Salomé tried to comfort her.

"Just leave."

Salomé left her alone at the grave.

Mary began to doubt herself. Maybe it was a delusion. Maybe Peter was right. Maybe someone stole the body for some nefarious reasons. Maybe she had become so emotionally distraught, she was seeing hallucinations. But the other women had seen the men too. They were not an hallucination. Maybe they were just tricksters who were playing with their minds.

"Woman, why are you weeping?"

The words broke her out of her whirlpool of confusion and tears.

He appeared to be the gardener. A kind looking man. Somehow familiar.

She said, "Sir, if you have carried him away, tell me where you have laid him, and I will move him back to his tomb."

The man smiled at her.

How odd. Why would he make such light of her pain and loss?

He said, "Mary."

Then she recognized him. "Rabbi!" She grabbed him and hugged him desperately.

He pulled away from her and said, "Do not cling to me. I have not yet ascended to the Father. Go to the disciples and tell them I am ascending to my Father and your Father, to my God and your God."

Her eyes dried with wonder. She touched him. He was real. She touched his face. His beard. She pulled it. He moved back, "Ow. Are you going to pull my hair out to be sure?"

She broke down into laughter.

"It is you! It is you!"

She dropped to his feet and worshipped.

She remembered the words he had spoken to the disciples. *Destroy this temple and in three days I will rebuild it.* She had always considered that a figurative statement. Like great leaders who still have an effect on their followers after they were dead and gone.

How foolish of her. Of course he had meant it. Of course he would rise from the dead to conquer the principalities and powers that had remained. Now it all made sense to her.

He pulled her back up to face him. "Go, tell them what you have seen. Though I suspect their thick-headedness is going to require a bit more on my part, before they get up off their rear ends and do what I told them."

It suddenly dawned on Mary why Jesus was going to Galilee up north to meet them. Beyond Galilee was the cosmic mountain of assembly for the gods of the nations. His resurrection gave him the power and authority to take back their inheritance as his own.

"You are going to Mount Hermon, aren't you?"

He didn't respond. But she could see it in his eyes.

•••••

Demas walked through the southern gates of the lower city of Jerusalem. He kept his hood up around his face in order to avoid being noticed. It was only days ago he was crucified before the world next to Jesus. Someone might recognize him. Someone who had been there to observe the spectacle of pain.

He soon discovered his efforts at discretion were wasted. He saw a large gathering around a market square at the Temple.

Four men stood on the steps near the Huldah Gate at the southeast entrance to the Temple. Hundreds had gathered around. One of them was speaking. He was an old man, but delivered his address with amazing strength of voice.

Demas recognized him from the underworld introduction. It was Moses.

"People of Israel, do you not know? I wrote these very words in the Second Book of the Law. For the Lord said to me, 'I will raise up a prophet like you from among their brothers. And I will put my words in his mouth, and he shall speak to them all that I command him. And whoever will not listen to my words that he shall speak in my name, I myself will require it of him.' That prophet was Jesus of Nazareth, whom you released to Pilate and had him crucified!"

The crowd's booing drowned Moses out. He waited until they died down. Demas recognized the three others with him. Joshua, Caleb and Othniel, Caleb's brother. They looked younger and stronger than their visages in Hades. They no longer looked as old as they were when they had died. Demas figured that their resurrection involved a return to their former selves at the height of their service to Yahweh. He felt it too within his bones. They had resurrection glory.

One heckler yelled out, "If you are Moses, why don't you part this crowd of people like you parted the Red Sea!" People laughed.

A man next to Demas grumbled to him, "These mad men claim to be our forefathers risen from the dead. Ridiculous fools." Then he turned back to the front of the crowd and yelled out, "Where is Abraham, Isaac, and Jacob to validate your witness!"

More laughs through the crowd.

"Right here," said a voice behind the grumbler.

Demas turned to see a hearty, vigorous Abraham and his resurrected descendants, Isaac and Jacob standing with arms crossed, glaring at him. The grumbler backed up, frightened that these crazy people may do something dangerous. He turned and ran to safety down the street.

Abraham smiled at Demas, who quipped, "I guess even resurrection from the dead won't persuade these hard-hearted idiots."

Abraham said, "They have the Scriptures. If they will not listen to them, They will not listen to God."

A young and strapping David stepped out from behind Abraham and said, "Jesus was right. They are sons of those who murdered the prophets."

His bodyguard, the loyal and sturdy-built Benaiah said, "Sons of Belial."

Demas said, "My lords, I need your help to find the rest of the risen ones in the city. We have to hurry. The Lord wants to meet us up north."

Abraham asked, "What is he planning?"

David said, "Well, he raised my thirty best mighty men, so I think it's clear. We're going to war."

CHAPTER 34

It took the resurrected saints just over three days on horseback to make the hundred mile trek up north from Jerusalem to Bashan. They had taken the Jordan Valley all the way, and camped a half mile outside the city of Caesarea Philippi.

There were over fifty of them. Patriarchs, warriors, kings and princes. Yet, they were led by the humble penitent criminal, Demas Samaras. They all knew it was Yahweh's way of using the least as the greatest. Many of them had started in life as the youngest, or smallest, or rejected of men. But Yahweh had often chosen the weak of the world to shame the strong, and the lesser to inherit the greater. David was the least of seven brothers in an insignificant family. Caleb was a Canaanite convert who became Joshua's right hand. Ittai the Gittite was a Philistine who became the most faithful of King David's warriors. Demas, was a lowly entertaining bestiarius who joined Jesus' side in Hades. Most amazing of all was the giant, Eleazar, the ten and a half foot Rephaim who had been redeemed by the very hand of Jesus.

How satisfying, thought Demas. *A seed of the Serpent redeemed and resurrected to fight against the Serpent. How God does have a sense of irony.*

But now, they were all being called upon for a final mighty act of giant-toppling faith. So they practiced with their weapons and fighting techniques in preparation.

David and his beefy bodyguard watched David's general, Joab and his brother Abishai lead his thirty mighty men in exercises. They were as youthful as they had been at the height of their service in David's kingdom.

Joab, David's gritty, ruthless general, yelled to the synchronized warriors in formation, "Pick it up, gibborim! These are more than giants we're about to face!" He glanced at the giant Eleazar by his side. "No offense, friend."

"Just glad I am not your foe," said Eleazar with a smile.

David stretched his sword arm and said, “We had best join them, Benaiah. We are after all, a thousand years out of practice.”

Benaiah grinned and they joined the others in the battle exercises.

Caleb and Joshua practiced with their weapons together in a forest clearing, as they had always done when they were alive. Caleb was bald, rugged and as strong as the commander of the armies of the Lord, twenty years his junior. He had been eighty years old at the peak of Joshua’s conquest of Canaan. But he moved with the fluidity and grace of an immortal angel. He spun, flipped and dodged Joshua’s thrusts and hacks with his sword.

Joshua strained for breath.

Caleb said breathlessly, “My lord, have you forgotten all I taught you?”

Joshua said, “I am only warming up.” Then he yelled, “Battle axes!”

They dropped their swords and picked up battle axes, in a continuous flow of battle form.

Joshua swung his ax in mighty arcs that would fell a giant. Caleb moved with his opponent’s flow and evaded every one.

Joshua burned red with frustration. “Javelins!”

They dropped their battle axes and picked up javelins and shields. In the heat of battle, everything could change in a moment, and one would have to adjust immediately. Their workouts had empowered them with the skills to clear the land of the mighty Anakim giants who had infested it in the days of Moses. But Joshua and Caleb had always been at odds with their fighting styles. Joshua overcame with brute force and ruthlessness. Caleb moved with faith, not force. He used the enemy’s momentum against him and had always told Joshua what he reminded him of now.

“Remember, a small amount of faith can move a mountain.”

At that very moment, Joshua danced and spun with a Karabu movement that took Caleb by surprise. He disarmed his partner of his javelin. Caleb moved fast to retrieve his weapon, but Joshua had bested him for that moment.

Joshua said with a smile, “When outweighed by skill, one must save their small amount of faith for just the right moment.”

“Well done, my general.”

A voice came from the forest edge. “Let us see how much faith the both of you have together.”

Joshua and Caleb turned to see a hooded monk at the edge of the clearing. They didn’t recognize him. They drew together protectively.

The monk took down his hood. He glimmered with the radiance of a Son of God. He had been in the presence of Yahweh Elohim in the heavenlies.

"I am Enoch ben Jared."

Joshua and Caleb looked at each other with wonder and curiosity. They of course knew of their ancient forefather who had walked with Yahweh. But they had never met him in Hades because he had never died. He had been taken into heaven.

Enoch said, "This is my son, Methuselah and his wife, Edna."

A hearty young Methuselah stepped into the clearing, accompanied by a heart-stopping woman that seemed to Caleb as beautiful as his beloved Rahab had been, which was almost impossible to believe. But this gorgeous one carried a sword and shield.

Her loveliness distracted Joshua as well. They may be resurrected heavenly saints, but they were still earthy men of flesh and blood.

Enoch said, "Let us see how warriors from the days of Moses do against warriors from the days of Noah—The original Karabu giant killers."

Joshua said, "A woman?"

Methuselah quipped, "Go easy on her and you'll be sorry."

Edna added with a smile, "Antediluvian beauty can be deceiving."

Caleb said to Joshua, "Let's show these primeval cave-dwellers how to fight, general."

The four of them engaged in battle.

Methuselah took on Caleb, Edna went after Joshua. Two teams of warriors moved with martial elegance, flowing in and out, working in tandem with one another. It was more a ballet than a battle. And it was beautiful Karabu at its finest.

Methuselah and Caleb were equals. They seemed to defy terra firma's grip, like dancing dragonflies.

Caleb shouted out, "If you were older like me, I'd have you by now."

Methuselah retorted, "Young man, I was killing Nephilim hordes at nine hundred."

Methuselah was his younger age now, but he had become famous in primordial days for being the oldest recorded age in the Scriptures at nine hundred and sixty-nine years.

Joshua had trouble keeping up with Edna. She was lighter and more nimble. He was beginning to regret his previous boastful words.

"Not bad for a woman, eh, general?" said Edna. Her graceful moves almost made Joshua dizzy.

But her strikes were not driven by Joshua's kind of strength. He struck her sword with such force, it flew out of her hand.

Joshua said, "I apologize for my condescension." But then he added, "So now I can stop going easy on you."

He launched on a series of blows so hard and so fast that Edna's arms shuddered with pain beneath her shield.

She backed up against a tree. Her shield cracked under the force of Joshua's strength. She tossed it aside.

Joshua smiled with sword raised at her. "Not bad for a woman." This time, he meant it with respect.

Methuselah kicked her blade up into the air at her. She caught it with ease. She released her own volley upon Joshua that surprised him, backing him up.

"Now I can stop going easy on you," she said with a twinkle in her eye.

Suddenly, the four fighters heard the sound of applause all around them. They looked around the clearing to see that they had drawn a crowd of all the resurrected warriors. The company watched their battle sparring like a gladiatorial game.

Joshua looked at Enoch and saw him smiling ear to ear.

Methuselah, ever the showman, gave a courtly sarcastic bow. Caleb followed suit.

Methuselah muttered to Caleb, "Not bad for an old man." Then he added, "But the truth is, you would have beat me when I was your age."

Caleb retorted, "I suspect our wives would be as equal in a competition of beauty."

Methuselah muttered, "I remember Rahab when we were below. I won't contest you there."

Joshua dropped his sword and walked over to Edna with open arms. They hugged, as the applause increased. He whispered to her, "I am happy to have you at my side, my sister in faith and battle."

She whispered back, "It is an honor, my brother."

"But under my command," he said with a teasing smirk.

"Under your command, general," she submitted with a smile in return.

And then she hit Methuselah in his arm while whispering, "Staring at Rahab in Sheol were you?"

Methuselah changed the subject, shouting out, "I don't know about the rest of you warriors, but this resurrection evidently didn't take away my earthly hunger. I'm famished, let us eat!"

The men and women laughed and made their way back to camp.

Enoch shook his head. Methuselah so enjoyed the earthly senses. It was something the two of them had fought about in antediluvian days. But not anymore.

Betenos, Lamech's wife, yelled to the men, "Everyone, dinner is served!"

The warriors made their camp alongside the Pharpar river, a mile outside Panias. Enoch had explained to them that he had been sent from heaven to gather the resurrected saints in Mesopotamia and bring them up the Euphrates river, where they marched across Syria and took the Pharpar down to this location. He introduced them to the saints of Israel in the Levant. Noah and his wife Emzara; The parents of Noah, Lamech and Betenos; Noah's sons, Shem and Japheth; Ham was noticeably absent; but not the burly metalworker Tubal-cain, and the brothers Jubal the shepherd, and Jabal the musician. In all, there were about twenty of them from the "land between the two rivers," making a total of about seventy righteous warriors ready to face the seventy unrighteous gods of the nations.

The group sat down to fill their stomachs with mutton and wine. They spun their tales of exploits in days of old. Someone asked who had killed the biggest giant. Caleb, never the shy one, launched in on his story of facing the mighty fifteen foot tall Ahiman, Son of Arba, Son of Anak, outside the walls of Kiriath-Arba. He had accepted the challenge of champions to decide the fate of their war with the city. They had faced each other, one on one, in hand-to-hand combat.

"So there I was, staring up at this big oaf, with his long Anakim neck swaggering about like a taunting cobra." Caleb swayed his neck to show them. It was a bit funny, so the men around the fire laughed.

Caleb saw Eleazar and said, "No offense, Eleazar."

Eleazar chuckled, "We Rephaim never liked those scrawny-necked Anakim either."

More laughs.

Caleb said, "You laugh, but let me tell you, I was not laughing. I peed my battle kilt." Everyone broke out in more laughter.

"You all know what I am talking about. And I wager you've done the same." Humbled murmurs of agreement ran through the group.

"So there he is, looking like a fifteen foot tower of stone, taunting me with his blasphemies about Yahweh. And I am just boiling with zeal for Yahweh's holiness. Then he makes his second mistake. He says what he is going to do with my wife after he kills me. My wife, the incomparably beautiful, unsurpassingly gorgeous Rahab, the nearest thing to a goddess."

The men all teased him with envious sighs.

Edna watched Methuselah who played dumb.

Caleb interjected, "My apologies to you gorgeous women here."

Edna and Betenos smiled.

"So I say to him, 'You have blasphemed my beloved and my god for the last time!' Keep in mind, the entire time I am praying my heart out to Yahweh to help me, because my words are far more cocksure than my actual abilities." More chuckles. Caleb was too modest about his skills.

"So I roll out Rahab. I take some chunks of flesh off of him. Just getting started. But wouldn't you know it? I wrap the blade around his arm and was about to cut it off, when the big old elephant yanks it out of my hands, flings it fifty feet away out of my reach. I'm flat on my back, without a weapon. He lunges in the air to crush me. I roll moments before I became flatbread." The men laughed again.

"And how do I defeat the gargantuan? With the heavenly whip sword I had become expert with? No. I kill him with a tiny dagger in the back of the skull. The tiny dagger my wonderful wife Rahab had given me."

The campfire was alive with gestures and words of affirmation.

Ittai barked out, "You did better with the whip sword than I. I lost her to the giant Ishbi ben Ob in the Valley of the Rephaim." Teasing taunts peppered the crowd.

When they quieted down. David spoke up. "It is not merely size of the giant that makes the defeat grand, but the disadvantage of the warrior."

Caleb said, "Of course, my lord. Your defeat of the Philistine champion in your youth was of far more import than any one of our battles."

"Oh, I am not talking about me," said David. "I am talking about Jonathan the Hawk's defeat of Argaz."

David's mighty men around the fire agreed with fervor.

Caleb looked over at the small, four foot, ten inch bowman. He was the smallest of them all. He turned red with shyness. He didn't like the attention.

"Jonathan the Mouse, as I used to call him," continued David, "became Jonathan the Hawk when he vanquished the fifteen foot tall Rephaim with a flurry of arrows."

Jonathan demurred, "They were like toothpicks in a cushion."

"But perfectly placed toothpicks," corrected David, "that bled out all his major organs. You should have seen that monstrosity. He was one ugly rock badger. His skin was burned over his entire body, from some past fire injury. His face almost looked like a skull. And our little Jonathan bested us all that day by cutting off the head of Argaz the Terrible."

Murmurs of agreement were outdone by Ittai shouting, "Argaz the Mouse versus Jonathan the Hawk!" More laughs.

Caleb noticed that Demas had left the fire and returned with something in his hands. When Demas approached him, he recognized what it was.

Demas handed it to him.

It was Rahab in her sheath.

Caleb's eyes went wide. He unfurled it like a loving father with his long lost child. "Oh, boys. You will never know the sweetness of harnessing this little serpent's bite. I had to rename her when I got her, because she had the same name as my wife. That would not go well."

Some men chuckled and gave cat calls.

Then Lamech, Abishai and Ittai got up, to stand by Caleb, asking to pass around their old weapon once more.

Betenos blurted out, "Men and their weapons."

Edna added, "They give them more care than their women."

The men all gave defensive "aws" and "nos." But everyone knew the women were not too far off the mark.

Demas said to Caleb, "You should have her. She deserves far more worthy hands than I."

"See?" said Edna. Chuckles followed.

Caleb sighed, and handed it to Lamech. "No. I was not the first to wield her."

Lamech caressed the smooth thin flexible blade with loving care. He snapped it at a tree branch and cut it off clean. Some of the men applauded.

But he smiled and handed it back to Demas. "Our Lord chose worthy hands for her to end up in."

Demas' eyes were wet with honor as he received her from Lamech. For the first time that evening, the men shared a moment of silence and awe.

Edna broke that silence. "Like I said…."

The men all gave moans and complaints of defensiveness.

A voice broke through, “I agree with Betenos and Edna.”

All eyes turned to see Jesus standing just outside their ring, flanked by seven armed paladin warriors. Archangels.

“But then again,” added Jesus, “women often give their parents more care than they give their men. So maybe you both have something to learn from each other.”

Betenos and Edna were not going to argue with their Lord.

He walked up to the fire with his archangel guardians.

“But the time for competition with each other is over. We have a battle to fight, and it is time to coordinate our plans. We strike tomorrow.”

CHAPTER 35

The moon was high and bright in the sky, lighting up the temple precinct of Panias. Jesus and the seven archangels walked through the now-empty graveyard into the cave of Pan. Since Jesus' mass exorcism there, it had been abandoned by the local inhabitants. They saw it as cursed of God.

The divine beings walked through the darkness back to the rear of the cave. They stopped by the huge golden statue of Azazel. With supernatural strength, they pulled the image down to the ground and carried it to the precipice over the large deep chasm. They launched it off into the darkness below.

"Good riddance," said Uriel. "Let it sink its way down to where Azazel resides."

Jesus said, "Now you understand why the mystery was kept secret for long ages from the principalities and powers in heavenly places. This mystery into which even you angels have longed to look."

"You can say that again," quipped Uriel.

The archangels gave him scolding looks.

Gabriel shook his head.

Jesus smiled and tousled Uriel's hair. "I would that more angels would have the curiosity and passion of Uriel. But what you will all need tomorrow is his fighting skill. We face a concentration of the enemy like never before. On their own turf, their own cosmic mountain. We will not have the element of surprise for long. So we must act speedily and surely."

The archangels nodded in agreement.

"Do you have your armbands?"

They showed their arms with the fine white Cherubim hair wrapped around them, ready to bind the gods.

"Are your weapons sure?"

"Yes, my Lord," they all said.

Jesus asked Uriel, "Did you pack the extra weapons I asked for?"

Uriel nodded. He was carrying a large satchel on his back wrapped tight.

Gabriel reached out and took the heavy bag off of Uriel's shoulder.

"Big brother, let me carry that weight."

"Big brother?" said Uriel. Everyone else was amazed as well.

"It is time I treat you with the respect you have earned."

"Thank you, little brother," returned Uriel, and he winked. They smiled affectionately.

Uriel helped Gabriel strap the satchel onto his back.

The seven of them tightened their belts and sandals, secured their weapons, and lined up at the cliff's edge looking down into the impenetrable darkness.

Jesus said, "Remember the appointed time. It is crucial to our surprise."

"Yes, my Lord," said Mikael.

Jesus said, "Tomorrow we bind the gods, and claim my inheritance."

The seven then leapt out into the void below.

Jesus left the cave before they even hit the waters of the Abyss.

•••••

Demas looked up at the stars. It was late and he couldn't sleep. He wasn't sure if it was because of the stakes of tomorrow's battle or because of the loud snoring of Tubal-cain and Caleb. He went a stone's throw away from the camp to be alone.

And that is how he felt, alone. He had noticed how so many of the warriors had their support from others. Moses had Joshua, Joshua had Caleb, Caleb had Othniel his brother, Jubal had Jabal, Methuselah had Edna, Lamech had Betenos.

But Demas had no one. His brother, his only friend left in life, had left God and therefore left Demas as well. He felt the least worthy of all those righteous men and women to be in this army of God. For what had he done? He had lived a life of anger and revenge. He had despised God and murdered men. He realized on that cross just how much he deserved judgment and begged for Messiah's mercy. But to be forgiven moments before one's death seemed so — unfair. Some of these warriors had fought for Yahweh most of their lives. They had been true to their Lord through trials and tribulations. And here he was, a capital criminal who spent his entire life in rebellion, getting a last minute reprieve and being given a commission of leadership in that army?

Demas heard soft steps approaching him from behind. He took Rahab's handle and turned to face the spy.

Jesus smiled at him.

"Master," said Demas.

Jesus said, “Cannot sleep?”

He nodded.

Jesus said, “I will be by your side, tomorrow, friend.”

Demas looked up at him painfully.

Jesus sat down. “Let me tell you a story, Demas. If it does not put you to sleep, it might help you to sleep.”

Demas smiled.

Jesus said, “The kingdom of heaven is like a master of a house who went out early in the morning to hire laborers for his vineyard. The first laborers he hired agreed to a denarius for a day’s work. So they went to the vineyard. About the third hour, the master went out to the marketplace again and hired more workers. Then at the sixth and the ninth hour, he went out yet again and hired more workers to complete the work of his vineyard. Strangely, he even went out at the eleventh hour and hired more again.”

Demas interrupted, “Did you not tell this parable to the disciples when I was with them?”

“Yes,” said Jesus. “But you didn’t listen the first time, so be quiet and listen now.”

Demas smiled, properly chastised.

Jesus continued, “Now, when evening came, he gathered the workers around him to pay them their due wages, beginning with the last up to the first. And much to the surprise of all the other workers, he gave those of the eleventh hour a denarius for their work. Then he gave a denarius to the ninth and the sixth hour workers as well. By the time the master came to those he hired in the first hour, they expected to receive more than a denarius, yet they too received a denarius for their work in the vineyard.

“So they complained to the master, ‘These last workers worked only one hour and you have paid them the exact same wage as us? We have borne the burden of the entire work day and sweated through scorching heat for you!’

“The master replied to them, ‘Friend, did you not agree to work a day for a denarius?’

“‘Well, yes,’ said the workers. ‘But, but, but….’

“‘Am I not allowed to do what I choose with what is mine?’

“‘Well, yes,’ said the workers. ‘But, but, but….’

“‘Do you begrudge my generosity?’

“Well, by now, the workers were tongue-tied and embarrassed, for they knew they were not justified.

"And the master finally told them, 'So the last shall be first, and the first shall be last.'"

Demas stayed silent.

Jesus said, "I do not hear you snoring, so you must have stayed awake.

Demas smiled sadly. "Even after receiving forgiveness, I still do not understand mercy."

Jesus said, "I will have mercy on whom I have mercy, and compassion on whom I have compassion."

"But it doesn't seem fair."

"If Yahweh was not merciful, if he was only 'fair,' then everyone would receive the fires of Gehenna and no one would be justified before him. For it is written, 'No one is righteous, no, not one; no one understands; no one seeks for God. No one does good, not even one.'"

Demas sat for a long silence.

Jesus spoke again. "You did not choose me, Demas, I chose you. From before the foundations of the earth. You were predestined for adoption as a son to God. Do you not think my Father in heaven knows what he is doing?"

Finally, Demas spoke in a hush, "I have nothing to offer but my gratitude."

"And your sword arm."

Demas glanced at Jesus who responded with an impish grin.

"That reminds me," said Demas.

He unbuckled his belt and offered the sheath of Rahab to the chagrin of Jesus. "I am not quitting. I am only giving you what is rightfully yours. We both know you would be the best with it."

Jesus sighed. Demas said, "I can handle a dozen different weapons against any beast from hell. You have been speaking of your wrath for the last three years. I just want to see you fight."

Jesus took the whip sword. "You are quite the penitent thief."

They shared a smile.

Demas said, "All I have now is my faith."

Jesus said, "Well, you know what my brother James often says. Faith without weapons is dead."

Demas smiled again. "I'll bring them."

Jesus turned sober. "Tomorrow will not be easy. You are resurrected flesh. But you are still flesh."

Demas said, "And flesh can die in battle."

Jesus said, "The Watcher gods are still in assembly. All seventy will be there. Except those already bound in Tartarus."

Demas asked, "Why are they gathered at Hermon?"

"Celebrating my demise."

"Fools."

"Immortal fools. Who will fight more viciously and ruthlessly than they ever have before, because they know what defeat will mean for them. Demas, we must hold them for the archangels to achieve their purpose. Not one can escape."

Demas looked into his master's eyes, and with all his soul, he said, "To the death, my Lord and God. Again."

CHAPTER 36

Jesus led the seventy resurrected warriors ten miles up to Mount Hermon. Though Demas was their general, they were divided up into three companies of about twenty-five men each. Joshua led one company of herem soldiers with Caleb. David and Joab led a second of David's mighty men, and Enoch and Methuselah the third company from Mesopotamia.

They stood and gazed up at the ruins of the ancient ziggurat temple of Ereshkigal, built halfway into the mountain. It was one of the gateways to Sheol. The structure was crumbling with erosion of the elements and time. Plants and foliage had grown up through the cracks, taking over its decay and dilapidation. But Noah could almost see it alive with idol worship as he had seen it millennia ago.

Noah said, "Brings back bad memories."

They could all see in their minds' eyes the human sacrifice up on the top ledge of the altar, where the now missing tophet had held the child's broken body, as the winged demon Ereshkigal, goddess of the underworld, rose to drink the victim's blood. It made them sick to their stomachs.

Jubal wrapped his arm around his brother Jabal. "It was inside that temple," he said, "that I lost my brother to the Scorpion Men. But not this time."

Tubal-cain said, "Do you think they will be there, guarding the entrance?" Scorpion Men were ancient magical and demonic soldier hybrids that Noah's company had faced before entering the assembly of the gods.

Enoch answered, "They are long gone in the mists of legend and time."

Methuselah added, "Along with the Seven Gates of Ganzir."

The primeval warriors from Mesopotamia all chuckled at the inside joke. The ancient Sumerian myth had spoken of seven gates of Ganzir to the underworld, but when they arrived, there was only one. Noah had responded with disappointment in being duped by the myth.

Methuselah recounted his sarcastic barb in the present, "If you prefer, we could re-enter the gate seven times to satisfy your penchant for the grandiose."

The primeval warriors all chuckled again at the retold joke.

Jesus said, "Let us go, army of God. We have a gate to crash."

They made their way up the long, crumbling stone "stairway to heaven" till they reached the top where the tophet was. This was a pit of sacrificial fire that led into the heart of the mountain where the assembly of the gods took place.

But the tophet was filled with boulders that blocked their way in.

"Is there a back door?" said Caleb with a touch of wit.

"Actually, there is," said Enoch. "I took it myself when I pronounced judgment upon the Watchers."

Jesus added "But we cannot get there in time."

Noah said, "We need some supernatural muscle to move these rocks."

Eleazar the giant stepped forward. "Stand back and let a repentant Nephilim pay his way."

"Of course," said Noah. The men cheered the giant on.

But Jesus announced, "You are not the only one in our midst with Nephilim strength."

Suddenly everyone knew who Jesus was referring to. They had all forgotten him, because he had stayed silently at the outer edges of their army, avoiding interaction with others out of shame for his failures in life.

The men parted now as a big bulk of musculature made his way humbly from the back to the front.

Demas opened his arms wide and said, "Samson. You and I have much in common, my friend." They embraced, and Demas knew he was not alone after all.

Like Demas, Samson had failed in his life. He too had found forgiveness moments before his death, through his single act of faith. He had been blinded and had his strength defeated with the cutting of his hair. But resurrection had given him new eyes and new strength. Samson pushed his long, braided locks behind his head so he could reach down and grab a boulder. It was a small one. Only the size of two horses. A mere warm up. Eleazar matched him with his own huge stone.

The two of them grunted and picked up the large rocks in a deadlift. They jerked them up above their heads with grunts and heaved them over the ledge of the temple with a simultaneous yell.

The men cheered as the rocks tumbled down the heights to the ground below with a crash.

Samson smiled. He muttered, "How is that for a dumb ox?"

"And a redeemed Nephilim," added Eleazar.

The men cheered.

The two strongmen began a kind of relay, heaving and lifting, heaving and lifting, until they had cleared a way through to the secret hallway below the tophet.

Jesus, followed by Demas, Enoch and the other leaders, David and Joshua, walked through the hundred and fifty-feet long pillared hallway toward a huge bronze gate.

Noah and his soldiers glanced cautiously into the shadows behind the pillars, looking for possible stingers and claws. Though Jesus had told them not to worry, their experience was still stark in their resuscitated memories.

The shadows seemed to move with their steps.

Something was not right.

The sound of claws scraped stone behind a pillar.

Noah's muscles tensed. He whispered, "Prepare for battle."

His team of Tubal-cain, Jubal and Methuselah drew their weapons.

But the shadow that showed itself from behind the column was not a Scorpion Man. It was Jabal, grinning from ear to ear, using his sword to scratch the stone.

"Gotcha."

Jubal fumed with anger. "Jabal, that is not funny. You were killed by one of those scorpion tails."

Jabal said, "Do not lose your humor, my brother. After all, death has lost its sting." He looked to Jesus for approval.

Jubal and the others groaned at the bad taste of their brother-in-arms. But they all secretly drew courage from the knowledge that he was right.

Jesus said from the front. "Warriors, keep it down. We are at the gate. Stand ready. Samson and Eleazar, we need you again."

The two strongmen stepped forward and peered up at the large bronze-armored gate towering over them.

Samson said with a grin, "Piece of raisin cake compared to the gates of Gaza."

Eleazar bowed and gestured to Samson. It was all his.

"Oh no," said Samson. "Let us make this a loud entrance with the both of us."

CHAPTER 37

Inside Mount Hermon, Belial looked over the bodies of the gods sprawled all over the cavern, all sixty plus divinities. Many of them were drunk out of their skulls, others were hallucinating with drugs of sorcery. Bodies of bloody, dismembered, dead humans lay all around, the victims of sexual debauchery and other unspeakable atrocities.

Disgusting, thought Belial sitting on the throne, looking out over it all. *Indulgent juveniles and morons. We have a world to rule and they are only now coming out of their stupor.* It had been a week-long celebration over the death of Messiah. *Yes, it was a victory. Yes, there is a time to celebrate. But these fools do everything to excess. They have no sense of discipline, moderation, restraint.*

A semi-sober Zeus stumbled up to him. "Belial, you really need to loosen up and enjoy our victory a bit. I did not see you rape or mutilate a single virgin, let alone the cult prostitutes and boy loves we brought in."

Belial narrowed his eyes at the teetering divinity. Was that "loosen up" remark a subtle reference to Belial's supernatural binding that had grown like a fungus over his body? If it was, there would be Gehenna to pay.

Zeus belched.

Belial turned his head at the putrid stench. "Keep your mouth shut, you stupid boar. This is not Olympus and your childish Greek parties. Pick up this mess. I want all the human body parts out of here and the blood scrubbed off those rocks. Have you no sense of the sacred?"

"So-rry, your majesty" said Zeus in a sing-song voice with a sarcastic salute. He pulled a poor young male from his impaling on a stalagmite and tossed the corpse into the black flaming waters of the Abyss. He clapped his hands loudly. "You heard the Prince of Rome. Let us clean up this mess!"

Some were already moving about. Others pulled themselves up off the vomit-filled floor. Anubis slipped on a pile of excrement and blood and fell on his rear end. He started laughing and cackling like a jackal. Others around him, joined in.

Suddenly the sound of pounding echoed throughout the hall.

Belial looked over at the large gate into their cavern. It hadn't been used in centuries.

More pounding again.

Anubis stopped howling. Everyone else stopped what they were doing.

More pounding.

But it wasn't someone pounding on the door. It sounded like someone was pounding *around* the door.

Watchers picked themselves up off the floor, looking for their weapons. Many of the gods had misplaced them in the celebration.

More pounding. Belial knew what it was now. Someone was hammering the hinges of the gate.

"Watcher gods, prepare yourself for battle!"

Lift up your heads, O gates!
And be lifted up, O ancient doors,
that the King of glory may come in.

Now someone pounded *on* the gate. It shook with defiance.

Belial stood in confusion, his mind racing with the possibilities of who it could be. Of *what* it could be.

The gates broke open with a crash.

Who is this King of glory?
Yahweh, strong and mighty,
Yahweh, mighty in battle!

Belial's eagle eyes could see a human, and a giant each take a door off its hinges and lift them up with superhuman strength. He recognized the human. But it couldn't be. He was dead.

"Samson?"

Marduk recognized the giant with the other door, and exclaimed, "Eleazar?"

The two muscleman threw the doors inward, crushing several gods that had tried to meet the visitors with weapons.

Lift up your heads, O gates!
And lift them up, O ancient doors,
that the King of glory may come in.

Belial's throat dropped to his stomach. Behind the strongmen was an army of warriors, led by someone wielding the infamous Rahab whip sword. Someone he recognized from any distance because he had come to know him intimately.

"Jesus Christ," he croaked.

Who is this King of glory?
Yahweh of hosts,
he is the King of glory!

The army of God poured into the breach and spread out, seeking their enemies with bow and arrow, battle ax, sword and javelin. It was almost too easy. Drunk and confused deities stumbled over themselves, others hid in fear, searching for their weapons.

Not all were completely overtaken.

Horus was the first to face Jesus sober. He stepped in front of the Nazarene. The falcon-headed sky deity yelled, "Son of God! You darkened Ra! But you will not bind the sky!" He was referring to the judgment of Yahweh on Egypt's deities in the days of Moses. The ninth plague was the darkening of the sun. Yahweh had punched out Ra's lights, and Horus had taken his status of power in the pantheon. But Horus was also the god of hunting and master with a spear.

Before he could engage with Jesus, Demas jumped in with his own shield and spear. Benaiah of Kabzeel joined him. In the days of King David, Benaiah had killed an infamous Egyptian Rephaim named Runihura with the giant's own staff. Horus was not going to get through this one unbound.

Jesus moved on, his eyes set on Belial and his throne across the burning black lake.

Belial sat anxiously considering his options. He was not much of a fighter. He was more of a legal attacker as the Accuser of Yahweh's heavenly court.

Jesus' path was blocked. He became surrounded by a trio of supreme Hindu deities, Shiva, Vishnu and Shakti. Shiva the Destroyer had a third eye on his forehead, a snake wrapped around his neck and he wielded a trident-like weapon. Vishnu was blue with four arms, and he carried a mace in his left hand and a discus in his right that contained serrated edges. Shakti, the mother goddess of power, had talons on her fingers that were as dangerous as ten daggers.

Jesus said, "I have had enough of this false trinity," and unfurled Rahab. He swung his blade in a circle to keep them at bay. But he was surrounded, and it was all he could do to keep the trident, mace and claws from piercing, crushing or cutting him.

Rahab snapped back and lashed out in defense. But Jesus finally got some room to breathe when arrows began to prick each of the three enemy gods. It was Jonathan the Hawk and his trusty aim from a rocky ledge above. Arrows would not stop the gods, but they would slow them down.

Methuselah and Edna faced down Odin, the bearded Norse god, with his mighty spear Gungnir. Too bad for Odin, Methuselah's specialty was the javelin.

Caleb and Joshua found themselves against the Toltec feathered serpentine god, Quetzalcoatl.

David took up combat with the Great Spirit of distant western lands, Gitchi Manitou, with Ittai at his back battling Zeus' lightning bolts with his double bladed battle ax.

Lamech and Noah fought the Persian deity Ahura Mazda, who had large wings and held a wheel blade between both hands. But the two humans moved aside and Ahura Mazda saw the giant Eleazar step up with shield and battle axe. Eleazar said, "You shouldn't have held me captive in Parthia, fool. A resurrected saint is not so easy to defeat." The god was thrown off by the surprise. It allowed his opponents, led by Eleazar, the advantage they needed to overcome him in short order.

What the invader's strategy had achieved was to focus the gods' attention on the attack from the gate. That way, they would not be ready for what happened next.

Behind the gods, seven beings exploded from the black waters of the Abyss. The archangels led by Mikael. Had they come with the humans, their supernatural presence would have been detected by the gods, and their surprise ruined. But because they traveled the secret depths of the Abyss from Panias all the way to Hermon, they had gone undetected.

They attacked the gods from behind, binding the easy prey of the drunk and the wounded while the human gibborim wore down the other Watchers.

Jesus dodged the trident of Shiva, but saw in the corner of his eye, Vishnu rearing back to throw his bladed discus. Jesus spun just as the discus flew where his head had been. It lodged in the rock behind him. He whipped Rahab around Shiva's trident, just as an arrow from Jonathan hit Shiva's third eye. Jesus yanked the weapon from Shiva's hand and snapped it behind him, to catch the claws of Shakti about to rip him open. The bite of Rahab was much mightier than her talons. The blade cut her hand clean off. She shrieked, holding her bloody stump.

Shiva tried pulling the arrow out of his blinded eye.

Jesus saw his moment and whipped Rahab around above his head. It drove like a windmill blade around him, and connected with all three of the gods' necks one after the other. Their severed heads fell to the ground in silent agony. Though the Watchers could not die, they could be incapacitated until their body parts could be reconnected for regeneration.

The archangels had them all bound before they could do so.

Belial stood from his throne as Jesus approached the other end of the black, viscous lake. He smirked, knowing that Jesus would have to run around the large body of darkness or swim through it to get to him.

Jesus did neither. He merely rolled up his sword, stepped out onto the lake and walked over the flaming black liquid without sinking or being singed.

"That's not fair," muttered Belial.

He stepped backward fearfully, and stumbled, falling back into the chair.

Jesus crossed the lake and made his way up to the throne. He stepped up to Belial with a stoic look and said nothing.

Belial wondered why Jesus did nothing. Then he realized it. "I have diplomatic immunity. I cannot touch you, but you cannot touch me." He grinned malevolently.

But then his eyes burned with a blinding brightness. He went dizzy.

•••••

When Belial opened his eyes, he saw that he and Jesus were no longer in the assembly of Mount Hermon. They were in the court of Yahweh's divine council in the heavenlies.

But something was very different. For all the millennia, the Accuser had pranced and bellowed from before the bar, as he prosecuted his enemies in the dock. Once, he had even put God in the dock, in an attempt to prosecute the Creator for covenantal unfaithfulness to Adam and Eve.

That was ballsy, he thought to himself.

But now, for the first time ever, the Accuser was in the dock, and Jesus stood before him at the bar. Belial panicked.

The sound of voices like many waters shook him out of his stupor.

"Holy, holy, holy is Yahweh Elohim Almighty. Who was and is and is to come!"

The trisagion of praise had come from the seraphim above the chariot throne of Yahweh Elohim, before which the Accuser now sat.

Their humanoid yet serpentine bodies had six wings. With two they flew, two covered their feet in holiness, and two covered their faces. Belial knew these beings well because he had once been one. A long time ago.

The Cherubim below the judgment seat were sphinx-like, with four faces and four wings, sparkling of burnished bronze. The faces were those of human, lion, ox and eagle. And beside each one was a wheel within a wheel of gleaming beryl that moved with the living creatures.

Around the throne were ten thousand times ten thousands of his holy ones, the Sons of God, who shone with the brightness of burnished bronze and flashes of lightning.

Silence enveloped the entire throne room. Normally, in a covenantal lawsuit, the Accuser would bring his prosecution before the court of the Most High. A defense would be offered, and Yahweh Elohim would render judgment of justification for one side or the other. Members of the divine council would then carry out any orders of the court.

But Belial knew in his soul that would not be happening this day. There would be no trial for him. This entire episode of crucifying Messiah was his trial, and he had failed to see it. This would be a summary judgment by the Judge of all the earth.

He heard a voice from nowhere and yet from everywhere call out, "Now the salvation and the power and the kingdom of our God and the authority of his Christ have come, for the Accuser of our brethren will be thrown down, who accuses them day and night before our God."

Belial's fear turned to slow burning rage. *How dare he appoint me as prosecutor for all these ages, and now turn around and punish me for it.*

The voice continued, "And they have conquered him by the blood of the Lamb and by the word of their testimony, for they loved not their lives even unto death."

That was it, thought Belial. *What I thought of as a groveling defeat of Messiah's death had been a crowning act of atonement. His resurrection became his justification of kingship. He tricked me, that heavenly coward. He didn't have the guts to battle me directly.*

The voice drowned out Belial's thoughts. "Therefore, rejoice, O heavens and you who dwell in them! But woe to you, O earth and sea, for the devil has come down to you in great wrath, because he knows that his time is short!"

Belial now realized he was not being thrown into Tartarus with the others. He was being spared, hampered though he was by the binding that grew over him. Well, if he still had the power of Rome, then he would use it. He thought of Yahweh, *You may have won this battle over Messiah and his mother, Israel. But I will make war on the rest of her seed. This Serpent will become a seven-headed dragon, a new Leviathan, whose head you will no longer be able to crush. Then what will you —.*

Belial stopped with painful shock. His eyes burned with the brightness of the throne of God. His ears were filled with a piercing ringing. Everything went white.

•••••

Jesus was returned from the divine throne room to the bowels of Mount Hermon.

The battle was over. The Watcher gods were defeated and bound by the angels, laying at the lake edge of the Abyss. The wedge tactic had worked. The gods were overcome in short order by the victorious forces of Mikael and the angels. The stakes had been high and the enemy fought with desperation like the stars of heaven. But they had been so inebriated and bamboozled that they were simply not capable of standing before the army of God.

Jesus yelled to the resurrected warriors, "Each of you, grab a bound deity. We are taking these sons of Belial down to Tartarus!"

•••••

When the burning brightness and piercing ringing stopped, Belial opened his eyes and saw that he was returned to earth.

He was in Rome in the palace of Caesar.

He looked around. *No. This could not be true. Could it?*

But it was. Yahweh had kicked him out of the divine council and took away his legal authority over the Seed of Abraham. He could no longer accuse or condemn the people of God. He could not stop their proclamation of the Kingdom of God and Messiah. He could not stop the great ingathering that had already begun. He was spiritually bound.

But Yahweh had given Belial back his earthly power. *Why?* he thought. *Is Yahweh a bullying child playing games? Does he need me like a pet of chaos in order to prove his power and control? Pathetic.*

Well, if Belial couldn't touch the people of God himself, he would simply get his earthly minions to do so. He would marshal his kingdom of iron and clay. He would kill them all.

CHAPTER 38

The bound bodies of the gods sank into the depths of the Abyss on their way down to Hades. They were tied in a train of defeat by the Cherubim hair of the angels. They were accompanied by the resurrected warriors who had defeated them.

When they broke through the watery sky of Hades and landed on the ground, Demas saw that they were on the huge mountain of the north. He remembered that this was the celestial storehouse from which flowed the rivers of Hades, including the River of Fire that Jesus had parted for them to cross to the Living Waters. To the south was Mount Zion and then Sinai, to the west was the Mountain of the Dead and Abraham's Bosom.

Jesus said to the warriors now guarding the train of captives, "We must journey to the far east, beyond the ends of the earth."

Demas knew where they were going: Tartarus.

The archangels ran ahead of them to prepare the way.

But when the train of captives made it down the foot of the mountain, they saw their way blocked by two huge twenty foot tall fiery beings. They appeared to be humanoid, but were covered in flames of fire that never consumed the figure. Then the two were joined by six more who seemed to peer down upon the company with cold observation. Like winged fiery serpents ready to strike.

Some of the warriors drew their weapons in fear. These gargantuans had flaming swords as well that were reminiscent of the "Flame of the Whirling Sword" in Eden. This would not go well for the resurrected humans. They felt outmatched by the divine. The whirling swords seemed to move and operate as independent beings, which effectively amounted to a doubling of their forces.

Jesus gestured to his company to put away their weapons. These were guardians of the sacred mountain. They were now under his authority.

The huge heavenly beings lined up in a pathway to the east and Jesus led the train out into the vast desert region leading to the Great Sea.

By the time they made it to the far ends of the earth and were on the shore of the Great Sea, the angels met them with large rafts they had made for their journey.

They linked the rafts together, and Demas saw Jesus on the waterfront with his hands raised in prayer. He wondered if the Son of God was going to part the Abyss as he parted the River of Fire. But the water did not separate. The only movement he saw was the spiny back fins and scales of a large serpent break the surface on its way toward them from the depths. Leviathan. The sea dragon of chaos had been tamed, domesticated by the Son of God, and put to his purposes, which now involved pulling their train of rafts to the outer reaches beyond the Great Sea.

The train of warriors and captives landed beyond the waters and Leviathan left them. They entered the desert wasteland of *Tohu Wabohu*. It was a world of chaos and disorder, of darkness and silence, with no sky above and no foundations beneath.

They made their way to a single large mountain of jagged rock, that stretched upward like a grasping hand: the prison-house of the Watchers.

Despite being in the company of mighty gibborim, Demas shivered. He knew that the Guardians of Tartarus were waiting for them.

The captive train arrived at the base of the mountain. They prepared to make the trek up the steep pathway. But an earthquake interrupted their plans and threw them all into the dirt.

Then the ground around them exploded open in seven places. Rocks and dirt covered the warriors and archangels as seven fifteen-feet tall warrior beings stood before them.

The primeval saints, Noah, Methuselah, and their kin recognized them. They were the Rephaim, souls of the giant warrior kings who had been thrown down to the underworld during the Titanomachy of primordial days. They were tall, powerful, and carried strangely shaped glaive weapons, crafted in the pit of Sheol. They were long blades at the end of a lance that the Rephaim could use to strike wide and long at a distance. They could take out entire groups of warriors with one swath.

Six Rephaim surrounded the train on either side, and one stood at the front. Strangely, it was a blinded Rapha who relied upon sound and smell to face its quarry. It didn't look any less intimidating.

The company of saints took defensive stances in their gauntlet of underworld giants.

Methuselah and Edna stepped into the front by Jesus and the archangels. The lead Rapha had killed Edna's family, and Methuselah had given him a permanent limp with his sword. Later in the days of Noah, Uriel had visited the guardian and taken out its eyes as a favor for Methuselah and Edna.

Methuselah said, "Let us help you with these, my Lord. We have a grudge to finish paying back."

Before any battle could begin, the Rephaim all knelt down to one knee and bowed their heads toward Jesus.

The humans were stunned. But they quickly realized what was taking place. The Guardians of Tartarus gave obeisance to their Lord, the king of heaven and earth and under the earth.

Methuselah and Edna felt their revenge transform into redemption.

The Rephaim chanted a haunting verse with their strange ghostlike voices as the captives passed through their gauntlet on their way up the mountain.

Sheol beneath is stirred up
to meet you when you come;
it rouses the Rephaim to greet you,
all who were leaders of the earth;
it raises from their thrones
all who were kings of the nations.
All of them will answer
and say to you:
'You too have become as weak as we!
You have become like us!'
Your pomp is brought down to Sheol,
the sound of your harps;
maggots are laid as a bed beneath you,
and worms are your covers.

They reached the cave opening a thousand feet above and led the Seventy inside to the pit of Tartarus.

It was said that Tartarus was as deep below the earth as the earth was below the heavens. It was the remotest point in the cosmos from Yahweh's heavenly throne above the waters.

It had changed somewhat since Noah had been temporarily held there in antediluvian days. The rock was still glass smooth, but the pit had been widened to accommodate the two hundred rebellious Watchers from the days of Noah. Its walls were covered with perpetual flames that did not produce light, like a chasm of fire that dissolved into the deepest darkness. No sounds could be heard from below, not merely because it was of incalculable depth, but because the acoustics of the pit were such that instead of creating an echo chamber for sound, it swallowed everything up in silence.

Now the last of those rebellious angels, the Seventy, were lined up along the rim of the chasm, still bound and in fear of their destiny.

Jesus nodded to Gabriel, who took out his trumpet and gave a long blast.

Then, the Archangels spoke, no, they sang a proclamation of Messiah's triumph.

Holy, holy, holy is Yahweh of hosts.
Who was, and is, and is to come.
The whole earth is full of his glory.
I have set my King
on Zion, my holy mountain."
Ask of me, and I will make the nations your heritage,
and the ends of the earth your possession.
For Messiah suffered once for sins,
the righteous for the unrighteous,
that he might bring humanity to God,
being put to death in the flesh
but made alive in the spirit,
In which he now proclaims victory to the spirits in prison.
He has disarmed the rulers and authorities and put them to open shame, by triumphing over them in him.
Angels, authorities and powers have been subjected to him.
The kingdom of the world has become the kingdom of our Lord and of his Christ, and he shall reign forever and ever.

It was the Messianic secret, the mystery hidden for ages but now revealed. That the Messiah, the Son of David, the Son of Man, the Son of God, would conquer the principalities and powers in the heavenly places as the Suffering Servant. That he would dispossess them of their allotted territories and inherit all the earth as the seed of Abraham, the Seed of Eve.

> *I will surely bless you, and I will surely multiply your seed as the stars of heaven and as the sand that is on the seashore. And your seed shall possess the gate of his enemies, and in your seed shall all the nations of the earth be blessed.*

> *Being made perfect through his suffering, he became the source of eternal salvation to all who obey him, being designated by God a high priest after the order of Melchizedek. As a high priest, he entered once for all into the holy places, not by means of the blood of goats and calves but by means of his own blood, thus securing an eternal redemption. For he has appeared once for all at the end of the ages to put away sin by the sacrifice of himself.*

This was the Messianic secret which God decreed before the ages for the glory of his holy ones. None of the principalities and powers of this age understood this, for if they had, they would not have crucified the Lord of glory.

Instead, those heavenly powers were now lined up along the precipice of their demise.

They were shoved into the pit.

They descended into the darkness and the silence to await the Great Judgment.

•••••

High above Hades, in the assembly hall of Mount Hermon, Jesus and seven archangels pulled themselves out of the black flaming waters of the Abyss. Uriel found the satchel of weapons he had left here during the battle of Mount Hermon. He pulled out the last weapon of the sack: the battle hammer of Ba'al.

He handed it to Jesus who took it in both hands. It was large and heavy, crafted for a god. It had been used for so much evil through history.

Now it would be used one last time for good.

He looked around the cavern at the sparkling gem laden stalagmites and stalactites. He saw the throne of the underworld across the lake, upon whose evil courtly majesty had sat Ereshkigal, Ba'al, and Belial. He peered at the flames flitting across the surface of the Abyss and the dark corners of this assembly hall of wickedness.

He said, “Good riddance,” and swung high the hammer.

It contacted with the floor of the assembly hall. A massive tremor spread from the epicenter and rattled the entire mountain around them. A crevice opened where the hammer had hit. Stalactites and rocky debris fell from overhead like dangerous missiles piercing the ground around their feet.

> *Yet once more, I will shake the heavens and the earth and the sea and the dry land. And I will shake all nations, so that the treasures of all nations shall come in, and I will fill this house with glory, says the LORD of hosts.*

Jesus dropped the hammer and they ran for the exit, the secret tunnel that led out to the foothills.

The rumbling and shaking of the rock around them made it difficult to make it through the tunnel. A small cave-in almost caught Uriel at the back.

“I am all right. Keep going!”

They stumbled their way out as the inside of the mountain imploded in a cascading landslide of stone and dust.

> *“Yet once more,” indicates the removal of things that are shaken—that is, things that have been made—in order that the things that cannot be shaken may remain. Therefore let us be grateful for receiving a kingdom that cannot be shaken.*

Mount Hermon rumbled as its rock and stone settled into place. The quake was felt for miles around.

The belly of wickedness had been disemboweled.

The assembly of the gods of the nations was no more.

CHAPTER 39

Simon the Zealot and Mary Magdalene made their way up the Mount of Olives. The eleven disciples, along with the seventy closest followers of Jesus had been called to meet there by the master.

These were the seventy that Jesus had appointed earlier in his ministry to go before him and proclaim the arrival of the Kingdom of God to unrepentant cities. They had been given the authority to tread on the Serpent and to have power over demons in his name.

Simon knew that this particular gathering would be very important. Because these seventy stood for the seventy nations whose principalities had just been dethroned. Would these seventy now become the new rulers over those nations as the twelve apostles would lead the twelve tribes of Israel?

Perhaps this was the final gathering, since Jesus had yet to bring those nations under his newly established kingdom. Simon knew that the prophet Zechariah had foretold this very location for his final battle.

> *Then Yahweh will go out and fight against those nations as when he fights on a day of battle. On that day his feet shall stand on the Mount of Olives that lies before Jerusalem on the east, and the Mount of Olives shall be split in two from east to west. Then Yahweh my God will come, and all the holy ones with him.*

Simon looked all around the valleys surrounding the mountain. There were no armies amassing to fight. None were in the distance marching their way toward the holy city. It was just another quiet, sunny day in all the land.

The seventy had gathered around Jesus, and made small talk.

Jesus quieted them down and announced to them, "What I told you earlier in Galilee, I tell you again. All authority in heaven and on earth has been given to me. Go therefore and make disciples of all nations, baptizing them in the name of the Father and of the Son and of the Holy Spirit, teaching them to observe all that I have commanded you. And behold, I am with you always, to the end of the age."

Simon frowned with confusion. Jesus had said in this very spot that the end of the age would be signaled by the destruction of the holy city and Temple, within their generation. But the city and Temple were still standing. He had used astronomical poetics to explain that when the ruling authorities, both in heaven and on earth, would fall, that Jesus would come like the storm god, "on the clouds of heaven," a sign of him seated at the right hand of God. This was a prophetic way of saying he would come in omnipotent power to judge.

Simon could not help himself. He blurted out, "Lord, will you at this time restore the kingdom to Israel?"

Jesus responded, "It is not for you to know times or seasons that the Father has fixed by his own authority. But you will be my witnesses in Jerusalem and in all Judea and Samaria and to the end of the earth. For it is written, that the Christ should suffer and on the third day rise from the dead, and that repentance and forgiveness of sins should be proclaimed in his name to all nations, beginning from Jerusalem."

This made some sense to Simon. The prophet Daniel had said that Messiah the prince would put an end to the sin that caused Israel's exile, to atone for iniquity and bring in everlasting righteousness. He had said that Messiah would put an end to sacrifice and offering. This atonement Jesus had accomplished to be sure with his death and resurrection.

But that was only the first half of the prophecy. The other half said that on the wing of abominations would come another prince, one who makes desolate. The abomination of desolation. Jesus himself had said to look for this abomination in the armies of the prince of Rome surrounding the holy city. The people of this prince would destroy the city and sanctuary of God.

But the armies of Rome were nowhere to be found.

But then Simon remembered that Jesus said these things would happen within a generation of his prediction. A generation was about thirty to forty years. It was still early in the gathering storm.

Jesus continued to explain, "You are witnesses of these things. And behold, I am sending the promise of my Father upon you. But stay in the city until you are clothed with power from on high."

Clothed with power from on high? thought Simon. *To do what? Proclaim the Kingdom of God? Who then would fight the armies of Rome?*

Simon swallowed with a dry throat and felt a pit in his stomach, because it was starting to become clear to him. Jesus had also taught the disciples regarding the abomination of desolation that when it came, they should not stay in the city but flee to the mountains. He was already familiar with such thinking. As an Essene at the isolated Qumran, he thought that they were the true remnant of Yahweh's holy people and all of Israel would be judged when Messiah came. But Messiah came and the Essenes rejected him. They were not the remnant. The Pharisees and Sadducees rejected him and along with the Herodians, led the people in crucifying him. None of them were the remnant.

That could only mean one thing. Israel was going to be judged. She had rejected her Messiah and Jesus was going to come on the clouds and destroy her through the armies of Rome, as he did through the armies of Assyria in Isaiah's day. Yahweh was going to protect his remnant of true believers, the followers of Jesus.

But how could this pathetic group of fishermen, ex-Zealots and plebeians draw all the nations into Zion if Zion was destroyed? Was Jesus himself the spiritual Zion, a heavenly mountain? His New Covenant kingdom, a heavenly Jerusalem?

Mary grabbed Simon's arm. He had become so lost in his thoughts, he wasn't listening closely to Jesus. But she had been listening. She had been watching Jesus closely to see what he was going to do. She had scanned the faces of the disciples all around, watching their reactions. Joanna, Salomé, and the other Mary stood beside her as they had done on Golgotha and at the empty tomb. They were inseparable.

But now, Mary felt herself separate from the others there. As if her body stayed in their midst, but her spirit seemed to stand apart. It reminded her of when she would go into trances at Panias. But this time it was not evil. This was from God, because in her hazy vision, she now saw what appeared to be a myriad of holy ones on chariots surrounding the Mount of Olives. Just like she had seen at the cross.

The chariots of God are twice ten thousand,
thousands upon thousands;
the Lord is among them; Sinai is now in the sanctuary.

She scanned the crowd of faces, and realized that none of the others had seen this heavenly vision. Only she.

But she had been so intent upon the heavenly vision in the distance that she almost missed the earthly miracle that happened right in front of her.

Jesus began to rise up off the ground before their very eyes.

Some went silent with awe, others screamed in fear, still others fainted. Someone cried out, "Jesus, don't go! Come back!"

As he ascended, he became temporarily obscured by the blinding sun behind him in the sky. Was this an apotheosis, a deification? *No,* thought Simon. *He had always been the unique Son of God, Immanuel, God among us.* He was born the Seed of the Woman *and* the Seed of the Holy Spirit. He had always been the true god-man, that which the fallen Watchers had sought to mimic, and by so doing, destroy his incarnation. But they had failed. And they had failed to stop his seedline through all of history. Now, he had conquered the powers. Now they were subject to him, as he ascended to the right hand of God, the very position of sovereign power and majesty. Simon knelt in awe as the resurrected messiah, Jesus, faded into the clouds above.

That was not all Mary saw as she watched the Lord ascend. She also saw into the spirit realm. She saw a train of what could only be ancient saints taken from the Bosom of Abraham, freed from their wait for Messiah in Hades, follow him up into heaven.

> *You ascended on high,*
> *leading a host of captives in your train*
> *and giving gifts to men.*

Silence permeated the crowd. No one knew what to say. They all knew this would be the last they would see of their Lord on this earth. He had told them before that unless he left them, the Holy Spirit would not come. But Simon wasn't sure exactly how the Holy Spirit would guide them.

Since everyone was looking up, no one saw the two men in white robes arrive in their midst. But Mary recognized them from the empty tomb. Angels.

One of them said, "Why do you stand looking into heaven? This Jesus, who was taken up from you, will come in the same way as you saw him go into heaven."

Mouths agape, minds bedazzled, the disciples looked amongst one another trying to understand just what was going on.

But Mary saw. And Simon knew. Jesus would return on the clouds of heaven within their generation as he promised. They had to be prepared. The Day of the Lord was coming.

CHAPTER 40

"I saw in the night visions, and behold, with the clouds of heaven there came one like a son of man, and he came to the Ancient of Days and was presented before him. And to him was given dominion and glory and a kingdom, that all peoples, nations, and languages should serve him; his dominion is an everlasting dominion, which shall not pass away, and his kingdom one that shall not be destroyed."
Daniel 7:13–14

The disciples returned to Jerusalem and replaced the twelfth apostle by drawing lots. Matthias would become Judas Iscariot's replacement.

It had been seven weeks since the Passover and the terrible events of that week. But Yahweh had established a new Passover with a new lamb, his Messiah, and now he was preparing to consummate his new covenant.

The feast of Pentecost had arrived and with it, another pilgrimage of Jews from all the nations into Jerusalem. This was the celebration of the harvest, but also the renewal of the covenant. Many offerings were made at the Temple to celebrate the original entrance into the Promised Land and the rich bounty that Yahweh had laid upon his people.

The seventy were gathered together at a home near the Temple gates, along with an additional fifty or so followers. Simon had been asked by Peter to share with them the story of the Tower of Babel. It struck him as strange, but he did so, having studied it quite deeply during his days in Qumran. All those hours of scrupulous reading of petty details came in handy sometimes. He missed those days of academic lectures at the community. But these days were so much better.

Simon looked at the faces of those around him as he told his story. "And so, Yahweh saw that the whole of mankind had once again rose from the muck and clay to make an idolatrous name for themselves. Nimrod, the mighty rebel before Yahweh, had built a tower, a cosmic mountain, that united heaven and earth. And all the earth spoke the same language back then. So in order to stop a united humanity from rising to incalculable heights of evil, Yahweh went down and confused their language so that they could not understand one another's speech. And from that land of Babel, Yahweh dispersed them as the seventy nations over the face of the earth. He placed those nations under the authority of the fallen Sons of God, allotted them as their inheritance, the gods of the nations. But he kept Jacob for himself. He was Jacob's inheritance, and Jacob was his."

Simon was about to tie it together and make his theological point when he was interrupted by the sound of a mighty rushing wind from heaven.

People exclaimed with fright as they saw tongues of supernatural fire rest upon each of them. Fear turned to awe when they saw that the fire did not injure their bodies or consume them. Awe turned to joy. And then to laughter.

They began to talk amongst themselves. But something even stranger had happened. They now each spoke in foreign languages unknown to them. Simon recognized some of them; Latin, Persian, Egyptian. But these were not known languages to these common folk who spoke them.

It dawned on Simon what was happening. He gestured for everyone to move out into the streets.

Peter led them across the street to the Great Arch, the stairway up to the southern gates of the Temple. He encouraged the followers to speak of the mighty works of God to those passing by. They spread out so as not to sound like a cacophony of confusion.

Simon realized that Yahweh was undoing Babel. He was reversing the curse. He had filled his new emissaries with the Holy Spirit and was using the tongues of nations to unify a new humanity, not in wickedness and violence, but in Messiah and his Spirit.

So this is how Yahweh would bring in the nations.

Simon saw Jews from every part of the diaspora, the Great Dispersion, stopping and listening all over the street. They were astonished to hear Galileans telling them of the mighty works of God in their own tongues. They were from Parthia and Media, from Elam and all over Mesopotamia. Judea, Asia, Egypt and Rome. Simon wouldn't be surprised if all seventy of the nations were represented here at this festival of pilgrimage.

Not all pilgrims were impressed. There were mockers as well. One of them yelled out like a horn, "These men are drunk on new wine!"

People laughed in the crowd. They started to murmur. Simon could see this sensitive moment of God's moving might so easily be ruined by the presence of hard hearts.

Peter took control at the top of the steps. He spoke with a supernatural presence. His voice boomed and curried attention.

"Men of Judea and Jerusalem! Hear my words! These people are not drunk on wine as this heckler suggests. But rather they are part of a profound movement of God that you had better consider for yourselves, or you will be sorry!"

The crowd went quiet. He had their attention now.

"These very events are what was spoken of through the prophet Joel:

And in the last days it shall be, Yahweh declares,
that I will pour out my Spirit on all flesh,
and your sons and your daughters shall prophesy,
and your young men shall see visions,
and your old men shall dream dreams;
even on my male servants and female servants
in those days I will pour out my Spirit, and they shall prophesy."

Simon knew the implications of this prophesy. In their patriarchal culture, only men were allowed the privileged status of such things as prophecy and spiritual leadership. But for God to say that even women, and worse yet, male and female *servants*, would be equally baptized in God's Spirit, was a scandal for their culture. A deeply offensive scandal. A spiritually liberating one. It marked the Last Days.

Peter continued his quotation of the prophet,

"And I will show wonders in the heavens above
and signs on the earth below,
blood, and fire, and vapor of smoke;
the sun shall be turned to darkness
and the moon to blood,
before the Day of the Lord comes,
the great and magnificent day."

Simon looked out upon the crowd. They had no idea of the terror that was coming. The last days of the Old Covenant were upon them, just as Jesus had said. The end of the present age, and the start of the age to come, the age of Messiah. The Day of the Lord was coming for Israel. Isaiah had used that phrase, "Day of the Lord," along with similar astronomical language when describing the destruction of Babylon and then of Edom. Ezekiel had used the same poetry for the destruction of Egypt. Now Peter was reiterating the same language to claim that the Day of the Lord was coming to Israel, just as Jesus had promised. Judgment was coming to Jerusalem.

But so was salvation for the remnant.

Peter continued, "'And it shall come to pass that everyone who calls upon the name of the Lord shall be saved!'"

As Simon listened to Peter, he watched the crowd become agitated. Peter spoke of King David, the forerunner of Messiah, and how he was dead and buried in his tomb, awaiting one of his descendants to sit on this throne. He explained that the Son of David was Jesus and that David had foreseen the resurrection of Jesus when he said Yahweh would not abandon him to Hades or let his flesh see corruption. He told of Jesus ascending to heaven and being exalted to the right hand of God, from where he poured forth the promised Holy Spirit upon his followers that the crowds were now seeing.

David himself did not ascend to heaven, but rather spoke of Messiah's apotheosis of deity, his crowning exaltation of omnipotence.

Yahweh said to my Lord Adonai,
"Sit at my right hand,
until I make your enemies my footstool."
Yahweh sends forth from Zion
your mighty scepter.
Rule in the midst of your enemies!
Adonai is at your right hand;
he will shatter kings on the day of his wrath.
He will execute judgment among the nations.

But then, Peter laid out his climactic accusation to the throng of people listening. "Let all the house of Israel therefore know for certain that God has made him both Lord and Messiah, this Jesus whom you crucified. This Jesus is the stone that was rejected by you, the builders, which has become the cornerstone."

Simon felt his mind clear with understanding. Jesus was the Messianic stone of Daniel's prophecy that would crush the iron and clay feet of Rome and grow to become the cornerstone of a new cosmic mountain that would fill the earth. Simon saw a similar understanding sweep over the listeners as agitation now melted into conviction. The Spirit of God had fallen upon this crowd. People began to weep. Others were crying out to ask what they should do.

Peter told them. "Repent and be baptized, every one of you, in the name of Jesus the Messiah for the forgiveness of your sins. You will receive the gift of the Holy Spirit. For this promise is for you and your children and for all who are far off, everyone the Lord our God calls to himself. Therefore, save yourselves from this crooked generation, upon whom judgment is coming!"

Some of the apostles led the repentant listeners south to the Pool of Siloam to be baptized. Hundreds of them. But Peter kept preaching as new people were drawn to the spectacle that had just occurred. Simon suspected that hundreds would turn to thousands that day.

The great ingathering had begun. The messengers of the Gospel of Jesus the Messiah were drawing in the elect from the four corners of the earth, before the great and terrible Day of the Lord. It was a day that Jesus had promised some of them would live to see. It would happen within their own generation. Days of vengeance, a great tribulation, was coming upon them.

> *"But when you see Jerusalem surrounded by armies, then know that its desolation has come near. Then let those who are in Judea flee to the mountains, and let those who are inside the city depart, and let not those who are out in the country enter it, for these are days of vengeance, to fulfill all that is written.*
>
> *"For there will be great distress upon the earth and wrath against this people. They will fall by the edge of the sword and be led captive among all nations, and Jerusalem will be trampled underfoot by the Gentiles, until the times of the Gentiles are fulfilled. "And there will be signs in sun and moon and stars, and on the earth. For the powers of the heavens will be shaken. And then they will see the Son of Man coming in a cloud with power and great glory."*
> Jesus in Luke 21:20–27

The Chronicles of the Nephilim continues with the next series, *Chronicles of the Apocalypse*.

APPENDIX A
Jesus and the Cosmic War

Jesus Triumphant is a dangerous novel. I knew it long before I wrote it. In fact, I had originally not intended to write it because, of all the *Chronicles of the Nephilim*, I thought it would probably be the most scrutinized and criticized with accusations of taking liberties with God's Word. Jesus and his story is the most prized of all Christian narratives—for me as well.

But the more I studied and the more I wrote of the *Chronicles*, I came to realize that I had to write this one because it is the true theological climax of the Biblical cosmic war of Christus Victor against the principalities and powers of this present darkness. Jesus Christ is the Seed which was prophesied in Genesis 3:6 to be at war with the Seed of the Serpent. Jesus Christ is the Seed to whom God made his Promises (Gal. 3:16). So how could I not finish my story with the conclusion I believed was in the Bible?

The premise of the series is to retell only those Scriptural narratives that touch upon the story thread of the Nephilim and the allotment of the Watchers (Sons of God) as described in the Divine Council worldview of the Bible. At first blush readers may legitimately ask the question "Where are there giants or Watchers in the New Testament?" But the reader of the entire series will not be so surprised as he sees key theological elements already established in previous *Chronicles* now show up in the New Testament in a way they had never seen before.

Chronicles of the Nephilim is primarily a theological saga that attempts to communicate a spiritual storyline that is behind the physical events and symbolic motifs and imagination of the Bible. So strap yourself in and get ready for a wild Biblical ride of theological imagination from the depths of Hades to the heights of heaven.

A Giant and Some Zealots

There may not be mention of giants in the Gospels, but I did find a giant placed in the same approximate time and location of Christ's ministry. One of my historical resources has been the ancient Jewish historian Josephus. His rich text, *Wars of the Jews*, is the only detailed source we have of the events that led up to the destruction of Jerusalem and the holy temple in A.D. 70. (this will be the subject of *Jerusalem Judgment*). Josephus is a non-Christian source that confirms Gospel details of Pontius Pilate, the Herods, John the Baptist, the apostle James, and even Jesus Christ.[1] Though his pro-Roman agenda is well-known, he nevertheless provides helpful reliable information for the historical inquirer.

One of those interesting factoids is the reference to a 10 1/2 foot giant Jew named Eleazar who was presented as a gift to Tiberius Caesar in the presence of Herod Antipas, by the king of Parthia, Artabanus III in A.D. 33 or 34.[2]

> When Tiberius had heard of these things, he desired to have a league of friendship made between him and Artabanus... Artabanus and Vitellius went to Euphrates...And when they had agreed upon the terms of peace, Herod the tetrarch erected a rich tent on the midst of the passage, and made them a feast there. Artabanus also, not long afterwards, sent his son Darius as an hostage, with many presents, <u>among which there was a man seven cubits tall, a Jew he was by birth, and his name was Eleazar, who, for his tallness, was called a giant</u>.[3]

Josephus doesn't tell us if the Jewish giant was a servant or a captive, but he was certainly chattel of some kind to be traded as a means of diplomacy between the two empires. It occurred on the shores of the Euphrates in a tent constructed by Herod Antipas, the tetrarch of Galilee at the time. Antipas inserted himself into the negotiations in order to ingratiate himself to Caesar. All this, the reader will recognize occurring in *Jesus Triumphant*.

Vitellius, the king of Syria and representative of Caesar, brought the "gifts" of his son and the giant to Antioch, where they were presumably shipped to Rome.[4] But were they? Josephus doesn't say. So, what if the giant

---

[1] His infamous paragraph describing Jesus Christ (*Antiquities of the Jews* 18.63-64) is controversial and some have argued that it is a later Christian redaction. But there remains solid scholarship for its legitimacy. For a balanced scholarly assessment see Steve Mason, *Josephus and the New Testament*, (Peabody, MA Hendrickson Publishers, 1992), 163-174.

[2] In *Antiquities* 18.106 Josephus places the trade around the time of the death of Herod's brother, Philip, who died in A.D. 33/34: Flavius Josephus and William Whiston, *The Works of Josephus: Complete and Unabridged* (Peabody: Hendrickson, 1987), footnote C.

[3] Josephus, *Antiquities of the Jews* 18.101-105. Flavius Josephus and William Whiston, *The Works of Josephus: Complete and Unabridged* (Peabody: Hendrickson, 1987).

[4] Josephus, *Antiquities* 18.105.

Eleazar escaped? What if he found his short way down to Caesarea Philippi, where Jesus was during that last year of ministry? Thus the creative license of the novel applying to historical characters in a feasible scenario.

But that is not all the novel drew from historical characters. Many Bible readers know the name of Barabbas as the one who the Jews chose to release at Pilate's offer instead of Jesus (Matt. 27:15-26). But what many casual readers of the Bible do not know is that Barabbas was a leader of a failed insurrection around that time in Jerusalem (Luke 2:19). He was no ordinary criminal. He was a zealot warrior, as he is in *Jesus Triumphant.*

The two "thieves on crosses" next to Jesus are another case of commonly misunderstood identity. "Thief" or "robber" makes one think of common criminals or kleptomaniacs caught stealing camels or jewelry. But the Greek word for "thief" used of the two on the cross is *lestai*, the same word used by Josephus to describe the zealous Jewish brigands in revolution against Rome. Crucifixion was the punishment for such organized sedition and insurrection. The "thieves" on the cross were actually revolutionaries in the tradition of the Zealots.[5]

Though the existence of bands of Jewish insurrectionists against Rome at the time of Christ is not in dispute, the exact nature and chronology of the infamous Zealots is. Some have argued they did not come into existence until around the fall of Jerusalem,[6] but others have shown that they originated in Judas of Galilee's failed insurrection of A.D. 6.[7] He made famous the slogan "No king but God," that came to mark the Zealot cause.[8]

Judas of Galilee's sons, James and Simon, went on to be executed as zealous rebels around A.D. 46.[9] Josephus also describes two Zealot-like leaders Eleazar ben Dinai and Amram, who were captured and banished around A.D. 45 by Roman procurator Fadus. Another brigand leader, Tholomy was executed.[10] Eleazar was captured again later and executed in Rome in A.D. 60.[11] This means that James, John, Amram, Tholomy and Eleazar had been rising within the ranks of the newly growing Zealot movement during the time of Christ. Thus, their presence in *Jesus Triumphant.*

---

[5] N. T. Wright, *The New Testament and the People of God, Christian Origins and the Question of God* (London: Society for Promoting Christian Knowledge, 1992), 178–180.
[6] Richard A. Horsley and John S. Hanson, *Bandits, Prophets, and Messiahs: Popular Movements at the Time of Jesus* (New York: NY, Winston Press, 1985).
[7] Martin Hengel, *The Zealots: investigations into the Jewish freedom movement in the period from Herod I until 70 A.D.* (Edinburgh: U.K., T. & T. Clark, 1989).
[8] Hengel, *The Zealots,* 108.
[9] Josephus, *Antiquities* 20.102.
[10] Josephus, *Antiquities* 20.4-5.
[11] Josephus, *Antiquities* 20.161. Under the procurator Felix.

Qumran, Essenes and the Dead Sea Scrolls

In 1946, the famous Dead Sea Scrolls were uncovered in caves near the ancient Essene settlement of Qumran on the northwest shores of the Dead Sea thirteen miles east of Jerusalem. They shed light on the early monastic community that had been previously found nearby, and written about by Josephus. Much discussion and debate surrounds these texts and the people who stored them in libraries.

One of the more interesting elements of their beliefs was the similarity of Messianic hope with what would end up being the New Testament claims for Jesus. Scholar Marvin Pate explains that, like many Jews of Second Temple Judaism, they too sought a Davidic Messiah to deliver Israel from her continuing exile under Roman rule.[12]

A more recent discovery of an ancient text on stone called "Vision of Gabriel," dated to the first century B.C., has revealed a unique correspondence with the New Testament notion of Messiah rising after three days. This is much more explicit than any Old Testament reference to such a thing. I incorporated this prophecy into *Jesus Triumphant* as part of the literature that persuades an Essene character of Christ's fulfillment. Several of the lines from the stone indicate this amazing correspondence.

> *By three days you shall know that, thus said Yahweh of Hosts, the god of Israel,*
> *the evil has been broken by righteousness...*
> *Behold, all the nations gather against Jerusalem...*
> *In just a little while, I will shake the heavens and the earth...*
> *My servant David [Messiah], ask of Ephraim for a sign...*
> *By three days, live/be resurrected, I Gabriel, command you, prince of princes.*[13]

This is not to say that the Vision of Gabriel should be considered Scripture. But it certainly adds outside corroboration to the understanding of the Jewish messianic hope fulfilled in Christ.

The Jewish expectation based on Nebuchadnezzar's dream in Daniel 2 was that Messiah would come and crush the nation of Rome in history. The

---

[12] C. Marvin Pate, *Communities of the Last Days: The Dead Sea Scrolls, The New Testament & The Story of Israel*, (Downers Grove, IL: InterVarsity Press, 2000), 107-132.
[13] Israel Knohl, "By Three Days, Live": Messiahs, Resurrection, and Ascent to Heaven in Hazon Gabriel, *The Journal of Religion*, Vol. 88, No. 2 (April 2008), pp. 147-158

Qumran community had a document called "The War Scroll" that describes in detail this War of the Sons of Light Against the Sons of Darkness, calling Romans by the symbolic name of *Kittim*.[14]

But as Josephus explains, the time period after Herod the Great's death in 4 B.C. was plagued with various messianic movements and revolutionaries, many that were deeply at odds with each other. They argued over whose interpretation was correct and what marked the true people of God. Pate argues that another element of distinction emerges in the Dead Sea Scrolls: they considered themselves the only true remnant of Israel. And when Messiah came, he would deliver the Essene Community alone, while destroying the rest of Israel with his holy army![15] This is remarkably reminiscent of Jesus' Olivet Discourse that describes God's destructive judgment of Jerusalem and the Temple (Matt. 24), and concurrent rescue of the remnant elect believers (Matt. 24:15-22; Rom. 11:1-10). Those Essenes were so close, and yet, so far.

N.T. Wright sums up this earthly expectation of why the Jews were looking for a physical conquering king rather than a suffering servant.

> Many if not most second-Temple Jews, then, hoped for the new exodus, seen as the final return from exile. The story would reach its climax; the great battle would be fought; Israel would truly 'return' to her land, saved and free; YHWH would return to Zion. This would be, in the metaphorical sense, the end of the world, the ushering in at last of YHWH's promised new age. From the perspective of covenant history, this complex event would be climactic, and not merely a paradigmatic example of a general principle (such as the importance of social justice). Moreover, this whole set of ideas and themes belongs together as a whole, not as a collection of abstract ideas, but precisely as a story.[16]

---

[14] Michael O. Wise, Martin G. Abegg Jr., and Edward M. Cook, *The Dead Sea Scrolls: A New Translation* (New York: HarperOne, 2005), 146–170.

[15] Pate, *Communities of the Last Days,* 113.

[16] N. T. Wright, *Jesus and the Victory of God, Christian Origins and the Question of God* (London: Society for Promoting Christian Knowledge, 1996), 209. N. T. Wright, Jesus and the Victory of God, Christian Origins and the Question of God (London: Society for Promoting Christian Knowledge, 1996), 209.

All this is not to say, as liberal scholars and Bible haters say, that Jesus was wrong in his apocalyptic declarations, but rather that, as the spiritual warfare motif of *Jesus Triumphant* points to, he was both suffering servant *and* mighty conqueror of a spiritual Armageddon, a covenantal "end of the age," for a kingdom not of this world, whose effect would ultimately be seen in history.

Caesar and Christ

But even pagans have their Christ prophecies too. It seems everyone wanted to be God. And the Romans were no exception. The language of Augustus Caesar reflected similar concepts of the divinity of their emperor, as the New Testament did of Jesus Christ. Inscriptions on coins and buildings throughout the empire called Augustus, "God, Son of God, Savior."[17] A famous proclamation of Augustus used phrases such as "savior," "god manifest," and "good news [*gospel*]."

> The most divine Caesar...we should consider equal to the Beginning of all things...; for when everything was falling [into disorder] and tending toward dissolution, he restored it once more and gave to the whole world a new aura...and who being sent to us and our descendants as Savior...and [whereas,] having become [god] manifest, Caesar has fulfilled all the hopes of earlier times... and whereas, finally, the birthday of the god [Augustus] has been for the whole world the beginning of good news concerning him [therefore let a new era begin from his birth].[18]

Early and Medieval Church Fathers were so impressed by classical wisdom, they sought to incorporate great Greek and Roman writers into their revealed wisdom of God. Some claimed that Aristotle or Plato were even saved through natural revelation. Augustine told a story in his *City of God* about a prophecy that was allegedly given by the Erythraean Sibyl to Augustus Caesar, but pointed toward Christ, not Caesar, as the world ruler.

---

[17] Stanley E. Porter, "Paul Confronts Caesar with the Good News," Stanley E. Porter, Cynthia Long Westfall, Ed., *Empire in the New Testament* (Wipf and Stock, 2011), 172-3.
[18] Richard A. Horsley, *Jesus and Empire: The Kingdom of God and the New World Disorder* (Minneapolis, MN: Fortress Press, 2003) 23.

As scholar Burke elucidates some of the lines of this prophecy as they appear in *Jesus Triumphant*,

> *"In token of judgment, the earth shall drip with sweat.*
> *A king destined to rule forever will arrive from heaven,*
> *present in mortal flesh, in order to judge the world."*[19]

Though these are fabricated legends by well meaning Christians, reading into Greek sibylline literature to bolster their faith, they point up the fact that sometimes, God does use pagans as instruments of prophecy or judgment (Num. 22:21-39; 1Sam. 19:21-24; Isa. 10).

Nephilim and Demons

Demons are a theological problem. Where do they come from? What are they? Why are they almost entirely absent in the Old Testament, and then all of a sudden, there is a flurry of demonic activity and possessions once Messiah comes to Israel? The casting out or exorcism of demons is so frequently linked with Jesus' proclamation of the Gospel that it seems to be more than a mere symbolic expression of his power over the spiritual world. It is an essential theological component of the New Covenant.

First, just what are demons? We see in the New Testament that they are evil spirits that possess or inhabit the physical bodies of living individuals (Luke 11:24-26), and who are cast out by Jesus and his disciples by the power of the Holy Spirit (Matt. 8:16; Luke 10:17). Their presence sometimes causes physical infirmities like blindness (Matt. 12:22), deafness (Mark 9:17-29), or epilepsy (Matt. 17:15-18), as well as mental insanity (Mark 5:15). Many of them can inhabit one body (Mark 5:9), and bring great strength to the host (Mark 5:4).

But where did these evil spirits come from? In the Old Testament, there is very little explanation of demons. God sends an evil spirit to torment King Saul in 1 Sam. 16:14. Based on Saul's insane behavior it is safe to say he was most likely possessed by that evil spirit (v. 15-23). 1 Kings 22:22-23 reveals that God sends a "lying spirit" into the mouths of false prophets. Demons? Maybe. But certainly subservient to God's interests. Even the satan is depicted as a circumscribed servant of God's will in the Old Testament (Job 1:12). As explained in other Appendices of the Chronicles, pagan idols

[19] Paul F. Burke, "Augustus and Christianity in Myth and Legend," *New England Classical Journal* 32.3 (2005) 213-220. From Augustine's *City of God* 18.23.1.

are sometimes referred to as demonic (Deut. 32:17; Psa. 106:34-37; Lev. 17:7) exposing the spiritual reality behind their earthly façade of graven images and foreign deities.

But other than these few examples, there is a dearth in the Old Testament of the kind of activity we read about in the New Testament, with raging demoniacs being exorcised by Christ and his disciples. It seems like the demons knew that the presence of Messiah was the final countdown of their own demise and they were throwing fits and tantrums. As if the Seed of the Woman was crushing the Seed of the Serpent's head and the body was wriggling in pain.

But they are never described as fallen angels in the Bible.

What then, are demons and from where do they come?

The church father Origen claimed that there was no clearly defined teaching on their genesis in the early church, but that a significant opinion was that "the devil was an angel, and that, having become an apostate, he induced as many of the angels as possible to fall away with himself, and these up to the present time are called his angels."[20]

This common Christian idea of the satan and demons as fallen angels is often proof-texted from Isa. 14:12-15, Ezek. 28:12-16, and Rev. 12:4. But as explained in the Appendix to *Enoch Primordial*, I do not believe these passages apply to a satanic fall from heaven.[21] Isaiah 14 is the likening of the monstrous pride of the king of Babylon to a Canaanite myth of arrogant deities. Nothing about the satan there. And there is no reference to any others joining him either. Ezekiel 28 is a condemnation of the king of Tyre by likening him to Adam's fall in the Garden, *not* the satan. This passage also fails to mention anyone in collusion with the arrogant prince. One has to import an alien notion of the satanic fall into these passages through eisegesis.

Lastly, Revelation 12 is not about a satanic fall or war in heaven *before the Garden of Eden*, or even in some future end of the world scenario. It is an apocalyptic parable that is describing the war of the satan *at the incarnation of Christ*, his ascension to the throne of authority over all principalities and powers, and his suppression of the satan's power as the Gospel goes forth into the world.

---

[20] Origen, "De Principiis," in The Ante-Nicene Fathers: Fathers of the Third Century: Tertullian, Part Fourth; Minucius Felix; Commodian; Origen, Parts First and Second, ed. Alexander Roberts, James Donaldson, and A. Cleveland Coxe, trans. Frederick Crombie, vol. 4 (Buffalo, NY: Christian Literature Company, 1885), 240.

[21] Brian Godawa, *Enoch Primordial* (Los Angeles: Embedded Pictures Publishing, 2013), 367-373.

So in the Bible there is no description of angels falling before the Garden of Eden. There *is* a satanic "fall" or a "casting out" of heaven (John 12:31) and a "throwing down" to the earth of the satan *during the time of Christ* (Luke 10:17-20). But that would be too late in the game to explain the few evil spirits in the Old Testament or their presence before the arrival of Messiah. The only other "fall" of angelic beings in the Bible is the Sons of God, the Watchers, in Genesis 6 coming to earth.[22]

But that presents another problem, namely that the ontological nature or "material being" of the angels as revealed in the Bible would seem to preclude these fallen angels from being the Old Testament or New Testament demons. While angels are multidimensional in their ability to traverse between the heavenlies and the earth, they are described as having flesh that eats food (Gen. 18; 19:1), and can have sexual congress with human beings (Gen. 6:1-4). This is a heavenly flesh that is different from human flesh (1 Cor. 15:39-40), but is flesh nonetheless. This would make angels or divine beings such as the Watchers unlikely candidates for incorporeal spirits seeking flesh to inhabit or possess.

There is no origin of demons detailed in the Bible. There is merely a description of their spiritual nature and evil activities. But there is a tradition of their origin that carries some weight beyond mere speculation. Regarding this origin, the *Dictionary of Deities and Demons in the Bible* says, "The most popular myth, however, is found in the Bible, intertestamental literature, the rabbis and the Church fathers: demons are the souls of the offspring of angels who cohabited with humans."[23] We are right back to that

---

[22] See the chapter "The Book of Enoch: Scripture, Heresy, or What?" in *When Giants Were Upon the Earth: The Watchers, Nephilim and the Cosmic War of the Seed* (Los Angeles: Embedded Pictures, 2014),.

[23] G. J. Riley, "Demon," ed. Karel van der Toorn, Bob Becking, and Pieter W. van der Horst, *Dictionary of Deities and Demons in the Bible* (Leiden; Boston; Köln; Grand Rapids, MI; Cambridge: Brill; Eerdmans, 1999), 238. Early church fathers who believed this are Justin Martyr, Athenagoras, Minuciux Felix, Irenaeus, among others: Bo Reicke, *The Disobedient Spirits and Christian Baptism* (New York: AMS Press, 1946), 80-81. Other Intertestamental literature that affirms demons as sons of the Watchers are Test. Of Solomon 5:3; 17:1; Jubilees 10:5; Dead Sea Scrolls 4Q510 v.5; 4Q511 Frag. 35; 4Q204 Col V.2-3 (1Enoch 10:15), that call the demons, sons of the Watchers or "spirits of the bastards." Florentino García Martínez and Eibert J. C. Tigchelaar, "The Dead Sea Scrolls Study Edition (translations)" (Leiden; New York: Brill, 1997–1998), 415, 1029, 1033-35. 11Q11 Col. V.6 calls demons "offspring of man and of the seed of the holy ones." DSS Study Edition, 1203. See Loren T. Stuckenbruck, "The 'Angels' and 'Giants' of Genesis 6:1-4 in Second and Third Century BCE Jewish Interpretation: Reflections on the Posture of Early Apocalyptic Traditions," Dead Sea Discoveries, Vol. 7, No. 3, *Angels and Demons* (2000), pp. 354-37; Ida Fröhlich,"Theology and Demonology in Qumran Texts," *Henoch*; Vol. 32 Issue 1, June 2010, 101-129.

ancient text that keeps rearing its head in the New Testament; the book of 1 Enoch. There we read that the giants had unique ontological status as hybrids of both human and angel. So when they died in the Flood, their spirits became roaming entities seeking bodily possession of humans.

> 1 Enoch 15:8-16:1
> [8] "But now the giants who are born from the (union of) the spirits and the flesh shall be called evil spirits upon the earth, because their dwelling shall be upon the earth and inside the earth. [9] Evil spirits have come out of their bodies. Because from the day that they were created from the holy ones they became the Watchers; their first origin is the spiritual foundation. They will become evil upon the earth and shall be called evil spirits… [12] And these spirits shall rise up against the children of the people and against the women, because they have proceeded forth (from them)… From the days of the slaughter and destruction, and the death of the giants… they will corrupt until the day of the great conclusion, until the great age is consummated, until everything is concluded (upon) the Watchers and the wicked ones."[24]

Chronicles of the Nephilim assumes this Enochic interpretation in its storyline as the last gasp attempt of the Seed of the Serpent to bite the heel of the Seed of Eve. Needless to say, their head is crushed in that attempt.

Gaia, Satyrs, and Pan

Surely, one of the more apparently outrageous imaginative elements that appears in *Jesus Triumphant,* in addition to previous *Chronicles of the Nephilim*, is the depiction of Gaia, the Goddess Earth Mother in the form of an immense tree, and her group of guardians. These guardians include Pan, the satyr goat god, along with the demoness Lilith, her children, and the huge serpent, Ningishzida.

Some may think this inclusion is completely alien to the Bible and its storyline of Christus Victor. That depicting these demonic monsters is theologically jumping the shark.

---

[24] James H. Charlesworth, *The Old Testament Pseudepigrapha*, vol. 1 (New York; London: Yale University Press, 1983), 22.

But they would be wrong. Theologian, correct thyself.

These creatures actually do appear in certain Old Testament texts in the form of poetic allusion to the demonic nature of the pagan world. So Jesus' ministry of casting out demons from the land of Israel is directly connected to these beings. First, we'll look at satyrs, then Lilith and Ningishzida.

Take a look at these prophecies of Isaiah referencing the destruction of Babylon and Edom.

> Isaiah 34:11–15 (The destruction of Edom)
> [11]But the hawk and the porcupine shall possess it, the owl and the raven shall dwell in it… [13]Thorns shall grow over its strongholds, nettles and thistles in its fortresses. It shall be the haunt of jackals, an abode for ostriches. [14]And wild animals shall meet with hyenas; the wild goat (*seirim*) shall cry to his fellow.

> Isaiah 13:21–22 (The destruction of Babylon)
> [21]But wild animals will lie down there, and their houses will be full of howling creatures; there ostriches will dwell, and there wild goats (*seirim*) will dance. [22]Hyenas will cry in its towers, and jackals in the pleasant palaces; its time is close at hand and its days will not be prolonged.

The passages above speak of God's judgment upon the nations of Babylon and Edom (symbols of all that is against Israel and Yahweh). A cursory reading of the texts seem to indicate a common word picture of Yahweh destroying these nations so thoroughly that they end up a desert wasteland with wild animals and birds inhabiting them because the evil people will be no more.

Nothing about mythical monsters like satyrs there, right?

Wrong. Because the English translation of the Hebrew word *seirim* as "wild goats," obscures the full ancient meaning. If we look closer into the ancient languages, we find a more expanded mythopoeic reference to pagan deities.

A look at the Septuagint (LXX) translation of those passages into Greek made by ancient Jews in the second century before Christ, reveals the hint of that different picture.

Isaiah 34:13-14 (LXX)
[11] and for a long time birds and hedgehogs, and ibises and ravens shall dwell in it: and the measuring line of desolation shall be cast over it, and satyrs shall dwell in it… [13] And thorns shall spring up in their cities, and in her strong holds: and they shall be habitations of monsters, and a court for ostriches. [14] And devils shall meet with satyrs, and they shall cry one to the other: there shall satyrs rest, having found for themselves *a place of* rest.[25]

Isaiah 13:21-22 (LXX)
But wild beasts shall rest there; and the houses shall be filled with howling; and monsters shall rest there, and devils shall dance there, [22] and satyrs shall dwell there.[26]

Wow, what a dramatic difference, huh? Of course, the LXX passages above are not in Greek, but are English translations, which adds a layer of complication that we will unravel shortly to reveal even more mythopoeic elements. But the point is made that ancient translators understood those words within their ancient context much differently than the modern bias of more recent interpreters. Of course, this does not necessarily make the ancient translators right all the time, but it warrants a closer look at our own blinding biases.

The LXX translates the word for "satyrs" that appears in these Isaiah passages as *onokentaurois*, from which we get our word "centaur." The *Greek-English Lexicon of the Septuagint* defines this word as "donkey-centaur, mythic creature (a centaur resembling a donkey rather than a horse)."[27]

In Isaiah 34:14 of the ESV we read of "the wild goat crying to his fellow," and in 13:21, "there wild goats will dance." But the underlying Hebrew (*seirim*) is not about wild goats, but *satyrs*, that were prevalent in Canaanite religion. Scholar Judd Burton points out that Banias or Panias at the base of Mount Hermon in Bashan was a key worship site for the Greek

[25] Lancelot Charles Lee Brenton, *The Septuagint Version of the Old Testament: English Translation*, Is 34:13–14 (London: Samuel Bagster and Sons, 1870).
[26] Lancelot Charles Lee Brenton, *The Septuagint Version of the Old Testament: English Translation*, Is 13:21–22 (London: Samuel Bagster and Sons, 1870).
[27] Johan Lust, Erik Eynikel and Katrin Hauspie, *A Greek-English Lexicon of the Septuagint: Revised Edition* (Deutsche Bibelgesellschaft: Stuttgart, 2003).

goat-god Pan as early as the third century B.C. and earlier connections to the goat-idol Azazel.[28]

The Bible writers considered these pagan *seirim* deities to be demons and thus called them "goat demons." So prevalent and influential were these satyr gods that Yahweh would have trouble with Israel worshipping them as idols.

> Leviticus 17:7
> [7] So they shall no more sacrifice their sacrifices to goat demons (*seirim*), after whom they whore. This shall be a statute forever for them throughout their generations.

> 2 Chronicles 11:15
> [15][Jeroboam] appointed his own priests for the high places and for the goat idols (*seirim*) and for the calves that he had made.

Not only did Israel fall into worshipping the *seirim* in Canaan, they even committed spiritual adultery with them in the wilderness! It is no wonder Yahweh considered them demons, a declaration reiterated in Moses' own prophecy that after Israel would be brought into Canaan by the hand of God, she would betray Yahweh by turning aside to other gods, redefined as demons.

> Deuteronomy 32:17
> [17] They sacrificed to demons that were no gods, to gods they had never known, to new gods that had come recently, whom your fathers had never dreaded.[29]

Siyyim and Iyyim (Demons and Goblins)

Moving back to the prophecies of Isaiah 13 and 34 we find additional spiritual creatures of chaos that are connected to the satyrs. We read of

[28] Judd H. Burton, *Interview With the Giant: Ethnohistorical Notes on the Nephilim* (Burton Beyond Press, 2009) 19-21. "Regardless of his [Azazle's] origins—in pre-Israelite practice he was surely a true demon, perhaps a satyr, who ruled in the wilderness." Jacob Milgrom, *A Continental Commentary: Leviticus: a Book of Ritual and Ethics* (Minneapolis, MN: Fortress Press, 2004), 169.

[29] The Psalmist also casts the gods of Canaan; Molech, Asherah, Ashtart, Ba'al, and others as demons as well in Psalm 106:37–38: "They sacrificed their sons and their daughters to the demons; they poured out innocent blood, the blood of their sons and daughters, whom they sacrificed to the idols of Canaan, and the land was polluted with blood."

hawks, ostriches, owls, and ravens was well as other unknown animals. But the English translations make it look like they are just more natural animals.

Not so in the Hebrew.

Let's take a closer look at the Hebrew words behind two more of these strange creatures, "wild animals" and "hyenas."

> Isaiah 13:21–22
> [21] But wild animals (*siyyim*) will lie down there, and their houses will be full of howling creatures; there ostriches will dwell, and there wild goats will dance. [22] Hyenas (*iyyim*) will cry in its towers, and jackals in the pleasant palaces; its time is close at hand and its days will not be prolonged.

> Isaiah 34:14
> [14] And wild animals (*siyyim*) shall meet with hyenas; (*iyyim*) the wild goat shall cry to his fellow; indeed, there the night bird settles and finds for herself a resting place.

The Hebrew for the words "wild animals" and "hyenas" are not readily identifiable,[30] so the ESV translators simply guessed according to their anti-mythical bias and filled in their translations with naturalistic words like "wild animals" and "hyenas." But of these words, Bible commentator Hans Wildberger says,

> "Whereas (jackals) and (ostriches), mentioned in v. 13, are certainly well-known animals, the creatures that are mentioned in v. 14 cannot be identified zoologically, not because we are not provided with enough information, but because they refer to fairy tale and mythical beings. *Siyyim* are demons, the kind that do their mischief by the ruins of Babylon, according to [Isaiah] 13:21. They are mentioned along with the *iyyim* (goblins) in this passage.[31]

---

[30] "Siyyim," Francis Brown, Samuel Rolles Driver, and Charles Augustus Briggs, *Enhanced Brown-Driver-Briggs Hebrew and English Lexicon* (Oak Harbor, WA: Logos Research Systems, 2000), 850.

[31] Hans Wildberger, *A Continental Commentary: Isaiah 28–39* (Minneapolis, MN: Fortress Press, 2002).

The demons and goblins that Wildberger makes reference to in Isaiah 13:21-22 and 34:14 are the Hebrew words *siyyim* and *iyyim*, a phonetic play on words that is echoed in Jeremiah's prophecy against Babylon as well:

> Jeremiah 50:39 (ESV)
> [39] "Therefore wild beasts (*siyyim*) shall dwell with hyenas (*iyyim*) in Babylon, and ostriches shall dwell in her. She shall never again have people, nor be inhabited for all generations.

The Dictionary of Biblical Languages (*DBL*) admits that another interpretation of *iyyim* other than howling desert animals is "spirit, ghost, goblin, i.e., a night demon or dead spirit (Isa. 13:22; 34:14; Jer. 50:39), note: this would be one from the distant lands, i.e., referring to the nether worlds."[32] One could say that *siyyim and iyyim* are similar to our own play on words, "ghosts and goblins."

The proof of this demon interpretation is in the Apostle John's inspired reuse of the *same exact language* when pronouncing judgment upon first century Israel as a symbolic "Mystery Babylon." But instead of using the words "wild beasts" and "hyenas," he uses, "demons" and "unclean spirits."

> Revelation 18:2
> [2]"Fallen, fallen is Babylon the great! She has become a dwelling place for demons, a haunt for every unclean spirit, a haunt for every unclean bird, a haunt for every unclean and detestable beast."[33]

Because of the exile under the Babylonians, Jews would use Babylon as the ultimate symbol of evil. So when John attacks his contemporaries in Israel for rejecting Messiah, he describes them as demonic Babylon worthy of the same judgment as that ultimate evil nation.

But regardless of one's eschatological interpretation, the "wild beasts" or "monsters" and "hyenas" of Isaiah and Jeremiah are interpreted as

---

[32] James Swanson, *Dictionary of Biblical Languages With Semantic Domains : Hebrew (Old Testament)*, electronic ed. (Oak Harbor: Logos Research Systems, Inc., 1997).

[33] Special thanks to Doug Van Dorn for this "revelation." Van Dorn, Douglas (2013-01-21). *Giants: Sons of the Gods* (Kindle Locations 3922-3925). Waters of Creation. Kindle Edition. In fact, his "Chapter 13: Chimeras" was helpful for more than one insight in this appendix.

demons, unclean spirits and detestable beasts, along with the unclean animals that will scavenge over the ruins of the judged nation.

Lilith

Another strange creature that occurs in Isaiah 34:14, *in the same passage as the satyrs,* is the "night hag," or "night bird" that "settles and finds for herself a resting place." The Hebrew word is actually *Lilith*, which the *Dictionary of Deities and Demons in the Bible* explains is a Mesopotamian demoness residing in a tree that reaches back to the third millennium BC.

> Here we find Inanna (Ishtar) who plants a tree later hoping to cut from its wood a throne and a bed for herself. But as the tree grows, a snake [Ningishzida] makes its nest at its roots, Anzu settled in the top and in the trunk the demon makes her lair... Of greater importance, however, is the sexual aspect of the—mainly—female demons lilitu and lili. Thus the texts refer to them as the ones who have no husband, or as the ones who stroll about searching for men in order to ensnare them.[34]

Lilith was also known as the demon who stole away newborn babies to suck their blood, eat their bone marrow and consume their flesh.[35] In Jewish legends, she was described as having long hair and wings, and claimed to have been the first wife of Adam who was banished because of Adam's unwillingness to accept her as his equal.[36]

The passage we previously looked at, Isaiah 34:11-15, after mentioning the satyrs, then talks about the "night bird" or "owl" that nests and lays and hatches her young in its shadow. But lexicons such as the *Theological Wordbook of the Old Testament* and *Brown, Driver, Briggs Hebrew Lexicon* contest this Hebrew word for owl (*qippoz*) with more ancient interpretations

---

[34] "Lilith," *DDD*, 520.

[35] Handy, Lowell K. "Lilith (Deity)". In *The Anchor Yale Bible Dictionary*, edited by David Noel Freedman. New York: Doubleday, 1992, 324-325.

[36] Ginzberg, Louis; Szold, Henrietta (2011-01-13). *Legends of the Jews*, all four volumes in a single file, improved 1/13/2011 (Kindle Locations 1016-1028). B&R Samizdat Express. Kindle Edition.

of an "arrow snake."[37] If they are correct, then the poetry of the passage would be more complete as the NASB indicates.

> Isaiah 34:14–15 (NASB95)
> [14] Yes, the night monster (*Lilith*) will settle there And will find herself a resting place.[15]The tree snake (*qippoz*) will make its nest and lay *eggs* there, And it will hatch and gather *them* under its protection.

The snake of verse 15 would match the Lilith myth (v. 14) with the snake in the roots making its nest. The correlation is too close to deny that this is another Biblical reference to a popular mythic creature that the Bible writers refer to in demonic terms.

The Dead Sea Scrolls of Qumran evidence a preoccupation with demonology that includes reference to this very Isaianic passage. In *The Songs of the Sage*, we read an exorcism incantation,

> "And I, the Instructor, proclaim His glorious splendor so as to frighten and to terrify all the spirits of the destroying angels, spirits of the bastards, demons, Lilith, howlers, and [desert dwellers…] and those which fall upon men without warning to lead them astray[38]

Note the reference to "spirits of the bastards," a euphemism for demons as the spirits of dead Nephilim who were not born of human fathers, but of angels.[39]

---

[37] 2050a, קִפּוֹז*Theological Wordbook of the Old Testament*, ed. R. Laird Harris, Gleason L. Archer, Jr. and Bruce K. Waltke, electronic ed., 806 (Chicago: Moody Press, 1999).

קִפּוֹזBrown, Francis, Samuel Rolles Driver, and Charles Augustus Briggs. *Enhanced Brown-Driver-Briggs Hebrew and English Lexicon*. electronic ed. Oak Harbor, WA: Logos Research Systems, 2000.

[38] 4Q510 Frag. 1. Michael O. Wise, Martin G. Abegg Jr., and Edward M. Cook, *The Dead Sea Scrolls: A New Translation* (New York: HarperOne, 2005), 527. Janet Howe Gaines, "Lilith: Seductress, Heroine or Murderer?" Bible History Daily, 08/11/2014, http://www.biblicalarchaeology.org/daily/people-cultures-in-the-bible/people-in-the-bible/lilith/, accessed 9/8/14.

[39] Loren T. Stuckenbruck, "The 'Angels' and 'Giants' of Genesis 6:1-4 in Second and Third Century BCE Jewish Interpretation: Reflections on the Posture of Early Apocalyptic Traditions," Dead Sea Discoveries, Vol. 7, No. 3, *Angels and Demons* (2000), pp. 354-37; Ida Fröhlich,"Theology and Demonology in Qumran Texts," *Henoch*; Vol. 32 Issue 1, June 2010, 101-129.

The God of This World

Chronicles of the Nephilim has largely been based upon the Divine Council worldview that has been explained in several previous Chronicles appendices. This involves the fallen Watchers from God's heavenly host who are called the Sons of God. They led the world astray in the Days of Noah, that led to the Flood as Yahweh's judgment. Deuteronomy 32:8-9, then speaks of how at the Tower of Babel, Yahweh divided the seventy nations according to the number of the fallen Sons of God and placed them under their authority. They became the "princes" (Dan. 10:13, 20-21) or "gods" of those pagan nations (Deut. 32:17; 4:19-21), rulers of those geographical territories.[40]

When earthly rulers battle on earth, the Bible describes the host of heaven battling with them in spiritual unity. In Daniel 10, hostilities between Greece and Persia is accompanied by the battle of heavenly Watchers over those nations (described as "princes").

> Daniel 10:13, 20-21
> The prince of the kingdom of Persia withstood me twenty-one days, but Michael, one of the chief princes, came to help me, for I was left there with the kings of Persia." …Then he said, "Do you know why I have come to you? But now I will return to fight against the prince of Persia; and when I go out, behold, the prince of Greece will come. [21] But I will tell you what is inscribed in the book of truth: there is none who contends by my side against these except Michael, your prince.

When Sisera fought with Israel, the earthly kings and heavenly authorities (host of heaven) are described interchangeably in unity.[41]

> Judges 5:19–20
> "The kings came, they fought; then fought the kings of Canaan…From heaven the stars fought, from their courses they fought against Sisera.

---

[40] See Appendix, "Sons of God," in Brian Godawa, *Noah Primeval* (Los Angeles: Embedded Pictures, 2011, 2012), 280-289.
[41] See also 2 Kings 6:15-17 where Elisha's servant has his spiritual eyes opened to see the myriad of heavenly warriors surrounding Israel preparing to battle Syria.

When God punishes earthly rulers, he punishes them along with the heavenly rulers ("host of heaven") above and behind them.

> Isaiah 24:21–22
> On that day the LORD will punish the host of heaven, in heaven, and the kings of the earth, on the earth. They will be gathered together as prisoners in a pit; they will be shut up in a prison, and after many days they will be punished.[42]

This notion of territorial archons or spiritual rulers is Biblical and carries over into intertestamental literature such as the Book of Enoch (1 En. 89:59, 62-63; 67) and others.[43] In the New Testament Greek world, heavenly rulers seem to transform into a more generic reference to spiritual "principalities and powers." The notion of the host of heaven being spiritual powers was foreshadowed in the Old Testament Greek Septuagint with the common translation of "Yahweh of Hosts" into "God of the Powers" (Psa. 88:9 LXX).[44]

Walter Wink points out that the picture of Watchers over nations is hinted at in 1 Cor. 4:9 where the apostle explains their persecution has "become a spectacle (theatre) to the world, to angels and to men." He explains that "the image of the Roman theater conjures up hostile and jeering crowds," and the angels are "heavenly representatives of the Gentile nations and people, who watch, not without malicious glee, the tribulations endured by the apostle to their peoples."[45]

The epistles speak of the spiritual principalities and powers that are behind the earthly rulers and powers to be sure (Eph. 6:12-13), but it appears to be more generic in reference. And after the death, resurrection, and

---

[42] Interestingly, this passage of Isaiah is not clear about what judgment in history it is referring to. But the language earlier in the text is similar to the Flood when it says, "For the windows of heaven are opened, and the foundations of the earth tremble. 19 The earth is utterly broken, the earth is split apart, the earth is violently shaken. 20 The earth staggers like a drunken man; it sways like a hut; its transgression lies heavy upon it, and it falls, and will not rise again." So this may be another passage that uses a Flood reference tied in with the Watchers and their punishment.

[43] See also Jubilees 15:31-32; Targum Jonathan Deut. 32, Sect. LIII; 3Enoch 48C:9, DSS War Scroll 1Q33 Col. xvii:7, Targum Jonathan, Genesis 11, Section II.

[44] Ronn A. Johnson, *The Old Testament Background For Paul's Use Of "Principalities And Powers"* Dissertation, (Dallas Theological Seminary, 2004), 46.

[45] Walter Wink. *Naming the Powers: The Language of Power in the New Testament* (The Powers : Volume One) (Kindle Locations 394-396). Kindle Edition.

ascension of Christ, these spiritual powers have been disarmed and overthrown (Col. 2:15, Luke 10:18), at least legally losing their hegemony (Eph. 1:20-23). The fallen angelic powers are still around, but have been defanged with the inauguration of the Messianic kingdom of God.

But there is one of those fallen angelic powers that seems to rise up and grab extraordinary authority in the New Testament: The satan (which translated, means, "Accuser"). The Accuser's choice of Belial as a proper name in *Jesus Triumphant* is well-attested in Scripture and other ancient Jewish writings, especially the Dead Sea Scrolls from Qumran.[46] He is also called Beliar, Mastema, and Sammael in other Second Temple literature.[47] Throughout the Old Testament, the Hebrew word *belial* is used as a personification of death, wickedness, and treachery, as well as "an emotive term to describe individuals or groups who commit the most heinous crimes against the Israelite religious or social order, as well as their acts."[48] The Apostle Paul uses the proper name of Belial for the satan (using language similar to the Dead Sea Scrolls) in 2 Corinthians 6:14–15: "Do not be unequally yoked with unbelievers. For what partnership has righteousness with lawlessness? Or what fellowship has light with darkness? What accord has Christ with Belial?"

Three times in the Gospel of John, this Accuser named Belial, is called "the ruler of this world" (Jn. 12:31, 14:30-31, 16:11), in 2 Cor. 4:4, "the god of this world." In Eph. 2:2 he is called the "prince of the power of the air, the

---

[46] Especially in the War Scroll (1QM) and the Thankgiving Scroll (1QH). Florentino García Martínez and Eibert J. C. Tigchelaar, "The Dead Sea Scrolls Study Edition (translations)" (Leiden; New York: Brill, 1997–1998), 113-178.

[47] C. Breytenbach (I, IV) and (I–III) Day P. L., "Satan," ed. Karel van der Toorn, Bob Becking, and Pieter W. van der Horst, *Dictionary of Deities and Demons in the Bible* (Leiden; Boston; Köln; Grand Rapids, MI; Cambridge: Brill; Eerdmans, 1999), 72; S. D. Sperling, "Belial," *DDD*, 169; J. W. van Henten, "Mastemah," *DDD*, 553. On Sammael: M. A. Knibb, "Martyrdom and Ascension of Isaiah: A New Translation and Introduction," in *The Old Testament Pseudepigrapha and the New Testament: Expansions of the "Old Testament" and Legends, Wisdom, and Philosophical Literature, Prayers, Psalms and Odes, Fragments of Lost Judeo-Hellenistic Works, vol. 2* (New Haven; London: Yale University Press, 1985), 151.

[48] S. D. Sperling, "Belial," ed. Karel van der Toorn, Bob Becking, and Pieter W. van der Horst, *Dictionary of Deities and Demons in the Bible* (Leiden; Boston; Köln; Grand Rapids, MI; Cambridge: Brill; Eerdmans, 1999), 169. "Such crimes include: inciting one's fellows to worship foreign gods (Deut 13:14); perjury (1 Kgs 21:10, 13; Prov 19:28); breach of hospitality (Judg 19:22; 1 Sam 25:17); lese-majesty (1 Sam 10:27); usurpation (2 Sam 16:7–8; 20:1); abuse of Yahweh's sanctuary by female drunkenness (1 Sam 1:13–17); and the cultic misappropriation and sexual harassment of women by priests (1 Sam 2:12–22). Refusal to lend money on the eve of the Sabbatical year (Deut 15:9) falls into the category of heinous deeds because it indicates lack of faith in the divine ability to provide." See also, Deut 13:13; Judg 19:22; 1 Sam 1:16; 2:12; 10:27; 25:17; 2 Sam 16:7; Nah 1:15 (2:1); 1 Kgs 21:13.

spirit that is now working in the sons of disobedience." In fact, when Jesus was tempted by the satan in the desert, he offered Christ all the kingdoms of the world for his own "domain and glory; for it has been handed over to me, and I give it to whomever I wish" (Luke 4:6). It seems as if the satan is the only Watcher god in authority over the nations, like he has all the power. What happened to all the other ones?

Walter Wink points out a possible key to the solution. In the intertestamental period "much tradition identified Satan as the angel of Rome, thus adapting the angels-of-the-nations idea to the situation of Roman world-hegemony. Since Rome had conquered the entire Mediterranean region and much else besides, its angel-prince had become lord of all other angel-princes of the vanquished nations. This identification was already explicit at Qumran, where Rome and the Romans (the 'Kittim' of the War Scroll) are made the specific allies and agents of Satan and his host."[49]

The Dead Sea Scroll 11QMelch interprets Psalm 82 as describing Satan/Belial as the chief of the gods in the divine council to be punished for his unjust authority over the nations.[50] Another Jewish intertestamental document, the Testament of the Twelve Patriarchs, lists in several places Beliar, synonymous with Satan, as holding captive mankind.[51]

In the post-New Testament religious text The Martyrdom and Ascension of Isaiah (1st century A.D.) the name of Satan is used synonymously with the names Sammael and Beliar.[52] But in the later text of 3 Enoch (5th century A.D.), Satan, Sammael, and Beliar are considered separate entities, with Sammael and Beliar being Satan's underlings (3 Enoch 26:12).

---

[49] Wink, *Naming the Powers*, Kindle Locations 409-412. Of the Qumran War Scroll, Davies says, "Using the term "Kittim," which in the Hebrew Bible is applied to Greeks and then (in Daniel) to Romans, it transparently identifies the Roman Empire as the ally of Belial, the spirit/angel of darkness, and of the "Children of Darkness," and describes their defeat in a great seven-stage battle… At present, there is little consensus on the literary history, though a date in the last quarter of the first century B.C.E. is widely accepted, as is the identification of the Kittim, allies of the "Children of Darkness," as the Romans." Phillip Davies, "The Biblical and Qumranic Concept of War," James H. Charlesworth, Ed. *The Bible and the Dead Sea Scrolls Volume One - Scripture and the Scrolls* (Waco: Baylor University, 2006), 223, 226.

[50] *11QMelch* (1st century B.C.) Geza Vermes, *The Dead Sea Scrolls in English*, Revised and extended 4th ed. (Sheffield: Sheffield Academic Press, 1995), 361.

[51] TDan 5:10-13; TZeb 9:8; TLevi 18:12; Test. Judah 25:3; Assum. Moses 10:1-3. These texts are from the 2nd century B.C.

[52] M. A. Knibb, "Martyrdom and Ascension of Isaiah: A New Translation and Introduction," in The Old Testament Pseudepigrapha and the New Testament: Expansions of the "Old Testament" and Legends, Wisdom, and Philosophical Literature, Prayers, Psalms and Odes, Fragments of Lost Judeo-Hellenistic Works, vol. 2 (New Haven; London: Yale University Press, 1985), 151.

But the real twist is that in this same text, Sammael is called *the Prince of Rome*, just as Dubbiel is called the Prince of Persia (remember the "Prince of Persia" from Daniel 10?).

> 3 Enoch 26:12
> Every day Satan sits with Samma'el, Prince of Rome, and with Dubbi'el, Prince of Persia, and they write down the sins of Israel on tablets and give them to the seraphim to bring them before the Holy One, blessed be he, so that he should destroy Israel from the world.[53]

Just like the satan in the New Testament, Sammael is called the "prince of the accusers who is greater than all the princes of kingdoms that are in the height [heaven]" (3 Enoch 14:2). And just like the satan in the New Testament, Sammael's name means "god of the blind" (2 Cor. 4:4).[54]

So in these texts Sammael is the Watcher prince over Rome under the authority of the satan, or Sammael is the name of the Watcher prince over Rome who also has the heavenly position of being "the accuser" (the satan).[55]

But what about this notion of the ruler (*archon*), or god of this world? Is the world something bigger than the realm of this satanic Prince of Rome? To answer that, we will have to look at the idea of *the world* as presented in the New Testament.

It is common in the Bible to refer to the Roman Empire as "all the world" (*oikoumene*) which meant the known inhabited world under Rome's power. Luke writes that when Caesar ordered a census of the Roman Empire, he made a decree that "all the world (*oikoumene*) should be registered" (Luke 2:1). Jesus said that the Gospel would be proclaimed "through all the world (*oikoumene*) as a testimony to all the nations" (Matt. 24:14). At that time, all the nations (and their allotted Watchers?) were under Roman rule. When Paul writes that within his own lifetime, the Gospel "has been proclaimed in all creation under heaven" (Col. 1:23), it is an obvious

---

[53] James H. Charlesworth, *The Old Testament Pseudepigrapha*, vol. 1 (New York; London: Yale University Press, 1983), 281.
[54] P. Alexander, "A New Translation and Introduction," in *The Old Testament Pseudepigrapha*, vol. 1 (New York; London: Yale University Press, 1983), 236.
[55] These pseudepigraphal texts do not have canonical status as Scripture. 3 Enoch is gnostic in its orientation. But they do illustrate an interpretive tradition that is in accord with the Biblical cosmic war we have been examining. Textual food for thought.

expression of *the inhabited world of the Roman Empire*, not the entire globe as we now know it.

Another Greek word occasionally used for the Roman world was *cosmos*. Cosmos was not the physical universe as we would understand it, but rather more like the zeitgeist or the godless "world system" or "world order" of estranged humanity.[56] And that world order was of course Rome. Paul writes that the very Gospel preached in the Roman Empire "has come to you, as indeed in the whole world (*cosmos*)" (Col. 1:6). The Roman Christian's faith had been "proclaimed in all the world (*cosmos*)" (Rom. 1:8), the Gospel "has been made known to all the nations" (Rom. 16:26) at the time of Paul's writing to those Romans in the first century.[57]

In the New Testament, the "world" (cosmos) and the "inhabited earth" (*oikoumene*) as well as other global language was used interchangeably to refer to the known inhabited world of the Roman Empire. All the known nations were encompassed in its power and worldview, so it seems those angelic entities over those nations would therefore also be under the authority of the Watcher of Rome.

If the satan therefore was "god" or "ruler" of that "world," then most likely he had become the angelic authority over Rome, and it would make sense that the New Testament would focus on the satan over the other Watchers. Rome had become the ultimate enemy of God's people and had authority over *all the nations of the world*. So much so that Daniel's vision was of the Messianic stone (Jesus) that would hit the Roman empire and ultimately crush it as the apex of godless empire (Dan. 2:44-45).

This theory is further evidenced in the book of Revelation where the Dragon of Revelation 12, clearly described as "that ancient serpent, who is the devil and the satan" (20:2), is the angelic principality of power that gives authority to both the Beast of the Sea (13:1-2) and the Beast of the Land (13:11-12).[58] Readers of the *Chronicles of the Nephilim* will be very familiar with the sea beast of Leviathan and the land beast of Behemoth. As explained in previous appendices, these are chaos monsters, symbolic of both foreign nations and rulers against whom Yahweh battles to establish his

---

[56] κόσμοςd Johannes P. Louw and Eugene Albert Nida, *Greek-English Lexicon of the New Testament: Based on Semantic Domains* (New York: United Bible Societies, 1996), 106.
[57] See Gary DeMar, *Last Days Madness: Obsession of the Modern Church 4th edition* (Powder Springs: American Vision, 1999), 87-89.
[58] Wink, *Naming the Powers*, Kindle Locations 407-417.

covenanted order.[59] Leviathan's sea dragon imagery is linked with the satan's serpentine chaos nature.

Revelation is notoriously difficult to interpret, and there are a plethora of interpretations of who or what the Land and Sea Beasts represent. But there is a common thread for the interpretation of the Sea Beast among most all the interpretive schools. Robert Mounce explains it:

> There is little doubt that for John the beast was the Roman Empire as persecutor of the church. It comes onto the land from the sea, just as the Roman troops did when they invaded the eastern Mediterranean. The beast is that spirit of imperial power which claims a religious sanction for its gross injustices."[60]

In his book, *The Beast of Revelation*, eschatology expert Ken Gentry points out that the Beast imagery of Revelation paints a fluid picture of both an individual and a kingdom of spiritual chaos and oppression. That kingdom is the Roman Empire that was also embodied in its emperor.[61] The third of other angels that the Dragon's tail cast with him to earth (Rev. 12:4) are then the Watchers of the other nations under Rome and therefore under the satan's authority.

In this understanding, When Jesus the Messiah arrives and inaugurates the kingdom of God, he does so by "binding the strong man" the "god of this world," the satan. His casting out of demons was a herald of casting down the satan's power (John 12:31; Matt. 12:28-29), and taking authority over his world. It was as if one fell swoop of the highest heavenly power over the nations brought down all the enemies with him. He destroyed the one who has the power of death, that is, the devil (Heb. 2:14). But why is he still prowling around like a roaring lion seeking whom he may devour? (1Pet. 5:8).

Because his overthrow is not absolute. It's a qualified binding. Let's take a closer look at the "binding" of the satan.

---

[59] Brian Godawa, *Noah Primeval*, 323-337. See also David E. Aune, *Revelation 6–16, vol. 52B, Word Biblical Commentary* (Dallas: Word, Incorporated, 1998), 732.

[60] Robert H. Mounce, *The Book of Revelation*, The New International Commentary on the New Testament (Grand Rapids, MI: Wm. B. Eerdmans Publishing Co., 1997), 246. See Steve Gregg, *Revelation, Four Views : a Parallel Commentary* (Nashville, Tenn.: T. Nelson Publishers, 1997), Re 13:1–4.

[61] Kenneth Gentry, *The Beast of Revelation* 2nd edition (Fort Worth: Institute for Christian Economics, 1994).

Magic and the Binding of Spirits

Through the entire *Chronicles* series, I have used a concept called "binding" of angels, demons, and Watchers. This binding is accomplished through imprisonment in the earth or Tartarus.

This binding notion originates theologically from the binding of Satan in the ministry of Christ as noted above in Matthew 12, as well as the binding of angels in "chains of gloomy darkness" in Tartarus in Jude 6 and 2 Peter 2:4. And these New Testament Scriptures are paraphrases of the Enochian narrative of the antediluvian Watchers who at the Flood were "bound" "for seventy generations underneath the rocks of the ground until the day of their judgment" (1 Enoch 10:12).

The idea of binding spirits is a common one in ancient religion and magic. Michael Fishbane notes that in the ancient Near East, incantations and spells were used by sorcerers and enchanters to bind people and spirits in spiritual "traps, pits, snares, and nets," using venomous curses from their lips like serpents. In response to some of these verbal sorceries, the Psalmist himself calls upon Yahweh in similar utterances to reverse the spells upon his enemies that they would be trapped, ensnared and bound by their own magical devices (Psalm 140; 64; 57:4-6).[62] Exorcists of the first century used incantations to cast out demons in Jesus' name (Acts 16:18), the same incantation used by Demons *against* Jesus before being cast out (Mk 1:27).[63]

Ezekiel 13:18 refers to a specific form of hunting and binding spirits in a practice of women "who sew magic bands upon all wrists…in the hunt for souls!" I reversed this pagan version of using magical armbands by creating a heavenly version of the archangels with armbands of indestructible Cherubim hair for their hunting and binding of evil spirits. The hair is wrapped as bands around the arms of archangels and used like a rope to bind the Watchers' hands and feet.

Scholars have pointed out that the binding of Satan that occurs in Matthew 12 is evidently not an exhaustive or absolute binding, since he is still active after the ministry of Christ and even into the New Testament era (Acts 5:3; Rom. 16:20; 2Cor. 12:7; 1Thes. 2:18; Rev. 2:13). But then how does this continuing satanic activity fit with the notion that Satan "was

---

[62] Michael A Fishbane, *Studies In Biblical Magic : Origins, Uses And Transformations Of Terminology And Literary Form* (Dissertation) Brandeis University, 1971. See also Edwin M. Yamauchi, "Magic In The Biblical World," The Institute For Biblical Research Lecture, 1981, *Tyndale Bulletin* 34 (1983).

[63] Graham Twelftree, *Jesus the Exorcist: A Contribution to the Study of the Historical Jesus* (Eugene, OR: Wipf and Stock, 2010), 95, 139, 159-60.

thrown down to the earth" (Rev. 12:9), "fell like lightning from heaven" (Luke 10:18), was disarmed and overthrown in triumph (Col. 2:15), destroyed along with his power of death (Heb. 2:14), and all of this accomplished through the death, resurrection and ascension of Christ (Matt. 12:28-29; Heb. 2:14)?

Revelation 20:2-3 provides a theological solution to the dilemma. It says that Satan is bound and thrown into a sealed pit for a thousand years, "so that he might not deceive the nations." *Deceiver of the world* is a Biblical epithet of Satan (Rev. 12:9; 20:7), ever since the beginning in the Garden (1 Tim. 2:14; John 8:44). So perhaps the binding of Satan is the muzzling of his deception over the world, as Jesus now has all authority, so that the Gospel can go forth into all the nations as it is now doing (Matt. 28:18).

This notion of Satan's binding is a problem for those who interpret that act as occurring in the Millennium, which they interpret as not having occurred as of yet. Revelation 20 is notoriously difficult to conclude any eschatological view. But we don't need Revelation 20 to make the point, because Jesus does in Matthew 12:

> Matt. 12:26–29
> And if the satan casts out the satan, he is divided against himself. How then will his kingdom stand?...But if it is by the Spirit of God that I cast out demons, then the kingdom of God has come upon you. Or how can someone enter a strong man's house and plunder his goods, unless he first binds the strong man? Then indeed he may plunder his house.

Jesus said that his ministry on earth of casting out demons from the Promised Land was a binding of the satan. The satan could not stop the kingdom of God (ie: the Gospel) from inaugurating on earth.

This binding is like a legal restraining order on the satan. In the Old Testament, the satan is a divinely ordained legal role as a kind of prosecutor within God's heavenly court. He would test God's law and righteousness through accusation against God's people (1Kgs. 22; Job 1, 2; Zech 3). In Rev. 12:10, it describes the satan's fall from heaven as "the Accuser of our brethren being thrown down," also at the inauguration of God's kingdom. With the advent of Christ, the satan/Accuser has effectively been exiled from the divine council of Yahweh and no longer has any legal power of accusation against God's people (Rom. 8:1-4).

Yes, many nations are still in the lap of the evil one, but whereas the Kingdom of God under the Old Covenant was exclusively located in a small patch of land in the Middle East, surrounded by pagan Gentile nations, now under the power of the New Covenant, people from every nation are getting saved from all over the earth. The entire earth is Messiah's inheritance, not merely the land of Israel (Psa 2:8). The Good News of Christ is currently drawing all nations into heavenly Zion (Isa. 2; Heb. 12:22). The kingdoms of man are right now becoming the kingdoms of God through the proclamation and spread of the Gospel (1 Cor. 15:24-28; Heb. 2:8-9).

Now, let's take a look at the anointing of that conquering king over the cosmic kingdoms of the satan and mankind.

The Gates of Hades and the Transfiguration

In Matthew 16:13-20 is the famous story of Peter's confession of Jesus as the Christ, who then responds, "I tell you, you are Peter, and on this rock I will build my church, and the gates of *Hades* shall not prevail against it" (v. 18). Shortly after, Jesus leads them up to a high mountain where he is transfigured.

In order to understand the spiritual reality of what is going on in this polemical sequence and its relevance to the cosmic War of the Seed, we must first understand *where* it is going on.

Verse 13 says that Peter's confession takes place in the district of Caesarea Philippi. This city was in the heart of Bashan on a rocky terrace in the foothills of Mount Hermon. This was the celebrated location of the grotto of Banias or Panias, where the satyr goat god Pan was worshipped and from where the mouth of the Jordan river flowed. This very location was what was known as the "gates of Hades," the underworld abode of dead souls.

The Jewish historian Josephus wrote of this sacred grotto during his time, "a dark cave opens itself; within which there is a horrible precipice, that descends abruptly to a vast depth; it contains a mighty quantity of water, which is immovable; and when anybody lets down anything to measure the depth of the earth beneath the water, no length of cord is sufficient to reach it."[64]

As scholar Judd Burton points out, this is a kind of ground zero for the gods against whom Jesus was fighting his cosmic spiritual war. Mount Hermon was the location where the Watchers came to earth, led their rebellion and miscegenation, which birthed the Nephilim (1 Enoch 13:7-10).

---

[64] *Wars of the Jews* 1:405, Flavius Josephus and William Whiston, The Works of Josephus: Complete and Unabridged (Peabody: Hendrickson, 1987).

It was their headquarters, in Bashan, the place of the Serpent, where Azazel may have been worshipped before Pan as a desert goat idol.[65]

When Jesus speaks of building his church upon a rock, it is as much a polemical contrast with the pagan city upon the rock, as it may have been a word play off of Peter's name, meaning "stone." In the ancient world, mountains were not only a gateway between heaven, earth, and the underworld, but also the habitations of the gods that represented their heavenly power and authority.[66] The mountain before them, Hermon, was considered the heavenly habitation of Canaanite gods as well as the very Watchers before whose gates of Hades Jesus now stood. The polemics become clearer when one realizes that gates are not offensive weapons, but defensive means. Christ's kingship is storming the very gates of Hades/Sheol in the heart of darkness and he will build his cosmic holy mountain upon its ruins.[67]

But the battle is only beginning. Because the very next incident that occurs is the transfiguration (Matt. 17:1-13). The text says that Jesus led three disciples up a high mountain. But it doesn't say which mountain. Though tradition has often concluded it was Mount Tabor, a more likely candidate is Mount Hermon itself. The reasons are because Tabor is not a high mountain at only 1800 feet compared to Hermon's 9000 feet height, and Tabor was a well traveled location which would not allow Jesus to be alone with his disciples (17:1).[68]

Then the text says, that Jesus "was transfigured before them, and his face shone like the sun, and his clothes became white as light. And behold, there appeared to them Moses and Elijah, talking with him" (Matthew 17:2–3). When Peter offers to put up three tabernacles for each of his heroes, he hears a voice from the cloud say, "This is my beloved Son with whom I am well pleased, listen to him" (vs. 4-5). The theological point of this being that Moses and Elijah are the representatives of the Old Covenant, summed up as the Law (Moses) and the Prophets (Elijah), but Jesus is the anointed King (Messiah) that both Law and Prophets pointed toward.

So God is anointing Jesus and transferring all covenantal authority to him as God's own Son. And for what purpose? To become king upon the

---

[65] Judd H. Burton, *Interview With the Giant: Ethnohistorical Notes on the Nephilim* (Burton Beyond Press, 2009) 15-23.

[66] Richard J. Clifford, *The Cosmic Mountain in Canaan and the Old Testament* (Wipf & Stock Pub, 2010), 1-8.

[67] Michael S. Heiser *The Myth That is True First Draft,* Unpublished book, 266.

[68] Clinton E. Arnold, *Zondervan Illustrated Bible Backgrounds Commentary: Matthew, Mark, Luke, vol. 1* (Grand Rapids, MI: Zondervan, 2002), 106.

new cosmic mountain that God was establishing: Mount Zion in the city of God. In the Mosaic Covenant, Mount Sinai was considered the cosmic mountain of God where God had his assembly of divine holy ones (Deut. 33:2-3). But now, as pronounced by the prophets, that mountain was being transferred out of the wilderness wandering into a new home in the Promised Land as Mount Zion (ultimately in Jerusalem). And that new mountain was the displacement and replacement of the previous divine occupants of Mount Hermon. Of course, just like David the messianic type, Jesus was anointed as king, but there would be a delay of time before he would take that rightful throne because he had some Goliaths yet to conquer (1 Sam. 16:13; 2 Sam. 5:3).

Take a look at this Psalm and see how the language of cosmic war against the anointed Messiah is portrayed as a victory of God establishing his new cosmic mountain. We see a repeat of the language of Jesus' transfiguration at Hermon.

> Psalm 2:1–8 (NASB95)
> [1] Why are the nations in an uproar And the peoples devising a vain thing? [2] The kings of the earth take their stand And the rulers [heavenly as well?] take counsel together Against the LORD and against His Anointed [Messiah], saying, [3] "Let us tear their fetters apart And cast away their cords from us!" [4] He who sits in the heavens laughs, The Lord scoffs at them. [5] Then He will speak to them in His anger And terrify them in His fury, saying, [6] "But as for Me, I have installed My King Upon Zion, My holy mountain." [7] "I will surely tell of the decree of the LORD: He said to Me, 'You are My Son, Today I have begotten You. [8] 'Ask of Me, and I will surely give the nations as Your inheritance, And the *very* ends of the earth as Your possession.[69]

Like Moses' transfiguration in Exodus 34:29, Jesus' body was transformed by his anointing to shine with the glory of those who surround God's throne (Dan. 10:6; Ezek 1:14-16, 21ff.; 10:9).[70] But that description is no where near the ending of this spiritual parade of triumph being previewed in God's Word. One last passage illustrates the conquering change of

---

[69] See also Psa. 48.
[70] Michael S. Heiser *The Myth That is True*, 65.

ownership of the cosmic mountain in Bashan. Notice the ironic language used of Bashan as God's mountain, and the spiritual warfare imagery of its replacement.

> Psalm 68:15–22
> [15] O mountain of God, mountain of Bashan; O many-peaked mountain, mountain of Bashan! [16] Why do you look with hatred, O many-peaked mountain, at the mount that God desired for his abode, yes, where the LORD will dwell forever? [17] The chariots of God are twice ten thousand, thousands upon thousands; the Lord is among them; Sinai is now in the sanctuary. [18] You ascended on high, leading a host of captives in your train and receiving gifts among men, even among the rebellious, that the LORD God may dwell there… [21] But God will strike the heads of his enemies, the hairy crown of him who walks in his guilty ways. [22] The Lord said, "I will bring them back from Bashan, I will bring them back from the depths of the sea.

In this Psalm, God takes ownership of Bashan with his heavenly host of warriors, but then replaces it and refers to Sinai (soon to be Zion). It is not that God is making Bashan his mountain literally, but conquering its divinities and theologically replacing it with his new cosmic mountain elsewhere. In verse 18 we see a foreshadowing of Christ's own victorious heavenly ascension, where he leads captives in triumphal procession and receives tribute from them as spoils of war (v. 18). He will own and live where once the rebellious ruled (v. 18). He strikes the "hairy crown" (*seir*) of the people of that area (v. 21), the descendants of the cursed hairy Esau/Seir,[71] who worshipped the goat demons (as depicted in *Joshua Valiant* and *Caleb Vigilant*).[72] He will bring them all out from the sea of chaos, that wilderness where Leviathan symbolically reigns.[73]

But first, the Messiah must descend into that sea to claim his victory.

---

[71] "Edom," Geoffrey W. Bromiley, ed., The International Standard Bible Encyclopedia, Revised (Wm. B. Eerdmans, 1979–1988), 18. See the Appendix on Satyrs and Seirim in Brian Godawa *Joshua Valiant*, (Los Angeles: Embedded Pictures, 2013), 310-314.
[72] Marvin E. Tate, *Psalms 51–100, vol. 20, Word Biblical Commentary* (Dallas: Word, Incorporated, 1998), 182.
[73] Heiser *The Myth*, 277-279.

Christ's Descent Into Hades/Sheol

One of the most difficult and strange passages in the New Testament is 1 Peter 3:18-22. It's oddity approaches that of Genesis 6:1-4 that speaks of the Sons of God mating with the daughters of men in the days of Noah and breeding Nephilim giants that lead to the judgment of the Flood. Perhaps its oddity is tied to the fact that it is most likely connected directly to Genesis 6 and therefore of particular importance for the Cosmic War of the Seed.

This 1 Peter 3 passage is notorious for its difficult obscurity and lack of consensus among scholarly interpretation. Views are divided over it with a variety of speculative interpretations to pick from. So, let's take a look at it more closely with an attempt to clarify its meaning.

> 1 Peter 3:18–22
> [18]For Christ also suffered once for sins, the righteous for the unrighteous, that he might bring us to God, being put to death in the flesh but made alive in the spirit, [19]in which he went and proclaimed to the spirits in prison, [20]because they formerly did not obey, when God's patience waited in the days of Noah, while the ark was being prepared, in which a few, that is, eight persons, were brought safely through water. [21]Baptism, which corresponds to this, now saves you, not as a removal of dirt from the body but as an appeal to God for a good conscience, through the resurrection of Jesus Christ, [22]who has gone into heaven and is at the right hand of God, with angels, authorities, and powers having been subjected to him.

The context of this letter is the suffering of believers for their faith under the persecution of the Roman empire (3:13-17). Peter is encouraging them to persevere in doing good despite the evil done against them because they will be a witness to the watching world just as Christ was in his suffering. He then launches into this section as an analogy of what Christ did for us in his journey of suffering, death, resurrection, and ascension.

The questions begin to pile up:

When did Christ go on this journey? (v. 18)

Where did he go to proclaim to the spirits? (v. 19)

What did he proclaim? (v. 19)

Who are the spirits? (v. 19)

Where is this prison that they are in? (v. 19)

I believe the answers to these questions are very much in line with the storyline of the War of the Seed.

When Did Christ Go on His Journey? When Christ "went" to proclaim to the spirits in prison, it says he was "put to death in the flesh but made alive in the spirit, in which he went..." In the original Greek, "he went" does not contain a notion of direction as in ascent to heaven or descent to hell. It can only be determined by the context.[74] So let's look at that context.

Some scholars interpret this being "made alive in the spirit" as a reference to the physical resurrection of Christ from the dead, repeated later in v. 21. As Bible commentator Ramsey Michaels says, "the distinction here indicated by "flesh" and "Spirit" is not between the material and immaterial parts of Christ's person (i.e., his "body" and "soul"), but rather between his earthly existence and his risen state."[75] Scholar William Dalton argues that the idea of being made alive in the spirit was a New Testament reference to the resurrection of Christ's physical body *by the power of* the Holy Spirit, not a reference to Christ's disembodied soul.[76] He writes, "General New Testament anthropology insists on the unity of the human person. Terms such as "flesh" and "spirit" are aspects of human existence, not parts of a human compound. Bodily resurrection is stressed, not the immortality of the soul."[77] This venerable interpretation sees Christ proclaiming to the spirits in Hades, as a resurrected body, sometime before he ascended.

Another scholarly interpretation is that Christ's journey of proclamation occurred in a disembodied state between his death and resurrection. While his body was dead for three days, his spirit was alive and in Sheol. This understands the flesh/spirit distinction as a conjunction of opposites. "Put to death in the flesh but made alive in the spirit" is not talking about the fleshly death and fleshly resurrection, but a fleshly death and a spiritual life. The "spirit" in which he was made alive in this view is not the Holy Spirit, but rather his disembodied soul in

---

[74] John H. Elliott, *1 Peter: a New Translation with Introduction and Commentary* (vol. 37B; Anchor Yale Bible; New Haven; London: Yale University Press, 2008), 13.

[75] J. Ramsey Michaels, *1 Peter, vol. 49, Word Biblical Commentary* (Dallas: Word, Incorporated, 1998), 204.

[76] Dalton lists these passages: Rom 8:11; Jn 6:63; 1 Cor 15:45; 2 Cor 3:6; cf. also Rom 1:4, For the resurrection as effected by the power of God, see 2 Cor 13:4; Rom 6:4; Phil 3:10; Col 2:12; Eph 1:19–20; Heb 7:16.Footnote 55, William Joseph Dalton, *Christ's Proclamation to the Spirits: A Study of 1 Peter 3:18–4:6,* vol. 23, Analecta Biblica (Roma: Editrice Pontificio Istituto Biblico, 1989) 137.

[77] Dalton, *Christ's Proclamation to the Spirits*, 64.

the spiritual realm. That "spirit" then corresponds to the "spirits" to whom he proclaimed in the very next verse (v. 19).

This view that Christ's soul or spirit went down into the underworld of Sheol between his death and resurrection is the most ancient and most traditional view, as attested in the Apostle's Creed.[78] The Greek for "made alive" is never used of Christ's physical resurrection in the New Testament, but it is used of the spiritual reality of the believer "being made alive" in Christ (Eph. 2:5-6).[79] Christ suffered the spiritual death of separation from the Father when he died on the cross (Isa. 53:4-6; 1 Pet. 2:24; Matt. 27:46). How the second person of the Trinity can experience separation from the Father remains a Biblical mystery. But in this interpretation, it is Christ's disembodied spirit that makes the journey to proclaim to the spirits, not his resurrected body.

But whether Christ proclaims in his resurrected body or in his immaterial spirit, the next question arises, who are the spirits to which he proclaims and where are they?

Who are the Spirits in Prison? The identity of the spirits has been debated extensively and falls into four possible categories: Human spirits, demons, Watchers, or a combination of the above.

John Elliott debunks the notion that "spirits" refers to human beings by looking at the Greek word for spirits (*pneuma*) in Biblical and Intertestamental texts. He concludes, "use of 'spirits' for human beings is very rare, and even then it is always qualified. In the Bible and related literature, when reference is made to deceased humans in Hades or the underworld, the term used is not *pneuma* but *psyche*."[80]

---

[78] The Apostle's Creed is the most universally accepted creed of Christendom. For the full text see http://en.wikipedia.org/wiki/Apostles'_Creed. Some of the earliest Christian apocryphal literature supported the interpretation of Christ's spiritual descent into Hades, such as *the Gospel of Nicodemus, the Ascension of Isaiah, the Testaments of the Twelve Patriarchs, the Shepherd of Hermas, the Gospel of Bartholomew, the Odes of Solomon*, among others. Church fathers from the second and third centuries who taught this view included Polycarp, Ignatius, Tertullian, Hermas, Justin, Melito of Sardis, Irenaeus, Clement of Alexandria and Origen. Alfeyev states that every major writer from the Eastern Church fathers of the fourth century "touched in one way or another, on the theme of Christ's descent into Hades," as well as Western Church fathers like Jerome, Ambrose and Augustine. See Metropolitan Hilarion Alfeyev, *Christ the Conqueror of Hell: The Descent into Hades form an Orthodox Perspective*, (Crestwood: NY; St. Vladimir's Seminary Press, 2009). Also, see Richard Bauckham, "Descent to the Underworld," ed. David Noel Freedman, *The Anchor Yale Bible Dictionary* (New York: Doubleday, 1992), 154-158.

[79] Jason M. Hauffe, *An Interpretation of 1 Peter 3:18-22*, Dissertation (Lynchburg, Liberty University, 2002), 46.

[80] Elliott, *1 Peter*, Page 314.

But another commentator, Ramsey Michaels, shows that "spirits" (*pneuma*) is used of demons frequently in the New Testament for those supernatural beings that Jesus often confronted in his ministry.[81] He points out that in 1 Enoch, *pneuma* is used of demons as the surviving part of the giants killed in the Flood.

> 1 Enoch 15:8-10
> But now the giants who are born from the (union of) the spirits and the flesh shall be called evil spirits [*pneuma*] upon the earth, because their dwelling shall be upon the earth and inside the earth. [9] Evil spirits [*pneuma*] have come out of their bodies…They will become evil upon the earth and shall be called evil spirits [*pneuma*].[82]

In this view, the "spirits in prison" are therefore the demonic souls of the Nephilim that are restricted to the prison "holding cell" under the earth until the coming of Messiah. (See below for the definition of "prison" as a holding cell). As 1 Enoch 15:10 reasons, "The dwelling of the spiritual beings of heaven is heaven; but the dwelling of the spirits of the earth, which are born upon the earth, is in the earth."[83]

But what of the angelic Watchers? Are they ever referred to as "spirits"? As the 1 Enoch 15 passage above shows, the spirits of the Nephilim hybrids comes from their angelic Watcher progenitors who are also called spirits. In verse 4 of that passage, Enoch condemns the Watchers for violating their heavenly being as spirits (*pneuma*) and defiling themselves with "the blood of the flesh begotten children."[84]

The Intertestamental book of Jubilees that drew from 1 Enoch also concurs with the spirits being fallen angels:

> Jubilees 15:31-32
> over all of [the nations God] caused spirits to rule so that they might lead them astray from following him. [32] But over

---

[81] "Matt 8:16; Luke 10:20; "unclean spirits" in Matt 10:1; Mark 1:27; 3:11; 5:13; 6:7; Luke 4:36; 6:18; Acts 5:16; cf. Rev 16:13; "evil spirits" in Matt 12:45//Luke 11:26; Luke 7:21; 8:2; Acts 19:12–13 (for the singular, cf. Matt 12:43//Luke 11:24; Mark 1:23, 26; 3:30; 5:2, 8; 7:25; 9:17, 20, 25; Luke 8:29; 9:39, 42; 13:11; Acts 16:16, 18; 19:15–16)." J. Ramsey Michaels, *1 Peter, vol. 49, Word Biblical Commentary* (Dallas: Word, Incorporated, 1998), 207.
[82] Charlesworth, *The Old Testament Pseudepigrapha vol. 1*, 21–22.
[83] Charlesworth, *The Old Testament Pseudepigrapha vol. 1*, 22.
[84] Charlesworth, *The Old Testament Pseudepigrapha vol. 1*, 21.

Israel he did not cause any angel or spirit to rule because he alone is their ruler.[85]

The only New Testament Scriptures that speak of imprisonment of spirits are Jude 6 and 2 Peter 2:4, *the very passages that most scholarship has revealed are literarily dependent on the book of 1 Enoch.*[86]

Jude	2 Peter	Enoch
Jude 6 (NASB95) And angels who did not keep their own domain, but abandoned their proper abode, He has kept in eternal bonds under darkness for the judgment of the great day	2 Peter 2:4 God did not spare angels when they sinned, but cast them into hell [*Tartarus*] and committed them to chains of gloomy darkness to be kept until the judgment...	1 Enoch 12:4; 10:12 the Watchers of heaven who have abandoned the high heaven, the holy eternal place … bind [the Watchers] for seventy generations underneath the rocks of the ground until the day of their judgment.

Jude not only quotes Enoch outright in Jude 4, but throughout his entire letter, he follows the progression of ideas in 1 Enoch and references memes and motifs of the angelic Watchers' sin and judgment in that ancient text.[87] 2 Peter 2 is considered a paraphrase of Jude with the addition of the word for *Tartarus* as the description of the location of punishment.

Tartarus was well known by the ancients as the lowest place of the underworld where the Titans were bound in pagan mythology. That underworld was referred to as Hades (Greek) or Sheol (Hebrew), and has obvious conceptual links to Jude and Peter's location of punishment (more on Tartarus and Sheol later).[88] It would make most sense that Peter's second

---

[85] James H. Charlesworth, *The Old Testament Pseudepigrapha and the New Testament: Expansions of the "Old Testament" and Legends, Wisdom, and Philosophical Literature, Prayers, Psalms and Odes, Fragments of Lost Judeo-Hellenistic Works, vol. 2* (New Haven; London: Yale University Press, 1985), 87.
[86] Nickelsburg, *1 Enoch: a Commentary*, 7. Also, E. Isaac, "A New Translation and Introduction," in *The Old Testament Pseudepigrapha*, vol. 1 (New York; London: Yale University Press, 1983); Robert Henry Charles, ed., *Pseudepigrapha of the Old Testament*, vol. 2 (Bellingham, WA: Logos Bible Software, 2004), 178.
[87] See Brian Godawa, "The Book of Enoch: Scripture, Heresy, or What?" in "*When Giants Walked the Earth: The Watchers, Nephilim and the Biblical Cosmic War of the Seed* (Los Angeles, Embedded Pictures Publishing, 2014), 1-30.
[88] See the Appendix of Brian Godawa, *Enoch Primordial* (Los Angeles, Embedded Pictures Publishing, 2013), 336-338.

letter about angels bound in the prison of Tartarus would have continuity with the "spirits in prison" he is writing about in this first letter.

Some scholars have argued that the link of this passage to 1 Enoch is so strong that it can only make sense if there was a scribal error that mistook the Greek word for "Enoch" as the very similar Greek word for "in which."[89] So Peter had actually written that Christ was made alive in the spirit in the same way as "Enoch who went and proclaimed to the spirits in prison" in 1 Enoch.[90] Even though there is no manuscript evidence for this scribal error theory, making it unlikely, the strong analogy to Enoch's descent into Sheol is undeniable. So much so that Bo Reicke argued that Peter is casting Jesus as a typological Enoch.[91] Dalton enumerates, "A survey of 1 Enoch reveals a striking and obvious parallel to 1 Pet 3:19–20. In this latter text we have 1. a journey of Christ, 2. a proclamation, 3. to the spirits, 4. in prison, 5. who rebelled, or disobeyed, 6. in the setting of the flood. Now it is precisely in 1 Enoch that we find all these elements bound together in the closest unity."[92]

The spirits are specifically indicated as being those who were disobedient during "the days of Noah while the ark was being prepared." That "days of Noah" is exactly the time period that 1 Enoch speaks of the fallen Watchers and their giant progeny receiving their comeuppance with a binding in Tartarus/Sheol at the Flood.[93]

Chad Pierce makes a convincing argument that the disobedient spirits are not just the Watcher angels, demons, or human spirits alone, but the sum total of all who defied God at that time because cosmic powers are often united with human powers in the ancient world.[94] In the Bible, the angelic power over Persia animated the human kingdom of Persia (Dan. 10:13), The Roman human kingdom in Revelation is granted its power from the satan (Rev. 12-13), and both are destroyed together in the Lake of Fire (Rev. 19:20; 20:7-10).

---

[89] J. R. Harris, "The History of a Conjectural Emendation," *Expositor 6* (1902): 387-390; E. 1. Goodspeed, "Some Greek Notes," *Journal of Biblical Literature 73* (1954): 91-92.
[90] 1 Enoch 18:10-19:3; 21.
[91] Bo Reicke, *The Disobedient Spirits and Christian Baptism* (New York: AMS Press, 1946), 100-101.
[92] Dalton, *Christ's Proclamation*, 167.
[93] This would tend to work against the demon view since the demons were released upon the earth *after* the Flood, not while the ark was being built. But it could be argued that 1 Enoch 15 conflates the demons with the Nephilim and the spiritual side of the Watchers. This would mean that Peter may be referring to the disobedient spirits in the Nephilim *before* the Flood while the ark was being built.
[94] Chad Pierce, *Spirits and the Proclamation of Christ: 1 Peter 3:18-22 in Its Tradition-Historical and Literary Context,* (Durham theses, Durham University, 2009), 215-218. Available at Durham E-Theses Online: http://etheses.dur.ac.uk/13/

Wink explains that the ancient mind of the Biblical writers was steeped in a macrocosm/microcosm of "what is above is also below." "Angelic and demonic activity in heaven was reflected in events on earth...These Powers are both heavenly and earthly, divine and human, spiritual and political, invisible and structural."[95] Reicke adds that the "fallen Angels... the Powers, the demons in general, can in a certain way represent the whole world of fallen angels."[96] And Pierce concludes, "the distinction between cosmic and earthly sinners is so blurred they cannot be distinguished. It appears that the author of 1 Pet 3:18-22 has left the recipients of Christ's message purposefully vague so as to include all forms of evil beings. The spirits in prison are thus all the forces of evil which have now been subjugated and defeated by Christ."[97]

1 Peter 3:22 concludes that the context of the proclamation Christ made was the subjugation of "angels, authorities, and powers." Heavenly "principalities, powers, and authorities" is a recurring concept in the New Testament (Col. 1:16, 2:13-15; Eph. 1:20-23). It is a concept that assumes earthly rulers and powers are animated and empowered by spiritual or cosmic rulers and power behind them.

Thus, Paul could encourage those Christians who were suffering from the earthly rulers and powers who persecuted them; "For we do not wrestle against flesh and blood, but against the rulers, against the authorities, against the cosmic powers over this present darkness, against the spiritual forces of evil in the heavenly places" (Eph. 6:12-13). In other words, the real enemies of the persecuted Christians were the spiritual powers behind their earthly persecuting powers. This is not a denial of the human evil, but rather a drawing back of the curtain to see the ultimate enemy with more clarity.

These spiritual and earthly "powers, rulers, authorities, and thrones," are the Seed of the Serpent that had been involved in the cosmic War of the Seed against Messiah. It is these rulers, *both heavenly and earthly*, who did not understand the mystery of the Gospel of redemption through Messiah's suffering. They thought that killing the Chosen One, the Messiah, would bring them victory.

> 1 Corinthians 2:7–9
> But we impart a secret and hidden wisdom of God, which God decreed before the ages for our glory. None of the

---

[95] Walter Wink. *Naming the Powers*,1552-1553, 182-183. Kindle Edition.
[96] Reicke, *The Disobedient Spirits,* 121.
[97] Pierce, *Spirits and the Proclamation,* 218. See also Reicke, *The Disobedient Spirits,* 121.

rulers of this age understood this, for if they had, they would not have crucified the Lord of glory.

So the focus on "powers and authorities" stresses the nature of Christ's cosmic mission against the heavenly powers. But the humans of Noah's day were certainly united in the rebellion of the Watchers and were also marked out by Enoch as being imprisoned along with the angels.[98]

Where is the "Prison"? One interpretation of the prison is that it is a metaphor for human beings on earth who are "imprisoned" in their sin. But the context of the passage mitigates against this view. When the New Testament refers to preaching the Gospel to people on earth, the Greek term for "soul," is used (*psyche*). But this is not a term about a ghost in a machine, but rather an expression of the life of an individual human, their inner being, their "person," or their "self." Thus, Peter writes in 3:20 that "eight persons (*psyche*) were brought safely through the waters" in the ark during the Flood. When Peter preaches the Gospel in Acts 2, it says that "those who received his word were baptized, and there were added that day about three thousand souls [*psyche*]… and awe came upon every soul [*psyche*]" (Acts 2:42-43). "Soul" could be used synonymously with "individuals" or "persons."

But in 1 Peter 3, the distinct Greek term for "spirit" (*pneuma*), not "soul" (*psyche*), is used in contrast to the physical flesh. And these "spirits" are those who were disobedient in the days of Noah (v. 20), so they could not be people on earth at the time of Christ. Christ was proclaiming to spirits. During the time of Christ, those who were around in the days of Noah could only be in one place according to the Old Testament: The underworld of Hades or Sheol.

Hades was well known in the Greco-Roman world as the holding cell of the spirits of the dead until the judgment. Sheol was the Hebrew equivalent for Hades so the two could be used interchangeably.[99] Prisons in that time period were exactly that, holding cells for punishment. So when Peter refers to a prison for spirits, this view concludes that he is referring to Hades, just as he did in 2 Peter 2:4 when he said that the disobedient angels were cast into Tartarus, the lowest point in Hades.

There are orthodox traditions of Christian scholars who have supported this passage as referring to Christ's proclamation as occurring at his physical

---

[98] 1 Enoch 9:10; 20:3, 6; 22:3, 6-13; 98:3, 10;103:4.
[99] Richard Bauckham, "Hades, Hell," ed. David Noel Freedman, *The Anchor Yale Bible Dictionary* (New York: Doubleday, 1992), 14.

ascension into heaven and others as referring to Christ's spiritual descent into Hades. I take the position in *Jesus Triumphant* that Christ spiritually descended into Hades. So did early church fathers like Tertullian, Augustine, Jerome, Clement of Alexandria, Irenaeus, Cyril, and Origen, as well as Medieval scholastics like Robert Bellarmine, John Calvin, Thomas Aquinas, and modern scholars like Charles B. Cranfield, and Bo Reicke.[100] But I also incorporate the post-resurrection interpretation when it comes to the angelic Sons of God (Watchers) reigning on earth.

William Dalton agrees with Reicke that Jesus is cast as a typological Enoch, but then argues that in 2 Enoch, Enoch visits the bound angels in the lower regions of heaven, not Hades.[101] This is true of 2 Enoch, but unfortunately, the text is of such late origin (2nd century after Christ) that it cannot have been part of the original Enochian corpus used as a source in the Bible.[102]

In contrast, 1 Enoch, which seems to be the source of the Biblical text, does in fact depict Enoch as visiting the place of the condemned Watchers who were "formerly in heaven" (1 Enoch 16:2), and that place is described as a "deep pit," in the bottom of a mountain, just like Tartarus of Hades (Sheol), "an empty place with neither heaven above nor an earth below" (1 Enoch 21:1-2).[103]

The descent of Christ in 1 Pet. 3:19 is poetically structured to counterbalance the ascent of Christ into heaven in verse 22. In the same way that Christ went down into Sheol, he later ascended up into heaven. But more importantly, if Christ makes a proclamation to the spirits in prison, those dead and bound prisoners are certainly *not* in heaven. They are most likely in Sheol.

Another passage, Ephesians 4:8 quotes Psalms 68:18 about Christ "ascending on high and leading a host of captives." Paul then adds a parenthetical,

---

[100] Pierce, *Spirits and the Proclamation,* 2-10.
[101] William J. Dalton, *Christ's Proclamation to the Spirits: A Study of 1 Peter 3:18-4:6.* Second Edition. Analecta biblica 23. (Rome: Pontifical Biblical Institute, 1989), 179-81.
[102] Francis I. Andersen, "Enoch, Second Book Of," ed. David Noel Freedman, *The Anchor Yale Bible Dictionary* (New York: Doubleday, 1992), 516–517. Philip S. Alexander, "Enoch, Third Book Of," *AYBD*, 524.
[103] Enoch has a dream vision and ascends to heaven in 1 Enoch 14 and 15. But then he is brought to the place of punishment in chapter 18:10-19:3, which is not in heaven, but is a mountain that leads him down into the pit of Sheol.

> Ephesians 4:9-10
> "In saying, 'He ascended,' what does it mean but that he had also descended into the lower regions, the earth? He who descended is the one who also ascended far above all the heavens, that he might fill all things."

Christ "descending into the lower regions, the earth" can legitimately be interpreted as referring to Christ's incarnation or even his descent in the Spirit on Pentecost.[104] But other scholarship argues that the phrase is better translated as "descending into the *lowest parts of* the earth," in other words into Sheol.[105]

This underworld (Sheol) interpretation would seem to coincide with the memes presented in 1 Peter 3. The contrast of the heights of heaven with the depths of Sheol, and the tying of Christ's death, descent into Sheol, resurrection, and ascension into the totality of his victory over the angelic principalities and powers.[106]

Psalm 68 says that after leading the host of captives, God "received gifts from men," a reference to the notion of ancient victors receiving tribute from their conquered foes. Paul changes that "receiving of gifts" into "giving of gifts" as a expansion of that victory over foes into a sharing of victory with his army, the people of God. Perhaps this is the meaning of the Old Testament saints resurrected at the time of Christ's resurrection (Matt. 27:52-53). They too were sharing in the long awaited victory train of Messiah to free them from Hades and ascend into heaven.

The context of conquest over the angelic powers is also apparent in Eph. 1:20-21, "when he raised [Jesus] from the dead and seated him at his right hand in the heavenly places, far above all rule and authority and power and dominion, and above every name that is named."

Christ's death on the Cross becomes the apparent defeat by God's enemies, led by angelic principalities and powers. But it turns around and becomes a disarming of those spiritual powers and the beginning of his triumph over them (Col. 2:15). In this view, Christ goes down into Sheol (in

---

[104] For a good survey of the defense of these views, see: Andrew T. Lincoln, *Ephesians, vol. 42, Word Biblical Commentary* (Dallas: Word, Incorporated, 1990), 244–247.

[105] "κατώτερος," Gerhard Kittel, Geoffrey W. Bromiley, and Gerhard Friedrich, eds., *Theological Dictionary of the New Testament* (Grand Rapids, MI: Eerdmans, 1964–), 640; Clinton E. Arnold, *Zondervan Illustrated Bible Backgrounds Commentary: Romans to Philemon., vol. 3* (Grand Rapids, MI: Zondervan, 2002), 325.

[106] Robert G. Bratcher and Eugene Albert Nida, *A Handbook on Paul's Letter to the Ephesians, UBS Handbook Series* (New York: United Bible Societies, 1993), 99–100.

his spirit or later, in his resurrected body) to make a proclamation to the original minions of evil, now held captive. After he raises from the dead, he ascends into heaven to be coronated as king over all authority and powers of heaven and earth (Eph. 1:20-21). And that victory over spiritual powers brings us to the next element of 1 Peter 3:18-22.

What was the Proclamation? Some have believed it was Christ preaching the Gospel to the Old Testament dead, as if they may have a second chance to repent because they died before Messiah, or even to Old Testament believers who did not yet have the historical sacrifice of Christ to apply to them yet. This brings us back to the human interpretation of the "spirits in prison."

Since there is no place in the New Testament that supports the notion of a purgatorial type of second chance after death (Heb. 9:27), then the proclamation that Christ makes cannot be the "preaching of the Gospel" unto salvation, but something else. That something else is most likely a triumphant proclamation of his victory over the angelic authorities and powers.

In the ancient world, kingly victors would perform a triumphal procession through the streets of a conquered city. They would parade their captive opponents, alive or dead, on carts to show off their power over their enemies. Thus the triumphal procession in Psalm 68 quoted in Ephesians 4:8 as "ascending on high and leading a host of captives." This would also be an encouragement for obedience from the vanquished inhabitants.[107] Triumphal language like this in 1 Peter as well as other passages, reflect this military type victory of Christ over the ruling authorities achieved at the Cross.

> 2 Corinthians 2:14
> But thanks be to God, who in Christ always leads us in triumphal procession, and through us spreads the fragrance of the knowledge of him everywhere.

This triumph is referred to in the next verse of 1 Peter 3:22. "Christ, who has gone into heaven and is at the right hand of God, with angels, authorities, and powers having been subjected to him." The subjection of the spiritual powers occurs sometime before or during the ascension in this

---

[107] Clinton E. Arnold, *Zondervan Illustrated Bible Backgrounds Commentary: Romans to Philemon., vol. 3* (Grand Rapids, MI: Zondervan, 2002), 387.

passage, most likely in the prison of Sheol. In Col. 2:15 we read that God "disarmed the rulers and authorities and put them to open shame, by triumphing over them" in Christ's death and resurrection. His death on the cross forgives us the legal debt of our sin, his resurrection unites us in our new spiritual life, and his ascension wraps it all up with a victory lap, towing the bound and defeated principalities and powers of the nations behind him.

One of the premises of the entire *Chronicles of the Nephilim* series is the Deuteronomy 32 worldview that spoke of the allotment of earthly nations to the fallen Watchers, at the time of the Tower of Babel (Deut. 32:8-9; 29:26). God granted territorial authority to these divine beings (Deut. 4:19-20; Daniel 10). But God kept Jacob for himself and then took the land of Canaan as his inheritance. So the picture is one of a world divided up into parcels of land underneath the authority of the fallen Watchers as false gods, with Yahweh having Israel in Canaan as his own.

And this allotment occurred at the division of tongues during the Tower of Babel episode (Duet. 32:8). But one day, the coming Messiah would ultimately take back that Watcher allotment and inherit the entire earth as his territory, along with the nations to be his people.

> Daniel 4:17
> [17] The sentence is by the decree of the watchers, the decision by the word of the holy ones, to the end that the living may know that the Most High rules the kingdom of men and gives it to whom he will.

> Psalm 2:7–8
> [7] The LORD said to me, "You are my Son; today I have begotten you. [8] Ask of me, and I will make the nations your heritage, and the ends of the earth your possession.

The proclamation that Christ made to the spirits in prison was most likely his proclamation of victory and authority over the angelic powers that once ruled the Gentiles. The first of those powers were imprisoned in the Days of Noah, but their fellow fallen angels continued to rule in their absence over the nations. This inheritance of the earth and the drawing in of the nations would finally commence on the Day of Pentecost when the Holy Spirit would literally undo Babel and the division of tongues and begin to draw those nations to himself (Acts 2).

But why would Christ have to proclaim authority or victory to those who were already imprisoned? Would that not be anti-climactic? Not if their fellow fallen angelic powers still ruled outside that prison on the earth, much like imprisoned Mafioso leaders are still linked to their fellow criminals on the outside. The angelic powers imprisoned at the Flood were the original rebels, the progenitors of the ongoing Seed of the Serpent that continued on in a lineage of evil on earth. They were in bonds, but the resultant War of the Seed that they spawned originated with their fall.

Christ's exorcism of demons becomes the picture of his cosmic authority casting out the occupying evil powers, described as an army (Luke 11;18). And that cosmic authority would ultimately crush the Serpent's head.

> Luke 11:20–22
> [20] [Jesus:] "But if it is by the finger of God that I cast out demons, then the kingdom of God has come upon you. [21] When a strong man, fully armed, guards his own palace, his goods are safe; [22] but when one stronger than he attacks him and overcomes him, he takes away his armor in which he trusted and divides his spoil."

The incarnation and ministry of Christ inaugurated the Kingdom of Messiah, the Kingdom of God. His death, resurrection, and ascension accomplished the atonement of sins for his people (Col. 2:13-15), the crushing of the head of the Serpent (Luke 10:17-19), and the victorious triumphal procession of binding his enemies, from Sheol up to heaven (1 Pet. 3:18-22), as he rose to the ultimate seat of authority over all kingdoms, rulers, and authorities: The right hand of God the Father (Eph. 1:21). From there Jesus reigns victoriously, in which he undid the Tower of Babel (Acts 2) evicted the spiritual authorities over the nations (Deut. 32:8), and began to draw those nations away from their gods unto the new cosmic mountain, Mount Zion (Isa. 2). This is the cosmic War of the Seed, a war of conquering Christ's enemies through the power of the proclaimed Gospel in history…

> 1 Corinthians 15:24–28
> [24] Then comes the end, when he delivers the kingdom to God the Father after destroying every rule and every authority and power. [25] For he must reign until he has put all his enemies under his feet. [26] The last enemy to be destroyed is death. [27] For "God has put all things in subjection under

his feet." But when it says, "all things are put in subjection," it is plain that he is excepted who put all things in subjection under him. [28] When all things are subjected to him, then the Son himself will also be subjected to him who put all things in subjection under him, that God may be all in all.

APPENDIX B

The Geography of Hades

When reading the words *Hades* or *Underworld*, most educated readers immediately conjure images of Greco-Roman myth taught in school: A misty and gloomy abode of the dead below the earth where all souls of mortals, both good and evil, went after death. It is ruled over by the god of the same name, Hades, and contains perilous landscapes and dangerous bizarre creatures. Though there is not perfect consistency of geography among the various Greek and Roman authors, some elements repeat.[1]

There are five rivers in the classical Hades. Styx is the most prominent one that circles the underworld. The second one, Acheron, is the one crossed by souls on a boat ferried by the ghostly boatman Charon to bring them to the gates of Hades. Each of the rivers represent what happens to the departed souls.

1) Styx: River of hatred.
2) Acheron: River of pain.
3) Lethe: River of forgetfulness.
4) Phlegethon: River of fire.
5) Cocytus: River of wailing.

The entrance to the underworld is guarded by the three-headed dog Cerberus and other chimeric creatures like centaurs. The rivers then divide the geography into multiple regions with different purposes.

1) Fields of Punishment: Where souls who committed sins against the gods are punished.
2) Fields of Asphodel: Where souls go who were insignificant, neither great nor wicked.
3) Vale of Mourning: Where souls go who were unloved.
4) Elysium: Where the spirits of heroes and the virtuous ended up.
5) Isles of the Blessed: For the most distinguished of souls for eternity.
6) Tartarus: The deepest pit of Hades where the rebel Titans were bound.

---

[1] For a brief introduction to Hades, http://en.wikipedia.org/wiki/Greek_underworld

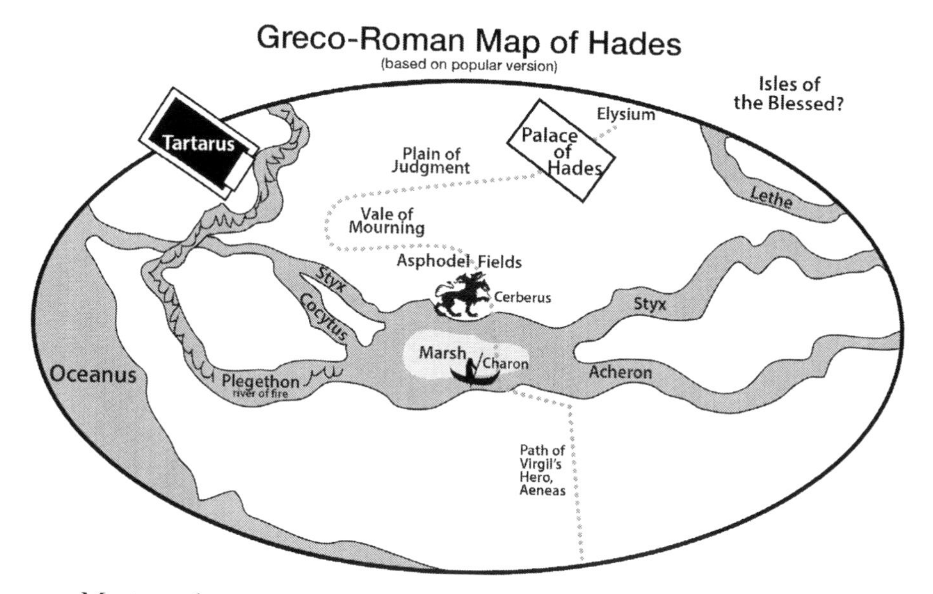

Most modern western pictures of the afterlife, or realm of the dead, come from the medieval punishments of Dante's *Inferno* and Milton's *Paradise Lost*. Levels of torture for sinners meted out by angels or demons, with Lucifer reigning over hell as a more interesting character than God. Sadly, these unbiblical notions have influenced Christian theology in some ways more than the Scriptural text itself. They make for colorful stories, but are not true to Biblical theology.

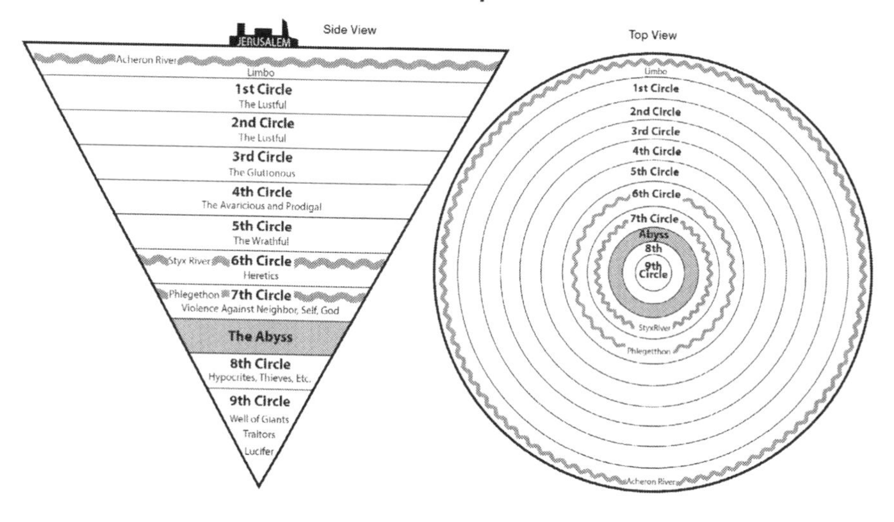

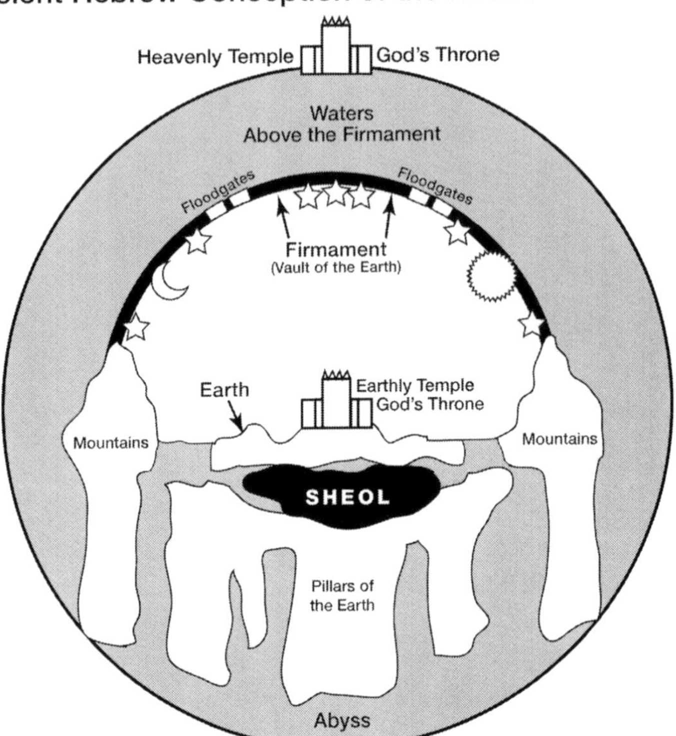

What does the Bible itself say about the underworld? The Old Testament Hebrew equivalent to the Greek *Hades* was *Sheol.*[2] Sheol could be a metaphorical personification of death (Hos 13:14; Isa. 28:15; 38:18, Ps. 49:15) or the grave (Psa. 88:11; Isa. 14:9-11), but it could also refer to a location beneath the earth that was the abode of the dead (Isa 14:9-15). The spirit of Samuel was called up from Sheol (1Sam. 28:13), and the sons of Korah went *down alive* into this underworld (Num. 16:33). People would not "fall alive" into death or the grave *and then* perish if Sheol was not a location. But they would die after they fall down into a location (Sheol) and the earth closes over them in that order.

When the prophet writes about Sheol in Isaiah 14, he combines the notion of the physical location of the dead body in the earth (v.11) with the location beneath the earth of the spirits of the dead (v.9). It's really a both/and synthesis. The term includes several concepts of imagination.

---

[2] "Sheol," *DDD*, p 768.

Here are some verses that speak of Sheol geographically as a spiritual underworld below the earth in contrast with heaven as a spiritual overworld above the earth:

> Amos 9:2
> "If they dig into Sheol, from there shall my hand take them; if they climb up to heaven, from there I will bring them down.
>
> Job 11:8
> It is higher than heaven—what can you do? Deeper than Sheol—what can you know?
>
> Psa. 139:8
> If I ascend to heaven, you are there! If I make my bed in Sheol, you are there![3]

These are not mere references to the body in the grave, but to locations of the soul as well. Sheol is a multi-layered term that describes both the grave for the body and the underworld location of the departed souls of the dead.[4] In Old Testament times, Sheol did not include any kind of punishment beyond its power to hold souls captive to death (Psa. 18:4-5), separated in some sense from God's presence (Psa. 115:17; 6:5), and one's misery of lost power and glory (Psa. 7:5; Isa. 14:9-16). But fire and bodily torture are absent from this Old Testament worldview.

Shades

One biblical term used for departed souls in Sheol is *rephaim*. It is sometimes translated as "shades," in English. As the *ISBE* puts it, "In Job 26:5 "the shades below" are the dead (cf. Ps. 88:10; Isa. 26:14). They dwell in "the depths of Sheol" (Prov. 9:18), where they live together in "the assembly of the dead" (Prov. 21:16)."[5] That assembly is described in 1Enoch

---

[3] See also Isa. 7:11; Matt. 11:23; Phil 2:10; Rev. 5:3, 13; 1Pet 2:4-5.
[4] "The ideas of the grave and of Sheol cannot be separated…The dead are at the same time in the grave and in Sheol…Where there is grave, there is Sheol, and where there is Sheol, there is grave." Theodore J. Lewis, "Dead, Abode of the," ed. David Noel Freedman, *The Anchor Yale Bible Dictionary* (New York: Doubleday, 1992), 103.
[5] P. K. McCarter Jr., "Shades," ed. Geoffrey W. Bromiley, *The International Standard Bible Encyclopedia, Revised* (Wm. B. Eerdmans, 1979–1988), 440.

as “four hollows” or pits under the mountain of the dead, where they await their judgment in the last days. One hollow is for the righteous; another hollow is for Abel and those unjustly murdered; a third is for the wicked unpunished in life; and a fourth for the wicked who were punished in life. The souls of the unrighteous dead thirst and are frightful of their future judgment (1En. 22:9), but they are not tortured by angels or demons. Righteous souls receive refreshment from a fountain of waters “with light upon them” (1En. 22:9; Luke 16:24).

Another Jewish text of the first century, 4Ezra, describes the departed soul’s entrance into Sheol as consisting of seven days to see the future results of their ways before being led to their habitation to wait for judgment. During this time period, the unrighteous…

> 4Ezra 7:80, 87, 101
> …shall immediately wander about in torments, ever grieving and sad…they shall utterly waste away in confusion and be consumed with shame, and shall wither with fear at seeing the glory of the Most High before whom they sinned while they were alive, and before whom they are to be judged in the last times… and afterward they shall be gathered in their habitations.

Another ancient Christian text, The Apocalypse of Zephaniah, describes the angels who draw the shades to their destiny as beings whose “faces were like a leopard, their tusks being outside their mouth like the wild boars. Their eyes were mixed with blood. Their hair was loose like the hair of women, and fiery scourges were in their hands.”[6]

This ancient legendary depiction is behind the confused, wandering zombie-like shades in *Jesus Triumphant* who are animated by maggots and worms (Isa. 14:11; 66:24) while wailing and gnashing their teeth (Matt. 25:30), before being brought to the Mountain of the Dead.

In Isaiah 14, a prophetic rant against the arrogant king of Babylon, the “shades” take on an additional meaning…

> Isaiah 14:9-11
> Sheol beneath is stirred up to meet you when you come;

[6] James H. Charlesworth, *The Old Testament Pseudepigrapha*, vol. 1 (New York; London: Yale University Press, 1983), 511.

> it rouses the shades (*rephaim*) to greet you, all who were leaders of the earth; it raises from their thrones all who were kings of the nations. All of them will answer and say to you: 'You too have become as weak as we! You have become like us!' Your pomp is brought down to Sheol.

The Hebrew word for "shades" here is *rephaim*, a word with ties to the Canaanite giants of Joshua's and David's time (Josh. 13:12; 2Sam. 22:15-22), and mighty warrior kings of Canaanite literature also called *rephaim*.[7] Isaiah's intent is to mock the pomp and vainglory of man, who will end up as humiliated as every other mighty being imprisoned in Sheol.[8] Thus, the appearance of the Rephaim guardians in *Jesus Triumphant.*

Hades in the New Testament

Because the New Testament is in Greek, it does not use the word Sheol, but the Greek word, *Hades*. Jesus himself used the term Hades as the location of condemned spirits in contrast with heaven as the location of redeemed spirits (Matt. 11:23). Jesus referred to the "Gates of Hades" (Matt. 16:18), a well-known underworld concept in ancient Near Eastern and Western Greco-Roman mythology. This was more than a metaphorical reference to the "power of death," because the sacred grotto in Caesarea Philippi, where he spoke those words, was considered a gateway to Hades.[9] The location had a cave with a deep chasm believed to lead to the Abyss and Hades.[10] In the book of Revelation, Jesus claims to capture the "keys of Death and Hades," which is a doublet separating the two words rather than identifying them (Rev. 1:18).

Hades was the location of departed spirits in Christ's parable of Lazarus and the rich man in Hades (Luke 16:19-31). It was from this parable that the term "Abraham's Bosom" came, that indicated the separated location of

---

[7] Mark S. Smith, "Rephaim," ed. David Noel Freedman, *The Anchor Yale Bible Dictionary* (New York: Doubleday, 1992), 674-75.
[8] Philip S. Johnston, *Shades of Sheol: Death and Afterlife in the Old Testament*, (Downers Grove: IL, InterVarsity, 2002), 128-130.
[9] Michael S. Heiser, *The Unseen Realm* (Bellingham: WA, Lexham, 2005), 267-271; Jimmy R. Watson, *The Religious History of Banias and Its Contribution to an Understanding of the Petrine Confession* (Hardin-Simmons University, Master's Thesis, 1989). 87; George W. E. Nicklesburg, "Enoch, Levi, and Peter: Recipients of Revelation in Upper Galilee," Journal of Biblical Literature 100 (December 1981): 598.
[10] *Wars of the Jews* 1:405, Flavius Josephus and William Whiston, *The Works of Josephus: Complete and Unabridged* (Peabody: Hendrickson, 1987).

righteous souls in Hades from the eternally thirsty wicked by a large chasm. This parable has been convincingly proven by some scholars to be a subversive polemic against the common motif of Hellenistic pagan journeys to the underworld and communication from the dead, not a literal geography of Hades.[11] But if it was good enough for Jesus, it's good enough for *Jesus Triumphant* in its imaginative depiction of Hades.

In Greek mythology, Tartarus was another term for a location beneath the "roots of the earth" and beneath the waters where the warring giants called "Titans" were bound in chains because of their rebellion against the gods. Peter uses a derivative of that very Greek word Tartarus to describe a similar location and scenario of angels being bound during the time of Noah and the warring Titans called "Nephilim."[12]

> 2Pet. 2:4-5
> God did not spare angels when they sinned, but cast them into hell [*Tartarus*] and committed them to chains of gloomy darkness to be kept until the judgment.

From Sheol to Gehenna

Despite this claim of a realm for the dead in both the Old and New Testaments, there is very little specificity of description of its attributes beyond "darkness" (Job 17:13; Lam. 3:6) and "silence" (Psa. 31:17–18; 94:17; 115:17). The one clear certainty about Sheol/Hades is that "he who goes down to Sheol does not come up" (Job 7:9; 10:21; 2Sam. 12:23). As Papaioannou describes:

> First, Sheol/Hades is where everyone goes at death. There is no distinction between the righteous and the wicked… Second, Sheol/Hades is not a place of eschatological

---

[11] Kim Papaioannou, *The Geography of Hell in the Teaching of Jesus: Gehenna, Hades, the Abyss, the Outer Darkness Where There Is Weeping and Gnashing of Teeth* (Eugene, OR: Pickwick Publications, 2013), 112. Richard Bauckham, *The Fate of the Dead: Studies on the Jewish and Christian Apocalypses*, (Leiden, Netherlands: Brill, 1998), 101.
[12] 1.25 ταρταρόω [*tartaroo*] Louw, Johannes P., and Eugene Albert Nida. *Greek-English Lexicon of the New Testament : Based on Semantic Domains*. electronic ed. of the 2nd edition. New York: United Bible societies, 1996. Bauckham, Richard J. Vol. 50, *Word Biblical Commentary : 2 Peter, Jude*. Word Biblical Commentary. Dallas: Word, Incorporated, 2002, p 248-249.

> punishment, but rather the destiny of all human beings... Third, there is no life or consciousness in Sheol/Hades. In contrast to some cultures that envisioned meaningful existence in the afterlife, the Hebrew Bible portrays Sheol as a place of silence and lifelessness where human existence has come to an end... There is no memory in Hades (Isa 26:14); neither is there any longer a communion with God (Isa 38:18). It is a place of silence, darkness, and oblivion (Job 17:13). Thus, a person who dies in effect ceases to exist (Eccl. 9:6)... With a belief in a bodily resurrection, Sheol/Hades is only a temporary abode—the dead remain there until they are raised.[13]

Richard Bauckham explains the change in understanding that occurred between the Old Testament and New Testament Scriptures regarding the abode of the dead. He points out that the older view did not involve active punishment of souls in Sheol, but merely involved holding the wicked in detention until the last judgment. The newer view, driven by apocalyptic literature included descents to the underworld, where increasingly only the wicked were located:

> The older view allowed for visits to the place of detention in Sheol (1En. 22), visits to the hell which is already prepared for but not yet inhabited by the wicked (lEn. 26:3-27:4; 2En. 10; 40:12; 2Bar. 59:10), and prophetic visions of the casting of the wicked into Gehenna at the last judgment (1En. 41:2; Bar 59: 11). But only the later view enabled a seer to see and to describe in detail the punishments actually being inflicted on the wicked in hell. The later view therefore spawned a long tradition of 'tours of hell,' in which a variety of different punishments appropriate to different categories of sinners is described.[14]

By the time of the New Testament, some Second Temple Jewish literature began to increasingly evidence the notion of punishment for the wicked and reward for the righteous in Hades *before the final judgment.*

---

[13] Papaioannou, *The Geography of Hell*, 87-88.
[14] Bauckham, *The Fate of the Dead*, 34.

Bauckham suggests this new notion of immediate recompense upon death in both Jewish and Christian writings may have been the result of Greek influence,"[15] but the fact remains that after the advent of Christ and his spiritual mission, the change took place with the growth of Christianity. In this sense, Christ's descent into Hades, and his victorious triumph over spiritual principalities and the powers of Death and Hades marked the inauguration of God's kingdom that may have included the beginning of rewards and punishment in Sheol/Hades.

The Greek word for "hell" used in New Testament translation is *Gehenna*. Some have believed that this was the name of a garbage dump outside Jerusalem that burned with perpetual flames, and Jesus used it as a metaphor for the fires of judgment. But recent scholarship tends to disregard this thesis as lacking both exegetical weight and hard archeological evidence.[16]

In fact, Gehenna is Greek for "Valley of Hinnom," the valley that bordered the south and western sides of Jerusalem.[17] This valley had a dark history in Israel's past as the location of tophets, or burning places for sacrifice to Molech, the underworld god. Israelites would "pass their children through the fire" as human sacrifice. God became so angry with this abomination that the prophet Jeremiah pronounced a fiery curse on the area destroyed by King Josiah around 632 B.C. (Jer. 7:29–34; 19:1–15). It would become known as the "Valley of Slaughter," and a synonym for future judgment/destruction of people and nations in this life as well as the next. Both Second Temple literature and Jesus' teachings used Gehenna as a reference to the future final judgment (Matt. 13:42, 30; 25:41).[18] So, yes it was a metaphor for fiery punishment, but a far richer meaning than a burning garbage dump. It provided incarnate location for the belief in the eschatological judgment of God upon evil.

Geography of the Underworld in 1Enoch

Apart from Jesus' parable of Abraham's Bosom (Luke 16:19-31), there are no descriptions of the actual geography of the underworld in the New Testament. Rather than drawing from pagan Greek myths to depict Hades in

[15] Bauckham, *The Fate of the Dead,* 36.
[16] Papaioannou, *The Geography of Hell*, 80.
[17] Duane F. Watson, "Gehenna (Place)," ed. David Noel Freedman, *The Anchor Yale Bible Dictionary* (New York: Doubleday, 1992), 926.
[18] See 1 En. 10:13; 48:8–10; 100:7–9; 108:4–7; Jdt 16:17; 2 Bar. 85:13.

Jesus Triumphant, I decided to draw from a respected Jewish source that did provide a "cosmic geography" or conceptual map of the universe that included the underworld. This geography of Hades can be found in the visions of the ancient book of 1Enoch.[19]

Though 1Enoch is not Scripture, I have argued elsewhere for the high regard that the New Testament gives the ancient text as a source for some of its own theological concepts and language.[20] The book consists of several "books," that recount an expanded version of the Genesis 6 story of the Watchers and Nephilim giants, as well as visions that the prophet Enoch allegedly experienced of angels taking him around the earth, up into the heights of heaven, and down into the depths of Hades (which are actually arrived at by going to the "ends of the earth" rather than descending down into the earth). Unfortunately, these visions are obscure, overlapping, and at times contradictory, so scholars have disagreed over their interpretation as well as their actual cosmic geography. I have attempted to use my own reading of the text and integrate it with several of these scholarly viewpoints that can be found analyzed in the book, *A Study of the Geography of 1 Enoch 17-19,* by Kelley Coblentz Bautch.[21] Imagination is required!

Since Enoch's "map" is cosmic, it includes Sheol/Hades as well as the heavens and the earth. But some scholars have argued that Enoch's entire journey is to the realm of the dead.[22] So I decided to use the ancient Near Eastern (and Jewish) notion of "on earth as it is in heaven" (Matt. 6:10) or "as above, so below," to apply to the underworld as well. In this way, the geography of Hades that Jesus follows on his underworld journey, is a reflection of the sacred geography of the earth above ("Sacred geography" means that it does not so much follow physical geography as it does theological meaning).

---

[19] Though 1Enoch does evidence Hellenistic influence, it retains a unique Jewish perspective throughout its literary style and content.

[20] See the chapter "The Book of Enoch: Scripture, Heresy, or What?" in *When Giants Were Upon the Earth: The Watchers, Nephilim and the Cosmic War of the Seed* (Los Angeles: Embedded Pictures, 2014).

[21] Kelley Coblentz Bautch, *A Study of the Geography of 1 Enoch 17-19: No One Has Seen What I Have Seen*, (Leiden, Netherlands: Brill, 2003).

[22] Glasson, T. Francis. *Greek Influence in Jewish Eschatology*. London: S.P.C.K., 1961, 8-11; Nickelsburg, *Jewish Literature between the Bible and the Mishnah*, (Philadelphia: Fortress Press, 1981) 54–55; 66, n. 26; also *1 Enoch*, 280; James C. VanderKam, *Enoch and the Growth of an Apocalyptic Tradition*. CBQMS 16. Washington, D.C.: Catholic Biblical Association of America, 1984.

Since the underworld was believed by the Jews to be under the earth,[23] and accessed by the waters of the Abyss,[24] that was the source of the waters above,[25] I have those waters work as a kind of sky in the dome of the underworld (though not in all places). The mountains below rise up from Hades to the earth above. So when Jesus is at Mount Zion in Hades, it rises up and penetrates the ceiling of Hades and becomes Mount Zion on earth above them. This fulfills the ancient Near Eastern notion of the cosmic mountains being an *axis mundi*, a connection between the heavens, the earth, and the underworld.[26]

The circle of Hades matches the circle of the earth above it and likewise has an ocean/river (the Great Sea or Abyss) at its outer reaches that extends beyond the "Four Winds" or "Four Corners" of the earth where the pillars of the earth support the heavens and the earth (1En. 17:5; Prov. 8:27, 29; 1Sam. 2:8; Mark 13:27).[27]

In this conceptual map, Jerusalem, or Mount Zion is at the center of the earth, and has "the accursed valley" (Gehenna) right next to it (Ezek. 5:5, 38:12; 1En. 26:1-2; 27:2).

North from that center resides Mount Hermon, the "rock" (mountain) that Jesus said God would build his new kingdom church upon.[28] This mountain is described as "reaching to the heavens" and as being the celestial storehouse of the luminaries and storms (1En. 17:3). Many rivers flow from it, including a river of fire and a river of "living waters" (17:4-8), and it is guarded by fiery beings who take human shape (17:1). This "source of the waters" is a reflection of the cosmic Mountain of Eden and it's source of living waters (Ezek. 28:13-14).[29]

In the south are seven mountains of precious stones arranged in a perpendicular layout. The central mountain burns with fire day and night, and is called the "throne of God," where God will come down at the final judgment. These elements suggest it is Mount Sinai (1En. 24-25).

In the west are "wintery winds" and the "great darkness," where another mountain hosts "hollow places" for the souls of all the dead. The righteous

---

[23] Amos 9:2.
[24] Ps. 136:6; Job 41:34 LXX.
[25] Wayne Horowitz, *Mesopotamian Cosmic Geography*, (Winona Lake; IN: Eisenbrauns, 1998), 334-348.
[26] Richard J. Clifford, *The Cosmic Mountain in Canaan and the Old Testament* (Wipf & Stock Pub, 2010). Also, Isa. 14:13-15.
[27] See also Isa. 40:22; Zech. 9:10; Job 38:4.
[28] Matt. 16:18.
[29] Bautch, *A Study of the Geography of 1 Enoch,* 64-69.

are separated from the sinners, much like the chasm separates the righteous in Abraham's Bosom from the sinners in the parable of Lazarus. (Luke 16:19-26; 1En. 17:6; 22:1-14).

In the east are "great beasts and birds" at the ends of the earth (1En. 33:1). Tartarus is further "beyond the edge of the earth," where the earth meets to uphold the vault of heaven (1En. 18:10).[30] This is where the angels who sinned in Genesis 6 are kept imprisoned in gloomy darkness (2Pet. 2:4; 1Pet. 3:18-20). They are in deep pits or chasms that are like fiery pillars. (1En. 18:10-16).

There is much more detail that can be quite confusing to follow, so I have included an illustrated map with some of the major elements adapted from Bautch and my own reading of 1Enoch.

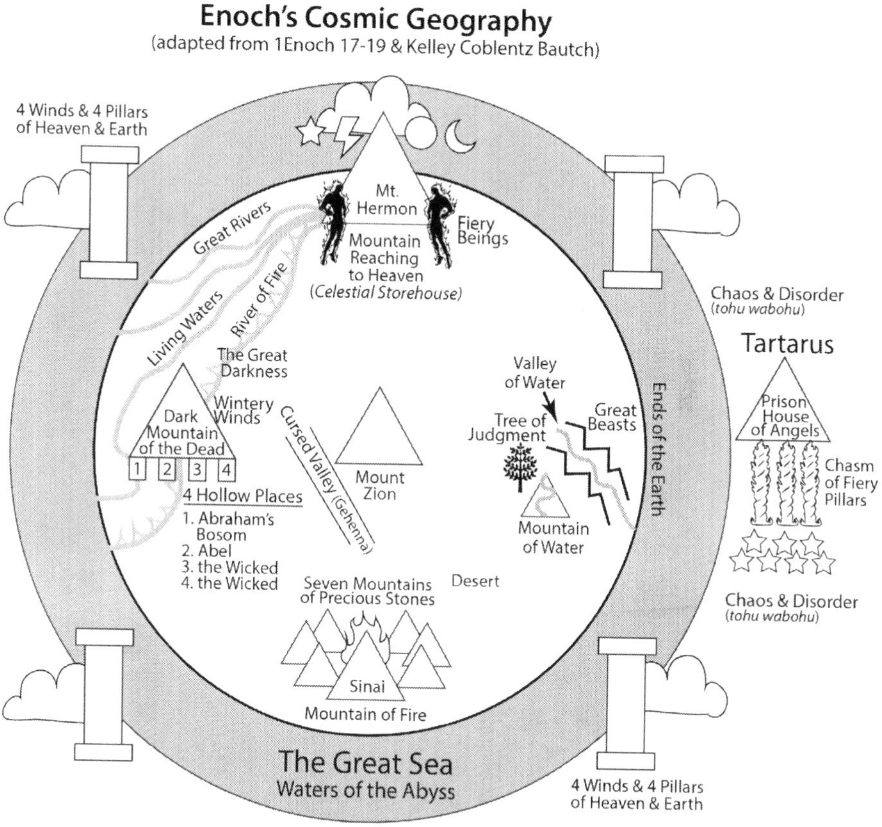

Enoch's Cosmic Geography

(adapted from 1Enoch 17-19 & Kelley Coblentz Bautch)

[30] George W. E. Nickelsburg, *1 Enoch: A Commentary on the Book of 1 Enoch, ed. Klaus Baltzer, Hermeneia—a Critical and Historical Commentary on the Bible* (Minneapolis, MN: Fortress, 2001), 286.

Can We Trust This Ancient Cosmology?

The ancient Biblical cosmic picture is a three-tiered universe with God's throne above the waters of heaven, a solid dome above the flat disc earth, founded on pillars, surrounded by a circular sea, on top of a watery abyss, beneath which is the underworld of Sheol, where souls are trapped in waiting cells for a final judgment.[31]

A natural question arises while examining this ancient cosmology: If the Biblical writers were so "scientifically inaccurate" in their understanding of the universe, then why should we trust what they write about God, the afterlife, and judgment?

Some well-intentioned Evangelicals seek to maintain their particular definition of Biblical inerrancy by denying that the Bible contains this ancient Near Eastern cosmography. They try to explain it away as phenomenal language or poetic license. Phenomenal language is the act of describing what one sees subjectively from one's perspective without further claiming objective reality. So when the writer says the sun stood still, or that the sun rises and sets within the solid dome of heaven, he is only describing his observation, not cosmic reality. The claim of observation from a personal frame of reference is certainly true as far as it goes. Of course the observer describes what they are observing. But the distinction between appearance and reality is an imposition of our alien modern understanding onto theirs. As Seely explains,

> It is precisely because ancient peoples were scientifically naive that they did not distinguish between the appearance of the sky and their scientific concept of the sky. They had no reason to doubt what their eyes told them was true, namely, that the stars above them were fixed in a solid dome and that the sky literally touched the earth at the horizon. So, they equated appearance with reality and concluded that the

[31] For a detailed examination of this full cosmology see "Appendix D: Mesopotamian Cosmic Geography in the Bible," in the first Chronicle of the Nephilim, *Noah Primeval* by Brian Godawa.

> sky must be a solid physical part of the universe just as much as the earth itself.[32]

If the ancients did not know the earth was a sphere in space, or that there was no underworld beneath their feet, they could not know that their observations of appearances were anything other than reality. It would be easy enough to relegate one or two examples of Scripture to the notion of phenomenal language, but when dozens of those phenomenal descriptions reflect the same complex integrated picture of the universe that Israel's neighbors shared, and when that picture included many elements that were *not* phenomenally observable, such as the Abyss, Sheol, or the pillars of earth and heaven, it strains credulity to suggest these were merely phenomenal descriptions intentionally unrelated to reality. If it walks a like an ancient Near Eastern duck and talks like an ancient Near Eastern duck, then chances are they thought it was an ancient Near Eastern duck, not just the "appearance" of one having no reality.

It would be a mistake to claim that there is a single monolithic ancient Near Eastern cosmography.[33] There are varieties of stories with overlapping imagery, and some contradictory notions. But there are certainly enough commonalities to affirm a generic yet mysterious picture of the universe. And that picture in Scripture undeniably includes poetic language. The Hebrew culture was imaginative. They integrated poetry into everything, including their observational descriptions of nature. Thus a hymn of creation such as Psalm 19 tells of the heavens declaring God's glory as if using speech, and then describes the operations of the sun in terms of a bridegroom in his chamber or a man running a race. Creative imagination is inescapable and ubiquitous.

And herein lies a potential solution for the dilemma of the scientific inaccuracy of the ancient cosmic geography in Scripture: *The Israelite culture, being pre-scientific, thought more in terms of function and purpose than material structure.* Even if their picture of the heavens and earth as a three-tiered geocentric cosmology, was scientifically "false" from our modern perspective, it nevertheless still accurately describes the teleological purpose and meaning of creation that they were intending to communicate.

---

[32] Seely, "The Firmament," p 228.

[33] Horowitz, *Mesopotamian Cosmic Geography.*

Though there is no literal underworld beneath the earth with rivers of fire and souls trapped in mountains waiting for the judgment, it still communicates the truth, transcendent of that ancient culture yet revealed through it, that those who have died await a future resurrection and judgment before the living God. Jesus' descent into that imagined underworld is a theological narrative explaining the transcendent truth that his death and resurrection paid the price for the sins of his people, and secured his victory over the spiritual powers who rule mankind, and from whom Christ has taken back his inheritance of the earth. Our modern worldview obsessed as it is with empirical science and human reason is so blinded to its own ignorance of transcendent reality and stunted imagination, that it amounts to idolatry, the limited, fallible human mind and senses as god.

Othmar Keel, one of the leading scholars on Ancient Near Eastern art has argued that even though modern depictions of the ancient worldview like the illustration of the three-tiered universe above are helpful, they are fundamentally flawed because they depict a "profane, lifeless, virtually closed mechanical system," which reflects our own modern bias. To the ancient Near East "rather, the world was an entity open at every side. The powers which determine the world are of more interest to the ancient Near East than the structure of the cosmic system. A wide variety of diverse, uncoordinated notions regarding the cosmic structure were advanced from various points of departure."[34]

John Walton has written recently of this ANE concern with powers over structure in direct relation to the creation story of Genesis. He argues that in the ancient world existence was understood more in terms of function within a god-created *purposeful order* than in terms of material status within a natural physical structure.[35] This is not to say that the physical world was denied or ignored, but rather that the priority and interests were different from our own. We should therefore be careful in judging their purpose-driven cosmography too strictly in light of our own material-driven cosmography. And in this sense, modern material descriptions of reality are more "false" than ancient pictures because they do not include the immaterial aspect of reality: Meaning and purpose.

But even more basic than that, human observation of the universe is always changing, from Newtonian physics to Quantum physics to String

---

[34] Othmar Keel, *The Symbolism of the Biblical World*, Winona Lake; IN: Eisenbrauns, 1972, 1997, 56-57.

[35] John H. Walton, *The Lost World of Genesis One: Ancient Cosmology and the Origins Debate* (Downers Grove: IL, InterVarsity Press, 2009), 23-36.

Theory. That change is less a change of more precise instrumentation than it is a change of ideas. What we think we see is more affected by our philosophical presuppositions (and theories) than empirical scientists are willing to admit.

Biblical writers did not *teach* their cosmography as scientific doctrine revealed by God about the way the physical universe was materially structured, they *assumed* the popular cosmography to teach their doctrine about God's *purposes and meaning*. To critique the cosmic model carrying the message is to miss the meaning altogether, which is the message. God's throne may not be physically above us in waters held back by a solid firmament, but he truly does rule "over" us and is king and sustainer of creation in whatever model man uses to depict that creation. The phrase "every created thing which is in heaven and on the earth and under the earth" (Rev. 5:13) is equivalent in meaning to the modern concept of every particle and wave in every dimension of the Big Bang space-time continuum, as well as every person dead or alive.

The geocentric picture in Scripture is a depiction through man's ancient perspective of God's purpose and humankind's significance. For a modern heliocentrist to attack that picture as falsifying the theology would be cultural imperialism. Reducing significance to physical location is simply a prejudice of material priority over spiritual purpose.

One of the humorous ironies of this debate is that if the history of science is any judge, a thousand years from now, scientists will no doubt consider our current paradigm with which we judge the ancients to be itself fatally flawed. This is not to reduce reality to relativism, but rather to illustrate that all claims of empirical knowledge contain an inescapable element of human fallibility and finitude. A proper response should be a bit more humility and a bit less hubris regarding the use of our own scientific models as standards in judging theological meaning or purpose.

For additional Biblical and historical research related to this novel, go to www.ChroniclesoftheNephilim.com under the menu listing, "Links" > Jesus Triumphant.

About the Author

Brian Godawa is the screenwriter for the award-winning feature film, *To End All Wars,* starring Kiefer Sutherland. It was awarded the Commander in Chief Medal of Service, Honor and Pride by the Veterans of Foreign Wars, won the first Heartland Film Festival by storm, and showcased the Cannes Film Festival Cinema for Peace.

He also co-wrote *Alleged*, starring Brian Dennehy as Clarence Darrow and Fred Thompson as William Jennings Bryan. He previously adapted to film the best-selling supernatural thriller novel *The Visitation* by author Frank Peretti for Ralph Winter (*X-Men, Wolverine*), and wrote and directed *Wall of Separation,* a PBS documentary, and *Lines That Divide*, a documentary on stem cell research.

Mr. Godawa's scripts have won multiple awards in respected screenplay competitions, and his articles on movies and philosophy have been published around the world. He has traveled around the United States teaching on movies, worldviews, and culture to colleges, churches and community groups.

His book, *Hollywood Worldviews: Watching Films with Wisdom and Discernment* has been released in a revised edition from InterVarsity Press. His book *Word Pictures: Knowing God Through Story and Imagination* (IVP) addresses the power of image and story in the pages of the Bible to transform the Christian life.

Find out more about his other books, lecture tapes and dvds for sale at his website **www.godawa.com**.

BOOKS BY BRIAN GODAWA

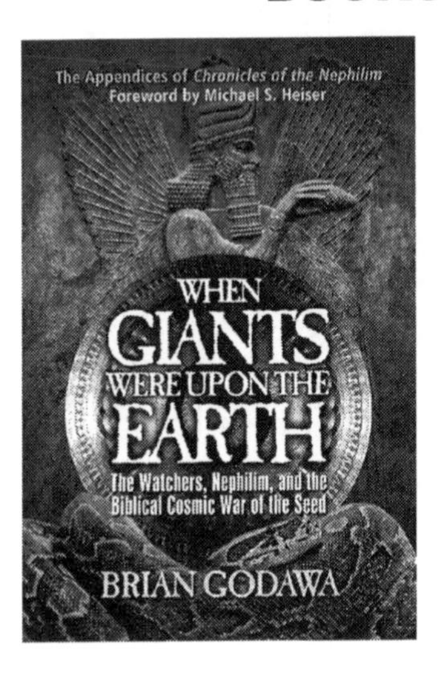

When Giants Were Upon the Earth: The Watchers, Nephilim, and the Biblical Cosmic War of the Seed

By Brian Godawa

The Appendices of the *Chronicles of the Nephilim* Together in One Book.

The bestselling Biblical fantasy novel series *Chronicles of the Nephilim* has opened a door for Christian imagination and theology like none other. But many have appreciated the appendices of each novel as much as the novels. In those appendices, author Brian Godawa shares the Biblical and ancient historical and mythical research that undergirds the fiction. Now all those appendices have been placed together in one book for those who want serious study of the topics of the Watchers, Nephilim, and the Biblical Cosmic War of the Seed.

This book has the special bonus of a previously unpublished chapter on the Book of Enoch, as well as a newly expanded chapter on the Sons of God. But it also contains the appendices of the last two Chronicles, *David Ascendant* and *Jesus Triumphant* before their release!

Chapters Include:

1) The Book of Enoch: Scripture, Heresy or What? (Bonus Chapter)
2) Sons of God (Newly expanded from *Noah Primeval*)
3) The Nephilim (from *Noah Primeval*)
4) Leviathan (from *Noah Primeval*)
5) Mesopotamian Cosmic Geography in the Bible (from *Noah Primeval*)
6) Retelling Bible Stories and Mythic Imagination (from *Enoch Primordial*)
7) Gilgamesh and the Bible (from *Gilgamesh Immortal*)
8) In Defense of Ancient Traditions (from *Abraham Allegiant*)
9) Mythical Monsters in the Bible (from *Joshua Valiant*)
10) Canaanite Baal and Old Testament Storytelling Polemics (*Caleb Vigilant*)
11) Goliath was Not Alone (from *David Ascendant*)
12) Jesus and the Cosmic War (from *Jesus Triumphant*)

To order books and products by Brian Godawa, as well as FREE articles, just go to the STORE at:

www.godawa.com

Hollywood Worldviews: Watching Films with Wisdom and Discernment
By Brian Godawa

With the sensibilities of an award-winning Hollywood screenwriter and the sensitivities of a thoughtful Christian, Brian Godawa guides us through the place of redemption in film, the "tricks of the trade" that screenwriters use to communicate their worldview through their stories, and the mental and spiritual discipline required for watching movies. *Hollywood Worldviews* helps us enter a dialogue with Hollywood that leads to a happier ending, one that keeps us aware of our culture and awake to our faith.

Endorsements:
"Provocative and challenging. Even when I find myself disagreeing with Brian Godawa in his evaluation of a particular film, his cinematé and sophisticated point of view command attention."
— Michael Medved, Film critic and author of *Hollywood Versus America.*

"Brian's analysis is insightful and stimulating. Our Biblical values are colliding with worldviews in the movies, and Brian shows us why. Those values are also illuminated by intersecting with movies, and I find that especially exciting. We might even understand the Bible with more insight from seeing these connections."
— Ralph Winter, Producer *X-Men 2, Planet of the Apes, X-Men*

To order books and products by Brian Godawa, as well as FREE articles, just go to the STORE at:

www.godawa.com

Word Pictures: Knowing God Through Story & Imagination

By Brian Godawa

In his refreshing and challenging book, Godawa helps you break free from the spiritual suffocation of heady faith. Without negating the importance of reason and doctrine, Godawa challenges you to move from understanding the Bible "literally" to "literarily" by exploring the poetry, parables and metaphors found in God's Word. Weaving historical insight, pop culture and personal narrative throughout, Godawa reveals the importance God places on imagination and creativity in the Scriptures, and provides a biblical foundation for Christians to pursue image, beauty, wonder and mystery in their faith.

Endorsements:

"Brian Godawa is that rare breed—a philosopher/artist—who opens our eyes to the aesthetic dimension of spirituality. Cogently argued and fun to read, Godawa shows convincingly that God interacts with us as whole persons, not only through didactic teaching but also through metaphor, symbol, and sacrament."
— Nancy R. Pearcey, Author, *Total Truth: Liberating Christianity from its Cultural Captivity*

"A spirited and balanced defense of the imagination as a potential conveyer of truth. There is a lot of good literary theory in the book, as well as an autobiographical story line. The thoroughness of research makes the book a triumph of scholarship as well."
— Leland Ryken, Clyde S. Kilby Professor of English, Wheaton College, Illinois. Author, *The Christian Imagination: The Practice of Faith in Literature & Writing.*

To order books and products by Brian Godawa, as well as FREE articles, just go to the STORE at:

www.godawa.com

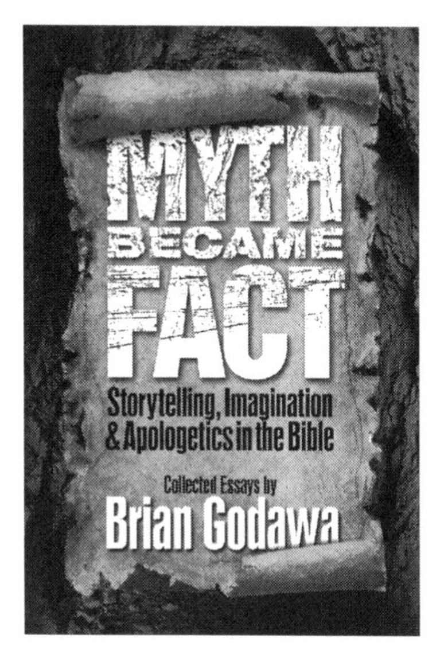

Myth Became Fact: Storytelling, Imagination & Apologetics in the Bible

By Brian Godawa

A collection of essays by Brian Godawa about storytelling, imagination, apologetics and the Bible. Some of them have appeared in the novel series, *Chronicles of the Nephilim* and some have been published in various magazines or journals.

The Christian reader will gain inspiration from these insights to use more imagination in their own approach to defending the faith and glorifying God.

Old Testament Storytelling Apologetics
Israel shared mythopoeic images with their pagan neighbors: The sea dragon of chaos, and the Storm god. These are polemical concepts used by Biblical writers to show the incomparability of Yahweh.

Biblical Creation and Storytelling: Cosmos, Combat and Covenant
Creation stories in the ancient Near East and the Bible both express a primeval battle called *Chaoskampf*, the fight of deity to create order out of chaos. But how do they differ?

The Universe in Ancient Imagination
A detailed comparison and contrast of the Biblical picture of the universe with the ancient Mesopotamian one. Does God communicate material structure or theological meaning?

New Testament Storytelling Apologetics
Paul's sermon to the pagans on Mars Hill is an example of subversion: Communicating the Gospel in terms of a pagan narrative with a view toward replacing their worldview.

Mythopoeia in Prophecy and Apocalyptic Genre
God uses mythical descriptions of future events to deliberately obscure his message while simultaneously proving his claim about the true meaning and purpose behind history.

An Apologetic of Biblical Horror
An exploration of the genre of horror to show how God uses it as a powerful moral tool to communicate serious spiritual, moral, and social defilement in the context of repentance from sin and redemptive victory over evil.

To order books and products by Brian Godawa, as well as FREE articles, just go to the STORE at:

www.godawa.com

LECTURES BY BRIAN GODAWA

Brian has spoken around the world on the topic of movies, worldviews, and faith. Now you can purchase some of his presentations on downloadable MP3 directly from his website, **www.godawa.com**! Here are a sample of presentations:

Art, Movies & Worldviews

6-Lecture Series by Brian Godawa

1. The Church and the Arts: Friends or Foes?
2. From Bezalel to Jesus: Art in the Bible
3. Kiss Kiss, Bang Bang: Sex & Violence in the Movies
4. That's More Than Entertainment!: Redemption in the Movies
5. Following Your Heart: Existentialism in the Movies
6. Losing Our Grip on Reality: Postmodernism in the Movies

Screenwriting for Christians

A 9-Lecture Series by Brian Godawa

Brian teaches the basic elements of storytelling used in writing screenplays from a Christian worldview, complete with examples and analysis of movies that illustrate the lessons. Comes with 30 pages of Student Handouts so you can follow along and take the class on tape! This was taught at YWAM's University of the Nations.

1. Introduction/ Sex & Violence & the Bible
2. Christian writer
3. Basic Structure/ Premise/Theme
4. Premise/Theme Part 2
5. Character
6. Plot
7. Scene
8. The Business and the Life of the Writer
9. Analysis of first 10 pages of "The Sixth Sense"

Storytelling, Worldviews & Persuasion

2 Lectures by Brian Godawa

Part 1: Incarnation

The modern Christian exclusive concentration on logic, precision and rationality has missed a fuller Biblical approach. In the Scriptures, truth and persuasion are mediated through imagination and storytelling as well. Brian addresses the power of incarnation used in Biblical storytelling and imagery. Examples from film clips are used to illustrate.

Part 2: Subversion

Brian examines the Biblical usage of subversion through storytelling as a means of engaging culture and capturing it for Christ. He shows how the Apostle Paul used subversion to retell the Stoic story in Christian terms.

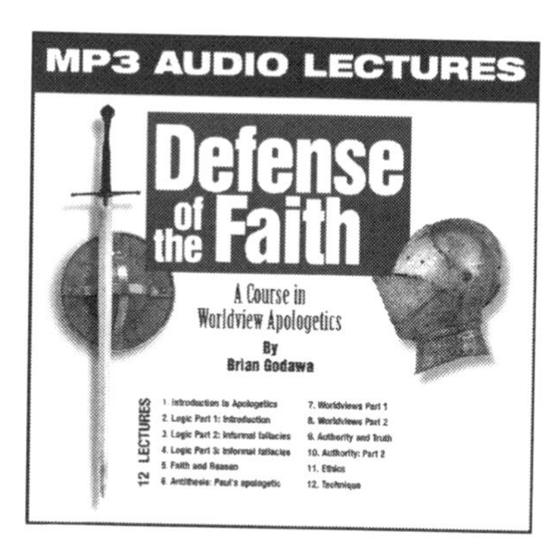

Defense of the Faith

12-Lecture Series by Brian Godawa

This is a different approach to apologetics than the typical way that "proves" a generic theism, then "proves" the Bible, then "proves" the resurrection. This series addresses the weaknesses of typical apologetics and explores how to defend the faith on a deeper level, the level of the worldview of the unbeliever.

1. Introduction to Apologetics
2. Logic Part 1: Intro
3. Logic Part 2: fallacies
4. Logic Part 3: fallacies
5. Faith and Reason
6. Antithesis: Acts 17
7. Worldviews Part 1
8. Worldviews Part 2
9. Authority and Truth
10. Authority: Part 2
11. Ethics
12. Technique

Bible Prophecy & the End Times: It's Not When They Told You It Is

10-Lecture Series by Brian Godawa

The Book of Revelation is more like an Epic Horror Fantasy than a sermon. Brian explores the creative literary imagery of the First Century writings used in Revelation. The Left Behind novel series has made a gazillion dollars based on a popular view of the End Times. What would shock some Christians is to discover that this view is not Biblical. Brian examines the common beliefs of the Left Behind dogma and compares them to the Bible. He shows how the Bible itself explains how most of these prophecies have already been fulfilled. A partial preterist approach to Bible prophecy.

Two options are available for purchase. You can either buy just the MP3 audio, or buy the DVD video versions that have the same audio, BUT ALSO lots of colorful and helpful PowerPoint visuals and film clips for a much richer presentation of the material.

1. Interpreting Bible Prophecy
2. Israel in Prophecy
3. The Last Days
4. The Rapture
5. The Great Tribulation
6. The Anti-Christ
7. The Beast
8. The Coming of Christ
9. The Millennium Part 1
10. The Millennium Part 2

To order these audio lectures and other books and products by Brian Godawa, as well as FREE articles, just go to the STORE at:

www.godawa.com

Sex and Violence for Christian Storytellers

Video or Audio Lecture with Q & A
by Brian Godawa
84 minutes

In this latest version of his "Beyond Sex and Violence" talk, Brian talks to Christian writers and storytellers about their craft (with a focus on movies). He examines the Bible to see just how it deals with the sins of mankind and draws principles how to apply that in storytelling for those who wish to be faithful to their Biblical values without being inauthentic in their picture of the world. A very frank and popular lecture.

Horror: A Biblical Genre

Video or Audio Lecture with Q & A
by Brian Godawa
80 minutes

God likes the horror genre, or else he wouldn't have used so much of it in the Holy Bible! Brian takes a look at examples of the horror genre in the Bible and in movies and explains how similar they can be as well as the differences. Though this is not intended to turn you into a horror fan, it will be helpful in gaining a broader understanding of the Biblical power and high value that God places on the horror genre in communicating original sin, human nature, the consequences of sin, and prophetic social commentary.

To order these audio lectures and other books and products by Brian Godawa, as well as FREE articles, just go to the STORE at:

www.godawa.com

Genesis To Revelation: Understanding the Bible as Story

6 Audio Lectures
Approx. 6 hours

The Bible is not a textbook of systematic theology. It is a story, God's story of how He saves His people. Genesis to Revelation: Understanding the Bible as Story is a 6-week class that provides a narrative approach to theology that will help you understand your own place as an actor in the unfolding drama of the Kingdom. You'll take a rollercoaster ride through the ups and downs of the narrative of the entire Bible, exploring some of its exciting plot twists and how it ultimately relates to our lives.

NOTE: A couple of the lectures had technical problems that caused some annoying sound problems, but all the lectures are entirely audible.

1. Story: Understanding God through Narrative
2. Creation: People, Land, Temple
3. Fall: Primeval History, Patriarchs: Abraham, Isaac & Jacob
4. Israel: Election, Exodus, Exile, Return
5. Messiah: New Covenant, New Creation,
6. Church: New Israel, New Temple, New Jerusalem, Resurrection
7. *Student Worksheet and additional reading material for each lecture included.*

DVD LECTURES by Brian Godawa

The Book of Enoch: Scripture, Heresy or What?

This dvd video lecture by Brian Godawa will be an introduction to the ancient book of 1Enoch, its content, its history, its affirmation in the New Testament, and its acceptance and rejection by the Christian Church. What is the Book of Enoch? Where did it come from? Why isn't it in the Bible? How does the Book of Enoch compare with the Bible?

Chronicles of the Nephilim: The Ancient Biblical Story

Watchers, Nephilim, and the Divine Council of the Sons of God. In this dvd video lecture, Brian Godawa explores the Scriptures behind this transformative storyline that inspired his best-selling Biblical novel series Chronicles of the Nephilim.

Horror: A Biblical Genre

Horror is not an inherently evil genre of storytelling. It can be used for gratuitous evil purposes, or for godly moral purposes. The Bible tells many stories using the horror genre in order to inspire holy fear of evil and admonish or chastise those in sin. In this dvd video lecture, Brian Godawa presents how horror movies can be biblically redeeming.

Sex and Violence for Christian Storytellers

In this dvd video lecture, Brian Godawa examines the issue of sin depicted in the movies and in the Bible. Should Christians watch or create R-rated movies, novels or articles? Are we sinning, or opening ourselves to sin, if we expose ourselves to dramatic visual images of sex, violence & profanity?

To order these DVD lectures and other books and products by Brian Godawa, as well as FREE articles, just go to the STORE at:

www.godawa.com

46370002R00202

Made in the USA
Lexington, KY
31 October 2015